**This gift
provided by:**

The
Seattle
Public
Library
Foundation

SUPPORTSPL.ORG

SCORPICA

◆ THE FIVE QUEENDOMS ◆

SCORPICA

G. R. MACALLISTER

SAGA PRESS

LONDON SYDNEY **NEW YORK** TORONTO NEW DELHI

SAGA PRESS
AN IMPRINT OF SIMON & SCHUSTER, INC.

1230 Avenue of the Americas
New York, NY 10020

First Saga Press hardcover edition February 2022

SAGA PRESS and colophon are registered trademarks of Simon & Schuster, Inc.

For information about special discounts for bulk purchases, please contact Simon & Schuster Special Sales at 1-866-506-1949 or business@simonandschuster.com.

The Simon & Schuster Speakers Bureau can bring authors to your live event. For more information or to book an event, contact the Simon & Schuster Speakers Bureau at 1-866-248-3049 or visit our website at www.simonspeakers.com.

Interior design by Jaime Putorti
Map design by Laura Levatino

Manufactured in the United States of America

10 9 8 7 6 5 4 3 2 1

Library of Congress Cataloging-in-Publication Data is available.

ISBN 978-1-9821-6789-9
ISBN 978-1-9821-6791-2 (ebook)

To Jonathan,
FINALLY

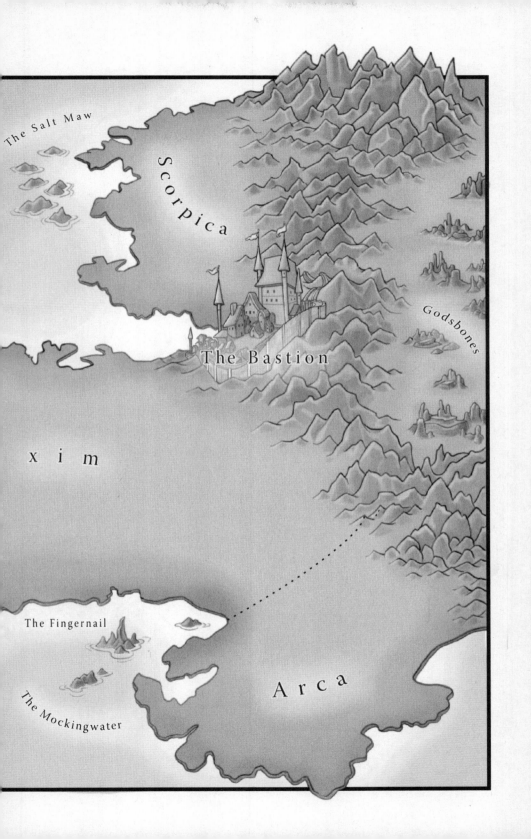

SCORPICA

Across the Five Queendoms of the known world, on an average day, roughly a hundred children were born. They rushed headlong from between the thighs of warriors and shepherds, farmers and courtiers, scribes and healers, thieves and queens. Some days brought more, some days fewer, but over weeks and months and years the newborns announced themselves in a constant cascade, squalling into life.

The Five Queendoms were the five fingers of a hand, crucially connected but distinct. Since the Great Peace had defined their borders five hundred years before, generations had known only harmony between the queendoms. The women who crafted the Peace drew the maps wisely: each nation had its gifts, its role. The scribes of the Bastion kept impeccable records and educated the most talented intellects of every queendom. Sestia was rich with grain and sheep. The desert of Arca grew only one thing, but that thing was magic, and it was enough. Paxim brokered the deals; the wheels of countless trade wagons wore ruts across its soil in every direction. And Scorpica had the strongest fighters, every woman a warrior, their commander their queen.

The balance seemed elegant, eternal, as solid underfoot as a natural stone bridge carved by water and time. Then one unnatural shift broke it open. Peace was not as solid as it had seemed.

Late on the fourth day of the fourth month of the All-Mother's Year 502, the day a headstrong kingling was born to the widowed queen of Paxim, four girls were among the world's newborns. One was the daughter of a warrior queen, another of a disgraced priest, yet another the offspring of a healer at the end of her line. One, born orphan as her mother's spirit left the world, was no one's daughter but the country's. At first, they seemed ordinary. If the next days had brought more girls like them, they would have been.

But the following day, every child born to the women of Paxim—senators to servants—was a boy. The same was true in the tents of the Scorpican warriors. Among the magicians of Arca. On Sestia's lush, sprawling farms. In the narrow stone fortress of the Bastion. All across the Five Queendoms, what happened was the same.

Infants were born squalling and silent, rich and poor, hale and weak, welcomed and unwanted. Their unfocused eyes looked out over bleak desert, rich green pasture, hilly wildwoods, impervious stone. They were gifts and they were accidents. They were blessed with excess and cursed with want. They were the ambassadors of future generations, hope made visible, swaddled in bundles of padded, wrinkling flesh. They were all things to all women. Except that not one of them was a girl.

Years would pass before another girl was born anywhere in the Five Queendoms.

More years would pass before anyone truly understood why.

PART I

BEFORE

THE

DROUGHT

CHAPTER 1

THE BARREN QUEEN

Midsummer, the All-Mother's Year 501

In the Holy City, Sestia

Khara

On the eve of the Sun Rites, Khara dha Ellimi awoke alone in the jet-black dark.

Despite the too-soft, too-large beds their Sestian hosts had set aside for her delegation, she'd fallen asleep quickly enough, soothed by the nearness of her fellow Scorpicae. The steady, measured breathing of a dozen warrior women at rest had been her lullaby. Yet she awoke to find silence her only companion. Soft, rumpled beds all around her lay abandoned.

Khara knew, of course, what her warriors had gone to do. She'd done it herself nine years running, in this very city, years ago. At ten-and-five she'd made her first journey to Sestia to celebrate rites. She'd returned to Scorpica with a belly set to swell, as did so many warrior sisters, their seed watered with a man's rain. The annual Moon Rites or rarer Sun Rites, in this sense they differed little: the Sestian priests, the Xaras, encouraged pleasures for all. Pleasures honored the God of Plenty and Her consort, they said. The warriors of Scorpica, hard-edged and lean with muscle, their dark hair shorn nearly to their scalps, laughed behind their hands at the long-haired priests' solemn piety. Some warriors believed in the God of Plenty and some did not. They pursued pleasure for pleasure's sake, not for Hers.

Khara felt as if the thick mattress were trying to swallow her slowly, like a fangless snake. She struggled upward and almost fell from the raised bed, not used to a perch so high. *Scorpion* mokh *these pilgrimages,* she thought. *Next time I'll stay home.*

But by the next Sun Rites, five years from now, would she still be queen? By then she'd be nearing her fortieth year. It would be fool-hardy not to consider passing the crown, though she had no daughter to receive it. So she had surveyed all her subjects, analyzed their strengths and weaknesses, planned for succession as she would for any campaign, and chosen as her protégée Mada dha Shodrei. Who had, like the others, vanished into the Sestian night.

Once steadied, Khara paced the dark room, her bare feet landing soundlessly on the cool stone floor. During the Sun Rites, the enormous, gleaming-white central building of the Holy City—both palace and temple—housed dozens, even hundreds, of visitors. Warriors could have their pick. Khara knew that some Scorpicae were strategic in their pleasures, choosing to bed particular men for their strength or intelligence, for traits they wanted in the next generation of warriors. She herself had never been so deliberate. But she suspected Mada would be. Her keen strategic mind was one of the chief reasons Khara had chosen her.

The other reason she'd chosen Mada was her daughter.

Tamura dha Mada was ten years old and already deadly with a bow, toting a swaying brace of red squirrels or plump rabbits home from the hunt even when far older hunters returned empty-handed. If Khara made her choice of Mada official—naming a woman who already had a daughter, and one clearly fated to grow into a talented warrior—the next succession, unlike this one, would never be in question.

The door opened with the faintest of creaks to admit a shadowed figure outlined by the lamp she bore, and Khara had the odd feeling she'd summoned Mada just by thinking of her. Instead it was Gretti, the youngest of their delegation at a mere ten-and-five, the keeper of the ceremonial blade. Even in the faint light Khara could identify her easily: slender in shape, her full lips pursed in concentration, her step tentative. Her sister Hana had been bladebearer five years before, an unusually capable one, but Gretti had none of her sister's easy confidence. She held both of her discarded sandals in one hand, strings dangling. Her leather vest had been tied in haste. Without looking at Khara she crept to her own bed, lifted the soft mattress. When she saw the muted glint of the metal underneath, she breathed an audible sigh.

"It was safe here," Khara said.

The girl wheeled, clearly surprised. She would need to learn awareness of her surroundings. "I was worried. So I returned."

With a wry look at the slapdash ties of her vest, Khara said gently, "If you'd told me you were going, I would have reassured you. Then you could have taken your time."

Before Gretti could respond, movement in the doorway caught Khara's eye.

Stepping into the room, sure and silent, was Mada herself. Even with cattle-hide sandals on her feet, her footfalls made no noise. A bit shorter than her queen and broader in the shoulders, with the long, ropy muscles of a born runner, she stretched luxuriantly as she came.

"My queen," she said. "It is time we were all abed."

"We all were, I suspect," said Khara. "Just not here."

Mada smiled with obvious satisfaction. "Just doing our part to serve the Holy One."

"Did you bed a Sestian, then?" asked Khara, an impolite question. She could see Gretti's jaw slacken in surprise out of the corner of her eye, but she kept her gaze on Mada, testing her temper. If she was too hotheaded to rule, it wasn't too late to choose a different successor. Nothing had yet been announced. "Did he call out Her name?"

Unruffled, Mada said, "I've more of a taste for Arcans, when I can find them. Do you remember what you used to choose, or has it been too long?"

She was saved from needing to answer—Mada seemed to want an answer, her eyes bright and expectant like a bird's—by the return of two more warriors, their lips swollen and limbs loose. There was no light yet from the single high window, but Khara knew that morning was growing closer. No more sleep for her tonight, then.

The returning warriors did not seem interested in sleep either, conversing in the low hum of bees drunk on sunlight, running a wet cloth from the basin across their shoulders or elsewhere, unpacking and repacking the bags they had carried with them from Scorpica in preparation for the long journey home.

Khara listened to their conversations while pretending not to and donned the ceremonial robe she would wear for the Sun Rites. The other queens would wear their hair loose, per tradition; hers was too short to wear any other way. Gretti polished the blade over and over and Khara had to force herself to look away. The blade was sharp and deadly. It did not need to shine to do its grim work.

In what seemed like minutes, a soft but distinct chime sounded through the thick wood of the door to their chamber. Every warrior's head rose.

"All ready," said their queen, a statement, not a question, and opened the door to admit the Queensguard.

Four warrior women, two closer to Khara's age and two to Mada's, stood arrow-straight in the hallway. The warriors of the Queensguard wore long cloaks of pale wool to show their current allegiance to Sestia, the swirl of a ram's horn stamped into the center of their leather shields. They were armored underneath.

"Queen," said the tallest. "It is time. You have the blade?"

Khara turned to the girl. It was her moment. "Gretti," she said.

In a flash the girl had sheathed the knife and brought it to her, turning the handle and presenting it, reverently, by the gleaming bone hilt.

Khara took the knife in her hands, then opened her palms with the sheathed blade flat on top, ready to bear it in front of her like an offering. Ever so slightly, she squared her shoulders.

"Will you follow me, please?" asked the shortest of the Queensguard, her tone hushed and formal.

"Yes," said Khara. "We are ready."

✦

The queen of Scorpica had three responsibilities during the Sun Rites. One was to make the long journey here to bring the holy blade to be used in the ceremony. No substitutes were accepted; the queen herself must attend. The second was to eat a ritual meal of fresh red cherries with the other queens the day before the ceremony and affirm her participation. The third was to attend the ceremony itself, bearing the blade and handing it to the High Xara to wield, which was Khara's least favorite of the three by far. The scent of blood alone did not disturb a warrior, and yet, how blood smelled to her depended so much on whose blood it was and how it had been drawn. Blood shed in the Sun Rites smelled like rust and rot, like overripe figs in a vulture's beak. Even as she saw it bright and fresh, shed in the moment, to her it always stank of decay.

But there was no option not to attend the rites, not for any of the five ruling queens. While only the Sestians worshipped the God of Plenty above all others, none of them knew what might happen if any queen ignored the summons. Were the Sun Rites a dam that kept back a flood of pestilence and famine? Did their own gods expect their participation, even if the sacrifice wasn't made in their name? They could not know unless they failed to attend. No one yet had thought her curiosity worth the risk.

So the queen of Paxim negotiated and secured promises of attendance, the queen of the Bastion brought the precious Book of Worlds to record the ceremony, the Arcan queen came as the messenger of Chaos, and she, the queen of Scorpica, delivered the holy blade. The queen of Sestia herself, the High Xara, would be the one to wield it.

As she followed the Queensguard out of the palace and toward the amphitheater, Khara could think only of how eager she was to have today's rites done with. Perhaps this would be the last time she'd ever walk this road. If she named Mada her successor and yielded the crown, she need not come this way again. She felt a pang of regret at the thought, but in the same breath, relief.

She would miss the cherries, though. Their like did not thrive in Scorpica's cooler, wilder northern clime. Perfectly ripe, bursting with juice, so fresh off the tree they were still warm from the sun. She knew the ritual was chosen for the symbolism—all five queens left the sacred grove afterward with stubborn crimson stains on their lips, on their fingers—but the taste was so exquisite, even the memory set her mouth to watering.

When they arrived at the amphitheater of gleaming stone, they surrendered their weapons to the guards—all but Gretti—and passed through the final gate. Then they descended the long, long stairs, heading for the dais where the ceremony would take place.

The ritual dances began as they approached.

The dancers, dozens of them, were dressed simply in flowing, short tunics, the girls and women with their hair piled high, the boys and men wearing headdresses of ram's horns. They acted out the beginning of history, beginning with the All-Mother creating the world, then birthing Her three daughters Velja, Sestia, and Eresh—Chaos, Plenty, and Death—to help Her create humans, animals, and plants to cover it. Sestia brought life, exhaling Her divine breath into mouths, bills, and snouts, placing feet and paws and hooves on the earth to explore far and wide. Eresh built the Underlands to welcome the spirits of humans, their shades, once their time on earth was done. Velja introduced all the things people most wanted and most feared—pain and longing, joy and satisfaction, hope, envy, despair—to create balance between life and death, ensuring that the only certain thing in this world would be uncertainty.

A horn sounded, bringing Khara back to herself. It was time. With the other queens she moved forward as the rest of their delegations stepped back, taking positions in the amphitheater's front row. The dancers slowed their movements, easing away, stepping aside.

The mood changed to a crackle of anticipation, a thousand spectators drawing in and holding their collective breath.

Eight muscular women strode into the gap where the dancers had been, each set of four bearing one of the ceremonial bone beds. These they set in place, one end firmly anchored to the platform and the notched end hovering above the open-mouthed bins of seed grain below. What happened in those bins would determine whether the next year's crop was plentiful or meager. All their hopes, not just Sestia's but the world's, rested in the golden cradle of that grain.

Then the sacrifices were led forward, their feet bare and cautious in the dust. Once on the dais, they were bound to the bone beds, each head fitting neatly into its notch, each long, smooth throat exposed. A girl on the cusp of becoming a woman. A boy on the cusp of becoming a man. Neither, thought Khara, was fated to live long enough to fulfill that promise.

Some years the sacrifices struggled and some years they didn't; Khara didn't know what made the difference and she couldn't let herself care. She only looked away from their accusing eyes, and when the four witnessing queens were called forward to test the bindings, she checked to make sure the knots were secure. It was bad enough to know you were going to die. It would be worse, she thought, to think that you had some chance of escaping that death and then meet it anyway.

"You are satisfied?" said the High Xara, officially beginning the sacrifice.

"We are," replied the other queens, as one.

The ceremonial horn sounded again, cutting through the air as dawn began to lighten the sky. The women and men in the amphitheater stood rapt. The horn's last long note faded and died above their assembled heads.

"Queen of Paxim, diplomat and dealmaker," the High Xara began. Though she addressed the purple-robed, dark-eyed woman, her words were for all, spoken in a voice nearly as sharp and resonant as the blast of the horn had been.

"Yes."

"Have you brought forth all five queens from across the known world to play their roles today?"

"I have," Heliane answered loudly, proud, firm. Her dark hair hung all the way to her waist; freed of its usual braids, it flowed down her back like a cloak.

After a pause, the High Xara turned to the next queen, her movements formal and spare. "Queen of the Bastion, the scribe of our holy rite."

"Yes."

"Stand you ready to record what we do here today?"

The oldest queen, her soft chin and cheeks crumpling inward like an overwintered apple, said, "I do."

"Queen of Scorpica, battle-driven and strong."

Khara raised her chin and met the priest's steady eyes, forcing herself to match strength with strength. "Yes."

"Will you bring forth the blade sacred to the Holy One for the sanctified task before us today?"

"I will," said Khara, using her voice of command.

"Queen of Arca," called the High Xara to the final queen in the semicircle, "I call upon you to speak with the lips of Chaos."

There was always a pause, a tension, at this moment in the ceremony. No one knew what might happen. Chaos Herself was here in the form of her earthly avatar. Even those who did not worship the God of the Arcans could not help believing in Her enough to fear Her caprice, deep down.

When the queens of Arca were called upon in these ceremonies, their god Velja moved some to take drastic actions and moved some not at all. Oft-told stories remembered the queen five generations before who'd leapt from the dais and thrown herself in front of the ceremonial blade, dying in place of that year's sacrifice. An earlier ruler had stolen a Scorpican pony and galloped through the rites as naked as the night her mother birthed her. The Arcan queen Mirriam standing before them today had ruled many years, her proud, hooked nose and bright, hawklike eyes unchanged for decades. And though she had ruled so long, they still did not truly know her. She might do nothing. She might do anything.

The silence lay over the crowd in the amphitheater like a blanket, stretching out, unbroken.

Then the queen of Arca said, with a faint, quizzical air of surprise, "I am moved to leave this place."

And she did just that, stepping off the dais toward the spectators, taking the long walk up the stairs toward the far exit. Heads everywhere swiveled to watch her as she went.

Khara looked at the High Xara, whose eyes did not drift from the dark-robed queen as she mounted the seemingly endless steps up and away. Once the queen of Arca was gone, it seemed to Khara that the High Xara breathed a sigh of relief. An instant later, the priest's face was blank and still as a mask. Perhaps Khara had imagined that moment of humanity.

"Let the God be fed," the High Xara's voice rang out.

It was time for Khara to fulfill her obligation.

She turned the blade in her hand, wrapping her fingers loosely around the leather sheath, and offered it to the High Xara. The priest took it in a smooth, practiced motion.

The crowd began to stir then, watching, shifting, breathing, and Khara knew there was no way she could have heard the sound of the sharp blade sliding out of the hardened leather. Yet that was what she thought she heard, the metal whispering, its parting almost regretful.

Khara bowed her head.

The High Xara struck.

A thousand pairs of eyes watched the bare blade come down, first into the chest of the girl-almost-woman, then into the chest of the boy-almost-man, but Khara's were not among them. She continued not to watch as both of the sacrifices' throats were slit, first the boy's cries silenced, then the girl's. She didn't need to see to know. Blood coursed down through the notches of the bone beds onto the seed grain, completing the ceremony, blessing the next year's planting. She never looked up. Instead she stared down at her hands, limp and unmoving, the juice of yesterday's cherries still staining her fingers a lingering, lasting red.

CHAPTER 2

THE ROAD HOME

Leaving Sestia

Khara

As the outline of the Sestian capital faded into the distance behind her, Khara felt both exhausted and elated. The landscape changed so quickly from the busy hubbub of the capital to the open countryside beyond. The countryside looked more like home. Once they were out of the city, the rolling green hills of Sestia were unbelievably lush, the air so sweet and clear. Khara let herself breathe deeply and leave the completed rites behind.

She rode in the center of the column, though she would have far preferred to be at the front. Next to her rode the other member of the delegation considered most vulnerable, the bladebearer Gretti. She was so young, thought Khara. Had she herself ever been so uncertain, so new to the world? How odd to have come so far, grown so strong—become queen!—and found herself banished to the center of the column again, next best to a near child.

Eight ponies rode ahead of them and eight behind, carrying the rest of the delegation as well as packs of trade goods, with senior warriors in the outermost positions. Bandits and brigands were always a risk on the long roads of Paxim, the constant stream of valuables a tempting source of rich plunder for the morally flexible. So the warriors kept their formation tight and their weapons at hand.

The shaggy, sturdy ponies they rode came from the wild red mountains that bordered Scorpica and Paxim on the east, the haunted land known as Godsbones. No other animals suited Scorpican riders so well. Khara had roped her own mount, Stormshadow, when she was only a girl. Now the horse was like an extension of her. The ride home across much of the known world was exhausting even in the best conditions, but her body could have no greater comfort than Stormshadow's familiar back.

Comfort for her mind was another matter. Khara wished, not for the first time, that she were riding alongside Vishala. But her most trusted councillor remained in Scorpica whenever Khara was not there, to represent her and make judgments in her stead. She and Vish had known each other since childhood, had learned together how to draw back bowstrings with their chubby fingers when both could barely speak words. She would have loved to name Vish her successor, but choosing a woman her own age was foolish. A queen who reached her forty-fifth year without handing over her power was always Challenged, or so the stories went.

And every year she grew more vulnerable. Her people respected her, but few truly loved her. Even at the beginning, when her mother, Ellimi, died, there'd been whispers. *Is she strong enough? Who will rule after?*

When Khara walked among her subjects, they nodded, fell silent in respect, lay their swords at her feet. When she walked alone, her ears far from their lips, she knew what those same warriors called her. The Barren Queen.

She rarely thought of those nine children born of her womb, year after year, all boys. Not a warrior among them. Once the midwife severed their link with the birthing blade, Khara had kissed their sweet, wet heads and handed them to Vish, who she trusted above all others to do what needed to be done. Vish would handle selling them to be raised in one of the other queendoms, where boys and men had roles to play. There was no place for them in Scorpica.

So many years, so long past. She had put it off too long already. Succession must be decided. She would put Mada to the test.

And it was Mada who led the column, her back straight as a sword even as she swayed in time with her mount. She was holding up well, especially for her first time in these strange surroundings, so far. But the journey back would be long. That was when Khara would show her the rest of what it meant to be queen.

On the way back to Scorpica—nearly a month's ride through Paxim and then a day between the high, stony gates of the Bastion—they would meet Khara's far-flung generals, the vast network of Scorpicae who managed protective forces hired out to the weaker queendoms. Anyone could train fighters, of course, and set them to the task. But Scorpica had been training, assigning, cultivating lifelong warriors for generations. That was their role, and no Scorpican had ever broken her sworn oath of loyalty to the nation where she was assigned. Trust was absolute, and the other queendoms paid handsomely for that trust.

To rule wisely as queen, it was not enough for Mada to fight brilliantly. She would need to understand each of the women she ruled, matching them to assignments that would shore up their weaknesses without wasting their strengths, naming a fair price for their services. A girl turning woman at ten-and-five might be ready for the high honor of an assignment as a foreign leader's Queensguard, or she might benefit from more training in Scorpica before she could even be trusted for straightforward guard duty in the nearby Bastion. It was not easy to know so many women so well. If Mada could grasp these matters, thought Khara, she would be ready. The best queens, the ones who ruled until succession without a single Challenge, were three in one: not just the nation's best fighter, but its best leader and best strategist as well.

Sunrise after sunrise, sunset after sunset, they made their way across the plains of Paxim toward home. The dozens of trading posts they passed through were all different, yet the same: a crier shouting the latest news, voice gone hoarse; citizens swarming like flies to the booths at the markets, settling upon anything they found sweet, then scattering again in a flurry; merchants by turns honey-toned and brusque, depending on what they had to sell and how they thought they could best sell it.

Mada was open-eyed with wonder, Khara observed, and yet she never relaxed her guard. She nodded and listened as Khara introduced her to important warriors. She cocked her head attentively as each spoke, naming which areas of the country had more unrest and required more vigilance, which were as placid as a forest lake.

Here and there among the posts and towns, inns dotted the countryside, but these had no appeal to Scorpicae. They bedded down along the roadside wherever they chose, rotating the watch and pillowing their heads on their packs. Most slept better than they had on the overstuffed mats where they'd lain their heads during their week in Sestia.

In the golden light of late afternoon, Khara estimated they were yet two nights from the gates of the Bastion, their last milestone before home. She held their position on the map in her mind, picturing them as a moving dot equidistant between two far-flung trading posts, when she heard a faint whistle, high and sharp. All twelve warriors knew it instantly.

An arrow.

"*Kii-yah,*" shouted Mada, the command to scatter, and her bow was already in her hand.

Ahead of them on the wide road stood a series of dark shapes, all human, all armed to the teeth.

The bandits were a random tangle of a dozen ruffians, cloaked in dirty brown rags; lean to a fault, looking like their last decent meal was but a distant memory. Khara's first thought was that they couldn't pose a serious threat, not against a team of trained warriors. That was before she realized that the arrow she'd heard whistling had lodged in her left shoulder, not nearly far enough for comfort from her heart.

Then, only then, came the pain.

The pain would have to wait. The battle was joined.

Mada's first arrow took the bandits' first bowman in the throat. Her second whizzed just over the head of the elfin, masked woman with the longsword. Quickly, they were too close for bows. Then hiss after hiss sounded, the sound of metal swords drawn from leather sheaths, as the Scorpicae readied themselves.

One of the bandits, a short man whose thicket of dark hair gave him a pronounced resemblance to a bear, seemed to reconsider. He turned and fled, his sword clanking hard against his hip as he ran for the far horizon.

Mada looked back at her queen and nodded once, then turned back to the fight with something that looked very much like glee.

Khara took one more moment to evaluate the scene, sizing up attackers and defenders, then reached out with her good arm to grab the bridle of Gretti's horse. Gretti's eyes were huge. Khara could not count on the untested young woman to keep her head and her mount in the fray.

"Hold on," Khara told her.

Then she clicked her tongue once, sank her heels into Storm-shadow's sides, and spurred her straight into a hard run. Gretti's mount followed suit.

The bandits were circling to array themselves both in front of and behind the column, and so Khara took them off the road immediately, due north, their mounts barely a pair of reddish streaks in the gathering darkness. She willed herself to ignore her stinging, burning shoulder for now. Once she could, she'd chew on the knot of willow bark from her pack, but only fools ranked comfort ahead of safety.

Behind, she heard the shouts of warriors closing to battle and wished she were riding at their head. Had she not been the Barren Queen, had there been a daughter at home ready to assume the mantle of leadership, she would have. *How different things could have been,* she thought grimly. Then she lowered her face into her mount's streaming mane and focused on saving the life of the young woman behind her. And her own.

As they rode hard, the shouts in the distance grew faint. Her eyes scoured the land ahead of her in the dwindling light. Farms in the far north of Paxim were small, growing only enough to sustain the families that worked them. There were no true cities for miles. She reached for the willow bark now and began working at it with her teeth, hoping it would dull the pain quickly. When she saw the squat, low shape of a dwelling on the horizon, she adjusted course, then slowed on the approach.

Suspicion must be their watchword. It was possible that the entire scene on the road had been staged to drive them into a second ambush. Then again, judging by the arrow in her shoulder—its stiff gray-white feathers bobbing as she moved—the attack had been very real indeed.

Keeping Gretti behind her, she scanned the house and the grounds. The figure of a man stooped outside the squat building, drawing up a bucket of water from a well.

As they drew nearer, he finished his task and turned toward the sound of the ponies' hoofbeats. He wore his wavy hair in a single knot at the nape of his neck. His clothes were those of a workingman, practical, well-used. She could almost read his thoughts as he looked up at their approach, his movements leisurely, and opened his mouth to utter a greeting. Then, noticing the arrow protruding from her shoulder, he let the words die unspoken on his tongue.

He hurried in their direction, and she put her hand on her sword, thinking, *Perhaps I will join in battle today after all.*

Then he veered past her toward Gretti. Belatedly she noticed the young woman was swaying in her seat, then slumping forward, her full weight against the neck of her mount.

"May I help her?" asked the man.

Even as he spoke, Khara was already dismounting from Stormshadow, supporting Gretti with her uninjured right arm, lowering the young woman's unconscious form to the ground.

"But your—can I—" said the man. He gestured to the arrow, its long straight shaft following Khara's every movement, the feathers ahead of her, the bloody arrowhead behind. "Do you need my help?"

The bark had blunted Khara's pain, and she could tell by the way the arrow sat in her shoulder that it hadn't taken her through the muscle. She could wait.

"Her first." She pointed to Gretti. The bladebearer had been untested, and no matter how they trained girls for battle, no training was the same as reality.

His dark brows knitting, the man nodded and knelt. He inspected the girl with care, gripping her chin without twisting it, pulling up one lid to gaze into the unseeing eye beneath.

"Are you a healer?" asked Khara.

"Of sorts," he said. "I do a little of everything, out here. Healing. Ranching. Trading. Teaching. Whatever needs done. Bandits on the road?"

"Yes."

"They get anything?"

"I doubt it very much."

He let out a noise that was something like a laugh, but not quite, and resumed his examination.

While he examined Gretti, Khara examined him. Body lean, fingers calloused from hard work. Likely close to her own age, she thought, perhaps a little younger. Face suntanned but not leathery, with faint spidering lines at the corners of his eyes. He moved with a deliberate, tense energy. She had the impression he was old enough to know himself, an age that came at a different point for everyone, but made for a greater happiness when it was reached. She had found it herself, finally, not that long ago.

She let him work in silence for another minute, and then said, "And how is she?"

"No wounds," he said. "Fainted from shock, looks like. She'll come around. Do you think your friends will be here soon?"

"My friends?" she asked.

"You're Scorpican warriors on a road direct to the Bastion," he said, "with the Sun Rites a month gone. I know who you are."

She sized him up again. Something in his smile looked like an invitation, though perhaps she was imagining it. Sometimes a person saw what she wanted to see. "You live out here by yourself?"

"My brother and I. He's gone to Melo—that's the nearest trading post—to swap the season's honey for some other goods we'll be needing for harvest. Back in a day or two, most like."

His eyes were on her again, appraising, appreciating. Perhaps she hadn't mistaken the invitation after all. She was enjoying the tingle of warmth in her limbs—a feeling long in slumber, starting to awaken—when she heard the sound of hooves approaching and stood, turning toward it.

"That'll be your friends, then," he said.

They arrived in a cloud of dust, a V formation, Mada at the point. The noise brought Gretti back awake. Khara saw her fight urgently to right herself before the other warriors arrived. The man reached out his hand and, in one smooth motion, brought Gretti to her feet. The three of them faced the new arrivals together.

"Bandits dispatched," reported Mada, sliding down from her horse quickly. There was no visible blood on her, but her quiver was nearly empty. "You're wounded, Queen Khara."

"So I am," she said, and couldn't help looking over at the man.

As she did, he dropped to one knee, bowing his head. He spoke to the ground at her feet. "Queen."

She told him, not unkindly, "Get up."

"I knew you were with the queen's party," he said, his voice changed. "But I didn't truly know . . ."

"We don't do that, you know," she scoffed lightly. "You do that for your queen here in Paxim?"

"Yes. We bow, at the least. Some lay their faces in the dirt. We lower ourselves to show respect."

"Queens are a little different in Scorpica."

"So I see," he replied, his face relaxing, returning to that lazy, inviting smile.

Mada, arms folded, interrupted sharply. "Look. If you're a healer, you can deal with the queen's wound instead of standing around with your cock on backward. Otherwise, we'll be on our way."

"I can help," he said, seemingly undisturbed by her insult. "I have a cutting tool to cut the shaft, and strong wine to wash the wound."

"You do not know the Scorpicae," Mada replied. "Warriors do not wash with strong wine. We drink it."

Khara did not care for the dislike pouring off Mada like rainwater, nor for her dismissive tone. Mada was already acting like the queen, already taking charge. That was troubling. The assembled warriors watched them both, their ponies pawing and snorting, waiting for the next command. And the pain in Khara's shoulder and back was beginning to burn. Now that the initial shock and hasty dose of willow bark had both worn off, that pain grew, radiated, spread. She gritted her teeth against it.

Khara turned her back on Mada deliberately and spoke to the man alone. "If you would share your water with my warriors, to refresh and wash themselves, it would be a kindness."

"May the All-Mother bless you, warriors," he said, addressing them all. "Any visitor is welcome here. You may avail yourselves of the well as you choose. And I will bring you some of that strong wine."

"We will rest here for the night," Khara said, her voice loud enough to carry, without turning. She added, "In our bedrolls. We travel lightly, and will not even put tent pegs in your ground."

"As I said. You are welcome."

Mada said, her voice forceful, "We can push on."

Khara turned to face her and the assembled warriors, taking her time. Perhaps Mada would be an excellent queen of Scorpica in the future, but it would do her good to remember who was still queen today.

When Khara knew she had the younger woman's full attention, she said, "Night falls. Tomorrow morning we push on. When none among us wears a bandit's arrow for ornament."

Behind her, the man added, "It is best to watch for poison, too. One never knows, around here, how a bandit has tipped her weapon."

Mada held Khara's gaze a moment longer, then said, "Tomorrow, then."

Gretti piped up, her voice bright, "Let the queen be healed now. I will go with our host to fetch the wine he promised."

Nods all around, and then the three of them walked into the gathering dusk toward the low, squat building, one lit lantern a beacon above its single door.

Inside, the hut was neatly kept, unadorned. One high table and one low, two chairs, two stools, and several shelves, all of mismatched wood. Two cots with thin mattresses and light blankets for the summer. A few stray rugs, undyed. A life without luxury, Khara mused. Then again, one might say the same about the life she and her sister warriors led, living in tents, moving their camp with the seasons.

As their host gathered several jugs of wine and a stoppered wineskin, Gretti pressed her hand into Khara's, leaving a small object there. When Khara looked down, she smiled to see that the girl had handed over her own stash of willow bark. Then Gretti took the jugs of wine from their host with a grateful nod and was gone.

The three of them were alone: Khara, the man, and the arrow. She asked, "The cot?"

He looked away from her when he said, "The table, I think."

"As you wish." She seated herself on the table, working her body backward into a comfortable sitting position without putting her left hand down, afraid to put any kind of new pressure on the wound. The wood was smooth under her thighs. She could feel it where her half-skirt slid out of the way, just above the backs of her knees. The fire in her shoulder was spreading, but she kept the bark in her hand. The longer she delayed chewing it, the more good it would do her when she did.

"You do not even seem to be in pain," he marveled.

"It should seem so," she said. "We are trained to bear it. Is it true that the local bandits use poison on their weapons?"

"It's possible," he answered. "I chose my words to smooth the way. Are you angry?"

"No." She thought of smiling to set him at ease, but the tension was an interesting tension, full of possibility. She let the silence linger.

"I'm glad. So. Do you want the strong wine on your body or in it?"

"Both, please."

He nodded and moved the wineskin onto the table within her reach. She watched him prepare, tracking his confident movements, precise in the small space. Strips of cloth in a neat stack near the table's edge, tiny pots and vials arrayed alongside. Once all was in readiness, he raised his cutting tool toward where the shaft of the arrow protruded from the front of her shoulder.

"No," she said, raising her fingers to stay his hand.

"No?"

"Not there, I mean. The back."

She was not sure he understood her reasoning, but that didn't matter, not as long as he obeyed.

"As you wish." He echoed her earlier words.

She let her hand fall. As he moved into position, she put the last piece of willow bark against her bottom teeth and began to chew, thankful for Gretti's gesture.

As gentle as he was, when he fit the cutting tool around the shaft still embedded in her flesh, she felt it. Despite her discipline, she was unable to keep her body from tensing with anticipation. There were things even a Scorpican could not control. The bark distanced the pain, but nothing—outside of Arcan magic, she supposed—could eliminate it completely.

As he clipped the shaft in a single, swift motion, she felt it shudder inside her. She heard the wood snap, the sound a sharp report in the small, close space, and felt him catch the cut-off section of arrow as it fell. As he bent down for a closer look at his handiwork, a stray lock of his dark hair nearly, but not quite, brushed her shoulder.

Before he could rise again, Khara took hold of the remaining shaft with her free hand, gripping it so hard she could feel her fingernails in her palm. Swiftly she yanked out what was left of the arrow and flung it away. A Scorpican trusted herself more than she trusted any stranger, amiable as he might be.

She looked down at the wound to satisfy herself. Yes, blood now flowed freely out of the narrow hole a handspan above her breast. She assumed the same was true of her back. The entire arrow was out, leaving a hole no bigger around than a slender reed. The cuts were clean. She might heal entirely, in time.

With gritted teeth, she said, "And now the wine."

He uncapped the skin for her and placed it in her hand. She raised it to her lips, taking a long, hard pull on the mouthpiece. She swallowed and grimaced as it burned its way down, not as sweet as she'd expected, a wild, harsh taste.

"This wine is not good," she gasped.

"I didn't say it was good," he said, pressing a wad of cloth firmly to her shoulder. "I said it was strong."

She took another long gulp and laughed, then held the skin toward him.

While he drank, she used her right hand to untie and peel off the soft leather vest she'd worn over her chest bindings, leaving her shoulders and neck bare. His eyes did not leave hers.

Between them, they cleansed the wound with wine and water, then covered it with patches of soft wool, bound over with a longer strip of clean nettlecloth. He wrapped the last bit of it around her shoulder and tucked in the free end, running his finger along the edge.

"It will bleed tonight," he said. "A few hours, I think, not more. We will change the dressing tomorrow."

The closeness of his body had been necessary as he worked. It no longer was. Yet he remained, and she was glad of it.

He asked her, "Will you return to the house at sunrise?"

A heady relief swimming over and through her, she was ready to speak her mind. The time had come for both of them to choose.

She answered him in a hushed tone. "I would not need to return if I did not leave."

The set of his jaw shifted. She could see him weigh his answer.

"With your wound, the ground will be hard for sleeping," he continued. "It would be better to have a softer place to rest."

"A softer place," she repeated.

Khara noted with satisfaction that his eyes flicked over to the cot, just for a moment, before meeting hers again.

She did not look away.

His voice even softer, he said, "But you are a queen."

Still holding his gaze, she answered, "But I am a woman."

Then he placed a hand on her knee, just where the split half-skirt ended. His fingers on her bare skin were blunt-tipped and warm.

He asked, "Will you stay?"

She lowered her hand to his. Briefly eyeing the door, she whispered, "And your brother?"

"He won't return tonight. And your warriors?"

"They'll stay outside."

He tilted his head forward and brushed his lips gently, oh so gently, on the bare skin of her shoulder above the bandage, next to her collarbone. He said, "I don't want to cause you pain."

She smiled at that.

"We are trained to bear it," she reminded him, and, lifting his chin with one outstretched finger, guided his mouth up to hers.

CHAPTER 3

THE WAY

The following spring, the All-Mother's Year 502
In Scorpica
Khara

The child was *makilu*, wrongheaded. There would be pain.

There always was, of course, in childbirth. Even for the Barren Queen, though in her previous births, she'd had an easier time than most. Her labors came on fast and strong, stripping her of breath and thought, but they did not last. Each of her babies had slipped from her womb as naturally as a scorpion molting, leaving her body behind like a shed skin, emerging new and soft and ready to embrace the world.

This one would not be so easy. She knew from what the midwives said and what they did not say. How many births had she witnessed, how many newborn warriors had she blessed? When childbed turned to deathbed, how many warriors' eyes had she closed, whispering the words to wing their spirits toward the great battlefield beyond? She knew the faces of Scorpican midwives. Had she been an ordinary warrior, they would have muttered as they poked her swollen belly, frowning, shaking their heads. *Makilu, makilu. Take care.* But for

Khara they pasted on brave, false smiles as they pressed and stroked the taut-stretched flesh over the shape of a compact backside, a head, a shoulder. *The child may yet turn.* She let them believe that she believed them.

A wail tore its way loose from her throat. The way was not open. Even as long as it had been, she could feel the difference. *Makilu.*

She reached out for Vishala's hand. "Vish?"

"My queen."

"Oh, but not now," she said, grunting out the words. "I am no one's queen when I am birthing."

Her friend's low voice, sweet like cream to Khara's ears, was as comforting as the grip of her strong fingers. "We will tell no one."

Most Scorpicae birthed with crowds of warriors in attendance, drawing on their encouragement, their support, their energy. When Khara was young, she had too. It seemed so long ago now. After the ninth birth, she hadn't entirely given up pleasure, but she had become selective about the pleasures she took with men, and the phase of the moon when she took them. The rites were the easiest but far from the only time. If one enjoyed their attentions enough to look for them, which Khara did, men could always be found.

But she looked rarely, after those nine births, after her mother, Ellimi, named her successor to the queendom. A ruler had little time for pleasure anyway. She had forces and generals to gather, warriors to train, decisions to hand down, a proud nation to serve. The next ten years she'd remained shorn, fruitless, remote.

This time only two other women squatted with her in the darkened tent, the two she had chosen: Vishala, the adviser dearer to her than any sister, and Beghala, the most experienced midwife in all Scorpica. She did not like Beghala, but liking was not important. That she and the child would both survive was her only hope. If the child remained *makilu*, Beghala might be the only one who knew the way.

And if only one of them was fated to survive, Beghala would know how and when to make the choice. The midwife had been trained in the Bastion and had served for decades since; there was nothing of midwifery she had not seen. When delivery came to a critical juncture, Khara trusted her not to hesitate.

Another pain began to gather low inside her, its dark wave rising, and Khara spoke to distract herself. "Who stands outside?"

"Everyone," Vishala said simply.

Khara began to imagine. It eased her pain to do so while she labored, setting her mind free to explore while her animal body did its work. The wave built, stretched, crested. She moved her grip on Vishala upward to the wrist, worried that if she tightened her grasp on Vish's fingers, she might break them.

"Howl if you like," came the voice of the aged midwife from farther away in the shadows.

"I. Do. Not. Like." Khara knew she would howl—she always did, she always had—but not yet. She struggled awkwardly to her knees and hunched forward, swinging her hips, hoping to free the way.

She tried again to picture the scene outside. Mada would be nearest the tent flap, eager and tensed and hopeful all at once, waiting to hear. If Khara never emerged from this tent, Mada would be their queen; as soon as they'd returned from the Sun Rites, Khara had officially named her as successor. Then again, Khara supposed, if she never emerged from this tent again, she would neither know nor care who reigned after.

The next wave of pain grew, crested, crashed. Khara imagined the warriors behind Mada, beyond her, stretching across the open land. Dozens, maybe hundreds, of Scorpicae. Muttering in clusters, passing hopes and rumors. Restless. No doubt those who believed in the God of Plenty were joining hands in prayer, close-cropped heads bowed and somber. She knew what they prayed for—a daughter—but she had no such hope. Many of these same women had prayed for her nine times before. She'd been just like this, crouched and lowing, and those prayers fell like seeds on hard-packed ground, never taking root.

The way was not open.

Another squeezing, wringing pain came on and she tried to make sense of what she felt at the core of the grip, the nut inside the shell. Was it the solid, compact mass of the head that her body squeezed toward daylight? Or a jumble of limbs, crushed and tangled with each other, nowhere to go? She would not ask the midwife. If the news was bad, she didn't want to know. Her sweat-drenched hair, grown long during pregnancy as tradition insisted, was in her eyes. She cursed it. She would be shorn again the sunrise after the child was born. If the child was born.

"Khara," whispered Vish, who rarely called her by her name, even with all the years of friendship between them. "Are you here?"

"Here," she grunted, though her head swam with stars. "Was I gone?"

"Just for a moment," said Vish, but worry was in her voice now, curdling the cream.

It had likely been longer than a moment, Khara realized. If she lost consciousness, if she could not shepherd this child into the world, who knew what would happen? She'd trusted her animal body to deliver the nine boys. It had, without fail. Now her body was different, the birth was different, the child was *makilu*. She could not trust her body. She needed her mind.

To Vishala she said, "Talk to me."

"About what?"

"Anything."

"My queen, I will not," said Vishala, her familiar voice stronger now, a strange harshness in it.

"What?" Khara struggled to focus. She saw Vish's face for a moment, the warm brown eyes, the dark halo of close-cropped hair, the thin lips set in a firm line. "What?"

"No. Not me. *You* talk."

She was in the rest between pains now, a blissful place like no other, and she laughed aloud. Of course her friend would know what to do. The midwife knew birthing, but Vishala knew Khara to her soul. "Trickster!"

There was no response, which she knew was deliberate.

"You want me to do the talking," said Khara, trying to make her voice teasing, light. "In my state?"

"Should she rise?" Vishala was speaking to the midwife now, not to her, but they both listened for the older woman's response. The rest between pains was short, the question urgent. In the next pain she might not be able to rise even if she wanted to.

"Let her do what her body asks of her," came Beghala's voice, which seemed to drift in her direction from very far away.

Vishala said to Khara, "You heard?"

"My body knows nothing," hissed Khara, and as if angry at the insult, her body instantly doubled forward, the rising wave of pain crashing on her like the full weight of a mighty sea.

Then she felt an irresistible urge to place her hands on the ground and raise her hips high. She obeyed the urge, folding her body at a sharp angle, bending forward as steeply as she could with such a heavy weight in her belly. Her dark hair pooled on the ground, blood rushing to her head. The pain encircled her hips like a band of iron; the child squirmed against the cradle of muscle tightening down upon it, fighting every inch. Khara's world shrank to those mere inches and she begged the child to win the battle, begged its head to drop into place and turn toward light.

At her ear, Vishala said, "What do you remember of him?"

It was a bold question, just shy of taboo. A warrior spoke freely of her pleasures if she chose to, but the choice was hers and hers alone. Details were to be volunteered, not requested. Khara would not have answered such a question from anyone else. But the answer came quickly to her lips. She remembered every one of them, from that first sweet-faced shepherd boy of Sestia, nearly a bumpkin, to the man she had joined with after the bandit skirmish, whose name she never had learned. In the morning, as he'd promised, he changed the dressing on her wound and treated it with a soothing, oily cream, and then she and her party went on their way.

"Everything," she panted to her friend, thinking her voice was soft, but not knowing.

"Tell me."

"Hair curly. All over. Fire in his eyes." The rhythm of her words became a chant now, a pulse to harken to, and she gladly embraced it as the pain crashed on her again, forcing her hips back down. She pushed up, straining. "Salt taste. Strong arms. Strong thighs. No fear."

What she did not say, but remembered—with exquisite clarity—was the remarkable ease of their joining. There had been no awkwardness, none of the nervous moments or self-conscious reserve of her younger years. They were both of an age to be confident, and neither mistook what the other wanted. All was clear. He offered himself up and she took him, setting a rhythm he quickly matched. She'd held his gaze as he groaned. Neither looked away.

His remembered groan fused with the groan that escaped her as her body fought her, the child fought her, her head swam again, she clutched Vishala's arms as if they were all that kept her tethered to the world, and then she howled an animal howl.

The child was coming.

Where was Beghala? she wanted to ask, but her words were gone, her breath was gone, the world was gone. She held on. Pain threatened to strip her from the world, hurl her through all five gates of the Underlands into the black darkness beyond.

A hand was—hands were?—on her belly. Was there a hand inside her too, or some other mass of muscle and bone? Child or midwife? She poured her pain into the howl, and it felt good to howl. She could do nothing else. The moment was upon them.

She was her animal body now, and she thought of the sacred scorpion her people and their hero were named for, its tail rising to strike, how nothing could stop that venomous sting once it was in motion, and it felt like that venom was coursing through her muscles and squeezing not just her birth portal and the bones of the child trapped inside but her heart, her poor heart, and then there was a great, echoing release and almost in that moment, it seemed, she heard the wail.

"My queen," said Vishala at her ear in a voice of wonder. "Your daughter is here."

✦

Sunrise light licked at the flaps of the tent when she heard the cheer rise up from the warriors outside. A new warrior had been born and the Barren Queen was no longer worthy of the name. The very thought brought a smile to Khara's lips. Humming a sweet, soothing music, Beghala had cut the rope of flesh between them with one silver flash of the birthing blade, then helped Khara dress in a loose shift of hemp cloth that would warm her without keeping her skin from the child. Now the child lay sleeping on her mother's chest, eyes closed, little shoulders rising and falling with the effort of early breath.

The tent flap parted as Vishala returned from making the announcement, moving almost without sound. She knelt at Khara's side. "My queen, it is time."

"I suppose I am queen again now," Khara said quietly, not wanting to disturb the child.

"You are," agreed Vish, "and when many years from now you tire, you have the next queen there in your arms."

Khara said, "Bless you."

Vish shrugged. "The Scorpion blesses you. I just stay by your side."

"And the Scorpion and I both bless you for that."

Vish reached out for the birthing blade. It was the masterwork of a long-dead armorer, its amber handle formed to mimic the ridged body of a deadly scorpion, its curved blade gleaming a wicked silver in the early dawn light. "Are you ready?"

"Ready."

Vish lowered the blade toward Khara's neck, swept a fistful of hair into her right hand, and began to cut away the dark locks. Sunrise was the most auspicious time to shear a warrior, doubly so after a birth. The child was safe. The mother was battle-ready again, or would soon be. Softness that had been hers while she carried and grew the child would melt away. Khara closed her eyes and leaned back, letting each clipped coil of hair fall to the ground, hearing their whispers as they landed. She was lighter already. She was surprised how vigorous she felt, even after the pain of labor, even after the panic and fear. The baby must have turned, at least partway, before she entered the world. Beghala told her she had not even torn. There was a great deal of blood, but there always was. Blood that soaked the earth, whether from birth or battle, fed the Eternal Scorpion, their half-immortal hero. The God of Plenty had Her days, but a warrior's years belonged to the Scorpion.

Finished, Vishala laid the curved birthing blade on its crimson leather wrapping, to be wiped clean and honed sharp, then blessed and stored against the birth of the next Scorpican warrior. "Are you well, my queen?"

Khara turned her neck this way and that, savoring the cool air on her ears and neck, the feeling of freedom. "We are."

The flap of the tent opened and a familiar form came through. Mada was dressed in the warrior's wrappings, a split skirt and vest of soft leather that would not hinder her movements on the hunt. Khara knew it was her without looking up and smiled absently, her attention closer to home. The baby sighed in her sleep and settled her round, soft cheek against her mother's breast.

"Queen," said Mada. A single word, a word she'd spoken to Khara a thousand times, but never quite like this. Never without *my* before it to indicate her allegiance, her fealty. And that voice, Khara realized. It was not her accustomed voice. Not the warm, respectful tone of a protégée, but something else altogether.

Something was very wrong.

Khara's body, so relaxed only a moment ago, began to hum with tension. Dread in her belly, she looked up. A true warrior could read an enemy's intent in a wordless instant, and though Khara had never before considered Mada an enemy, the message of the younger woman's body was unmistakable. A knot in her jaw, a clenched fist, weight balanced on the balls of her feet. The queen caught a flash of what Mada might intend, an explanation for her bristling anger. She hoped desperately that she was wrong.

Without preamble, Mada began, "I speak the Words—"

"No!" Khara had never been so sorry to be right. Mada was angry, and anger made warriors foolish. What a loss it would be—but perhaps it was not too late.

She struggled up to her knees, then to her feet, holding one hand palm outward toward the younger woman, the hand that was not cradling the downy head of the child. She fought off the surge of vertigo that threatened to pull her back to the ground. These moments were crucial. She could not be weak, not now.

Vishala stepped forward into the narrowing space between them. "Mada, no."

"I do not speak to you, Councillor," the younger woman said, her eyes flashing fire. Her right hand settled on the grip of the short sword sheathed at her waist. The leather thong used to secure the sheath closed was dangling loose; she could have her sword out in barely a blink if she wished it, and Mada was excellent with a sword.

Vishala said, her low voice nearly a growl, "You know I will protect my queen."

"In this, you know the queen is honor-bound not to accept your protection," said Mada. "In this she has only her own."

Vish looked to Khara.

Khara nodded with a confidence she did not feel and addressed the younger warrior. "Before you do this, Mada, think. There is no going back. Think of your daughter." Tamura was now ten-and-one, gaining skill and strength by the day, clearly an iron-willed warrior in the making. No matter what weapon was put in her hands, she learned it and loved it. She took after her mother in that way.

Mada did not flinch. "It is my daughter I think of."

"You will leave her motherless."

"I will make her queen."

Vishala interrupted again. "Someone else must stand for you as your second. Who stands for you? Who will make the case that you are fit to rule?"

Khara knew Vish was right—the Challenge ceremony required such an action—but at the same time, insisting on protocol would change nothing.

"I will not require it," said the queen wearily. "I myself could make that case. I chose her once as my successor. To claim she is not fit would make me a fool."

Mada nodded in response, not in gratitude, only acknowledgment.

Khara saw it clearly, the inevitable. For years the rule of Scorpica had passed peacefully from mother to daughter, but any queen was vulnerable to Challenge. That was the law of the land. A queen could not be Challenged while she wore her hair long to signify life growing inside her, but as of this very minute, Khara was shorn. Anyone could speak the Words of Challenge to her. And Challenge had only one outcome. One of them would walk from this tent the queen of Scorpica, and the other would be carried out to her grave.

When she'd decreed Mada her successor, she'd used the official words, passed down through generations. *Because I have no blood successor, I choose my successor by name. She will command when I pass to the battlefield beyond.* But there was a blood successor now, and the decree was instantly void. The new daughter—so new she was not yet named—had changed it all.

Mada said, "To you, Khara dha Ellimi, I speak the Words of Challenge."

"Mada dha Shodrei, I do not wish to accept."

"Wish? What fig should I give for your wishes?"

"Please," begged Khara in a softer voice, "please." The baby stirred again in her arms, seeking warmth, seeking her heart.

"The Challenge has been issued," Mada said, her face impassive, each word like a blade. Her hand still rested on the hilt of her sword. "Battle or forfeit."

"I will not forfeit."

Vishala broke in. "Mada! She is freshly birthed! Where is your mercy?"

"She is shorn, is she not?" Mada gestured to the fallen curls on the ground. "You promised me the queendom. I am ready to lead. I will not let you break that promise. Challenged queen, choose your time."

Dread welled within Khara. She had the right to choose any day or time up to three sunrises hence, by the law of Challenge. The choice of weapon was hers as well. Queens who were Challenged won more often than not, or at least the stories said; but of queens who were Challenged the sunrise after childbirth, Khara could recall no stories.

Mada had chosen to speak words that could not be unspoken. Now it was Khara's turn to choose—from nothing but impossible options. So she made the only choice she could, the only path forward. Any other choice meant certain death; only this one made death slightly less certain. She would likely die anyway, but she would die fighting, as befit a warrior.

So Khara rose in a clinging veil of pain, her first step unsteady, and handed the downy-headed newborn to Vishala. The child cried faintly in her sleep, a bleat like a goat's, then settled against the other woman's shoulder. Khara could not look Vishala in the face. But Mada was too good at strategy, too good with too many weapons; if she gave the younger woman a chance to plan their battle, she would surely lose. And so.

"I choose *now*," spat Khara, and swept the birthing blade from its resting cloth with one hand, driving the other hand down low toward Mada's stomach, knocking the younger woman off-balance and onto the ground.

Vishala cried out and leapt back from the fighting pair, both arms encircling and sheltering the nameless newborn child. Beghala fled the tent. Khara was dimly aware of their movement, but once she was sure they were out of reach, she focused all her energy and attention on the fight. She imagined herself parting the veil of pain that wreathed her, splitting it like a tent flap and stepping through the gap into the light, so she could see her way clear. Her opponent was wasting no breath on protest or shock but simply reacting, brawling, readying herself to bring their battle to a swift, fatal close.

She'd been smart, of course, Mada; instead of fighting Khara's momentum she rolled with it, already working to unsheathe her short sword as she rolled across the dirt toward the far end of the tent.

Khara threw herself against Mada before she could stand, landing as hard as she could on the younger warrior's right wrist, preventing her from getting her sword out for one more crucial moment. She knew in such close quarters she could not get her own blade in position to strike, but she raised it anyway. As she hoped, Mada moved to block the blade, and Khara landed a sharp elbow in the soft hollow of Mada's throat, leaving her gasping for breath. Khara gasped too, the pain in her core radiating outward like heat from a fire, but she summoned every scrap of strength left to her, knowing even that might not be enough.

Now the element of surprise was gone. They were matched.

Mada threw her off and rolled to her feet, coming up against the side of the tent but still eking out enough space for a ready crouch. The sword was in her hand. They were in full battle, warrior against warrior.

They traded blows and parries, no sound but breath. A feint to the right, another to the left, a slash at the belly, a spring, a hard drive, a fast spin. Every attack had an answer, every counter a dodge. Khara's choice to fight in the moment had denied Mada the chance to don armor, and although her own nursing shift offered no actual protection, it at least obscured her shape. The nearest of Mada's blows hissed impotently through fabric instead of meeting flesh. But the birthing blade was no longer than a handspan; it was deadly sharp, but small. Khara would have to get closer, much closer, to land any kind of blow. So far Mada had kept her at a distance. Pressing in would be a risk, especially as her steps inevitably slowed.

She felt blood she could ill afford to lose trickling—coursing?—down the inside of her thigh, knee, ankle. At least she would be slippery with blood if Mada tried to grab her and hold her in place. Should she press in?

The short sword swung through the air so near her ear she heard it whistle.

Mada had a gift for strategy, but Khara knew no strategy was needed here: just wear the bleeding, weakened queen down to nothing. That would do. Khara's strength would give out quickly; she was already down to the last of her reserves, and one mistake was all it would take to end her. Even making it this far was a small miracle. Scorpica was not known for miracles.

For now, both were still on their feet. Mada forced her backward, swinging the sword in arcs Khara had to dodge, driving her toward the pole of the tent. She edged to the left to avoid it. Then the young woman was coming faster, faster, her blade flashing, too fast.

From near the tent's front flap, the child's sharp cry split the air.

It was only a moment, but it was all Khara needed. Mada turned a fraction of her attention toward the sound. The weight in her left foot shifted sideways. Her elbow on the right side went ever so slightly up.

Now.

Khara drove hard forward, grunting, diving as she swung her knife hand up, putting all the strength left in her body behind the short, curved blade of the birthing knife as she thrust it just under the protection of the younger warrior's lowest rib.

At the initial stroke, the soft flesh gave no resistance and the blade sank all the way in. As the weight of Mada's body dragged on the blade, Khara continued to pull upward, willing her arm to give her just these last moments of strength to do her fatal work. The birthing blade's sharp curve opened the flesh of Mada's belly the length of a thumb, then two, then three, everything red and glistening below the skin exposed.

Khara was falling, Mada was falling, Mada was screaming with pain, she was swinging the short sword even as she fell. The flat smacked against Khara's temple and bounced off, its impact resonating in her skull, and she swung her free hand wildly at it, all instinct. The sword fell from Mada's grip, skittering across the ground, and slid to a halt against the pole of the tent, where it raised a faint powder of dust. Both women landed hard but not together.

Khara's world exploded in a shimmering darkness.

For a moment, she thought she was dead. There was no sound, no light, no breath. Perhaps she was on the way to the battlefield beyond, where her ancestors would welcome her with a feast of deer and wild boar and lily wine. She had fought well. If nothing else, there was that.

But then there was sound again. The child's cry.

And she could see. Mada's still body lay in a heap a few feet away, her face mercifully turned from view. The stench of blood had already been in the tent, but this new blood, fresher, more like metal, was overwhelming. The Scorpion would feast on this blood as well, so much of it soaking into the ground, so much life that could have been and now would never be. The battle was over.

From the ground, Khara gazed up at the roof of the tent, hearing the cry of the child and her own ragged breath. Her body was all pain, from her core to her head to the hand she'd sliced open as she slapped the falling sword away, like a fool. But she was alive. She would weep over Mada's death—all that lost potential, the warrior who could have served her nation so faithfully—but not now, not today.

The child would have to be named. As she lay on her back in the bloody dirt, the name came to her. In the Old Language, in the incantations the warriors whispered before and after battle to invoke the strength of the Scorpion, there was a word for a beloved blade: *amankha*. It was not a name, but it could be. Yes. That would do.

Amankha dha Khara. Amankha, daughter of Khara. Her daughter. Her own.

The daughter whose cry the no-longer-barren queen now recognized. Hunger.

Now here was Vish, kneeling next to her, her voice thick with relief. "Your daughter, she needs you," she said, and laid the child on Khara's chest.

As if to fulfill her words, the child's mouth sought out the nipple. Khara would not have thought herself strong enough to move, but her hand rose. Her palm cupped the back of the baby's head, guiding her. As the baby nursed, Khara hung on. The tiny skull in her hand was an accusation, a promise, a dizzying possibility. This fragile, hungry creature was the future queen of Scorpica—if Khara could stay alive long enough to keep the queendom safe for her, until she came of age.

"I will tell your warriors of the outcome," said Vishala, and swung the flap of the tent wide to walk out into the morning. A warm breeze stirred the stale, bloody air, promising something beyond. Khara turned her head to watch her friend go, her eyelids heavy, her heart torn.

Along with a slice of blue sky, through the open flap she glimpsed the crowd, a crowd that not an hour ago had cheered the birth of their queen's only daughter, an unforeseen blessing. Now they were arrayed and waiting, grim, stone-faced. They all wore weapons, which was not unusual, as most warriors did—weapons for the hunt, for practice, for boasting. But a weapon could be put to any purpose, and now every weapon looked like a threat.

A cluster of younger warriors stood closest to the tent, young women who had trained with Mada, who had been passed over in her favor by Khara as they grew. When Vishala told them that Mada had died and Khara lived, would they hiss in disappointment or shout with joy? This was the last moment before they knew. One rubbed her face with her palm; one crossed her arms, planting her feet, glaring. How many of these women were loyal to Mada and not to her? How many of them, now that the queen had been Challenged, would be next in line to speak the Words of Challenge themselves?

She'd thought that after the birth of the *makilu* child, whatever happened, she would be able to rest.

She saw now she would never truly rest again.

CHAPTER 4

THE HEALER

In the village of Adaj, Arca
Jehenit

The desert sky of Arca was alive with stars. Grateful for their light, Jehenit moved deliberately from roof to roof across the buried houses of her village, counting each roof so she would know her destination. She was grateful, too, for the evening breeze, and for the distraction that drew her from her own house to the stranger's. What she was not grateful for was her disobedient body. Her swollen feet dragged like bricks, every step an effort, the low weight of her enormous belly tilting her forward and shoving her knees out into a waddle. Even a year ago, a woman grown and married with more than two decades on the earth, she could skip lightly across these rooftops as freely as a child. The indignity of her leaden movements now vexed her beyond the limits of her patience, which had once been considerable.

Given enough sand and life force, combining their talents and skills, the magicians of Arca could do almost anything. Jehenit herself had sealed countless wounds, reattached half a dozen fingers, brought more than one child from the brink of death back to full health in the time it took to breathe. Not every woman in Arca could call forth the light of ten thousand lamps with a snap of her fingers, as the village's most talented fire magician had done, but nearly all were born into some sort of magic. Fire, earth, air, water, body, or mind. Each Arcan could harness one of these in a specific way, according to her talent, to accomplish some goal. To dry a wet garment, calm a harsh wind. To soothe a fretful child. To cool water or to warm it. To spark a hearth to life.

And yet not a one of them could make a baby come when it did not want to come.

When she found the fifth rooftop from the end of the market road, Jehenit paused and counted again to be sure. The houses here were meager and narrow, the rocks and pots that defined their borders drawing ever closer together. The impression was as if Velja, God of Chaos, had taken three regular-size houses between Her palms and pressed them together into the space of one.

Jehenit herself was hardly rich, but she had a house twice this size to herself and her husbands near the center of the village, three levels deep. Her mother, chief healer before her, had used it, and she would bequeath it to the next healer after her. Hopefully, the child in her belly would be that healer, if she—Jehenit asked Velja daily for a she—would ever give up her comfortable perch and consent to enter the world. As if in answer, the child turned inside her, a sharp elbow or knee stretching the drum-tight skin painfully, and settled into a new position square against Jehenit's hip bone.

She could not lower herself to her knees to knock on the door, so she muttered an apology under her breath, and thumped her foot against the wooden square below her to ask for entry.

As she waited, Jehenit contemplated the house. There was much one could tell from a roof. It had been swept recently, so despite its compact size, it was clean and neat, well cared for. Whoever lived here had neither money nor status; no one who had either would live so far from the village center. But healers didn't take coin for their labors, so it didn't matter what the woman here was able or unable to pay. Besides, Jehenit was no longer sleeping. No matter how she lay, there was no position in which the child didn't weigh on some vital part of her. If she could not rest, she might as well work, and bring someone else the peace she could not have for herself.

The wooden door next to her feet swung open at last, banging on its hinge. She looked down into the square, dark opening.

Two faces looked up at her. Nearer, she saw a young boy on the ladder, long lashes fluttering on his cheeks. Below him and behind him, in the half dark, she caught a glimpse of a woman's upturned face. The resemblance suggested they were son and mother.

Still panting from exertion, Jehenit took a moment to find her voice. "I am told healing is needed here. May I come in?"

A lamp flickered and swung in the interior, and the woman's face came more clearly into view. Now Jehenit could see the grim yellow cast to her smooth, unlined skin. Her face almost glowed against the darkness.

"Please," the woman said. Then, a heartbeat later, "Excuse me, I need to lie down."

"Of course."

The boy stepped aside. Jehenit tugged her calf-length tunic up and knotted it loosely at one thigh so she had more freedom to bend her knees without losing the use of one hand. She needed both to grasp the wooden side rails. She began to lower herself down the ladder with care, putting both feet on each rung, making sure she was stable before lowering her foot to the next. She knew every home's ladder was made to stay strong under the weight of the entire household if needed, but she still felt a fluttering shiver of fear that it might not bear her.

When she made it to the bottom, relieved to feel packed earth under her sandals, she oriented herself to the half-dark room. There was little to see, not much more than a low couch, a faded rug, a table made of sand bricks, and the guttering lamp. Shelves and sconces in one wall held what the household needed, a few jugs and bowls. On the highest shelf sat their household figure of Velja, the most common one, with one arm ice and one arm fire.

The yellowed woman lowered herself onto the couch and closed her eyes, her arm dangling onto the rug's faded patterns of rust red and coppery brown.

Jehenit lay two fingers across the woman's trailing wrist and found her pulse. Not as weak as she'd expected, but not strong. Gods-bones, it was uncomfortable to crouch on a floor, her knees creaking, belly resting on her rapidly tiring thighs. She'd have to beg the boy's help in order to rise again once this was all done. And then there would be the ladder afterward. She pushed down the resentment and forced herself to focus.

"Sister, what is your magic?" she asked the woman.

"Does that matter?" The response was defensive, sharp.

"I only wondered," clarified Jehenit, "what enchantments you'd cast recently, maybe something stronger than usual. Some women drain their own life force without meaning to. Is that possible?"

The woman sighed and turned her face toward the wall. "I'm only a minor water magician," she said. "Drop me on the dunes of an un-mapped desert and I'll dowse you three wells by sunset. But here, where there's no water to find? I'm useless."

"You're not useless, Ma," the boy said, but it sounded like he had made that exact protest before. His voice lacked conviction.

Jehenit shifted her weight to her knees, which at least released the tension in her aching ankles, but brought new strain elsewhere. There was a shimmering feel to the flickers and twinges in her abdomen, a sense that one pain was racing another around the circle of her womb, like fox kits at play. She shifted again, moving sideways, with no relief. Knitting her brow, she forced herself to concentrate. She cast her gaze around the room, hunting for clues to the woman's condition.

What else could cause this sort of bone-deep weakness? Something in her food or drink? Was another magician sapping her life force, either by accident or with intent? Jehenit had seen that before. She'd done it herself without meaning to, in the early days. Like anything else, good magic took practice.

Her eyes settled on a spot near the ill woman's dangling hand; the color of the rug there had changed. Gingerly, Jehenit lay her own fingertips on it. Damp. She raised her wet fingers to her nose, but it smelled like nothing. Not the musk of sweat or the tang of urine. How odd. Did it have something to do with the water magician? Had she lied about the exact nature of her powers?

"And what's this?" she asked, pointing.

Neither the woman nor the boy responded.

Jehenit clarified, "This wet area on the rug. Sweat from a fever, perhaps. How long has it been here?"

"That's not . . ." The boy trailed off, looking down and away under his long lashes.

Puzzled, Jehenit looked down at the damp rug again. Too far from the couch to come from there, now that she looked closely. Why hadn't she seen it when she first crouched down? Then she felt the lower part of her tunic clinging to the flesh of her swollen thighs. It, too, was wet. Everything came together. The boy hadn't wanted to tell her where the water came from because it came from her.

Birth waters.

She'd thought the twinges in her body were the usual pains and protests, but it seemed she hadn't recognized what they really were:

the beginning of the end. At last, and at the wrong moment, the child was coming.

She began to struggle to her feet, attempting to brace her weight against the sand-brick table, but a spasm ripped through her belly and stole her breath. Her arms gave out. She pitched forward. There was no room for her, and she barely managed to miss the table with her chin.

Down she went, all the way. She heard the ill woman gasp.

She felt the ragged scratch of wet wool against her cheek. Her knees were caught under her belly, her body curling in on itself, even as the pain radiated everywhere.

"The child," she managed to groan.

"Do you need help?" asked the weak woman, though she did not move. "Should we call another healer?"

"None to call," said Jehenit, every word a struggle, and another sudden cramping wave seized her. There was no question of getting to her feet. She could not even feel her feet. She couldn't spare the energy to magic the pain away. She would have to bear it. Besides, if she took the pain out of her body, it would have to go somewhere. She wouldn't torture either the woman or the boy. Her pain was her own.

The ill woman's fingers spidered across the back of her hand and then interlaced with Jehenit's. She had no energy to grasp, but she gave Jehenit something to hold on to, and that would have to do.

Jehenit panted through the waves of contractions, the woman above her holding her hand, calling out encouragement in a faint voice, for she had no idea how long. It was an eternity and just a moment. Had the boy gone for help? Would he come back? She saw nothing beyond the small circle of rug on which she lay. She had never felt such pain and she tried her very best to welcome it. They said that if you welcomed it, if you rode it, things were easier.

She'd never birthed a live child. The ones that hadn't lived were smaller, younger, less formed. There had been two, one from each husband, and she'd looked only once at each before their small forms were wrapped for burial under the hearth. From what she remembered—and she tried not to remember—their passage had been easier. There had been pain, of course, but other healers had been there to help. Only five years ago there'd been a half dozen of them with healing magic, including both her sisters, all touched with valuable power. Now the village had only Jehenit. If this child was not a girl, if this girl were not a healer, Jehenit's family line would die out. She worried that would condemn her village to die too.

At long last, in the wringing, wrenching pain that might have lasted minutes or hours or days, she felt something like a pop. She understood that this was the child fighting its way into the world. The head was out. Then more pain, and another pop—shoulders, body? For a moment, nothing moved.

All at once the room was bathed in blinding blue light, sparks exploding outward in a fierce, glowing burst.

Jehenit closed her eyes instantly but could still see the stunning, reeling brightness all around. No heat came with the light, only that rain of blue sparks, and a concussive force that sucked the air out of Jehenit's chest with a *whomp*.

If there had been air left to her, she would have screamed.

The light vanished as suddenly as it had come on; not dimming, just disappearing. Then there was only faint lamplight, as if she'd imagined the whole thing.

Panting, Jehenit struggled for breath. The ill woman on the couch panted too, but neither of them spoke. Now she could hear the angry howling of the newborn and reached down between her spread thighs for the squirming body. She saw no wounds on the child, nowhere on its small, still-bent arms and legs or on its bald crimson head. The only blood streaked against its newborn skin was its mother's.

Her mother's.

The girl child wailed. The shower of blue sparks had not shocked her into silence, as it had the women. Jehenit heard a faint sound of crying from elsewhere. Likely the boy, but she could not see him from where she was, afraid even to turn her head.

The cool night breeze was on her then, cooling the hot blood on her thighs, and she realized the square door atop the roof had been blown open. Or off? From the top of the ladder, a square now open to the starry sky, night air drifted in.

Finally the ill woman found her words. "What was *that*?"

"Dry lightning," Jehenit said, the lie coming to her lips with surprising speed. "But it has passed."

Still dazed, the woman seemed satisfied with the answer.

It was the first time Jehenit swore to herself that no one would know the truth, and over the years to come, she would swear it over and over again. No one could know.

The baby had done it.

Her long-awaited baby was a girl, as she'd asked, but not the girl Jehenit wanted. More than likely, she would never be a healer. She had all-magic.

Jehenit saw now she should have known better than to pray to Velja for what she wanted. Velja was the God of Chaos, after all. It was Her way to give you what you wanted in such a way that you didn't want it anymore.

And though it was too late, Jehenit wished—wished it with the fierce fire of all those blue sparks her newborn had conjured into the world—that the girl had stayed inside her body just a little bit longer. That she could have lived one more day in a world where this was not so. An all-magic girl. Far worse than no girl, no child, at all.

The baby's cries were quieting, changing into some other, less angry sound. Her unfocused gaze drifted away from her mother's face and roved the dim, spare room. What burbled out of her wide, toothless mouth next sounded eerily like a laugh. Her hands flailed loosely, exploring the air.

Jehenit could have sworn that at the girl's chubby, flushed finger-tips she saw the haunting trails of a few more blue sparks, streaking out of and back into nothingness.

Praise Velja. Curse Velja. An all-magic girl. No one could ever know.

◆ CHAPTER 5 ◆

Binding Magic

Five days later

Jehenit

Jehenit could not stop thinking about Daybreak Palace.

Five days after she bore her all-magic daughter, Jehenit awoke out of a fitful sleep with a husband's hand cupping the bone of her hip, with no inkling whether it was Koslo's or Dargan's. Her mind was a muddled cloud and had been for days. Baby Eminel slept little and Jehenit slept less. She was always exhausted, but not because of the baby. Or rather, not because of the baby's cries or her need to be fed and rocked back into slumber.

Whenever she lay on that pallet, night or day, in light or darkness, the image sprang up insistently behind her closed eyelids. Daybreak Palace gleamed golden, its sandstone curves and columns hewn from the smooth mountainside, its spires and arches soaring. Its front gate loomed in shadow. Then a wave of scuttling creatures poured forth, streaming down the steps and onto the sand like beetles, ugly, black, and low. Her heart rose up in her throat to choke her. Seekers. They would come.

Real Seekers were women, not beetles, and Jehenit had never

seen Daybreak Palace with her own eyes, but nothing would drive away the vision. And there was no mistaking its meaning. If they were lucky, that first blue-sparked surge of power had escaped the palace's notice. If not, Seekers might already be on their way.

Every queen of Arca since the very first, Kruvesis, had been born with all-magic. The songs said she was descended from Velja herself, daughter of a daughter of a man so beautiful even divine Chaos was wild to wrap her legs around his waist. All-magic did not descend only through specific matriclans, but popped up unexpectedly, as befitted the gift of Chaos. Wherever and to whomever she was born, every all-magic girl had an equal claim to the throne. So the queens of Arca regarded all-magic girls of the next generation with far more than idle curiosity.

It was assumed by all that the most gifted Seekers, the fastest and most accurate, were employed by the palace to retrieve all-magic girls. But even discussing such powerful magic felt like a dangerous risk, out here in the broad desert miles of Arca, where your own magic and your neighbor's often formed the thin, brittle wall between life and death.

Especially in a dying village like Adaj, with its best days in the past. Once they'd had a dozen healers, said the old women, able to handle any crisis, make any injured person whole. Once, they said, there had been an earth magician who grew an apple tree right through the center of her house and out through the roof, and every single day of her life, that tree budded, grew, and ripened one juicy, speckled apple. Once there had been a line of water magicians whose gifts were so strong they diverted a stream's path into new banks, steering it alongside the houses of Adaj, so close one needed only kneel there to drink her fill. The line had died out, and with it, the stream. It was gone mere days after they buried the last of the matriclan under the hearth and spoke the words of homegoing.

But even in this tiny, fading village, Jehenit knew, an all-magic girl could be found. That was why she could not stop picturing Daybreak Palace, why she was consumed with possible plans to keep the girl safe. Could she shield her from detection? Hem her in until she could learn for herself not to use her dangerous gift? In those long predawn hours, one dark-haired husband or the other slumbering peacefully beside her, her unsettled mind returned again and again to the problem. Jehenit was not sure she could do it. She certainly couldn't do it alone.

Then, inspiration: What about Jorja?

The instant she thought of her neighbor, Jehenit rose, slipping out from under Koslo's arm, for it was Koslo, as he slumbered on. She would have to do this just right, she thought. She would not get a second chance.

So she began with an offering to Velja, asking her blessing first, kneeling at the shrine. Their household figure of Velja was an unusual one, truly unique, a stone shaped by water and time instead of human hands. As a child, Jehenit had found it one day when she thrust her hands into the cool water of the stream—that year, but not the next, there had been a stream—to search the pebbled bed for mussels. The stone face's expression was powerfully reminiscent of the god, somehow both merry and watchful, disapproving and tolerant, and so it occupied the shrine's place of honor.

Most honored and powerful Velja, she said. *I prayed to You for this girl, and You brought her to me. My gratitude is infinite. Now I humbly ask one more boon: do not take her from me. Do not let her be stolen by Daybreak Palace. Let me keep her gift close, hide it from view, until she is old enough to take on its mantle.*

Lack of sleep still muddied her thoughts, but focusing on the task gave her new energy. Next she coaxed the sleeping baby from Dargan's arms, fed her without waking her so she would be content and drowsy. Then, cradling the girl against her chest, she ascended the household ladder out into the cool, dry air of dawn.

Jorja answered her knock promptly despite the early hour, welcoming her inside with a smile.

"You brought the baby," she said with delight when Jehenit descended, setting her feet firmly on the entry-room floor. "Ohh, let me see, let me see."

Jehenit handed Eminel over, watching her friend watch the baby's face. Jorja's own sons had been grown and gone for many years. The woman must be lonely. Her house smelled faintly of oil of olives, salt, and the white flower known as *klilia*, but the air was always a little stale, a little close. It was too much house for a woman alone, and if Adaj hadn't been dying, a larger family would've claimed it. But with houses standing empty, no one had disputed Jehenit's insistence that Jorja remain, though that was likely only because of Jehenit's standing. Jorja herself lacked a gift that could help the village. She could only build walls of air. It might have been a useful form of battle magic once upon a time, but no raiders had attempted to attack Adaj for years. There was simply nothing valuable to take.

But the very thing that made no difference to Adaj could now make all the difference in the world to Jehenit.

"I would not ask this favor of anyone else," began Jehenit, tentative, anxious. "But I cannot share this with Koslo or Dargan. And I have no family left here, no mother, no sisters. You are the closest I have to family."

Jorja seemed touched by the sentiment, her friendly expression sobering. She set a reassuring hand on Jehenit's shoulder. "Anything. You need only ask. What is it?"

Eyes on her slumbering daughter, Jehenit confessed everything. The flash of blue fire, her unsettled nights since, her hopes of weaving a web to trap the simmering magic within Eminel's body. Jorja's eyes widened in surprise over and over again, but she listened in steady silence, taking it all in.

"You understand," Jehenit said quietly, "I cannot let her go to Daybreak Palace."

"Of course not," said Jorja. She glanced around, upward, as if fearful that even inside this house there might be someone watching, listening. Her gaze flicked over to the image of Velja in the shrine, the one that showed the kindly face of Chaos, an open grin with two outstretched palms. Then she eased the slumbering child back into her mother's arms. For a moment Jehenit was afraid Jorja wouldn't help, that she was too frightened, too unsure.

"Only you can help me keep her safe," said Jehenit, trying to be bold, babbling in her worry. "I think we can do it. Make a kind of a shield over her. My body magic, your air magic. Woven together. To keep the magic in."

Jorja looked thoughtful.

"I hope we will be enough, but I'm not sure," Jehenit went on. "Maybe we need a third. Someone to make the shield strong. Provide the power to sustain it, even when we are not there."

Jorja's expression shifted from thoughtful to resolute. She said, "We have the third. It's her."

Hope bloomed in Jehenit's chest. Yes. She saw what Jorja meant, the simple logic of it. Harnessing all-magic to trap all-magic, using the very power of the girl to sustain the spell that contained her power. "Do you think it will work?"

"If Velja wills it," said Jorja. In a softer voice, she said, "Do you have the strength? You look so tired."

"I'll find the strength," Jehenit responded.

Jorja said, "The sooner the better, then," and gestured to the open space in front of her hearth, under the watchful gaze of the household god.

Jehenit set the wrapped, sleeping baby down. Aloud, as she always did when beginning an enchantment, she said, "Velja, be with me."

Then they began.

Jehenit always worked in silence, so she was momentarily startled when Jorja began to sing. The song itself was unfamiliar, the words unclear, but its rhythms matched Jorja's movements. Jehenit watched the older woman, rapt. She'd never seen magic quite like this. Jorja's sweeping motions seemed to scoop and shepherd the very air around them, gather it somehow, into a denser material that hung invisibly within the other woman's reach.

The rhythms of Jorja's song shifted. She quickly swung her arms so that her elbows faced in opposite directions and her palms lined up fingertips to heel, heel to fingertips. With an expression equal parts wonder and fear, she nodded to Jehenit.

Next, Jehenit summoned her power to her own hands with a speed born of long practice and carefully, slowly, lowered both hands to hover just above the surface of her daughter's skin.

Her magic tangled with Jorja's, struggled, seemed to clash, and their wide eyes met as they scrambled to fit their enchantments together. A dozen times Jehenit was sure her own spell was on the cusp of dissolving into nothingness; a dozen times she regained the upper hand just as it was about to slip away. She scrambled to gather the life force she needed, depleting her own though she could ill spare it, tapping the reserves of her sleeping husbands nearby, trying to draw only a very little bit from other women and men in the village. She'd never needed this much life force to heal someone, but this was an enchantment she was making up as she went along, and if it sputtered and dissolved, all would be lost. It occurred to her she had no idea how much life force Jorja needed for her own spell or where she was drawing it from. She hadn't asked. But she pushed the thought away. Even if this spell had dire consequences, she would bear them. In this moment, nothing else in the world mattered.

The girl awoke, twitching, fighting free of her blanket, but Jehenit did not rewrap or soothe her. She drew her focus back to the magic and continued.

Jorja gasped, the fingers of one hand twitching uncontrollably, but with a grim expression, she forced them to steady again. Jehenit felt the air grow heavy, solid.

The two magics fused at last, sliding to fit into one another like grasped hands, locked tight.

Jehenit felt the web settle into place exactly where she wanted it. Jorja must have felt it too; she gave a faint cry of what sounded like relief. But one more thing was needed. If the third magic didn't work, thought Jehenit, all this effort was for nothing. She nodded to Jorja, who nodded back. They were ready.

Heart pounding, Jehenit reached out with one hand. She covered the girl's eyes. She waited.

At first the naked baby lay still, but when Jehenit did not pull the hand away, she soon began to squirm. The hand pressed harder and would not leave. The child saw only darkness. She struggled. She swatted her ineffective arms at the hand, tried to move her head away and failed, flopping like a bird with a broken wing. Jehenit did not think she could hold her much longer. Something built in the air, an energy like the sky before a storm, almost too much to bear.

All at once a blue *something* rose from the girl, too slow to be light, too fast to be mist, and Jehenit braced herself for impact. It did not come. The magic rushed into the trap they'd set for it, simmering and roiling, caught just above the girl's skin.

Jehenit took her hand away and smiled down at the baby, showing her everything would be okay.

With one last sniff, the baby calmed. The blue glow around her faded, settling, though an occasional shimmer still could be seen skimming over her tawny little body. Jehenit hoped this would fade with time. For now, the important thing was, it was done.

Jorja's exhausted eyes locked with Jehenit's.

Barely able to form words, her power spent, Jehenit murmured, "Thank you."

Jorja shook her head as if to say thanks were not needed. She placed her hand on Jehenit's. "Family," she said.

"Family."

By the time Jehenit stood on her own roof with her daughter in her arms, the baby's blue shimmer had already faded from sight.

When she descended the ladder, Koslo reached out his arms for the girl, and she gratefully yielded the small, fragrant body to him. If he noticed anything different about the baby, he didn't say. He rested her little head against his shoulder and cooed, beginning to walk when she fussed, jiggling her gently as they crossed one room and walked into the next.

Dargan handed Jehenit a bowl of porridge and a spoon and she ate it standing, scooping the warmth of it into her mouth eagerly.

From the far room she could hear Koslo's voice—he had such a lovely voice—telling her daughter a story. She couldn't catch every word, but it sounded like one of the oft-told stories of Queen Kruvesis and her sister, how two girls born with the same gifts could grow up to be so different, how a prideful woman might pay for her arrogance and a humble one find herself chosen to rule as queen.

She felt Dargan take the empty bowl from her hand—she'd finished it without noticing, distracted by the story and her own fatigue—and replace it with a cup of hot, sweet tea. She didn't want it, but didn't know how to say so. Now that she'd eaten, her body wanted nothing but sleep.

He read her expression and took back the cup. She felt his lips gently brushing her forehead.

"Go rest," he said.

Shuffling into the nearest sleeping chamber, she lay down on the pallet fully dressed and closed her eyes.

Softer now, farther away, she could hear Koslo singing a familiar tune. She heard no sound from Eminel. Perhaps the baby was listening intently, eyes bright. Perhaps she was already asleep. The murmuring sound was so reassuring, so lovely. That old song, she thought. That old, reliable lullaby. She relaxed into the first lines, as known as her own skin, as her husband sang.

When an Arcan calls on all her magic
And the answer's a thousand leagues deep . . .

But even before Koslo's warm tenor voice sang the next line, Jehenit was finally at rest, seeing nothing behind her eyelids but darkness.

CHAPTER 6

THE DROUGHT OF GIRLS

Across the Five Queendoms
One year later

Only some disasters *strike*. Others roll slowly, rippling in wide, lush waves, creeping unnoticed as their poison spreads. Their victims awake one dawn to find not that disaster has struck, but that it has long since crept into their pallets alongside them, nestled inside their clothes, settled itself to live upon their skin. It has dwelt unseen in their houses for days, weeks, months. They have already breathed in the disaster like air.

So it was with the Drought of Girls.

Logically, the scribes of the Bastion should have noticed it first. Ever since the Great Peace, it had been their duty to record every known birth in the Five Queendoms. Seemingly endless lists of names, dates, and locations were written down in their vast library of record books, shelved forever. Scribes assigned to every nation discharged this duty faithfully. Yet these lists were initially scattered, kept in smaller logbooks tucked into a pack, a knapsack, a pocket. These records might not make their way back to the Bastion for a full year—what was the rush, for history? The junior scribe who transferred birth records into a central book saw a pattern but said nothing, afraid the anomaly was in his work, not the facts themselves.

It was in Scorpica that the pattern became obvious first, then, and at first it looked like good fortune. Trading away or selling newborn boys to other nations brought in goods, money, and food, and more boys meant more gain. Their stores of wine, for the first time, threatened to overflow the storage jugs; the councillor responsible for coin realized that, for the first time, she needed a second warrior to help her lift the chest. Quickly, there was more of everything. Except newborns who would grow into warriors, the one resource they could not do without.

In Arca, every village kept its own counsel, too concerned with survival to take notice of what villages across the miles might have or do. They mourned their own lack of girls, yes, but spoke to no one outside the village about it, not on the road, not at the river. The queen, Mirriam, could certainly have figured it out, if she cared to. She only noticed she'd heard no reports of all-magic girls in a while, but that was all to the good. In her view, there were altogether too many all-magic girls already.

In Sestia, the farmers and boneburners had work to do. They gossiped when they met, but they met rarely. And their priest-queen, the High Xara, did not concern herself with children. Priests of the Holy One were sworn to forgo pleasures, in honor of the celibate life their god had led after her consort descended to the Underlands. There were rites to plan and manage, the nation's storehouses to maintain, the god's standards to uphold. Life outside the walls of her temple-palace remained just that: outside.

For its part, Paxim was too far-flung to put the pieces together. The senators were occupied with the things that always occupy senators: laws and rules, arguments and debates, jockeying for power and position. Their widowed queen had her own all-consuming concern, worrying as her infant son, Paulus, grew. Every day, as she watched him learn to stand, walk, speak, she never lost sight of the clash that was to come when she insisted on making him the first-ever king to rule a queendom.

And so it went that the Drought of Girls spread across the Five Queendoms unheralded. It did not look like a disaster, not yet. To those who lived day to day, it simply looked like life.

PART II

DANGER

The All-Mother's Year 505
Three years into
the Drought of Girls

✦ CHAPTER 7 ✦

A DAUGHTER

The All-Mother's Year 505
In Scorpica
Khara

Tamura's spear sang through the air, making a perfect arc. Its sharp point flew toward the painted straw target as surely as if drawn there with a string. A moment later, its heavy iron head struck the innermost circle with a satisfying *thwack*. It sank deep and stuck hard, vibrating.

The sound was no doubt satisfying, that was, for the girl who had thrown it. The queen who watched the girl felt something less like satisfaction. Closer, indeed, to alarm.

Khara wasn't sure why she found herself returning over and over again to watch Tamura dha Mada train. She got a sick feeling in the pit of her stomach every time. But perhaps that was the reason. She knew that one day, a spear from Tamura's hand would fly with this same accuracy, this same savage precision, aimed for Khara's head or throat or heart. She could not afford to forget.

Or perhaps it would not be a spear. In the past three years, she had seen Tamura demonstrate remarkable—and still growing—skill with a dagger, a longsword, a hatchet, a staff. She'd even seen the girl lose her weapon in a fight and wrestle an armed opponent to the ground, then subdue her, with no weapon at all. Some of the younger warriors had taken to calling her Tamura the Barehanded. When the day came for Khara to choose, she thought, all she knew was that she would not choose the hatchet. She rarely dreamed, but when she did, that hatchet was her nightmare.

"Less than a year," she said to Vishala quietly. "That's all I have."

Her old friend cut her a look. "Are you so sure?"

"I am," said Khara. "As soon as she is old enough to speak the Words of Challenge . . ."

"She will have to find a second."

"Seconds are not so hard to find. Not for a girl with her talents."

They watched as Tamura trotted up to the target, bare heels flashing, calling something over her shoulder to another girl her age. She yanked out the spear with one hand and thrust it upward toward the sky. The other girl's face twisted with discontent. Tamura laughed, mouth open, throat long.

At this age, training was still a merry occasion, at least for the talented. And perhaps the mere thought of victory delighted Tamura. Some embraced their role as warriors despite the need to do violence, thought Khara, and some because of it. She wondered which one Tamura would be. Whatever her feelings, her path was clear: Tamura would pass her ritual that fall at ten-and-five, taking her place among the ranks of sister warriors.

And just as surely, she would take aim at the woman who had killed her mother. Without delay. Without mercy.

They watched from a distance as Tamura trotted back to her starting line, then aligned herself with the other girl, who hefted a spear of equal size. Tamura said something, her chin high. The other girl nodded. Tamura moved five paces farther away, and both sighted the target once more, arms raised and ready.

"And do you think I have any chance of winning?" asked Khara softly.

Vish's eyes were on the girls and their friendly competition. "You defeated Mada from your childbed, at the weakest you had ever been, despite her strength. Anything is possible."

"But not probable."

All at once the two girls unleashed their spears, grunting as they threw. Both weapons soared toward their targets. The other girl's spear sank into the straw target near the edge, just a moment before Tamura's, which thwacked once more into the center of the inner-most circle.

Tamura's laugh rang out again across the distance, a dark, harsh bell.

"No," said Vish. "Not probable."

"And if you were me, what would you do?"

There was an immense sadness in Vish's eyes as she said to her friend, "But I am not you, Khara," and reached out to clasp her hand.

✦

The years since her daughter's birth had been odd, worrying ones for Khara. She loved the girl beyond the telling of it. There were not words enough in the world. The child herself was no cause for worry: sunny, strong. But when weeks, then months, then years passed without another warrior's birth, Khara feared that the tribe might turn against young Amankha. When her time came to rule, would they regard her with too much suspicion? Did her status as the last girl born in Scorpica mark her, somehow, as unlucky?

After Amankha, warrior after warrior had birthed boy after boy. The increased income from trading away the boys had been the first sign, but the effects rippled out in countless other ways. The murmurings and whispers of worry increased as the camps rang less and less often with the cheerful babbling of the very young. Goat's milk had once been reserved only for feeding the babies of mothers who could not do their own nursing, but now there was enough goat's milk to make cheese to store for winter. Anyone could partake. Rarely were these truths spoken aloud, but everyone knew them. And they would only grow worse over time—differences growing into divisions, and eventually, into disaster.

The scope of that pending disaster paralyzed Khara. She knew she should take action, make changes, prepare her people for what might come. But it felt impossible to her, somehow, that the Drought of Girls could keep going. Every time a warrior gave birth—though far fewer did, now—there was still a spark of hope in her chest that the child might be a girl. But once the newborn's wail greeted the world, the midwives' faces telling all the tale that needed telling, that tender, vulnerable spark of hope, once more, died.

When she returned home from watching the girl she expected to kill her someday, her own daughter was curled peacefully on a cot in their tent. The child's dark hair formed a wild cloud all around her little head, obscuring her sleeping face. Spring had come early and they had moved from winter camp to summer camp two months before the annual rites—the lesser Moon Rites, this year—began in Sestia. And so the two of them had their own tent, with no need to gather in larger numbers to stay warm at night. Amankha could wander freely while her mother took care of other tasks in the camp; other mothers would keep her out of the worst of dangers. Now she was here, deep in a sound sleep, and Khara almost fell to her knees at the sight of her tender, vulnerable back, visible as soon as her mother the queen lowered the flap behind her to block out the sunlight.

The spot she loved most on her daughter's body was the small, sun-shaped birthmark between the girl's shoulder blades. Her broad cheeks, her merry eyes, her chubby knees and wrists, all were loved, but it was the round brown mark smaller than the child's fingernail that always made tenderness well up in Khara's bursting heart.

Khara kissed the birthmark and lay down next to the sleeping girl, curling around the small back with her own, much larger form. Her heart was still hammering, too loud and fast. She hoped the weight of the warm, breathing child resting against her would help to calm her again.

She had lost her nerve before. She had wanted to ask Vish the ultimate favor, to charge her with a sacred duty, but she could not form the words. She would do it tomorrow. Or if not tomorrow, then soon.

Because if Tamura defeated Khara and won her queendom, Khara knew exactly what the young woman's next move would be. Kill the mother, yes, then kill the daughter. That was what Khara herself had lacked the heart to do. Now she saw what came of it, when the daughter was as ambitious as the mother had been. For Tamura to leave the girl alive was to risk falling victim to another version of herself, to start the cycle again: a victor who lived, but lived in fear, dreading the day her victim's daughter grew old enough to make the victor, in turn, the next victim.

✦

Khara spent the next morning away from camp, allowing time with her daughter to distract her from questions of state. But those same questions distracted her in return. When she was a queen but not a mother, she had been wholly a queen. Amankha had changed her. She had seen queens who were able to put thoughts of their daughters, their lovers, their families aside when they ruled. She had discovered in the past few years that she was not one of them.

She'd intended to spend the morning teaching Amankha to move silently in the woods, preparing her for the hunt, but her distraction was contagious. The three-year-old had failed to focus. They'd ended up crashing through the brush instead and making a new game of it. If she couldn't yet teach her daughter stillness, Khara decided, she would at least teach her speed, and they played run-and-chase between and among the trees.

By the time they returned to the camp, the sun was already high, time for the council to meet. Today they would discuss the Drought of Girls, not for the first or last time, and Khara approached the meeting with slow, reluctant steps. If this drought dragged on, would it disrupt the peace between the queendoms? It was the largest question any of them would likely face in their lives, and no one had the answer.

And when she walked into the meeting tent, she blinked. To a woman, the group was already assembled. Was it her imagination, or did her councillors give each other furtive glances? Not just some, but all: Mirha to Gretti, Gretti to Vish, and on from there. Perhaps it was just their disappointment that she'd arrived late. Perhaps their discontent ran deeper. Dread spiraled inside her, fanned through her blood, though she let none of it show.

"Let us speak today," she said, the traditional words, almost like an incantation. "Let us speak freely. Let us speak truth. And today, let us speak of the Drought of Girls."

She waited. Any one of them could speak; any one could suggest a course of action, without judgment, without malice. It was in her hands to call a vote, but until that moment, their thoughts and impressions were all weighed equally.

"No one wants violence, but if it comes, we must be ready," said the warrior Mirha, who had served with Khara's mother, Ellimi, her tones measured, steady. She had always been conservative. Khara was shocked to hear her speak first on a topic so radical. "We must look first to our own strength."

"What do you suggest?" Khara said mildly.

"I will leave it to others to make their suggestions," said Mirha, backtracking. "I only think it important that we strengthen Scorpica."

"Scorpica is strong," scoffed Vish.

"Is it?" blurted Gretti. "We are thousands, but we are scattered everywhere. Wouldn't we be stronger together?"

The former bladebearer had grown into her womanhood, her first and only son sold shortly after Amankha was born. At ten-and-eight she was young for the council, the youngest here, but she had shown her worth. She and Khara did not always agree, but no one disagreed more respectfully.

"You are heard, Gretti. But could you explain what you mean?" asked Khara, doing her best to maintain a still face, one that gave nothing away.

"I don't quite know how to do it," admitted Gretti. "But something has to change. We have so few young warriors, and everyone knows it. Couldn't we make better use of the ones we have by bringing them home?"

Some nodded, some shook their heads. Khara looked around the circle, observing. Should she count who agreed, who disagreed? Should she speak her own mind or wait longer, listening?

Vish spoke into the silence, saying, "It must at least be considered."

"And we will consider it," Khara said. "But are you suggesting we need our sisters here to defend us?"

Gretti nodded soberly.

The queen shook her head. It was time to take a stand. "I will not precipitate a war no one is planning by taking a rash action."

"We wouldn't recall the Queensguards, of course," said Gretti, apparently speaking every thought that came to mind. "We wouldn't want to send the wrong message."

"Any withdrawal would send the same message—prepare for

war!" said Ekhrin, another of the older council members, more force-fully than she usually spoke. "It is the wrong message. We must leave our warriors in place."

There was some muttering, but no one spoke up for a while, either to agree or disagree.

At last, Mirha said, "If we did withdraw, which I think we can do carefully and wisely, since Paxim negotiated the original agreements, we'll need to ask them to negotiate withdrawals."

"Will we?" said Khara.

Mirha met her gaze with steely eyes, seemingly searching for what motivated Khara's objection: uncertainty or fear? "It would be the safest course."

"Not so safe as all that," said Vish, a little sharply. "If they said no, where would that leave us? Or if they brought us a bad deal? It's our decision, not theirs."

The older warrior weighed in. "Better to ask forgiveness than permission."

"Better not to ask at all," Vish said, "and just do."

Others spoke up, and though no one shouted or harped, Khara could feel the tension simmering underneath every word. Eyes darted around the circle, hands clenched into fists, heels ground in the dirt. Judgment in words was hard for women who spent their lives otherwise judged only by their actions. Council was fraught on a good day, and these were not good days. The Drought forced them to confront the possibility of important, irrevocable movements, any one of which could be a grave misstep. Unfortunately, they would never know what the true misstep was until long after they'd made it.

Khara let her council speak, but she had no intention of making a choice on such a weighty matter without more time to think. She had no idea how she would choose even given infinite time. For today, formally, she spoke the words of closing. "You have spoken well and wisely today. Thank you for your counsel. May the Scorpion bless your minds with wisdom and your arms with strength. Until we meet again."

The women dispersed, but the tension remained, and Khara was the last to leave, falling into step silently next to Vish. She thought she might discuss the meeting with Vish, as she often did, to get a sense of whether both had read the mood in the same way.

When they crossed near the practice fields, she lifted her head and automatically scanned the crowd. She did not see Tamura there. Next to her, she heard Vish draw in her breath, long and slow, then let it out the same way. The sound put her on her guard, but she was still not prepared for what came next.

"I know you are looking for her," said Vish, "and she is not here."

Of course Vish knew. But what did she mean? Khara's suspicion began to grow. "Where is she, then?"

"I wanted to tell you myself."

As if by unspoken agreement they clung close to the supply tents, lowering their voices so no one else could hear, but continuing their slow walk in the public eye, as if they merely chattered of nothing.

With dread, Khara said, "Tell me."

"She has been assigned."

"Assigned? But she's not old enough!"

"She is an extraordinary warrior. An exception was made."

Khara's mind was racing. "An exception? Whose exception?"

"The council. They agreed. We all agreed, Khara." Vish's tone was level, determined. But not at all guilty. There was nothing of fear or regret. It seemed obvious that she was completely convinced she had done the right thing.

It came to Khara in a flash: the whole time Vish had been talking in that council meeting, when it sounded like she was talking about recalling assigned warriors, that wasn't what she'd meant at all. She'd spoken in favor of acting without asking for permission—because that was what she herself had done. She knew if she'd asked Khara whether she wanted Tamura sent away, Khara would have forbidden it. Then, mere months in the future, she would have simply walked out of her tent on the day Tamura came of age, ready to fight and die.

The scope of what Vish had done struck Khara, hard, square. She made no attempt to hide her anger, which flared hot and high. "You did this behind my back? Convened a council, as if you had the right?"

"I did."

"I am *your queen.*" She had never spoken so to Vish, but she didn't know what else to say.

Vish simply agreed, "You are."

"I should—I should—" She should punish her. That was what she would have done to anyone else, even a council member, but it was Vish. Her oldest friend in the world. Her burning anger melted into guilt, equally intense. "Vish. I never would have asked this of the council. Of you. She is just a girl."

"An extraordinary girl. And not for long."

"Custom is custom, rules are rules. If we don't have those—"

"I know."

"You did not have the right."

"I know." Still no regret, no guilt, in her tone.

Khara's thoughts stuttered and tripped, but when she found the words, her question was sharp. "Where did you send her?"

Then and only then did Vish's resolute calm seem to flag. Her gaze went down, seeking her sandals in the dust. "The Fingernail."

"*Mokh,*" Khara breathed out, a sharp rebuke. The Fingernail was a prison island off the coast of Arca, full of hardened criminals. A guard's position there was the most challenging assignment a Scorpican warrior could draw. Half the women who got it wanted it desperately, and even they returned daunted by its challenges. The other half trembled walking through its gates on the way in and again on the way out, fearing how bad it would be and then shaken by how bad it had been. The Fingernail always lived up to its grim, dark promise.

Vish set her jaw and put her hand on Khara's arm. "You are angry with me, I know. My hope is that time will help heal the wound. There is a hunting party leaving soon, camping in the lower mountains overnight. I will join them." She turned and was gone before Khara could reply.

Khara continued walking with her head down, turning in the direction of her own tent, her steps deliberate and slow. She was glad Vish left her to think, but still, how much time did she need to come to the right conclusion? Mere minutes.

Vish had only delayed the inevitable. Tamura would come back even angrier, even more ready for combat, even more the warrior.

Even so, thought Khara, she was grateful beyond words.

She would have two more precious years with her daughter. And no matter what, those years were a gift. She could not be angry at the prospect of watching Amankha's face grow and change over the days, the weeks, the seasons. To see the girl's eyes dance with delight at both the sparkle of winter snow and the sun-kissed summer grass. To see the girl bring down game and sew her own leathers, to come into the promise that was only now hinted at in her sharp eyes and strong legs. Khara would never have sent Tamura away like this herself, would never have given Vish permission to do it.

Thank the Scorpion that Vish had not asked permission.

Tamura would come for her, as she'd always known the girl would, ever since Mada sighed her last breath at Khara's feet. The next Challenge would grow from the last one like a tree's branches from its root. Blood—possibly a great deal of it—would be shed. Only one of them would survive.

But not yet, she thought. *Not yet.*

CHAPTER 8

HEALING LESSONS

The All-Mother's Year 507
In the village of Adaj, Arca
Jehenit

Jehenit lived in hope until the day the winged girl fell from the sky. For the first few years of Eminel's life, as the girl grew, Jehenit did her best to teach her healing. Eminel was a roly-poly dynamo of a child, always trying something new, collecting bruises, scratches, scrapes along the way. These, Jehenit easily could have left to heal on their own. Instead she crouched next to her daughter, her hands hovering a few inches above the scraped knee or singed fingertips, her manner intent.

While she had the girl's attention, she patiently explained how healing magic worked. She reminded Eminel that both sand and life force were needed to produce magic, that in the absence of both, even the strongest gifts would fail. Each magician had to understand both her potential and her limits. Then she'd put the lesson into practice, murmuring an incantation, demonstrating hand motions that helped focus the healing energy. She'd bend the girl's fingers into the right positions over and over, repeat the words as Eminel stumbled. She tried to teach the girl to heal herself.

Tried.

The thing about all-magic was that it included all six magics—air and water, fire and earth, mind, and yes, body. So Jehenit knew there was a good chance her daughter had some healing power. But that neat and breathing web she and Jorja had woven, dampening the field of the girl's all-magic, kept everything inside. This sharpened the challenge as Jehenit tried to teach the girl the one aspect of magic it was not just allowed, but necessary, that she have.

Jehenit struggled to remember how she herself had learned healing; it seemed to her no one had ever tried, on purpose, to teach her. Her mother had turned nearly all her attention to her eldest daughter, Rissel, shining on her like the sun. Then there had been her second daughter, Yidini, and a beloved son, Mijar. Jehenit herself was much younger, lingering far behind. In some ways Rissel had nurtured her more than their mother had. Most of the time Jehenit had been cared for by her mother's husbands, and of course they had not taught her to heal, though at least she'd known they loved her. Love was nothing to take lightly.

The one time Jehenit remembered her mother touching her was to build her tattoo, a swirling pattern of black sand embedded under the skin of her left wrist that marked her as a healer so all would know. Even while she was doing it, her mother had not soothed her or reminded her that she could, if she wanted, displace the pain. She had simply pressed her thumbs against Jehenit's palm, bending it back to bring the wrist taut, and wordlessly driven each grain of sand through and under her daughter's skin until the wheel-shaped design was complete. Jehenit would have sworn she felt each single grain like the tiniest of blades. If anyone had ever asked her. No one had.

Now, there were no other healers—her grandmother and mother dead, her sisters and cousins gone—leaving Jehenit alone to heal any injury, large or small, in the village. If she could not train Eminel as her replacement, there was no future for Adaj.

Or perhaps another healer could be found. Once a year, Jehenit hired a scribe to help her write and send messages in every direction. Her words went to the far eastern hamlet of Bryk, famed for its glass castle, a masterwork of heartbreaking beauty raised by a uniquely talented earth magician of old—but it got so hot in the sun it was uninhabitable, no good for anything but looking at, and that from afar. Her words went as far north as Sjinja, almost to the border of Paxim, known as a hospitable and lovely place, one where there was always plenty because of the deals struck by their diplomatic neighbors: magic for goods, goods for magic. Her words went to a village on the southern coast so old it had no name, the village where the ancestors of Jehenit's line had been born in the long-ago days before the Great Peace. She sent her pleas to these far corners, knowing the nearer villages had nothing to give, hoping against hope she might find a new healer the way an animal digging in the dry dirt hopes it might unearth a hidden spring.

She shared none of this with Koslo and Dargan, not wanting to worry them, knowing there was nothing they could do to help. All they could do was what they already did: share the domestic duties, watch the girl while she worked, provide pleasure and respite in the calmer hours of the night. She knew her preoccupation with keeping Eminel's secret was straining her, distracting her, but if they noticed it, they said nothing.

Until the day of the winged girl.

It was a rare quiet day. Dargan was gone on his yearly visit to his mother and sisters, and she'd taken Koslo and Eminel to picnic in the shade of the high caves overlooking the village. Just as they were finishing their meal, an unusual shadow streaked the ground in front of them, moving fast. Koslo remarked that it looked too large to be a hawk, but when Jehenit looked up, she lost the shape in the gleam of the sun. Broad, feathered wings, then nothing. She would've thought no more of it, but only minutes later, a long-legged boy came charging up the path. He could barely form words, but panted, wild. "My sister. Five years. Wings. She fell."

Jehenit understood instantly. The winged figure in the sky had not been a hawk at all. She had never herself seen a body magician whose gift was to add physical features, but she knew they existed. Five was a common age for a girl to discover her power. It was all too easy to understand how a girl so young could, without considering the consequences, give herself wings and take flight.

"Take Eminel home, please?" she asked Koslo. Assuming she knew the answer, she rose, brushed off her tunic and leggings, and made to follow the boy.

It surprised her when she heard her husband's voice behind her saying, "No. You take her."

"What?"

"She should see you heal."

"The girl is only—"

Koslo rose. "Eminel. Take her."

The boy, wild-eyed, said, "Quickly. Please."

There was no time to waste arguing. She grabbed the five-year-old's chubby hand. Perhaps Koslo was right. If Velja willed, the girl could still be a healer someday, and if so, she would see far worse than this. Maybe it would even help her understand.

She hefted Eminel onto her hip and picked her way down the rocky path, following the nimble boy, the tingling fear in her blood driving her just fast enough to keep up.

When they arrived, a dozen villagers were already gathered, more coming by the moment. As the years of Drought advanced with no sign of respite, injuries to young girls lit the village with terror. And this girl—small for her age, narrow-hipped, her hair cut close—had a stunning pair of wings unfurling from her back, brownish feathers thick and dull like a winter sparrow's. She lay on her back with her eyes closed. Both wings were spread out against the sand, one lying wide flat, one bent at an unsightly crooked angle.

Jehenit rushed to the girl's side and crouched there. The girl was breathing, but only lightly, and could not be roused.

At her shoulder Jehenit heard the girl's mother, desperate, manic. "She fell so far—we didn't know, she had never shown—before we even knew, she—help her, please, help."

Jehenit turned and laid hands on the mother, gripping her shoulders lightly, before she even touched the child. Sometimes the patient was not the only one who needed healing.

"Please," she said, using her most soothing voice. "Do your best to be calm for her. She will look to you the moment she wakes."

The mother was able to settle her body, kneeling next to Jehenit, though her eyes darted wildly around. On Jehenit's other side crouched Eminel, already imitating her mother, sober and small and quiet.

The healer examined the winged child. The shallow breathing was worrisome, but it was impossible to tell the extent of her injuries at a glance. How far had she fallen, and how had she landed? No way to tell. She might get up and walk away in mere minutes. She might never walk again. She might not, in fact, survive the hour.

Jehenit looked around. There was plenty of sand, of course, and villagers from whom she could borrow life force, though she always checked first for other options. Here they were scant. A short, dry-looking tree stood nearby, a few crows perched and staring from one of its gnarled branches. Not likely to be enough.

A man came running toward them, most likely the mother's husband, and made as if to lift the child. Jehenit held up her hand, raised her voice. "No! Don't disturb her! She must remain just this way."

He still reached for the child's prone body, and Jehenit stood to block him with her own, to shake his focus. Make him see her.

In doing so, as she rose to her feet, she turned her back on the mother and child, as well as the child she'd forgotten was even there: her own. Young Eminel had been watching silently, a small shadow. When her mother turned away, Eminel reached out and placed her hand on the injured girl's chest.

Jehenit did not see what happened next, but she felt it. She felt the web of magic she'd woven over her daughter rip just a little, like a cloak caught on a thorn. It made no sound, but what followed made plenty.

The first crow landed with a thud on the sand. The second and third fell only moments later. Two more thuds, dense and muffled. Then the branch upon which they had stood turned as black as their feathers and cracked from the tree with a thundering snap. This echoed, crackling through the bright sky. The stench of burnt feathers hung in the air.

Jehenit spun away from the mother's husband, back toward the girls, and fell to her knees. She wrapped her hand around her daughter's tiny wrist, terrified and uncertain. What would happen if she pulled the girl's hand away in the midst of a spell like this? Would magic continue to pour out? What kind of magic? She hesitated, terrified of what would happen if she acted, what would happen if she didn't.

Eminel's gaze slid from the tree to her mother. In the moment their eyes locked, Jehenit felt the cold. The girl broke eye contact and her gaze moved on, beyond.

Then Jehenit heard the husband gasp.

His gasp was not shock or surprise, she realized almost instantly, but a frantic, desperate bid for air. For a long moment, he clawed at his throat, eyes wide. She felt movement under her grip and turned to see the winged daughter's chest rising, filling, as the father struggled. *Sweet Velja.* Every breath the girl took was a stolen one. Whatever the consequences, she had to stop it. She yanked hard on Eminel's hand, breaking her contact with the other girl's body.

"Ma-ma," the child whined. "Let me. I want to help."

"Not now. Sit over there. Watch." And the healer did her best, though she was far from certain it would be enough.

As she always did before healing, Jehenit said quietly, "Velja, be with me," then began.

Whatever amount of healing her daughter had managed to do in those short moments, even while wreaking havoc, it did seem to have helped; Jehenit could feel the injured girl's heart beating. Her breath was better, and she continued to breathe, even now that her mother's husband was breathing on his own again. A faint color was creeping back into her cheeks. The healer drew from her own life force, some of the mother's, and even a little of Eminel's—perhaps it would keep her quiet, dampen her—to bring the fallen girl from the brink of death back the rest of the way toward life.

Jehenit did not look up at the villagers, but she could sense their energy, their tension. They had seen what happened. Did they understand it? Could they tell that Eminel had tried to heal the winged girl? That she had reached for life force and gone too far?

Then something else was happening. A deep blue bruise formed on the injured girl's chest, above her heart. Both Eminel and Jehenit had touched her there, but Jehenit knew this was not her doing. Then there was another bruise, and another. The bruises kept blossoming outward, blue on blue on blue. The fallen child moaned softly. Whether from her previous injuries or these new ones it was impossible to say.

Jehenit turned toward her daughter. Brushed to the side, the fussy child was playing a game with her fingers, flicking the nail of her index finger against the pad of her thumb to make a faint whispering sound. It looked like something any bored child might do to amuse herself. But it wasn't. To her horror, Jehenit realized that with each flick of her daughter's fingers, a new bruise formed on the other girl's skin.

She wrapped her arms around Eminel and squeezed her, hoping the parents of the injured girl would see it as an outburst of emotion, the healer's thankfulness to Velja that her own daughter was safe. More than anything else, she hoped it would distract the girl enough to stop what she was doing.

"Ma-*ma*," her daughter whined again, quietly this time, into her ear. "There are places in her she says need fixing. I'm fixing them."

Jehenit focused on the web of magic around her daughter, finding the tiny hole through which the all-magic had poured. She could not knit it back up on her own. She needed to get the girl to Jorja right away.

Had anyone else heard Eminel's words? What could she do if they had? Nothing.

Just then, the injured girl's eyes opened and she let out a cry, echoed by her parents' cry of happiness to see their child revived, and an answering wave of relief through the crowd behind. Jehenit turned away from her daughter to look over the small body, inspecting every inch with great care.

"The fall was great," she said to the parents, doing her best to keep her voice steady. "I cannot tell you whether your daughter will walk again, but bless Velja, I believe she will live."

She wanted to stay, to reassure them, to check the girl over again for deeper damage. But she knew the longer she stayed here with Eminel, with that pinhole of all-magic let loose, the more she courted disaster. Too tired to carry her, she grabbed her daughter's hand and tugged her along toward home.

She went straight to Jorja's. First she only told her the minimum— she needed a hole knit up, could she help?—and then later, after the girl fell asleep in the midafternoon light and the women sat nearby drinking tea, she told her everything.

Jehenit stammered, "She said—I think she . . ."

"What?" said Jorja. "You can tell me anything."

"I think she went inside a girl's mind," Jehenit confessed. "Her all-magic. How powerful must it be?"

Jorja wrapped her arms around Jehenit, who pillowed her head on the other woman's shoulder and let herself sink down. They stayed like that for a long time, while the tea cooled and the silence stretched on and on.

A little later, Jehenit descended the ladder into her own house alone, step by weary step. Jorja had insisted that she leave Eminel napping, since the girl was already asleep; Jehenit accepted gratefully. She hadn't even turned her head to see Koslo before she heard his voice.

"Did she die?" asked Koslo.

"What? She's with Jorja."

"I meant the girl you went to heal," said Koslo, biting off his words, "but I suppose your own child's all you ever think of."

"What?" repeated Jehenit, exhausted, trying to make sense of her husband's words. When she looked at him, she saw how he was dressed, and she knew what was happening. He wore a traveling pack over both shoulders, full to brimming. He intended a journey. And he would not come back.

"It's been much worse since the girl was born, but I understand now, I was never really happy," said Koslo. "I loved you, but it wasn't enough."

He looked to her for a response. She had none.

"I'm going back to my mother's family," he said, voice sharp.

She had so many questions, but none would come to her lips. She watched him, stunned, dry-eyed.

He took her silence as encouragement to go on. "You said you loved me, but did you? You barely even saw me. You didn't try. You never tried."

At last he seemed to tire of her blank look, sighed heavily, and stepped around her to reach the ladder. He passed so close she could have reached out and touched him. But she couldn't find it in herself to move.

Afterward she wished she'd lashed out in return, repeating his accusations: *You should have done more. You were never enough.* It would all have been lies, but at least she would have left him with some impression.

When Jorja brought Eminel back an hour later, the girl rubbing the sleep from her eyes with chubby fists, Jehenit had already finished crying. And when she lay down to sleep that night with the girl's body curled against hers on a single pallet, it was not Koslo's words that echoed in her ears, but Eminel's.

There are places in her she says need fixing. I'm fixing them.

There would be rumors. No one but Jorja knew what Eminel was, not even Eminel, but the community didn't need to know in order to suspect. Jehenit had healed hundreds of people in plain sight before today, and not one of them had bruised like the winged girl. If anyone made the connection to Eminel, whispers would fly. Jehenit could not take it if anyone decided her daughter might be a danger to other girls. In these years of want, there could be nothing worse.

She saw only two options. They could go, leave Adaj behind, before anything else happened. Then Eminel would be safe. But Jehenit's duty was so ingrained, so deeply felt, she couldn't just abandon the village to its fate. Without a healer, its scant handful of girls left vulnerable, Adaj would be gone within a generation.

The other option, then, was the only real one. She would have to work harder. Make herself indispensable. Make no enemies, ensure everyone in the village owed her a debt. That way, gossips would be hushed, goodwill overcoming rumor, because the town would love Jehenit too much to speak against her.

She could save both the village and her daughter, she was sure of it.

She would just have to try harder.

✦ CHAPTER 9 ✦

THE HUNTED, THE HUNTER

Long ago and now
On an island off the coast of Scorpica
Sessadon

First they slew her friend Alish, whose turn it had been to lead the party, with an arrow in the throat. Skilled hunters, their enemies. Swords and spears took out the next half-dozen of her comrades in a flurry of merciless speed. Then the warriors chased down two stragglers, the first dying with a wild cry, the second felled in silence. In what felt like five heartbeats only Sessadon, fighting for her life, remained.

That life hung by a thread. Bleeding from half a dozen wounds that would have killed a lesser fighter outright, wounds that could yet bring her down in minutes or hours or days, she sprinted through the unfamiliar forest. She knew her blood left a clear trail any fool could follow. Still, finding herself hunted like any common, doomed fox, she did what prey does. She fled.

Behind her they called to each other, their shouts too close, always too close, tracking her progress through the trees. Driving her forward so she had to run or die. When she stumbled out of the forest's ragged edge to find herself poised high over the roiling, roaring threat of the Salt Maw, their shouts grew merry, taunting. They were sure they'd won.

So she made the choice that was no choice at all. When, grinning, they pressed her to the stark white cliff's very edge, she gathered herself and leapt.

Her soaring body left the land behind, arcing first through the empty air, then down through the water and down, down, down. Gone she was, swallowed by the white-capped sea. They did not follow because only death waited in the Salt Maw's waters. Its roar was all around her as it closed over her head, her world turning murky, salt-stung blue.

Later, the sea that had swallowed her spat her up upon an even less familiar shore, no other land in sight, a lonely island. Sky. Sand. Silence.

She awoke with only the outline of her earthly form, a kind of body that was not a body, though it once had been. She'd faded almost to nothingness, but there was magic here. Something powerful, something charmed, kept her spirit anchored so it wouldn't slip away.

Should she bother clinging to that anchor? She was so alone. Her friends murdered, her far-off homeland twisted into something unrecognizable, everything she had been promised gone, gone, gone.

But she heard power singing in the solitary island, in its outcropping of glistening quartz, in the mouth of a cave nearby. A dark yawning mouth against the searing blue sky. Out of the light, out of the weather. If she could make it that far, she told herself, she could wait there. Either death would find her or something else would. Slowly, so slowly, she crawled toward the cave's welcome darkness. Once inside, she lay her spectral cheek against the sandy ground and let her awareness of the world go dark.

An unknown time later—minutes? days? years?—she awoke.

Her body had none of the functions that bodies should have: no breath, no pulse, no heartbeat. Her blood had dried up in her withered, parched veins. Yet something of her remembered earthly form was there. She needed to bring back both her body and her purpose; the one would serve the other. If only she weren't alone. If she had no one at all in the world, she thought, remembering the circumstances that had driven her here, there wasn't any reason to live.

So she focused on her purpose first. Gathered the kernel of her power, guarded it like a smoldering coal. Murmured the words of an enchantment and sent it out over the sprawling land, searching, hoping.

There. Far off, so far, so faint she almost missed it. A drop of blood that sang to her blood, as fresh and new as hers was dried and wasted. A descendant of her line. It came to her whole, then. A purpose. A goal. She reshaped the enchantment, drew every drop of power she could muster. In a silent frenzy she painted the far-reaching spell against the cool hard ceiling of the cave and stretched, thickened, pressed it there like fresh dough on a hot stone. To achieve her purpose, she needed to encourage certain possibilities and cut off others, and this spell would shape the future she burned for.

Spent, she rested, and did not wake again until the hunter came.

✦

No one else would have noticed the hunter. Her movement through the forest was like a water bug's path across a silvered pond, almost too seamless to be seen. She moved with easy confidence born of experience, an arrow ready, at any moment, to let fly. Her prey didn't stand a chance. More than likely, they would never even know she was there.

But the woman in the cave knew.

When she woke, she saw the passage of time in the island around her, though she still did not know how long she'd slept, or how long it had been since she'd first washed up on shore. The foliage of the overhanging trees seemed longer, heavier, the beach itself a bit wider where the sea had worn more sand away. But two things had not changed. The spell she'd painted onto the ceiling of the cave hovered above her reassuringly, and her weakened form had become no more solid. She would need help to bring life back to the body. To feel the desiccated lungs not just plump up and regain their spring, but fill, blessedly, with air. Now that she remembered her purpose, she longed to bring the feeling back to her fingers and the smile to her face. Now someone young and strong, bursting with life force, was here to keep her company. Now she was no longer alone.

Careful not to siphon too much power from her main spell, remaining hidden, she placed a tickle of her voice just behind the younger woman's ear.

Good hunting, she whispered.

The hunter froze, not twisting her body to search high and low for the source of the voice, but remaining as still as the trees that flanked her. A good hunter knew ears told more than eyes ever could. She remained still, and while she was still, Sessadon seized her moment.

It had been an eternity since she had practiced this brand of magic, but she needed to do it now, and do it right. She would only get one chance.

She delved into the mind of the young hunter, swimming through its murky depths like the cold currents of the Salt Maw. The mind was all around her and she caught its stray ideas and memories in flashes like silver fish darting, flickering, rushing by. The hunter knew what year it was and now so did Sessadon; five centuries had passed, she realized with a jolt, though she could spare no time to consider the revelation. Instead she dove deeper, reassembling the woman's disjointed thoughts into sentences, listening as the hunter, without conscious intent, revealed the truth of who and what she was.

I am Hana dha Rhodarya, ran the hunter's story. *This morning I killed three ibex, a mother and her kids, and I am remembering the location of the tree where I hung them to bleed so that on my way back to the camp, I can finish dressing them and packing the meat for travel. My favorite things in life are the bloom of the* argaut *flower in spring, the breathless freedom of riding a wild pony at a hard gallop across flat land, and the knowing smile of sweet, shy Marbera when I whisper at her shell-pink ear with dark and luscious promises.*

Of the six talents any given Arcan magician might have—air or earth, water or fire, mind or body—mind magicians were the least understood, the least trusted. Not every mind magician had the power to control other minds; of those who could, it was widely believed that they could take charge of only one mind at a time. But then, whose word could any magician take for it? One could not trust the untrustworthy to be honest about their own nature. Only the mind magicians, and the queens who ruled them with all-magic, knew the truth for sure.

When she'd been young, before she was marooned in this forsaken land, Sessadon had discovered that she had more power than she'd ever thought possible. It was an accident, the first time. She'd only meant to explore the servant girl's mind, not crack it open like a green almond and slurp up the knowledge inside, leaving the girl gibbering, senseless. She quickly learned to take more care. With practice she could send her mind into others' like thread through the eye of a needle. She could even slip into her sister's mind undetected, once she got good enough. That was when she realized how much her sister feared her. Her sister could never hate her, those unveiled thoughts made clear, but she could never trust her either.

Their differences, at last, drove them apart. Proud, fierce Sessadon had been chosen to lead their tribe, but then the architects of the Great Peace decreed that queendoms would replace tribes. And they'd asked the more charming, cautious Kruvesis to reign as queen of the fledgling Arcan nation. One sister's rise was the other's fall. It was hard to say whether Sessadon left or was driven out, but it amounted to the same thing. She gathered a small group of angry fellow magicians and headed north, and only months after the borders of Arca had been defined, they found themselves far beyond them.

Kruvesis's fear was not the only thing Sessadon had plucked from the recesses of her sister's mind. A secret had also been shared with Kruvesis by the women who designed the queendoms: though Arca had been established in the southeast to draw on the sand that enabled Velja's worshippers to cast their magic, the same minerals were highly concentrated in quartz deposits in the islands off the northwest coast of the newly defined nation of Scorpica. Sessadon and her friends, like Alish, intended to investigate these deposits, and possibly even harvest and carry off the quartz. If they could show that these divisions between nations were arbitrary, even counterproductive, they could weaken the new nations before they had a chance to calcify. Tribes were the natural order of things, not queendoms. Velja had never wanted them to gather in communities any larger than a few matriclans or to limit where they might wander. The quartz islands proved it. But before they'd even made it off the mainland, the Scorpican hunters ambushed them, and only Sessadon had survived to set foot on the islands they'd journeyed so far to reach.

Now she reached for that quartz, drew on its enormous potential, and called up her mind magic. She had never found the limits of her abilities when she lived the first time, all those years ago in Arca; she had only one mind to play with now, but she would make the most of it.

She started with a single thought: *the woman in the cave is my friend.*

A smile tugged at the corners of Hana's lips. There. It was already working.

Sessadon nudged again, with a soft suggestion.

I do not need to hunt now. I will visit my friend.

Hana moved into the cave as soundlessly and easily as she'd moved through the forest, her body tensed but her mind open.

Ah, there she is, ran her thoughts. *My friend. I cannot see her well, but I know her.*

In the darkness of the cave, using only her mind magic, Sessadon beckoned Hana closer. The gentlest of suggestions, just a hint, a whisper.

The hunter approached, making her way toward the back of the cave. The pleasant sensation had no cause that she could identify, but she did not question it. Why would one question such a warm feeling? All was well. All was right. The warm darkness cradled her, and her friend was here. It was right to feel a balance to the world.

A simple test, thought Sessadon. Just to see. It could open the door to all sorts of intriguing possibilities.

This time, without thinking, only commanding, the sorcerer sent her mind into the mind of the hunter and moved her.

The fingers of Hana's right hand rose through the air, adjusted the leather strap that held the quiver of arrows on her back, and then settled down at her side again. The young woman didn't seem bothered by the fact her body had just done something she didn't intend it to do. Her thoughts were untroubled, still friendly, still open. Through the power of manipulating the hunter's mind, Sessadon now had access to move and use her body.

The sorcerer smiled.

Without really understanding why, so did the hunter.

CHAPTER 10

TRIALS

The All-Mother's Year 507

Daybreak Palace, Arca

Mirriam

From high above the maze, Queen Mirriam of Arca, Well of All-Magic, Master of Sand, and Destroyer, cheered.

She wore no crown. Queens of Arca never did. Instead, around her neck lay the gleaming snake of blue glass every queen since Kruvesis had worn, its pearl eyes shining with what looked, on some days and in a certain light, like intelligence. Nor was the snake necklace truly glass. Real glass did not slither. But today the snake merely rested in its comfortable coil, warmed by the heat of the queen's body as she called out. She urged on the pair of racing girls on the course below, the dark sleeves of her robe falling away from her raised arms like the petals of an exotic flower.

Dozens of finely-dressed courtiers, eager and thrilled, faced down onto the maze. Like their queen, they called out, cheering one girl or the other, shouting encouragement, disappointment, surprise. Their eyes flicked over to the queen's face regularly, measuring her, observing her, so they could change their own behavior to mimic hers. She was their model and their muse.

And Mirriam hated every single one of them—every woman, every man, no matter their rank, no matter their talents—with a singular, burning passion.

The only people on the high seats she did not hate, her husbands, sat at her left side. Rijs sat closest as the senior husband, then Ever next, as the junior. On her right was an empty place for her daughter, Mirrida, who did not like to attend the trials, but Mirriam would not give her place of honor to any other at the court. It would upset the delicate balance. She placed the highest-ranking women close enough they could hear her speak but not so close they could hear her whisper; it was an important distinction, and one she had been observing for years.

Keeping her enemies close was a wise course of action, and she never diverged from it. Her mother had given her that counsel nearly a century ago. But closeness was as much curse as virtue. Her court of rivals crackled with magic that verged on danger every day and every night. Such constant pressure wore on a woman, especially after this many decades. The courtiers themselves changed over time, but the danger never did.

Mirriam's mother had been Solaji, Well of All-Magic, Master of Sand, Destroyer of Enemies. Solaji's own mother, for her third title, had worn Destroyer of Injustice. When Mirriam chose her titles, she had chosen simply Destroyer. It struck the right note of fear: limitless.

But this morning, in front of the assembled court, she was all kindness. She cheered for both of the all-magic girls competing in the maze, choosing no favorite. Both were about ten years of age, the roundness of youth in every limb, dark hair pulled back from their small, determined faces. The taller one was dressed in a white tunic that reached to her knees; the shorter one wore an identical tunic, dyed black as night.

They'd seemed evenly matched, both demonstrating their ability to see through illusion, to leap over fire, to breathe in water, to build a bridge of earth. Now, ragged, tired, and wet, they parted ways, searching for the exit, for the solution to the maze. It was not enough to survive the maze's dangers, though some girls failed there, if their magic was not strong enough. A girl must race and win and find her way free. If she could not do that, she failed the trial, and every courtier here knew the penalty for failure.

The tall girl in white, bedraggled hair plastered to the sides of her face as she panted, came up against another blind wall. She would have to pass through the fire again to find her way back to the next turn; Mirriam could see her energy flagging, see the doubt plain on her face. Could she gather enough life force, enough strength, to cast an enchantment that would see her safely through? To jump or fly over the fire, to make her skin impervious and pass through it, to find some other way?

The girl in black had taken a different turn, found herself faced with her own failure: a wall had turned, changing the course, and now she had blind walls on every side. Like a mouse she skittered to one corner and then another, searching for a way out, finding only flat space.

Then the sound of a crashing wave turned every head: the girl in white had summoned water, a great gush of it, and extinguished the fire in front of her. She raced through the ash, its gray paste clinging to her bare feet, and with two more right turns, she was out of the maze and free.

The courtiers, led by their queen, roared.

Mirriam rose to her feet, applauding, and descended to the exit of the maze. She kept the broadest of smiles on her face. When she faced the girl who had won, she lowered her head in a slight nod to honor her hard-won victory. From a queen, that was meaningful.

"Congratulations," she said to the girl. "Rest well. Tomorrow you will run again."

Mirriam could see the question in her eyes—*So soon?*—but she said nothing. Good. A girl who could not hold her tongue could never rise to be queen.

This girl would never rise to be queen anyway, but she did not need to know that. The trials were not really about the girls. The trials were about the court: the management of its energies, its shifting alliances, its teeming power.

The courtiers did not have all-magic, but the powers of magic they had were the strongest of their kind. The best water magician in the court could disrupt the vast expanse of the Mockingwater; the strongest earth magician could roil the earth in a quake that buckled and snapped any building that stood upon it. Their skills were the most developed, their clothing the richest, their baubles the brightest-gleaming, and their husbands the most beautiful.

And some of the husbands even had a flicker of other magic, the type that only the most talented men of Arca had: some variation on illusion magic that touched not just their own appearance, but the appearance of others. Benica's husband Duveen could make flickers appear in the corners of others' vision, distracting or unsettling them. Dolse's husband Ijahn could project a wash of color over any room, casting everything in a light as green as grass or red as blood. He was much sought-after for banquets and other social events, though no one had worked out a practical purpose for such a gift. Husbands were not, in any case, generally chosen for their practicality.

Mirriam, queen of Arca, turned the victorious girl toward the waiting faces of her court and said, "This all-magic girl has earned your praise! Let her hear how she has pleased you."

The stands erupted in applause. Benica and Duveen, the girl's sponsors, descended. They grinned at her and she grinned back, wearily, as they guided her from the arena back to her quarters.

Then Mirriam turned to the other girl, the one in black.

"I'm so sorry," she said gently. "Your all-magic is not strong enough. You cannot be a queen of Arca."

Tears streaked the girl's face, but to her credit, her voice was steady. She faced her queen and spoke with only a slight tremble. "What will I be?"

"For now, you will work in the kitchens," said Mirriam. "It is a good life."

"What if I want to go back to my family?"

"The kitchens first," Mirriam said. "In repayment for all we have given you, you understand. For how we have hosted and clothed and fed you all these months while you trained, giving you the chance to rise. The trade is fair. If, after six months in the palace's service, you still wish to return to your village, you need only say so."

The girl looked up at her solemnly and nodded. Mirriam placed a hand on her shoulder and gestured to a man in a midnight-blue robe who would take her where she needed to go.

"Your efforts were not in vain," she told the girl before taking her hand away. "All here today have seen what you can do. Velja has blessed you. We will not forget."

Her words were kind.

Her words were a beautiful lie.

✦

It was absurd, thought Mirriam, that you could grow a living creature inside your own body and have no control over what they became once they were out. She'd given birth to Mirrida nearly thirty years before and still found her daughter incomprehensibly foreign. Mirrida had been an undersized, thin-limbed slip of a child, flooding into the world too soon, as if she could not stand to call her mother's body home any longer. Their discomfort with each other, even from those early days, was mutual.

And yet her daughter was one of the very few people Mirriam trusted. They were bound together by blood, which meant a lot in this world, and by the all-magic gift the mother had passed to the daughter, which meant even more. Mirriam had a grudging respect for Mirrida, who had proved time after time that no matter how frustrating she could be, she was also very clever. They had that, at least, in common.

"Queen?" Mirrida said, her voice sharp, and Mirriam realized it was not the first time that she had said it. The queen's attention had wandered. It often did, trying to get through these conversations. As little as Mirrida cared to witness the trials, she frequently invited her mother to her own chambers afterward to discuss them privately over a midday meal, and Mirriam had never yet turned down her invitation.

"I was saying"—Mirrida leaned in—"given the Drought, don't you think we should make the trials a little easier?"

"I don't make them anything," Mirriam lied. "The trials are what they are. If Velja does not make girls strong enough to pass them, it means that today's girls are not strong enough to be a successor to the throne. But what do I need another successor for, anyway? I have you."

"I'll be dead long before you are."

Her voice cross, Mirriam said, "Such a lovely day. You need not spoil it by reminding me what a mule you choose to be."

"I have no intention of extending my life," Mirrida said, her tone devoid of emotion. "I have told you a thousand times. Do not make me say it again."

You don't want to know what I could make *you do,* Mirriam thought and did not say.

"Is that all you came to tell me? That you think the trials are too hard?"

"I came to tell you people are asking how you are going to counter the Drought."

Mirriam threw up her hands. "Counter it? Is that my personal responsibility?"

"Well," said her daughter with infinite dryness, "you are, after all, the queen."

"What I mean is, I didn't cause it. Do they think I caused it?"

"Some of them, yes."

"Why would I? If girls are never born again, eventually Arca will run out of magic. We'll be a nation of pretty men and dead women. And sand."

"Eventually, yes. But the time horizon . . ."

"Yes, yes, I understand." Mirriam waved her hand dismissively, her mind already picking up the rest of her daughter's argument. "Some of the more talented women of Arca live longer than the women of other queendoms. If our bodies stay young enough to bear children, no matter how old our minds are, we can still birth babies. Once girls are born again, we'll make up the gap."

"It's the warrior nation that will die out first," said Mirrida, and her tone was no longer flip. "The other nations are somewhere in between the two, but all are unsettled. Paxim is already tied up in knots arguing about whether men can be allowed to vote, let alone serve in public office, and their queen has only a son. Their men are . . . eager to claim a larger share of power."

"And our men? Are they similarly eager?"

Mirrida looked down. "I've heard some rumblings."

The queen's daughter's official position was chief councillor, but anyone who was anyone knew that also meant she was the spymaster, and any rumblings she'd heard were not mere rumor. She would not have mentioned it if it were not something the queen needed to know.

"I'll keep that in mind," said Mirriam.

She left her daughter and walked quickly down the golden sandstone halls of Daybreak Palace, headed for her own chambers. At some point in the future, the men of Arca might band together to do something about their discontent. Today's rumblings could become tomorrow's rebellion. Then again, the gap between feeling powerless and risking one's very life to grab for that power was vast. Life was not so bad for these Arcan husbands, when you got down to it. If it became a problem, she would fight the threat.

But for now, she had another use for men in mind, and two husbands waiting.

One for the head and one for the bed, the saying went, but Mirriam did not choose her husbands for the traditional reasons. She took no companion who could not satisfy her in both body and mind. When they'd been younger, she had chosen Rijs more often, but now, she sought her pleasures most frequently with Ever. They each had their own rooms within her rooms, so she could choose at will. She rapped lightly on Ever's door and opened it without waiting for an answer.

He lay waiting for her, stretched out on the softest couch near the window, long bare legs tawny against the pale cushions.

"Napping?" she asked.

"Hoping," he said, and rose to meet her.

She pressed her lips to his, exploring his warm, familiar mouth, and lay her hand on his chest. She pushed gently and he fell back against the cushions again.

"And that's what I was hoping for," he said with a sly, welcoming smile.

They spent the afternoon in pleasures, baring themselves to each other, as the sun outside the window sank toward, and then below, the horizon.

Mirriam happily lost herself in the sensation of skin on skin, setting aside all thoughts of Droughts and trials and tensions. Her husband stroked and licked her, building her pleasure like a fire: kindling first, then flame, then a long, slow burn of banked coals with a lasting, luxurious heat.

Whenever a worry sprang into her nimble mind, Mirriam simply forced it away, telling herself there would be other days. Weeks and months and years of them.

Queen Mirriam of Arca, Well of All-Magic, Master of Sand, and Destroyer, who had already lived more than a century, had a long life yet to live.

CHAPTER 11

A CHALLENGE

In Scorpica

Khara, Tamura, Vishala

Two years earlier, five warriors had been sent on assignment to the faraway prison island called the Fingernail. One day in late summer, four returned.

Summer camp was already half-dismantled. Big-game season was upon them, and dozens of unassigned warriors were set to journey into the middle mountains, hauling home meat that would see them through the winter. Smaller game—red squirrels, coneys—came easily enough in other times of year. But this was the best time to bring down larger animals. Each single death could fuel dozens of lives. Time spent hunting brown bears or mountain aurochs was time well spent.

That was the way it had always been, and Khara followed the pattern. She sent the full complement of warriors, exactly the same number as the previous year, even though not as much meat was needed; the Drought had lessened their numbers, and the Scorpicae could get by with less. She knew she was clinging too tightly to the old ways. And yet she clung. She heard the murmurs of those who disagreed with her, the ripple of discontent. But it felt too much like surrender to recognize how the world had changed. She let herself postpone the reckoning. Next year, she thought. Next year she would send fewer warriors to the mountains. Perhaps by next year it would be clearer what the future would bring.

The group from the Fingernail had been expected back nearly a month before, but travel through four nations was vulnerable to uncertainties, and given the unsettled times, delays were expected. No one had yet expressed serious concern. These women were survivors, or they never would have been sent to the Fingernail in the first place: all strong, stubborn, fighters to the core. After two years in the crucible, headed home at last, even misadventure was unlikely to keep them too long from their destination.

When four figures were spotted in the distance, the rumors began instantly. *Why only four? Which four?*

Bohara walked into camp, as did Larakhi, Nikhit, and Ibis, but not Tamura dha Mada. Whispers flew. She'd been killed by an inmate, said one version of the story. She'd defected to the Arcans, said another. Within mere hours of the four guards' return, countless strains of baseless gossip spread to every corner of the camp. The rumors called the unseen Tamura noble and venal, faithful and faithless, dead and alive.

When the next day dawned, they saw the truth with their own eyes.

Tamura dha Mada sat twenty handspans from the front flap of Queen Khara's tent, cross-legged on the ground. The angles of her face had sharpened, her body grown leaner, the last traces of childhood softness worn away. She'd left with her hair in the plait of youth; it had been trimmed to a warrior's crop, but not recently, and her short, dark curls sprayed out around her head like the rays of the sun. Two handspans from her lay a well-used, bone-handled dagger—her mother's—pointing straight ahead.

Khara knew then that there would be no question of the young woman lacking a second, lacking support from other warriors. No guards had raised the alarm when Tamura came into camp overnight; no one told Khara she was here. There had been no warning. She had to look out the tent flap into the rosy tint of dawn and see the young woman for herself. All during the Drought she had heard countless whispers of discontent and she had ignored them, assuming she would know when the simmering anger grew truly serious, and that once she chose to act, she would have time. Now she knew time had run out.

Not far off, two of the other former Fingernail guards were lurking. Khara could see the stout, steady form of Bohara and the more angular outline of Nikhit. The studied casualness of their positions was, she knew, not casual at all. They were on guard for Tamura. They were ready.

Two years had not been enough to prepare herself to meet Tamura in battle. No stretch of time would ever have been enough.

Lowering the flap of the tent and returning to her cot, Khara stroked her daughter's hair and pretended nothing was wrong. Amankha turned in her sleep, not quite waking, pillowing her head on her mother's thigh. Khara shifted underneath her. The girl's head in her lap was a welcome weight, the curve of her small cheek impossibly dear. Her mother looked down at her for a long time.

Khara wanted to linger here, in this dreamlike moment, forever. The stillness of the morning was all around them. It would have been a peaceful morning, as so many of them had been, but for the enemy waiting.

When her daughter began to stir awake, Khara kissed the girl gently, cradled her, tickled her chin. Her tiny, radiant smile was like the sun and stars. Khara felt a pang in her heart then. Perhaps she should have run. Perhaps it was not too late. Perhaps the young woman could be reasoned with—but no. The time for reasoning had passed. The challenger had taken up a confrontational position. The moment they'd all known to be coming was here.

"Did you sleep well, dear child?" Khara asked.

Young Amankha considered the question, blinking, sober. "I'm still sleepy."

"Close your eyes, then."

"I can't. Too much to see," said the little girl, looking around in wonder.

"There's nothing to see but me," Khara said. "You've seen me before."

"You've seen me before too. Many times! But you look at me all the time anyway."

"That's true." She nuzzled and kissed the girl's hair, inhaling her smell.

"You've kissed me before too," Amankha pointed out, her high voice firm and instructive, with that unearned certainty common in the very young.

"Also true."

"So sometimes we do things over and over."

Khara confirmed, "Sometimes we do."

"Why?"

"Sometimes, because we can," said her mother, and planted a loud kiss on the girl's brow, smacking her lips together to make Amankha laugh.

But even as she cherished what she fully expected to be her last minutes with her daughter, Khara was careful not to hug her too tightly. At the end she did not say goodbye. Even when Vishala entered and the two women bent their heads together in an intense discussion, they were careful to keep their voices low.

They murmured so softly Amankha could not make out their words. She only knew her mother and auntie gripped each other's forearms as they spoke, a warrior's embrace. With their faces pointed downward they looked like they could have been sisters, even twins. At a greater distance, she might not even know which was which. She snuggled back into her bedroll while they talked. Perhaps she would sleep a little longer, she thought. Her eyelids were heavy. The day could wait to begin.

"Thank you," Khara said at last, her voice hushed, thick.

"May the Scorpion bless your path," Vishala said in return, her head down. Without looking her friend in the eye, she departed.

When Vishala exited the tent, bursting into the open air like a hawk taking wing, she headed straight toward Tamura. She closed the space between them with sharp, quick steps, then planted her feet very near the point of the girl's dagger. She said nothing. Nor did the girl respond. One might even think she did not see the other woman at all. The two of them only hovered there, in opposition, each silently willing the other to take a different path.

After a long, stony silence, Vishala bent down and put two fingertips on the worn bone handle of the dagger. Without appearing to rush, Tamura reached out her own hand and put her fingers on the back of Vishala's hand. Despite this, Vishala did not stop what she had started. Slowly, almost gently, Vishala turned the point of the dagger back toward the girl who had laid it on the ground.

"You don't have to do this," Vishala said in a whisper.

Tamura's long, coltish legs were still crossed, her mouth still set in a hard line, her body a raised flag of readiness. She did not say a word.

At length, Vishala departed, disappearing behind the queen's tent. Tamura reached out and turned the dagger back to point at the front flap of the tent again.

Warriors had begun to gather. Word spread. They came in a hush, saying nothing. There was nothing to say.

The flap of the tent opened and Khara dha Ellimi, her head bowed, stepped through.

The queen pointed back toward the tent and raised a finger to her lips before lowering the flap to cover it again and loosely tying the string. There had been only a glimpse of a shape in a bedroll, covered by warm blankets.

"I speak the Words of Challenge," said Tamura, just as her mother had said five years before. No one had challenged the queen in the meantime; despite their discontent, as if by agreement, they'd left it to her.

Khara said, "It doesn't have to be this way."

"It does," replied Tamura coolly, dagger in her hand. "Will you insist on seconds? With my mother, I am told, you did not."

The queen shook her head soberly. "You are not your mother. Yes, we will hear from your second."

The woman who stepped forward out of the silent crowd was the warrior called Bohara. She was wide in the shoulders and hips, aggressive and tenacious. Her face was almost flat in profile, her nose broken and healed several times over. It was rumored she had the strength of an ox. If Tamura lost her Challenge, Bohara would be killed or exiled, and Khara feared that further lives could be lost in carrying out either sentence.

"Mada should have been queen," Bohara said in a direct, cutting voice. "Tamura should be queen. She is our bravest and most able warrior. You, Queen Khara, have shown yourself unwilling to confront threats to Scorpica and protect your nation. You have turned away as blind as a cock while our numbers dwindle to nothing. The time has come for Tamura dha Mada to rule."

Tamura narrowed her eyes at Khara. "My Challenge stands. Choose your time and your weapon."

Khara took a long pause, looking down at the dagger Tamura had pointed in her direction, her brows drawn together. She had considered this question many times. She had only gotten as far as dismissing the hatchet that terrified her. But the girl was too good; any weapon would be her last. It was an awful thing to be beaten to death with a staff. Khara was not particularly strong with a longsword. A duel with bow and arrow was strange and ugly, though she'd heard of them in past reigns, when circumstances called for it. In one long-ago Challenge, or so the stories went, a queen weakened by wasting disease knew she could lift neither staff nor sword repeatedly, and so took a chance with the bow. Luckily, her opponent was not a particularly talented archer. The queen had managed, through luck, to make her second arrow fatal and win the victory. The current queen did not hold out much hope for a similar outcome in this case.

All in a flash inspiration struck. It would not be enough, thought Khara, not without a miracle, but it was something.

Khara said, "I choose the shield."

"Sword and shield?"

"No."

Tamura cocked her head and considered the older woman. Khara thought she saw a hint of a nod, but it might just have been the wind tugging at the girl's cropped hair, which was wild around her head.

At last Tamura said, "I see. Let us call the armorer for shields, and begin."

"Wait." Khara knew she had few advantages, and she would need to take every one of them. Tamura was not the strategist her mother had been. She had a temper, quick to flare.

"Do not try to dance away from this, Queen," said the young woman. "We both know it will happen."

"Yes," Khara said, eyes blazing, "but I am your queen, which we also both know. And as the Challenged, it is my right to pick not just the weapon, but the time and place."

"You slew my mother where she stood," spat Tamura. "Do you not want to do the same to me? Or die trying?"

Khara stayed silent, forcing her to wait, watching her anger grow.

At last Tamura said, "How could you be unready for me? You've had years to prepare. Years I spent suffering in the Underlands aboveground. Years subduing prisoners who would have gladly eaten my eyes from their sockets. Years in a place where even sleep brings no rest. And in those years—years!—you did nothing to save our ailing nation. You need more time? Scorpion *mokh* your time."

"I am not unready," said Khara, her voice strong with a boastfulness she did not feel. The previously quiet crowd began shifting, whispering, around them. Would there be no fight today? "I claim my right."

"No. You are not claiming. You are dancing."

"A warrior listens. A warrior knows there is also strength in words."

"Words are for fools!" shouted Tamura, fists clenched, her eyes now as wild as her hair. "Fight me! I have Challenged you!"

There. The girl was good and angry. Khara said, "Very well. Let us begin."

The armorer presented each of them with identical shields, the standard type carried by any Scorpican warrior: long strips of wood bound into a circle with an iron ring around the outside and an iron boss at the center. The shield could either be held by the boss, to protect the hand, or strapped onto the forearm, which was better for absorbing blows. Shields were not meant to be weapons, but Tamura was good with every weapon she'd been trained in, and so Khara had made this unexpected choice. Besides, iron was iron. If wielded with intent, anything could be deadly.

Khara could see the young woman watching her closely to see how she would hold the shield at first. *Scorpion* mokh *her eyes,* thought the queen. Her challenger was too smart. Choosing shields gave her a temporary advantage, much as rushing into the battle had done for her when she fought Mada, years past. It was not at all clear whether she could, as she had before, turn that slim advantage into victory.

The warriors made a circle around them, once again soundless and vigilant, their eyes wide and their hands clasped behind their backs. None would interfere. No matter what happened from this moment on, no matter whose victory they prayed for and whose they feared, they would no more touch the combatants than they would slit their own throats in the Bastion's marketplace. They would watch, unmoving, until one was dead and one was queen.

"Begin," cried Khara, her shield neither gripped nor strapped. Instead she flung the shield with both hands at the feet of her enemy.

The shield struck Tamura in the ankles, hard enough to jar but not fell her, and the discarded shield lay a tempting target at her feet. She had just begun to bend to pick it up when the impact of the shield was followed by the impact of Khara's foot hard on her hip, a flying kick that sent the younger woman sprawling. Now both shields lay in the dirt.

Khara spun up first and grabbed her shield, this time sliding her arm into the double strap. She held the shield in front of her, high enough to protect her body but low enough so that she could see over it, ready for her opponent's next move.

Tamura took her time, rising slowly, and mirrored the queen: watchful, shield strapped and held high, beginning a circle of slow, measured steps within the larger boundary circle of motionless warriors.

The younger woman lunged. In response the queen bashed her shield hard against Tamura's, pushing, pushing with her considerable strength, and Tamura staggered backward.

Khara tried to press her advantage, but Tamura sidestepped out of her stagger, using the shield to push her opponent along, and she reached out a hand for Khara's retreating back until she got a fistful of vest.

Khara flipped her shield up over her back and bashed the girl's hand away.

Tamura let out a sharp bark of pain but did not let herself be driven off, her guard still up, undaunted.

They closed again and again, pressing and shoving each other, an ugly, close-in fight. Silent warriors watched and listened as the melee dragged on. Cries of pain, shouts of anger, the thudding sound of iron and wood on flesh. The longer they fought, the better they learned how to fight, and Khara hoped she could keep just a hairbreadth of advantage. She hoped she might step in behind Tamura's guard at some point, in the moments before Tamura could figure out how to win.

She never got the chance.

The next time they neared, Tamura reached out for her opponent's forearm and seized it, her fingers gripping tight as talons.

With the other arm, where her shield was strapped, Tamura attacked.

She drove hard in an arc, whipping her arm upward too fast to follow, bringing the shield up under Khara's chin in a deadly amber blur.

Khara struggled away as best she could. A flicker in her mind told her what her challenger intended. While most of her body was trapped by Tamura's iron grip, immobile, she gained enough purchase to yank her head back.

It wasn't enough.

The iron edge of the shield cracked hard on Khara's jaw with deadly upward momentum. Only her dodge at the last moment kept the overwhelming force from shattering the bone as it struck.

But the momentum was enough to carry her backward, and Tamura let go of her arm at last, so all the force of the blow shoved her back and down, horribly down, and then she was sprawling on her back in the dirt.

The shield was off Tamura's arm. The shield was in Tamura's hands.

The shield came down, its iron edge descending toward Khara's neck before she had any chance of moving aside or putting her hands up or doing anything to stop it. Perhaps she didn't even see it coming.

Tamura did not see the look on Khara dha Ellimi's face as she drove the iron edge of the shield through the flesh and bone of the Barren Queen's neck over and over again, driving it with all her strength, deeper each time, until the iron blunted on the dead woman's unyielding spine. Tamura's eyes were closed.

When she opened them, she was queen.

If there were cheers or shouts, she did not hear them. The blood was surging, rushing in her ears. The stench of fresh death was in her nose. She felt nothing: no relief, no remorse, no joy, no sorrow. Perhaps it would come, later. For now she had another task, just as unavoidable, just as ugly. She flung down the bloody shield.

Queen Tamura dha Mada picked up the dagger she'd left on the ground, barely taking a moment to savor its familiar weight in her hand before she turned in the direction of the queen's tent.

Now she did hear whispers. She ignored them. Nothing would move her from this goal, as unpleasant as it was. It simply followed the other as the sun followed the moon, night followed day, consort followed queen.

She strode into the tent through the front flap and headed straight for the small bedroll. Should she simply stab down into the bedroll with the point of her dagger or open it first? Did she want to see the girl's terrified face? Should she say to the girl, *Your mother slew my mother, and so I killed her, and now I am killing you?* She wanted to cause that pain, the pain of all her younger years, the pain she even now could tell was not subsiding just because she had given death for death. Where was the elation she'd assumed she'd feel? The satisfaction? The numbness was wearing off, emotion flooding back, and she recognized not the smug pleasure of victory but a grim, cold panic.

Yet the girl was just a girl. Tamura herself had ten-and-one years when her mother was slain; this girl was barely more than half that. She would not understand, even, what she was being told. Perhaps it would be mercy just to stab her in her sleep.

But with the bulk of the blankets, it was difficult to tell exactly where the girl's head and heart lay. She might miss, and it was not the way of the warrior to miss. It was that thought that made Tamura reach down and grip the edge of the blanket, and with no further delay, yank it back.

Inside the blankets were only more blankets. There was no girl.

Springing to her feet, Tamura dashed about the small space, overturning what few objects remained: a heap of clothes, a chest, the dead woman's spare breastplate and greaves. A poppet someone had made the girl out of a discarded corner of worn tent cloth, eyes stitched from domed black beetles. Tamura flung it away. Nowhere was there enough space for a girl, even a girl a handful of years old, to hide.

The only thing that kept Tamura from screaming aloud was the nearness of the warriors who awaited her outside the tent. If they heard, they'd know she had been fooled. That was no way to start a reign.

Her heart still pounding from the fight, she struggled to clear her mind. Thought back. Vishala. What had she done, and why? Vishala had put her hand on the dagger, turned it toward her, and then walked off. Tamura struggled and then recalled: she had disappeared behind the tent instead of walking away in the direction of her own dwelling. Vishala had distracted Tamura, drawn her attention to the dagger and her last-minute plea, when that had nothing to do with Vishala's intent.

It had been a ruse to spirit the girl away.

Now the girl Amankha was gone, and there was no way for Tamura to hunt her without it becoming a distraction. Tamura was too important now to waste her time searching for a child, even a child who would one day become a warrior, if she lived.

Tamura dha Mada, queen of Scorpica, tucked her sword back into her sheath. Her hair, not short enough, thronged around her face in a wild arc. She would have to have someone shear it closer to her head. She'd been hoping to force Vishala to do it, to get the woman to swear allegiance, but now that was not a possibility. If Vishala showed her face in Scorpica again, Tamura would kill her, as surely as she would have killed the girl.

Tamura exited the tent to the cries of her subjects, a strange and lovely music. She had avenged her mother's murder by slaying her murderer. It was a triumph. She had to remind herself it was a triumph.

She swallowed her confusion, let none of her uncertainty show. She had done it. The only queen she'd known was dead. There was a before and an after now. By slaying Khara in a fair fight, she had brought the first, most terrible period of her life to a close. Now the new phase, her own reign as queen, was beginning.

✦

The red mountains of Godsbones were not welcoming, and yet, Vishala dha Lulit breathed a sigh of relief when she saw their red dirt under her feet. Given the impassable high mountains to the north, the natural barrier that blocked the unknown land beyond the Five

Queendoms except through the slim neck of the Scorpion's Pass, there were only three ways to leave Scorpica.

The usual way lay due south through the gates of the Bastion. Pilgrimages to the rites always went through the Bastion, as did all trade, and even warriors traveling for pleasure—or pleasures—were welcome to pass through the gates without fanfare. But the scribes of the gate were incorruptible, inflexible pedants who insisted on inking the names of every woman or man who passed the gates in their endless stacks of books, recording them for history. Today, Vishala wanted nothing put down in ink. She could easily have lied, inventing a name—two names—but she was obviously Scorpican, and so was the girl. If the queen of Scorpica asked to see the books, the queen of the Bastion would grant her request, and the deceit would be quickly revealed. Even false information would be too much. Wherever they went and however they went, the most important thing was that they leave no trail.

The second route was by boat, and Scorpican warriors were like cats, their distrust of open water deep and abiding. Hunters in search of a challenge sometimes climbed aboard round wooden *kuphai* to hunt on the isolated islands off the coast, but even these became rarer after Gretti's older sister Hana, a highly capable and experienced hunter, sailed off one day and never returned. Vishala herself had no *kupha*, so even had she wanted to flee by water, that route was not open to her.

That left the third way, by far the most dangerous. She undertook this path reluctantly, knowing there was a good chance neither she nor the girl would make it out of Godsbones alive. But a chance was more than she'd have any other way, and so she took it.

The green mountains and plains within the borders of Scorpica were hospitable, home to all sorts of game and vegetation, a place where warriors could ground their tents in good earth and live near cool rivers under fruit trees. Godsbones, by contrast, made every trespasser an enemy. Yes, there were the wild ponies the warriors pursued into the red hills when new mounts were needed, but the other animals there were too dangerous to hunt. Golden mother lions with sharp claws, their eyes glowing, their steps silent until they were upon you and it was too late. Outsize rats that hissed and snarled, scuttling along the red earth on fat, soft bellies. Vultures the color of old, drying blood, their eyes so black they seemed to soak up any surrounding light. If there were more typical animals in Godsbones, like the red squirrels and nut-brown coneys the warriors of Scorpica hunted in their own lands, they kept themselves well-hidden. The only animals a warrior saw in those borders were either waiting for trespassers to die or eager to do the killing themselves with sharp teeth, sharp beaks, sharp claws.

And animals, fierce as they were, were far from the only reason to fear. Rumor had it that the entrance to the Underlands themselves, the first of five gates, was located in Godsbones. Legend said it was the blood of the dead and dying that had stained the mountains red. Anyone who wanted to rescue a loved one from the Underlands must first find the entrance and fight their way through those five gates that sealed off the world of the dead from the world of the living. For every story of a hero who'd fought her way there and back, there were ten stories, perhaps twenty, of those who'd tried and failed.

Yet Vishala had brought the girl here, hoping to take her through and out again. Because it was the only way.

When her oldest friend, her queen, had asked Vish to spirit her daughter away, she'd had no choice but to say yes. Tamura was simply too strong, too fierce to be defeated. So Vish snuck into the back of the queen's tent and took the girl by her tiny hand while Khara walked out the front to confront the challenger who had finally, inevitably, come for her.

She and Khara had both long known the day would come. She and her oldest friend had no secrets from each other. She'd had the pack ready to go even while Tamura served out her assignment in the Fingernail, just in case the young woman showed up unexpectedly. She'd taken it with her from summer camp to winter camp and back again, repacking it regularly with provisions that would last in the wilds. Dried fruit, jerked meat, anything preserved that wouldn't weigh her down. She had hoped never to wear it; now that she did, its contents were not the hardest part of the weight to bear.

Later in the day she would pause and give the girl a drink from her waterskin. For now she pushed through, wanting as much distance as possible between the two of them and the land they both loved.

But the land wouldn't be the same with Tamura in charge of it, and with the rash young woman as queen, both of them would be in constant danger. This way they chose their danger, or at least she had, thought Vish. Amankha had chosen nothing. She had simply been born into an impossible position: blessed with intelligence and spirit, wanting for nothing, but doomed to lose her mother almost as soon as the woman's beaming face was fixed in her young mind. At least they'd had a few years. At least the queen had survived her childbed challenge and lived long enough to meet this one with strength and grace.

They were three days into Godsbones, Vish already worn to a nub from a lack of sleep, when the lion found them.

The border of Paxim was not yet in sight, but Vish could smell it in the distance, the scent of grass so different from the rock and scrub she'd been smelling the past several days. They were not so far from the wide-open plain of the largest of the five queendoms. They'd circled far east of the Bastion so they wouldn't be seen, and would circle south of it through Paxim. A few more days on foot from here, their destination awaited.

She took the girl's hand and smiled. "Just a little farther," she said.

Amankha, too young to be as stalwart as her mother, made a soft, wordless whine.

"If we meet women and men on the road," Vish said, "we will need to tell a story. You cannot tell anyone who you truly are."

The girl's voice was still a whine, but this time, she formed a word. "Why?"

"A bad woman wants to do you harm."

The girl's tiny hand tensed in Vish's own. She was so small, already so far from home, soon to be much farther. Quietly she asked, "Who?"

"You must be suspicious of anyone. Anyone could be the enemy. That's why you must keep your secret to yourself."

"Only you and I will know?"

"Only us," Vishala confirmed. "And we will call you a new name. Ama. If anyone asks your name, what will you say?"

"Ama."

"Good girl."

"But you will keep me safe, won't you, *tishi* Vish? From the bad woman?"

But Vishala's attention was elsewhere.

Somehow, in the soil and scrub around her, she sensed danger. She felt the presence on the hillside before her conscious mind saw or heard anything, her warrior's body attuned to signals beyond the sensory.

"Ama," she said softly, hoping the girl would respond to the new name without protesting. "Get behind me."

The lion rose above them on the hill, well within leaping distance, her eyes golden and menacing, her right paw and jawline already dark with dried blood from some previous kill.

To her credit, the girl not only listened, but she slipped in behind the warrior's body without a sound. She rested her fingertips in a five-pointed star on the small of Vishala's back, a hunter's signal: *I am here, but the kill is yours.*

The lion raised her eyes and growled, a low, throaty hum full of promise and danger.

Vishala growled back at her, an almost perfect imitation of the sound the animal had made, and grimly drew her sword.

◆ CHAPTER 12 ◆

STRENGTH FOR
THE SORCERER

On an island off the coast of Scorpica
Hana, Sessadon

The hunter dashed through the forest, fleet and silent, her feet barely touching the ground, more wind than woman. The boar ran ahead of her. She chose her moment. When it came, she tossed the rock in her hand to the beast's left, correcting its course. Skittish, the boar lowered its tusks and curved its path away from the sound. The two of them sped on among the trees.

Yes. This. Let's go.

Hana used to wonder whether certain thoughts in her head were her own or the voice's, but she had come to understand there was no real difference. She and the voice were one. Together, they hunted. Today, together, they ran.

Another rock. Another mile. Almost there.

Flinging another rock just beyond the nose of the boar made it snuffle, confused. Then it turned in the direction she and the voice wanted it to turn. *Faster now,* she thought. *To the end.*

All at once the forest broke and they were on a cliff above the water, and Hana planted her feet to wrench herself to a halt, too late for the boar to do the same.

The animal plunged over the cliff into the empty air. After a long moment and a terrible, ear-piercing squeal, it landed on the wet rocks below.

Very good. Now bring it to me.

Hana descended the cliff eagerly, her nimble fingers and feet finding grooves and niches. The next part was the hardest. But it was the only way to bring an animal of this size back the way the voice commanded: not fully alive, not fully dead. Over weeks and months she'd fetched back creatures from all over the island, ibex and grouse, crakes and serpents, and the voice had thanked her for each and every one. But boars were the largest, liveliest prey on the island, and for these, the voice was the most grateful.

At the base of the cliff she roped the thing's legs, drawing its feet together. Then she clambered back up the cliff with the long rope in her teeth, jamming her hands and feet into the holds she'd memorized along the way. She looped the rope around a short, thick tree trunk in order to pull the animal up after her, foot by agonizing foot. The beast made awful noises as it rose, some loud, some soft, all deeply unpleasant.

Once the half-dead animal lay at the top of the cliff, still groaning, she considered stopping for a rest, but she feared disappointing the voice. If the boar died on the way, this would all be for naught. She rolled it onto the broad leather tarp she'd left waiting and grabbed the poles along each side, then heaved her body forward, dragging the low-squealing, writhing animal behind. At least her own panting was so loud in her ears it made the beast harder to hear.

When she at last descended into the darkness of the familiar cave, she laid the boar like an offering in front of the still form where the voice resided, then fell to her knees by its side.

For you, she thought.

Instantly a warm happiness bloomed through her, starting in her chest and radiating outward. She lived for this feeling. It was all worth it, all the labor, for this. This deep, nearly overwhelming bliss, a happiness she'd never felt any other way, not even with Marbera's touch in her most secret places. She had not thought of Marbera in some time; her life before was a poor, distant shadow. This was the ultimate bliss. The ultimate reward.

Very good. Now you may end it.

Hana dragged the knife across the throat of the struggling boar, cutting short a last agonized squeal, and blood poured onto the sand. Hana understood by now that it was the life force, not the blood, that mattered. As that force poured out of the animal's body along with its last breath, the shell glowed a faint blue, and Hana knew the force was entering the shell and strengthening it.

Her efforts would help make the shell into a body again. She wasn't sure what would happen after that, but the voice told her not to worry. *Haven't I shown I know how to reward you?* Yes, of course, yes. Another wave of bliss surged through her, almost too delicious to bear.

When the light faded, Hana undertook one more task, dressing the boar meat to eat later. She carved and peeled, separating skin from flesh and flesh from bone, every movement practiced and precise. She stored the meat on a high shelf within the cave to keep it dry. Tomorrow she would cut some into strips to dry for jerky, but for now, she was exhausted. She lay down her head to rest.

The sorcerer used short, small bursts of magic to give Hana sweet dreams, then left her to rest; she used as little magical energy as possible on the everyday. Lucky for her she'd found this particular hunter, both talented and malleable, to assist her. And, she admitted, to keep her company. To live on this island alone, deserted—well, she never forgot that she'd considered not bothering to live at all. She lived so much of her time in Hana's mind that she sometimes forgot she wasn't Hana, but then her own memories would roar in like a summer storm, and she'd remember that this same hunter's ancestors had slaughtered her friends and driven her off a cliff to die. A tiny fissure inside her opened up every time, and she could not make the halves meet. Her only friend, her cherished companion, if she knew the truth, would cut her throat in a heartbeat.

She needed to get off this island.

The spell, then. She banked most of the energy Hana brought her to strengthen her earthly form, but after a hunt was always the best time to check the spell for any signs of weakness. She searched for holes or errors or connections that were beginning to fray. Any such flaws could spell doom.

The blue glowing web of her magic stretched across the entire ceiling of the cave, shimmering a nighttime sapphire in some places and, in others, in small steady points of light as bright as stars. The star-shapes perfectly mirrored the sky above the Five Queendoms, all the constellations of the night sky replicated here in miniature: the curled form of the Scorpion, the curves of the Dreamer, the lines of the Cauldron and the Cup. If one stayed perfectly still, it was possible to see that the entire spell breathed in time with its creator, each of its thousand lights pulsing almost imperceptibly, rippling with a constant flow of energy.

The form of the spell was only partially related to its purpose; Sessadon had made it beautiful because she chose to, not because she needed to. Any ugly spell could have kept the women of the Five Queendoms from bearing girls. It didn't even need to be visible. But she had chosen to make it beautiful because she liked it that way.

For now it still required her presence, but with enough stored life force, she would have two things: a body ready to leave this place, and a spell that could survive without her, feeding on its own energy, once she'd gone. Once her young heir reached womanhood, she would no longer need the spell, she'd decided. The girl would be the last leader of her generation. She was too young yet, but oh, how Sessadon longed to meet her, once the time was right.

Then she would have a true companion. A girl from her own bloodline, heir to the immense power she intended to reclaim. The one person in the world who could truly understand how she'd been wronged, all those years ago, and how fiercely she burned to make it right.

If the architects of the Great Peace had chosen her instead of her sister, she would have been the first queen of Arca. She had not approved of the making of the queendoms at all, but they hadn't known that; they were only judging reputation, character, personality. Not what a woman did or wanted, but who she was. Kruvesis had been selfless and open where Sessadon herself had been reckless and ruthless. To women who hoped to shape a fragile harmony from the ashes of perpetual conflict, her sister's traits had been more valued than her own. But there was no true north for any culture, the sorcerer knew. Values changed. Times changed. Qualities that defined treasured leaders in one era could be disastrous in another. And look at her now. Her power grew every day. Hundreds of years had passed, and she was here, and her sister was not. So who, in the end, was meant for greatness?

For now, she would wait, but it was not a passive waiting. Every day she built her future, one small death at a time. She nurtured and tended the net of enchantment she had spread across the world. She strengthened her earthly form, steadily, like an inexorable march. One day she would rise. And come that day, this meager cave would not hold her.

Nothing would.

✦ CHAPTER 13 ✦

BETRAYAL

In the village of Adaj, Arca
Jehenit, Eminel

Five years and countless letters into the Drought, no healers had come to Adaj. Jehenit no longer even bothered to try.

In the early years, on occasion, they'd written back. She saved up the messages for the scribe's return and paid to have each one read to her. When Eminel was a baby, she'd received kind messages, sent by fellow healers with good intentions. There was a cousin showing promise, they said, or a second sister whose gifts might grow into something worthy. Perhaps one of them might wish one day, wrote the hopeful healers, to seek her fortune in a village like Adaj.

But this deep into the Drought, five long years in, any offer of help had dried up. Sometimes they wrote to say things had not turned out as they'd expected; more often they did not write at all. Every village, every matriclan, held on to the resources it had. There was no longer anything to spare. Perhaps there would be girls again one day and things would change for the better. But for now, not a single Arcan, knowing their lives were ruled by the God of Chaos, was willing to count on it.

Jehenit knew the one place she refused to write—Daybreak Palace—would have sent a healer in a heartbeat, but she would have had to relinquish the only thing left she treasured: Eminel's secret. For a fresh, untested all-magic girl, one of the nation's youngest remaining, surely the palace would have given almost anything. They could have had half a dozen healers there with a snap of the queen's fingers. Yet was it worth putting her child in danger? It wasn't, Jehenit had decided. Nothing was.

Jehenit did her best to shoulder the burden. Healers of her line were strong, durable; they could heal themselves, after all, and unlike physical strength, magical strength increased with age and experience. When her grandmother had developed a breathing disease, so her mother told her, she'd stripped it from her body in one fell swoop. She'd worked with a water magician to boil the nearest lake until every full-grown fish in its waters yielded up their life force at the same moment, which the healer harvested for her own desperate need. The village feasted and her grandmother lived another twenty years.

Jehenit did nothing so dramatic, but she'd tweaked her body in a hundred little ways, boosting her energy, smoothing her sleep, keeping herself in the best condition she could. In addition to healing the life-threatening injuries in her village, she was constantly doing favors; word had gotten out that she'd even travel to nearby villages to help out a friend, and all she asked in return was gratitude. Her generosity was famed, her time treasured.

And all of it weighed on her like stone. Her healing gift was strong, but her daughter's gift was something else entirely, and the effort of concealing it was crushing her, hour by hour, day by day.

More often than not now, within minutes of coming down the ladder into the house, she headed straight for her pallet to sleep. She might exchange ten words in a day with her daughter, sometimes twenty, sometimes none. Sometimes when she came home to find Eminel asleep, she curled her body around her sleeping daughter's, not sure which of them she was trying to comfort. It was only the two of them now. Dargan had not bothered to conceal his delight when he found that Koslo had disappeared; in the months immediately following, he'd been overjoyed to have Jehenit all to himself. He'd lavished attention on her, bringing her trinkets, taking his time with her favorite forms of pleasure, making himself especially lovely for her.

But over time, he realized that even when he no longer had to share her attentions with another man, she still had nothing left to give. She had no energy for him, not at the end of a long day when she'd been healing—or worse, when she was spent, failing to heal—their neighbors and the children of their neighbors. Within the year, Dargan, too, was gone.

Thank Velja for Jorja, who knew her burdens. Who'd been there when Koslo left, soothing her, reassuring her, and then doing the same when Dargan followed. Who fed Eminel when Jehenit failed to return at the promised hour and tucked her own childhood poppet in with the girl to help her sleep. Without her, Jehenit would have left long ago, even with the powerful duty she felt to Adaj. The healer was at her limit all the time now, and she knew it couldn't last, but she kept trying. One more day, and then one more day after that. She'd gone on for months that way.

And there were good days too. Like the day she brought home a basket of ripe, sweet peaches, and she and Eminel sat on the roof eating them with the juice dripping down their chins, laughing. All the weight of her burdens lifted when her daughter smiled. She lived for those smiles.

Sometimes she even dreamed of them, when she dreamed.

✦

Eminel looked at her sleeping mother, facedown on the second pallet. Her hollow stomach rumbled. Perhaps there was bread in the kitchen, she thought. Her mother sometimes brought back food when she'd been out healing, if she remembered. Bread, oil, cheese. The grateful often paid in trade. She remembered those peaches, last summer. There had been too many of them, a hairbreadth from rotting, and the woman and girl had eaten themselves sick. The pattern was feast or famine. Today had been no feast.

Nothing at all, when she looked. The shelf was bare. She knew she shouldn't, but she headed for the ladder.

It was dark already, the sky starry-bright. She tried not to bother Jorja after night fell. But there was no helping it. And the woman always welcomed her, no matter the hour. Not too long ago, she'd dreamed Jorja was her real mother, and she was ashamed. Not because of the dream itself, but because she woke up with a warm feeling of delight. And because for a week afterward, every night as she lay down, she wished to dream that dream again.

She rapped her small knuckles on Jorja's door and called out her name. Jorja called in answer for her to descend, and so she did, scurrying down, certain-footed.

Jorja looked drowsy. Maybe she had been asleep too? There were shadows under her eyes, under her cheekbones. But she reached out for Eminel, giving her a quick squeeze. "Hello! What a surprise, so late. Where's your mother?"

"Sleeping."

"Poor thing. She works so hard."

"I wish she didn't have to," said Eminel. She couldn't say such a thing to her mother; the only time Jehenit raised her voice was when Eminel asked why she had to leave so much. *Because I am the only healer here. If I don't answer a call for help, someone could die. Don't be selfish.* So Eminel had stopped asking, which didn't mean she'd stopped missing her.

"Me too, dear. Some tea?" asked Jorja.

"Yes, please. And do you have any food?" Eminel knew she was not being polite. Her mother had told her many times it was not polite to ask for the thing you most wanted. But she was hungry. And her mother was not here.

Jorja's brow creased, which Eminel thought probably meant she was unhappy. But she reached into a shallow bowl on a high shelf and produced an orange, a rare treat. Eminel's mouth watered.

As Jorja began to peel the orange, its bright, juicy scent rose in the air. She separated it into segments and made two little piles, one for herself and one for Eminel. Eminel made herself wait one, two, three beats before reaching out and slipping the first sweet, sharp segment into her mouth. It burst on her tongue like sunshine.

They ate in silence, each slowly chewing and savoring. Eminel thought she felt Jorja looking at her, watching her. She didn't say anything. She didn't want her to take the orange away, so she didn't look up until she had finished every last bite.

Jorja asked gently, "Do you really wish your mother didn't work so hard?"

"Yes," Eminel said. "I want her to spend time with me."

"It's hard for adults. They have to make choices."

"I wish she chose me."

Jorja's brow lowered farther. "She did, you know."

"No," said Eminel, feeling the beginning of tears welling up in her eyes. "She never chooses me. She forgets I'm there. If I went away, she'd be happier, because she could just be healing all the time."

Jorja said nothing, but it looked a little bit like she, too, might be on the verge of crying. The sharp, acid flavor of the orange burned the inside of Eminel's mouth, now that the sweetness was gone.

Eminel said, "Healing and sleeping. She doesn't have time for anything else."

"When does she pray?" There was surprise in Jorja's voice, and something else the girl couldn't identify.

Eminel searched her memory. "I don't think she does."

After a long pause, Jorja said quietly, "I don't think she wants to be healing all the time. She's afraid to say no. She doesn't want anyone to have anything bad to say about her, because . . ."

Eminel sniffed, waiting, but the woman didn't seem eager to finish the sentence. "Because?"

Then Jorja seemed to make a decision. "Never mind that. Let me see your hand."

"Which one?"

"Either."

When Eminel held out her little hand toward the older woman, palm up, Jorja held it in her own. She spread the fingers flat and stared down at the palm for a minute. Then she grabbed a space just off the tip of Eminel's middle finger and twisted. Eminel started. Even though Jorja hadn't touched her, she *felt* that twist.

Now Jorja was looking into her face, watching her expression closely.

"Do you feel different?" the woman asked her. "Strange?"

"A little strange."

"Tell me what it feels like."

"It doesn't feel like anything," Eminel began to say, and then the oddest thing happened. Not a feeling, but a knowing.

She knew the words that Jorja was thinking inside her head.

There, it's done. Now they'll find her, for better or worse. And good luck to them both. Poor thing. Does she have any idea? thought Jorja. *Has her mother told her?*

"Told me what?" Eminel asked.

It was Jorja's turn to start. Her eyes went wide in surprise, her jaw slack, and a cry strangled itself in her throat.

She can hear me. Velja's lower beard, she can hear me, ran her thoughts, as clearly as if she'd spoken them aloud. Eminel hadn't seen an adult look so panicked since the day the winged girl fell from the sky.

Just then, a rap sounded on the door above, sharp and insistent.

"Jorja?" called a familiar voice, breathless. "Is Eminel with you? Hello?"

"Yes, Mama," called Eminel before Jorja could move. She could hear the woman's thoughts: *Oh no.*

Her mother descended the ladder. As soon as her feet touched ground, Eminel felt a rightness in the world, a soothing. Her mother was here. Everything was strange, but it was all right. Nothing could go too wrong when Jehenit, ever capable, was here to manage it.

Jehenit said, the tautness to her voice unfamiliar to Eminel, "What is happening here?"

She was staring at Eminel's hand. They all were. There was a faint blue light coming from the tip of Eminel's middle finger, the one Jorja had not-quite-twisted.

No one answered the question hanging in the air.

"Step back, Eminel," Jehenit said, walking toward them both slowly, something coming over her face. Confusion. Alarm.

"We were just talking," Jorja said.

Jehenit said, unsteadily, "Eminel?"

Eminel saw nothing to do but tell the truth. "I can *hear* her, Mama. What she's thinking, I mean. Why can I hear her?"

The alarm on her mother's face did not resolve, but she kept her voice steady. "Let's go home and talk."

Eminel moved toward her mother until they stood together at the base of the ladder, but Jehenit did not move to ascend. She stood in silence, wrestling with something. The three stared at each other.

Without taking her eyes off Jorja, Jehenit said to Eminel, "Tell me, *cheru*, what is she thinking now?"

"That she wants me out of her mind," the girl reported. "That she's afraid you'll realize she's made it so the Seekers will come."

"Seekers!" Jehenit shouted so loud the household image of Velja trembled. She backed against the ladder, holding Eminel by the shoulder, but she stayed facing toward Jorja, shaking with—something, Eminel wasn't sure what. Anger? Fear?

Maybe she could help if she could tell her mother more. She could feel the tension and it was almost unbearable. She wanted to make it better. Could she?

Eminel pondered, raised her finger, turned back toward Jorja. "She says you'll be better off. You'll remember who you're meant to be, what you're meant to do. Without me." The girl seemed to hear her own words only after she'd spoken them, lowering her tiny brows, looking back and forth between the women. "Without me?"

Jehenit stared at Jorja over Eminel's head, mouth agape. "You want them to take her from me? I thought you were my friend!"

"Family!" shouted Jorja. "That's what you said, you said we were family! Velja be blessed. But you don't even—the girl said you don't even pray anymore?"

Eminel looked up at her mother's face, worried Jehenit would feel betrayed, but her focus was completely on Jorja.

"That isn't your business." Jehenit's voice was lower, darker.

"Velja blesses you with this gift, this all-magic girl? And you don't even thank her for it? You hide it instead. You wear yourself out hiding it. You've driven everyone away and I'm all you have left, and you give me no more thought than that ladder." Jorja gestured sharply. "Only ever thinking about where I can get you. Assuming I'll always be there."

"She's my daughter. It's my choice," Jehenit hissed.

Jorja stared at Jehenit, angry and silent, but her thoughts rang out clear to Eminel. Still desperate to help, the girl spoke them for her. "You made the wrong choice, she says. From the beginning. So she's fixing it. Doing what she should have done in the first place. Letting Daybreak Palace come."

Jehenit said, her eyes brimming with tears, "After everything, you would let them take her?"

Confused, Eminel said, "Take who? Take *me*?"

Jehenit realized the girl was speaking as herself this time; Eminel did not know, did not understand, what she was. Now that she was in Jorja's mind, though, she might see the truth. How did this mind magic work? Did she know everything, or only some things, that Jorja knew? How could a five-year-old navigate the mind of a grown woman, the memories, the experiences far beyond her reckoning?

Jehenit told her daughter gently, just as she would tell her to step away from an unknown dog baring its teeth, "Come out of her mind now, *cheru*."

"Yes, Mama."

Eminel blinked and Jorja blinked and that was the only sign anything was different. There was no crackle of magic, no apparent pain. Her daughter had been inside the other woman's mind and now she wasn't. The magnitude of it terrified Jehenit.

"We have to go," she said to Eminel, and reached for her hand.

"And leave me alone?" Jorja cried suddenly. "Now, after everything?" It was startling to hear her voice so desperate, so emotional. In all their years of friendship, Jehenit had never heard her speak this way.

Jehenit bent toward her daughter and placed the girl's hand on the ladder. "Climb up, *cheru*, and head home. Lie down to sleep. I will be there soon."

"Yes, Mama," the girl said without hesitation, and was gone.

When the two women were alone, they faced each other, and Jehenit could give voice to her anger. "How *dare* you? How dare you be angry I'm leaving you alone, as you put it? Because of you, they're going to find her."

"Without me, they would have found her years ago." Jorja's eyes burned, her voice thick with emotion. "You owe me and you've given me nothing. All these years, nothing. We were family, you said. But did you welcome me into your house? Share your bounty with me? Never."

Jehenit was stunned. "My house? You've been in my house a thousand—"

Jorja cut her off with a sharp gesture. "You were happy to accept my help, of course, as if I were a third husband, but you never even asked me to stay the night. Never offered me hospitality. After I kept your secret, consoled you, cared for your child. Never asked me to sit at table with you. And after your husbands both abandoned you, for good reason? When people gave you food and goods in trade for healing? You kept everything to yourself. Never offered me a single bite. You never once thought I could be starving."

Still reeling, Jehenit said weakly, "You could have asked."

Proudly, her chin high, Jorja said, "I shouldn't have had to."

After a long silence, Jehenit said, "I'm sorry. I had no idea. Now that I know, I can—"

"Stop," said Jorja, her voice sharp but now sounding weary. "You never realized, and now it's too late. I did what I did. Your daughter is leaking magic. And for her sake, I beg you not to say another word. Because when the Seekers get here, in days or weeks or months, anything in my mind will be theirs."

Jehenit stared at the woman: her protector and her betrayer, friend and enemy, a woman to be pitied and feared.

Without a word, she turned to face the ladder and ascended. She climbed toward the night sky and did not look back.

That same night, only hours later, they left. They took little. A spare tunic and leggings for each, preserved food, a copper spoon, a small stone crow one of her husbands had carved for Eminel, though Jehenit no longer remembered which one. She could not help but tuck their household image of Velja into a shoulder pack, but other than that, the house would forever look as if they had just stepped out for a moment. When they did not return, the villagers would come and take the furniture, the blankets, anything remaining of value, re-distributing to each according to their need.

As they eased through the darkness to slip the village's limits, Eminel finally spoke. "What's going on, Mama?"

"Hush, no questions, *cheru.*"

"But if I can't ask you, who can I ask?"

"That's right," Jehenit said, half to herself. "I will explain every-thing when I can. Right now we need to go."

"Yes, Mama."

They were leagues down the road before Jehenit thought of the right answer to her daughter's question. Not truly the right answer—there was no right, here—but the only way she could think to answer it for now.

"The thing that you can do," Jehenit began. "That you did back there. Not everyone can do it."

"Everyone has a gift. Isn't it my gift?"

"Not a gift," her mother said sadly. "A curse."

"Oh," said Eminel, her small brow creased in thought.

"So you must do all that you can not to use it. Until we get where we are going. Then you will not be able to use it, even if you try."

"Where are we going?"

"Somewhere without sand," Jehenit said.

"But there is always sand," the girl said, pointing to her mother's wrist, to the wheel-shaped black sand tattoo.

"There will be less," Jehenit said.

That night on the road, as Eminel slept, Jehenit used her healing magic one last time. Every grain of black sand burned coming out of her skin the same way it had burned going in. When only a bloody wheel remained, she heated the copper spoon in the campfire, then held it to the wound like a brand, searing away the pattern. By morning the spot on the inside of her wrist was a sun-shaped, bright red coin. She knew she could displace the pain, but she held on to it. The pain would remind her what she was fighting for. The pain would remind her they could never go back.

CHAPTER 14

THE ORPHAN TREE

Entering Paxim

Vishala

"Y ou are a proud Scorpican," Vish whispered into the girl's ear, her breath coming hard and fast, almost panting. "If you remember nothing else, remember that."

The girl seemed to nod, but it might just have been the swaying of the pony upon whose back they rode. Vish gave thanks to the Scorpion for the animal, without whom she never would have made it this far. The lion's long claws had torn deep into Vish's body twice before Vish had managed to bring her down. The wound in her throat had come closer to killing her in the moment—another inch deeper would have done it—but now, it was the leg wound that worsened by the hour. Even before they'd left Godsbones, the crusting red blood had begun to blacken. Now the leg was pulsing with heat and so swollen she feared the flesh would split. Had she needed to walk on it, she doubted she could have made it more than a couple of leagues.

But the Eternal Scorpion or the All-Mother or someone, maybe even the God of Plenty, had provided them a mount. At first it had seemed like a disaster when the girl's tired fingers fumbled the pack and sent a handful of barley cakes skittering down a steep hill. Then, while Vish was still wondering whether it was worth climbing down the hill to retrieve them, they'd seen a pony wander into view, drawn by the grain. At least one god must have intervened for their sake, because the pony had not started at the girl's approach. Once Ama led the pony up the hill with the promise of more barley cakes, Vish managed to loop a rope around the animal's neck, and they had themselves a willing mount for the last stage of their journey.

They had nothing else left by now. The horse cropped grass lustily whenever Vish allowed her to stop, but the humans had no such option. She'd fed the last of their food to the girl, taking no more than a few ropy dried figs for herself. And even rationing the willow bark, chewing a small strip every few hours and sucking the dried wad when it could be chewed no more, she'd run out by the previous sunset. So the food was gone. The painkiller was gone.

And soon, Vish believed, she herself would be gone.

But not before she got the girl to her destination.

Vish had always loved stories of other queendoms. Her heart was fiercely Scorpican, devoted to her country and her queen, but she also collected tales of other lands like a magpie collected treasures for its nest. It was not the stories of gods that arrested her, but of places. From the time she was young, she'd waited at the feet of recently returned warriors to hear tell of the places they'd been. When she was older, she'd journeyed to some of these lands with the newborns her fellow warriors delivered, handing the boys over to new parents who gifted her with coins and treasures in return. These journeys were not for pleasure, but she still found pleasure in them: she'd visited many corners of the five queendoms her fellow warriors would never see.

She knew of the steep cliffs of Western Sestia, so white and sheer they were like enormous teeth in the land's open mouth. She knew of the villages of Arca, buried underground like rabbit warrens so the rooms remained cool even at blazing midday. And she knew of one place that belonged to the Bastion but stood outside the Bastion's enormous, impenetrable walls. A place that she could take the girl. The only place she would be safe.

And so she whispered into Ama's ear while they rode, heading for a destination Vishala had heard of many times but never herself visited. She doubted the tree could be as grand as it was described in the tales, but she would see it for herself. By her calculations, they were getting close now, very close. Every part of her throbbed, not just the wounds but her head now too, a painful light dawning like a small, angry sun behind her eyes. The pony plodded forward, her soft nose pointed over the next ridge, the woman and the girl on her back huddled so tight together that from a distance they might have been mistaken for a single person.

"Tell me what you remember," she whispered to the girl.

"I'm so tired, *tishi* Vish."

"So am I, sweet girl, so am I. But tell me, so I will know."

Clinging with both fists to the pony's mane, the girl gathered her breath and answered. "I am from Scorpica but I will tell no one. I am a proud Scorpican but a secret Scorpican. For the rest of the world, I am an orphan who does not know her story. For them, my name is Ama."

"Yes," said Vishala, her pride equally mixed with sadness. In another world, if things had unfolded differently in Scorpica, this girl never would have had to deny her heritage. But they didn't live in that world. All they had was this one. "Very good."

They crested the ridge, the pony's hooves taking them up the road and over. At the top of the hill, on either side of the roadway, clusters of scrub trees marked the path for a few hundred yards more down the way. Beyond, broad fields stretched into the distance, and behind that, the dark walls of the Bastion, which they now approached from the south, formed a smear on the horizon.

At last Vishala saw their destination, and she gasped. As many times as she had ridden south through the gates of the Bastion into the other queendoms, she had not detoured east to see this particular sight. When boys had been valuable, she had never had occasion to bring one to the Orphan Tree. She had imagined the tree many times over, and what she imagined paled in comparison to the reality before her now. It was not as grand as it had been described in the tales. It was far, far grander.

The Orphan Tree was an immense, spreading elm, unbelievably huge. Its trunk was a pale tan spotted with gray, its broad expanse of bark almost ghostly. Its branches reached out, split and reached, split and reached until their infinite scope seemed to blot out the very sky. No other trees were near it, just flat grassland, leaving no doubt whatsoever in Vish's mind that she had found the right place.

The tree's leaves were a silvery, almost shimmering green, numbering in the thousands. The wind stirred them softly, ceaselessly. When she first caught sight of the tree, she could only see the motion, but as they rode closer, Vish could hear the sound the stirring leaves made. They murmured and muttered. They hissed what sounded like words a little too hushed to hear clearly, a conversation held just around the next corner. They sounded like a vast number of voices with urgent but opaque things to say, a chorus of constant whispers.

She felt Ama straighten up a little, her small back pressing against Vish's chest and stomach, her head coming up higher to the base of Vish's neck.

"What is that tree?" asked the girl, in awe.

"Our destination." Vish looked to the right and left, taking stock of their surroundings in a thorough, detailed sweep, and then drew the pony to a halt. They were still hundreds of yards away, but if they rode closer, there would be no cover. She lingered near the last of the scrub trees and stared out at the magnificence of the tree.

For a moment she thought she understood the whispers. *Here, here, here, she's here, her, here.*

In the next moment the sounds were just the whispers of leaves in the wind again.

She knew it now; her fever was worsening. Along with the bright light behind her eyes and the pain that hovered with it, this was a very bad sign.

The girl tapped on Vish's good leg with two fingers, and the woman realized she had probably spoken her name several times to get her attention. "This is where we're going?"

"Yes."

"Then why did you stop?"

"I need you to walk from here."

"Walk?" the girl moaned.

"You are strong," urged Vish. "You can."

"But your leg. Can you?"

It might have been another sign of the fever, but Vish thought she could feel the exact moment of her heart breaking, a shimmering *snap* inside her aching chest. She could no longer delay. "I cannot come with you."

"No! You have to! *Tishi* Vish!" The girl twisted in her seat to look up into Vish's face as she protested. It was surprising how strong the girl's voice was now that she was upset. Vish chose to take joy in that. She could not let herself feel the other emotions. There would be time enough to feel when she turned the horse around.

"Hush now," Vish told her, as gently as she could. "You will always be a warrior. You will grow up in the world of the Bastion, and you will be one of them in your body and maybe even your mind, but you will always be a Scorpican in your heart."

"No. I will stay with you," Ama said, still looking up, her tiny chin quivering.

"You will not. I am . . . not staying."

"Where are you going?"

"Back to Godsbones," said Vish, although she knew it was a death sentence to cross that border again. She already stank of death. She was certain that the claw marks in her leg were festering, a black, rank smell coming from under the ragged edge of her skirt. Any worthy healer would cut the blackness out to stop its spread, carving flesh and muscle away. If the wound at her throat festered in the same fashion, there would be no saving her. Blackness would spread down through her chest and belly, swallowing up her vital organs like moss swallowed a fallen, rotted tree. A miracle might save her, but nothing short of that, and even a miracle might not be enough if she walked into the cursed red lands of Godsbones, crawling with predators, already reeking of rot and blood.

But if she were to die, that was the place to do it. Word of a dead Scorpican found close to the Orphan Tree would reach the ears of the Scorpican queen, which by now must be Tamura. The angry young woman would surely send assassins after Amankha, and they would find her, even in the warm bosom of the Bastion, deep in its maze of nearly endless halls and rooms. There was nowhere Scorpicae could not reach. If Vish were to live, she could do it anywhere, but if she died, only one choice could save the girl. Vish would ride directly back into the hostile world of Godsbones. As soon as she had done what she came here to do.

The girl opened her mouth in what looked like the beginning of a cry, but Vishala shushed her.

"Get down now," she said in a firm voice.

The girl cooperated like a good young warrior, without resistance, without delay. She released the horse's mane, flung her foot over, and slid down to land softly on the dirt of the road, raising barely a puff of dust. Once on her feet, she wavered. Vish worried hunger might overtake her. But she straightened up again and turned up her face to Vishala's like a sunflower.

Vish looked down at the girl, who looked so small at that distance, and told her, "Remember. You are strong."

"I am strong," Ama said in her high, childish voice.

"Walk to the Orphan Tree," Vishala told her, gesturing toward the enormous oak. "Wait beneath its leaves. There you will be found."

"And they won't know who I am?"

"It is forbidden to ask questions of a child who comes to the Orphan Tree. The Bastion is sworn to welcome any such child. The Bastion raises its young in nurseries, finds what they are meant for, trains them for that purpose. Leaders and artists, teachers and scribes. Scientists. Midwives."

"Warriors?"

"Guards, I think they call them. But warriors, yes. They find a place for everyone. They will find a place for you."

"Until you come for me?"

"Child," said Vish, the breaking feeling in her chest again, "I think you know I cannot come for you."

Ama's voice was soft, thin. "And my mother?"

"She cannot either. The danger is too great. It is because she loves you so much that you can't ever go to Scorpica again." She could not tell the girl her mother was dead. Not because she hoped Khara was still alive—she had no such hope—but because she had already taken away the rest of the girl's world. She could not take that, too.

The girl nodded. "I understand."

They both waited in silence for a long moment. Then there was nothing left to say but the one word Vishala said. She put all her sadness and pride into it, all her hope and longing, all her love. "Goodbye."

Instead of replying with the same word, the girl gave a gesture that brought tears to Vishala's eyes.

She did not say goodbye. She raised one hand and flicked her index finger inward, somewhat like a warrior drawing a bowstring tight, then quickly twisted her hand upward in a fist toward the sky.

Good hunting.

Blinded by tears, Vishala clicked her tongue and pressed the knee of her working leg against the pony's side, then turned her in the direction they had come. Back to the red sands. If she could die deep inside Godsbones, with the scavenging creatures drawn by her rotting scent, she could leave no body at all. Just a hearty meal for vultures and blowflies. Not the most glorious death for a warrior, but fitting. A warrior who died after setting out to keep a promise, to do what she meant to do, might still hope to rise to the battlefield beyond. If she did, she hoped she would see Khara there.

If not, if the legends were true, she knew her path. The stories said that deep in the Underlands, if they chose, shades could visit the Oak of Unknowing. The oak's bark was white as bone, its leaves black as night. When shades drank from the still, clear pool that fed its roots, the tree itself drank away their memories. They forgot their earthly lives. If Vishala did not ascend to the battlefield beyond, forgetting herself would be a blessing, and her shade in the Underlands would not have to mourn the afterlife she did not earn.

Perhaps in Godsbones, she told herself grimly, she would find that fabled entrance to the Underlands. Perhaps she would climb down into the afterworld without having died, the way the God of Plenty had, the way the old stories said that heroes had when they loved so much they would do anything to follow their lost loves. The underworld was as full of fields and farms and mountains and rivers as the world above the ground. It would be a pleasure to explore, thought Vish, almost laughing. In life, she had always loved to explore.

Her fever was rising again, she realized. That was what the giddiness, the spiral of delight, really meant. Was it the black rot in her leg that was sickening her, or had her throat begun to rot too? Did it matter? The sunlight in her head now threatened to blind her. She considered tying herself to the pony, but should she die on its back, the body she left would make a macabre burden. The sure-footed pony had appeared in a moment of great need and served Vish and Ama so well. She deserved to run free back in her homeland once her last rider was gone.

Most of the old stories of quests to the Underlands ended with tragedy, but Vish had heard enough to know that on occasion, when you least expected it, one might bring joy instead. On occasion, when the love was pure enough and the hero brave enough, she might get a happier ending than she deserved. So Vish told herself that if she saw an archway in Godsbones that looked like the entrance to the Underlands, she would lower herself from the pony, say a prayer as she dropped her weakening body into the red dirt, and crawl right through that gate.

It seemed that one way or another, the world of death was her next destination.

CHAPTER 15

THE BANDIT GOD

The All-Mother's Year 508

On the roads of Paxim

Jehenit

On certain days, in certain places, the gazes of an entire crowd would follow every move Eminel made. Heads would swivel to watch her, from the left and the right, from near and far. Her mother found it deeply unsettling. No matter that the girl did nothing of interest, rarely even spoke a word with others present. She was a young girl in a public place, and people seemed to consider it a right, even a duty, to stare. At the first sign that a bystander moved to do anything beyond staring, Jehenit would take the girl's hand and begin to walk away. But she lived in fear of what would happen if the person just kept following, following.

Jehenit had not realized just how conspicuous they would be, a woman traveling with a six-year-old girl, especially one small for her age. Young girls were now the rarest of creatures. There were few good reasons for them to be traveling on the open road, but Jehenit had not thought of a better place for them to be. Nowhere seemed safe.

Had Jehenit been traveling alone though Paxim, the road would have been easy. She would have traveled from town to town offering her services as a healer, powering her magic with a sand-filled *psama* around her neck. Hundreds, maybe thousands, of Arcans had done it before. In that way she could have paid for a bed at an inn, a hot meal from a cart in the city, the comforts travelers of means could earn. She could have moved easily through Paxim and found herself welcome everywhere she chose to go.

But Eminel, as she had from the moment of her birth, changed everything.

Of course Jehenit could not carry a *psama*. Sand might activate Eminel's all-magic, sending up a signal as bright as a bonfire. If Seekers were on their trail, it might already be too late to escape, but she would try. Even stumbling across another magician could put them both in danger.

And so the two of them traveled, fearful but determined, with no clear destination but to stay as far from Arca as they could. Paxim was the most hospitable country to explore, the nation where wanderers found themselves most welcome. The roads that cut through its plains and hills and forests offered more paths than they could ever explore before Eminel grew to womanhood.

The road they were on was clearly well-traveled, shallow ruts worn by laden wagons layered over each other, dozens of tracks intersecting in complex, repeating patterns. Wheat and wool traveled north and east from Sestia, with payment flowing back along the same path. Travelers headed for the Bastion, intending to consult the Books or deliver students to be educated, also went north. From the west and north souls streamed southeast toward Arca in search of help: the magicless seeking the magical, trading hard-won money or goods for the gifts certain sorcerers could pluck, as easily as ripe fruit, from nothingness.

There was a rhythm to it, a pattern. For everything that went south, something of equal value returned north, and so on. Travelers in search of something returned from whence they'd come—with or without the thing they'd sought, it was impossible to tell—and these roads carried them in both directions.

Because their mere presence drew such unwelcome interest, Jehenit and Eminel skirted the larger cities, where a pallet for the night came dearly and thieves haunted the unattended alleyways. At least along the roads, when no other shelter was available, roadside temples offered a safe roof, a clean floor.

It was a temple that changed everything.

In Arca only Velja was worshipped, but in Paxim worshippers seemed to seek comfort from every god in the pantheon, major or minor, every god Jehenit had heard of and then some. Like any good child of the Five Queendoms, she knew the first three levels of the pantheon by rote: the All-Mother gave birth to Eresh, Velja, and Sestia, then each of those three gods had daughters and sons of their own, including Hunger, Sleep, and Wealth for Eresh, Luck and Trickery for Velja, Birth and Spring for Sestia. Those she had memorized long ago.

But once the first three levels were passed, the minor gods numbered into the dozens, their family trees quickly becoming complicated. The Bandit God was the grandson of both Velja and Eresh, for example, via Eresh's son Wealth and Velja's daughter Trickery. Some said Beauty had sprung fully formed from Sestia without benefit of a father, others that she'd been conceived when Sestia comforted Eresh's consort Death while he wept, then found herself impregnated by him—not with his man's rain, as was the usual way, but with his tears. Jehenit found most of the far-fetched stories difficult to remember, let alone to believe, and she had not bothered teaching them to Eminel.

Then there were the half-immortals, like the Eternal Scorpion that the Scorpicae were always going on about. They were not quite gods but not quite human, often worshipped, even more often honored in song. The famous Scorpion was supposedly the daughter of the God of War and a human man, a skilled hunter who competed with her in an archery contest and neither won nor lost, earning her respect without claiming to have bested her. She had a whole country that venerated her, but no temples either within or outside its borders.

The night when everything changed started with a day like any other. Jehenit and Eminel worked their way along a trade road toward what seemed to be north, nibbled a stolen seedcake in the narrow shadow of a lone tree when the half-shrouded sun was high, played a game that was not a game by guessing how many steps it might take to reach the horizon. The land was more or less flat here, grassy green, with no landmarks to distinguish their progress or lack of it. By late afternoon, when the clouds overhead spat a temperamental drizzle, Eminel began to complain.

"Tired, Mama," she said.

Jehenit was always a little startled to hear her daughter's voice these days. She realized she, too, had mostly given up speaking. There just didn't seem to be much cause for it. She worried that it might be bad for the girl, all this silence, but then she remembered: nothing would be as bad as losing her to Daybreak Palace. Keeping her safe mattered. Everything else was secondary. She rubbed the slick, aching spot where her healer's tattoo used to be.

"Mama," Eminel said, louder this time. "Can't we rest?"

Jehenit looked around. They were well and truly alone on the road. They were too far from the last trading post to go back, with no idea how far away the next might be.

"Yes, *cheru*," Jehenit said. She tried to say yes whenever she could, mindful of how often she had to say no. "Soon. I'll find us somewhere."

It was another hour before Jehenit caught sight of a small building in the distance. Whatever it was, it seemed the most they could hope for. The rain grew heavier, the sky darker, as they came. Peering through the wet gloom toward the shape, finally she could make out more than just its outline.

It was not always possible to tell which god was honored by a particular roadside temple, but Jehenit had learned to read the signs. Temples of the God of War were guarded by fierce-looking women and men with weapons polished to a gleam; a miniature temple to an unnamed forest god, only large enough for one person and even then only if she stooped, was hollowed from a dead tree trunk swallowed by twining ivy leaves; a temple to Eresh's consort Death was crafted entirely of long, dry, sun-bleached bones, its entrance framed by clusters of small white flowers known as death's fingers; and so on.

This was a temple of the Bandit God, resembling nothing so much as a magpie's nest in building form. The material from which the temple itself was made could not be seen, covered as it was by hundreds, probably thousands, of small objects. She saw coins and ribbons, cheap amulets on leather thongs, nuggets of incense, wads of brightly colored paper soaked by rainwater until their color ran down the walls. Buttons, bells, medallions. In the midst of brighter treasures she saw what looked like the perfectly trimmed and tanned hide of a shrew.

Even lawbreakers were safe in the temple of the Bandit God, thought Jehenit, which was a reason both to stop and to keep moving. Any other travelers seeking shelter here could well be the unsavory kind. But they didn't have to stay long. Just an hour or two out of the rain, that was all they needed. A rest. Just for now.

There was no door, only a doorway. She ushered Eminel in first, her hand on the girl's damp back, then followed. Once over the threshold, the constant patter of the rain softened to a muffled whisper. Jehenit looked around.

It was dim inside, no lamp visible. From what she could make out, the interior walls of the small temple were decorated just as thickly as the exterior walls, all sorts of small treasures nailed, pegged, and glued from floor to ceiling. Up high she thought she saw a fistful of coppers tacked far too high to reach. At her eyeline lay a clutch of gorgeous, exotic feathers each as long as her thumb, their crimson so brilliant it shone even in the half darkness. Farther down were humbler treasures: a white stone polished smooth, a few dried spears of lavender woven into a perfect circle no larger than a child's wrist. The floor itself was unadorned. She took off her wet shoes and left them near the door. The girl followed suit.

As Jehenit walked across the wooden floor, bare feet swishing lightly against the planks, she felt something underfoot that caught and held her attention.

A crack in the floor, a long one, perpendicular to the planks' lines. Narrow and perfectly straight. No accident.

She dug her fingers in, feeling along the crack's length for any curves or imperfections, and her reward came quickly: a popping sound, then a release. Then she saw it. In the shadow of the altar she crouched not on a floor, but on a sizable wooden door, hinged on one side with nearly invisible hinges.

It took all her strength and several tries, but she heaved the door in the floor open to bare what lay beneath.

She'd revealed a wood-lined, shallow hole slightly larger than her own form, perhaps four or five handspans deep. In the hole lay a beautiful length of cloth, folded over on itself again and again, its color the rich, rare blue of larkspur.

"A blanket, Mama," said Eminel. "I want to lie down."

"So do I, *cheru*," Jehenit told her. And they climbed into the hole on their hands and knees, lying down in the cozy hollow, pulling the rich cloth over their huddled, damp bodies. She did not close the door over them, worried she might lack the strength to open it again.

After that, she let every thought fall from her mind like dishes from a shaken table.

They were almost instantly asleep.

When Jehenit awoke with a start, she realized two things: it was pitch-dark outside—night had come—and they were no longer alone.

There was a light above them, a flickering, bobbing light, which cast new shadows.

"Is this the one?" a young man's voice said, but he wasn't speaking to her. She realized there must be two of them, at least. Without moving, she let her gaze drift upward. On the wall danced two shadows, the same size and height, cast by a hand lamp.

"It should be . . . ," said one voice, and then another one answered, except it sounded like the same one over again, "If it's empty, I swear . . ." and then more words she couldn't hear.

The sound of footsteps, a faster flash of light, and then an oath.

"Velja's lower beard!" came that voice again, this time right above her.

The hand lamp was mere feet away now, so close she could feel its warmth. Jehenit caught her breath and looked up to see who held it.

Both men had the same face, identical in every way. Twins. She'd heard of twins, of course, but had never met any. The effect unnerved her, making the men seem a little less real, more like figures in a dream.

So she was able to study them in silence, keeping panic at bay. They had heavy brows and short hair cut straight across their foreheads. Their eyes were wide with curiosity, their muscular bodies surprisingly relaxed: startled, not afraid. Their clothing was not identical but might as well have been, dark and close-fitting, unremarkable.

The unadorned hilts of their short swords protruded from identical metal-tipped leather sheaths that differed only in placement: one worn on the right hip, one on the left.

After the initial shock had passed, the one who recovered first said, "Excuse me. We'll be needing that, please."

He seemed at first to be pointing at her daughter, and Jehenit's heart pounded; then she realized he meant the blue cloth, which was tucked and rumpled around them.

She raised a finger to her lips to shush the twins, gesturing to Eminel, who still slept. In the flicker of the light, she was surprised to see them obey.

Reality was sinking in now. In this unknown place, she and Eminel were fully vulnerable. Her mind swirled and leapt. Who were these strangers? If they weren't going to harm her or her daughter—and they gave no signs of wanting to, not yet—might they help her instead?

She took her time easing her body out of the hollow, moving first one handspan away from Eminel's smaller form, then another. As she moved, she took the opportunity to look more closely at the twins' faces. They were young, she realized. Ten-and-eight perhaps, or ten-and-nine. Certainly no more than twenty, around a decade her juniors. Perhaps she could use that.

Then there was another voice, a loud one. "What in the infinite Underlands is taking so long? Caught your cocks in a rattrap?"

As she finished straightening up, her feet firmly on the temple floor, an enormous shadow seemed to loom above her. Then the shadow came into the lamplight and resolved into more than a shadow.

Jehenit looked up. And up. And up.

The woman was a veritable giant, at least two heads, maybe three, taller than Jehenit, and wickedly scarred. A long, raised scar as thick as a thumb cut from just above one ear across her chin and neck, down her breastbone, disappearing under the low neckline of her tunic somewhere south of her opposite shoulder. The overall effect was one of the enormous woman's body having been severed and put back together, and not quite correctly. The ear where the scar began was at least half an inch lower than the other. Her jaw was also out of true, the shape of the scar lying like a rope between her lower lip and chin, so half her face was lumpen and awkward where the other half was sharp and lean.

The scar bisecting her face gleamed silver, catching and reflecting the dim lamplight to create an unearthly, haunting glimmer against the dark.

Jehenit knew she was gaping and absolutely could not help it.

The giant said, "One coin to look, five to touch."

"Sorry," Jehenit said, then added a moment later, "ma'am."

"Ma'am?" The enormous woman's eyebrow rose.

"I don't know your name," said Jehenit.

"Name's Fasiq. You must have heard of me. Terrifying giant with her band of Rovers? Dead a dozen times over but always rises again?"

"Sorry," said Jehenit. She was at a loss. They were all waiting, but nothing happened. So she thought about what the giant had said, then asked, "Is the dying part true?"

"More or less," the giant went on merrily. "I mean, there isn't much difference between death and near death. Everything gets dark, and if you're lucky, it gets light again. And it makes a much better story. People think twice about killing you if you won't stay dead."

Jehenit tilted up her chin. She swallowed hard and met the giant's eyes, wincing only on the inside at the way the remarkable silver scar rose from the woman's skin like a welt, like a rope, like a snake.

"Clearly," she said, "someone tried."

Fasiq ran her fingertip along the scar, almost lovingly, beginning with the ear and gliding all the way to the opposite armpit, the trail's presumable end. "And very nearly succeeded, she did. Some deaths leave a mark and some don't. I've been drowned, stabbed, frozen, hanged. Still here. You're sure none of this is ringing a bell?"

Jehenit said again, "Sorry."

"Really? I'm so disappointed," the giant said, in apparent sincerity.

Eminel began to stir. When Jehenit looked down at the girl, she could think of nothing but how vulnerable her daughter was, how they were both at these strangers' mercy. She thought about reaching down to stroke the girl's hair, but that would mean climbing back down into the hollow.

Another voice came. "They're not from around here, Fasiq."

Jehenit turned back. Another man emerged from the shadows. The shadows themselves were starting to pale; dawn was already coming. The lamp was still necessary, but the outlines of the group became clearer, the details of their faces more visible, moment by moment. Jehenit caught sight of a knob-shaped object just behind Fasiq's undamaged ear: the pommel of an enormous broadsword, she realized, worn on the giant's back.

"What makes you say that, Hermei?" asked the giant.

The man who stepped forward was old enough to have sired any one of them, thought Jehenit. She wondered if he might be related to the twins, but there was no resemblance. He had deep grooves in his face and nimble, graceful fingers that almost seemed to be twirling an imaginary coin. Like the twins, he dressed to disappear. Of the entire group, only the giant wore memorable clothing, her tunic the dark, shimmering green of a bottlefly, its low neckline chased with silver that matched her silvered scar. Perhaps because there was no hope of her blending into a crowd, she'd chosen her own ways to stand out.

Hermei said, "Just guessing. But I'm pretty good at guessing, you know."

Then Eminel, blinking, said, "Mama?"

"Hush, *cheru*," Jehenit said to her daughter. But the girl sat up in the hollow at their feet, looking wide-eyed at the strangers above her.

The giant lowered her body to sit on the open door next to the hollow, bringing her face closer to Eminel's, the enormous sword slung diagonally across her back banging hard against the wood just once as she settled.

"Don't be afraid, child," she said. "We won't hurt you. We do need that cloth you're holding, though."

The girl looked down at the gorgeous blue cloth and said, "But it's my blanket."

"You can have another. Right now we need to leave before—"

But there was a clanking in the doorway, and even before Jehenit fully understood what was happening, the bandits had closed ranks in front of her, blocking Jehenit's view of the new arrivals, and their view of anything behind her, including the hollow and Eminel within.

"Bessemer," said one of the twins. "There's nothing here for you."

"Isn't there?" came a deep voice.

Fasiq rose, moving smoothly to stand between the twins, and Hermei pivoted to press his back to hers. He reached out, almost casually, for Jehenit's wrist and wrapped his hand around it. He raised his finger to his lips to shush Eminel, but though the girl tried to muffle her squeak of fear, she did not completely succeed.

"You'll want to move on," Fasiq said loudly, firmly, in the direction of the doorway.

"Will I? Or will I want to take a look at that girl you're hiding?"

The giant said, "She's with us. So you won't need to look at anything but the open road. Maybe check out the pickings up toward Scorpica."

"With you? A *girl*?" The voice was cool and dark as a nighttime riverbank. Jehenit felt a tight knot of worry in her chest. As Fasiq shifted, Jehenit turned her head, catching only a glimpse of the man in the doorway, of an arm thickly furred, almost as if the rival bandit were not a man but an animal.

The sound of Fasiq's enormous sword sliding out of its sheath seemed to go on forever. Metal scraped against leather for two beats, three beats, four.

"With us," confirmed Fasiq. "So you best be on your way."

The silence was deafening. Jehenit's eyes met Hermei's. He gave the smallest possible shake of his head. The silence stretched, pooled, became a tangible thing. Jehenit could feel it weighing her down. She felt sweat beginning to bead on her wrist. Hermei's grip tightened, probably without intent.

Then, at long last, the tense silence broke. Jingling and clanking broke out, something like a dramatic sigh, then the sound of retreating footsteps. Then there was another silence, during which Jehenit checked Hermei's face—he looked relieved, thank Velja—and finally a long wait as the footsteps grew softer, softer, softer until they were gone.

Turning back toward mother and child, Fasiq broke the silence. "I guess you'll be riding with us. I'm sure you wouldn't want to make me a liar."

Jehenit said, "That was—very kind of you."

"I don't do things to be kind."

"Why, then?" asked Eminel, the valuable blue cloth now draped around her shoulders, and her mother's stomach plummeted. She could not think of a good answer to the question, which was why she had not asked it.

Fasiq grinned. "You two seem like a nice change of pace. I'm guess I'm sick of all this male company."

Then she leaned down toward the girl and said in a loud, mock-conspiratorial whisper, "You know what they say about too much time among men. Makes you soft as a scrotum."

Eminel's eyes widened in surprise.

The giant laughed at her reaction, a warm, heavy sound, like buckwheat honey.

Jehenit said, "We're in your debt."

"Yes," said the giant. "You are. Now let's be on the road. In case old bear-breath changes his mind. He's not too much to look at himself, but I hear he's got some savage new friends. Nasty bunch. Hermei, would you go and track him a few leagues, make sure he doesn't double back? We'll want to go wherever he's not."

"Happy to," said the man. Before he released his grip on Jehenit's wrist, he looked down at it one more time, then met her gaze again. When he let her go, she understood why.

At the exact spot where he'd placed the center of his palm lay the scar that had once been her tattoo.

✦

Jehenit had lived in fear and uncertainty for so long that it was an utter relief to fall into line behind Fasiq's determined, no-nonsense commands. In gratitude for the Rovers' protection, she worked quickly to make herself useful. She could not use her healing powers, but she had other practical skills. From the first, she handed around food from their supplies at mealtimes and lit a fire when one needed lighting. Within two weeks she had taught herself to brew the strong, bitter tea Fasiq favored, making sure the pot was already bubbling over the fire before the giant even awoke. Within three she had mended the twins' clothes to perfection, stitching countless rips, splits, and fraying seams, though new damage seemed to appear almost daily. She was not an expert with the needle, but the bandits were complete novices, and as her mother had sometimes said, *In the land of the blind, the one-eyed woman is queen.* By the end of the first month, Hermei—who turned out to be the party's thief, and a

talented one—asked her to sew concealed pockets in his cloak, places
he could tuck purloined trinkets. When her designs proved successful, he rewarded her with a few stolen coppers and a delicate cuff of
hammered silver the pockets had helped him carry away.

Fasiq herself was friendly but never intimate, jovial but never
carefree, generous but never selfless. In quiet moments she regaled
them with tales of former lovers, of whom there seemed to be a near-
infinite number: women and men and people who were both or
neither, sheltered scholars and wandering actors, wanton lapsed Sestians and noncompliant Bastionites, learned intellectuals and beautiful fools. These stories always seemed to reinforce the point that
Fasiq was both magnetic and coldhearted, but there was something
about the way she pronounced her departed companions' names that
sounded ever so slightly like regret.

Jehenit understood that in order to lead them, the giant always
had to hold some part of herself back. Even in the close quarters in
which they found themselves, traveling together as they did, Fasiq
was always a little apart. She hated to be seen without her scar silvered. She did this herself every morning immediately upon waking,
patting a new layer of silver dust onto the twisting, raised scar from a
green glass jar that dangled from her belt, the shape and size of a fig.
This was the one task Jehenit never offered to do, knowing her help
would not be welcome.

Of the group, Jehenit found the twins to be the best company.
Their names were Elechus and Luben and she could not tell them
apart, not even close up, except that Elechus was right-handed and
Luben left-handed. They generally acted as a unit in any case. They
poked gentle fun at her and all the things she didn't know about life
as a bandit. Once she learned each new thing, they found something
different to mock her for. So she learned that thing, whatever it might
be. In this way, she became familiar with all the ins and outs, all the

necessities, until she was a productive member of what felt very much like a family.

She never asked Fasiq directly why she had taken the two of them in, but it was impossible to miss how protective the giant was of Eminel. Jehenit saw the giant crack walnuts with her teeth and kick one enormous foot clear through a hut's doorframe, but when Fasiq cradled the girl's cheek, her hand exerted no more pressure than a breeze on a leaf.

After Hermei rewarded her for her sewing skill, she finally worked up the nerve to ask him some of the questions that had been burning in her mind since the Bandit God's temple.

"Who is Bessemer?" she asked first.

"No one important," Hermei said, but she could read the tension in his voice. "All-Mother willing, you'll never cross his path again."

"But he knows now. That there's a girl traveling with Fasiq. She stuck out her neck for us."

"That she did. Partly to be contrary, I suppose. She wouldn't want Bessemer to get a leg up."

"That's why she took us in? To be contrary?"

"Like I said"—he eyed her—"partly."

"And why did you?" She turned her wrist upward and extended it toward him, the shiny coin-shaped scar beginning to pale with time. He had hidden it from them all, Fasiq and Bessemer alike, in the temple of the Bandit God. "How did you know?"

He said, "Does it matter? I know."

"I was a healer," she said. "Back home."

"I thought it likely."

"Do you want to know why we left?"

"No," he said, "I don't. The more I know . . . well, you shouldn't want me to know."

A chill went through her blood. He was thinking of Seekers. Not even knowing Eminel's power, not knowing the story of Jorja's betrayal, his mind had still run to the possibility of their being hunted. The fear, she realized, never really went away.

She asked him, quietly, "You're from Arca?"

He did not look at her. "Born there, yes."

"So you're . . . ?"

"Yes." His tone was matter-of-fact. "The standard type. With the power to make myself beautiful."

"But you aren't," she blurted without thinking. In the day's light, she examined his face in detail. Everything about him was grimly ordinary, the faint stubble of grayish whiskers around his chin, his deeply lined forehead, his too-large ears. He looked like a man the world had used and forgotten.

"No. I'm not." He smiled. "I have no wish to be. Beautiful is not useful. I would much rather be useful."

Jehenit said, "And you don't . . . you don't carry a *psama*, do you?" She was sick to her stomach, realizing how long she had gone without knowing. She should have asked that first, the very first thing. All this time, all these miles, they could have been sending out a signal that would lead the Seekers right to them. She had never even suspected.

"I don't," he confirmed. "Please, be calm. I can't promise you'll be safe forever, but I can tell you that Fasiq will do anything in her power to protect that girl of yours. You two are good for us and we're good for you. I believe Velja set our paths to cross."

"Me too," said Jehenit. "How long do you think the giant will let us stay?"

"How long do you think the Drought will last?" asked Hermei.

Jehenit answered, lowering her brow, "That's impossible to know."

Hermei laughed without mirth. "She's no easier."

"So we should . . . be careful?"

"You should be ready for anything," he said, reaching out for her wrist, his thumb pressing the shiny pink coin of the scar. It no longer hurt, even when he pressed it, but it still served as an ever-present reminder. "And even so. You're only as safe as she can make you."

Jehenit heard the unspoken corollary as clearly as if he'd said it aloud. *As safe as she can make you is not the same as safe.*

✦

They identified the treasury wagon by the deep ruts it laid, the heaviness of its cargo pressing its wheels into the hard ground. In order to travel undetected, the drivers had to treat the incredibly valuable wagon like it wasn't valuable at all. So they did what they would have done with a wagonload of barrel staves, fertilizer, or secondhand ash: they left it unattended in front of the local inn while they supped inside, the oxen only loosely tied. But the Rovers knew the wagon instantly; the deep tracks led right to it.

The twins wore hoods that cast shadows over their faces, and while one snuck up into the driver's seat, the other passed into the inn through the front door to give anyone who turned something else to look at. At the same time, Hermei ambled past the hitching post, untying the oxen without even seeming to pause. The wagon was gone before its drivers could even stand up to object, and they had no idea who'd absconded with it; despite its size and heft, it was as if the wagon had been spirited away by shades, its heavy tracks disappearing into the nearby river, which was rumored to hide a path to the Underlands. Once the bandits redistributed the gold among themselves, the wagon floated, and gold and wagon were reunited in a quiet patch of woods many leagues away.

Nearly as shocking as how easy the treasury wagon was to steal was what Fasiq ordered afterward: the twins and Hermei would immediately return the wagonload of gold to the capital, claiming to have wrested it from the actual thieves, while the giant, Jehenit, and Eminel stayed behind in the quiet woodlands. The girl was used to hiding in the Rovers' wagon by now, every day by daylight and even by night on the busier roads. She was a full shade paler than her mother, so rarely did she see the sun. Jehenit cooked oats over a fire and ladled up three bowls. Eminel snatched hers, scampered up into the wagon one-handed, and pulled the curtain tight behind her.

Taking her own bowl, with her own extra-large spoon, Fasiq turned to Jehenit. "It's plain on your face you're bursting with questions. Go ahead. Ask one."

Feeling a fool, Jehenit asked, "Why steal a wagon we're going to return?"

"The treasury pays out a percentage on returned property," the giant explained, scooping oats but letting the spoon hang in the air while she finished her thought. "Encourages thieves to turn on each other, take each other out. And we may have kept just a bit for ourselves. Which we'll blame on the low-down bandits we'll claim to have rescued it from."

"And the twins and Hermei will . . . be all right?"

"Of course. Why wouldn't they be?"

She said carefully, "It just seems like something could happen."

"They've been ambushed before, yes. Turned out well enough. For them, anyway."

Jehenit looked for another way to express what she meant. In the end she simply blurted it out. "But how can you trust them to come back?"

"For one thing, they're smart enough to watch their own hides. The treasury would never let a whole wagon of gold vanish. If they couldn't track the thieves when they tried to spend the bars—which they would, someone would report it in a heartbeat—they'd send Seekers."

A shiver ran down Jehenit's spine. She hid it, played dumb. "Seekers?"

"Yes," Fasiq said. "Bless your little heart. Never had to worry about Seekers where you come from?"

"No," lied Jehenit. Even as careful as she'd been, she still half expected to see the grim face of a Seeker when she opened her eyes each morning. Only by the grace of Velja had none materialized.

"They hire themselves out," explained Fasiq, "magicians who are good at finding things. Plunder every mind in their path to hunt their quarry, they say. But don't you worry. The wagon's getting returned. So no Seekers, no Scorpican enforcers, none of that. Besides, those three would never betray me. They know if they did, I'd spend the next few years hunting them down."

But they're your friends, thought Jehenit.

As if she'd heard the other woman's thoughts, Fasiq said, "No matter how dear they are to me, I would kill them if they did me wrong. I had to do it before, with others. I didn't like it, but I did it."

Jehenit did not ask for details, but Fasiq took her silence as invitation. "The twins weren't with me then but Hermei was, and he will have told them. So they know."

Again, Jehenit did not ask. Again, Fasiq went on. "Before the twins, I had a mother-and-son team as the muscle. You don't need all the details, but they cheated me out of my fair share of something. I hung one from a tall tree and hung the second from the first. You may wonder about the mechanics of that, but I assure you, the tree was very tall."

Jehenit could think of nothing to say to that. The silence was heavy now, leaden. She stared down at the pot of oats on the fire. She had forgotten to stir it, and the bottom had scorched. She could not see the brown, burnt mess on the bottom of the pot, but she knew it was there.

"Anyway," Fasiq said, "they'll be back soon enough."

Jehenit scraped the unburnt oats into another bowl for later and soaked the bottom of the pot, then scrubbed it clean. They rolled bones and talked of nothing. Eventually the sun sank below the horizon. Jehenit had not passed a sleepless night since joining the Rovers, but tonight she was not sure she would be able to rest. The story stuck with her.

But when Jehenit bedded down inside the Rovers' wagon with her daughter that night, she found herself bone-weary. She felt Eminel, limp and trusting, sleeping without fear. And she heard the buckwheat-honey voice of the giant singing from the ground beneath them, quiet and gentle and exceptionally out of tune.

When all Paxim is done with their deals
Your honor's the thing that you keep.
When a girl helps a girl helps a girl
Peace be upon the land, and sleep.

✦ CHAPTER 16 ✦

WARRIORS

In Scorpica

Tamura

After only a year, Tamura felt like she had been queen for an eternity. The three dark years after Khara slew her mother had crawled by, seemingly endless, as she hungered for the moment she could finally trade mourning for revenge. Then that *kheq* Vishala had thwarted her for another two years—another wait that felt infinite— by assigning her to the Fingernail. Even so, Tamura had come to terms with the delay. Each of those years had strengthened her and taught her. By the time she issued her Challenge, she'd become a weapon herself, honed to a fine point, forged in fire.

But she had only wanted to deal death to her mother's killer, with no awareness of what awaited beyond. She had not been prepared in any way to rule a nation. Now, her thirst for blood still burning, she was expected to spend her days managing supply lines and as-signments, councils and disputes. When she rode off by herself to hunt, she had only a few blissful moments of silence before hoofbeats sounded: someone always rode after her, insisting she needed protection. The life of a queen was limiting, and every day she wished she were free of it. But the only stories of women willingly giving up the queenship of Scorpica were stories of weaklings and cowards; she would not be one of them.

She almost longed to be Challenged. Anyone who could best her deserved to rule Scorpica more than she did. No matter how she shirked her duties, ignored the constant requests to make decisions, give orders, the warriors still looked to her for guidance. Tasks that were absolutely necessary, she delegated; the rest, she ignored. Every day she waited for an angry, able warrior to come for her, the way she'd come for Khara, but so far, none had dared.

The Drought had unsettled everything, everyone. Time itself chipped away at the future of her country like a daily drumbeat. She wished she had a clear solution, a path to the brighter future they all longed for. Instead she listened to daily reports stone-faced and left her councillors guessing. Warriors remained on assignment throughout the Five Queendoms, continuing to train and strengthen themselves, even as skirmishes became more common between those warriors and the people they'd been hired to patrol and protect. Owners of large farms in Paxim and Sestia had long welcomed boys from Scorpica as half-sons, half-laborers, but with more boys born in their own countries, they traded or paid less for each one. How it had always been was no longer the way it would be. Scorpica could welcome it or resist it, but either way, change would come.

It would come for her, too, Tamura knew. The rumbling discontent would twist and grow into blame. She would be held responsible. But every day it seemed easier to muddle along, to postpone any major decisions or declarations, to ignore the burdens of being a queen she'd foolishly put upon her own unwilling shoulders.

Until one crisp autumn morning, a year into her rule, when the visitor appeared.

Tamura heard the hubbub outside well before anyone came to present themselves at the flap of her tent. They had moved down from the mountains onto the flatlands near the border for their winter camp this year; the augury had said the snows would be worse than the winds, and so the flatlands were safer. Her tent was in the center of the others. No one could reach it unnoticed. But sound traveled far more easily than people, and so the murmurs and shouts interrupted her peace. Curious, she listened for more.

All she could hear were warriors' voices, chattering and abstract like far-off geese. Just words. No swords, no arrows. Even the shouting settled, over time, into a dull roar. When she tired of waiting for someone to call at the flap of her tent, she flung it open herself and emerged into the brightening daylight.

Larakhi dha Hulia, her second-in-command—Tamura had chosen her more or less at random, early in her reign—stood with her hand on the arm of an intruder. On his other side was another tall warrior, grim-faced, gripping him just as intently. Both women were on the taller side for Scorpicae, but the man was taller and wider than either, his shoulders several handspans above their shoulders, their shoulders narrower than his chest. She evaluated him quickly: no more than twenty years of age, lightly armed with a single short sword in a scabbard and belt so unscuffed it might be his first time wearing them. His hooded eyes looked almost eager. In short, not a threat. And likely not used to using his sword if he hadn't drawn it on the Scorpicae who now held his arms immobile.

At her approach, the man straightened, clearly knowing who she was, trying to look dignified despite his inferior position. Raising his chin, the man said, "Queen Tamura. May the All-Mother bless you."

She did not return the blessing.

Though she had not asked his name, he offered nervously, "I am Balicon. I was raised in Paxim, in a town called Elom, but I was not born there. When I came of age, my parents told me they were not my parents. They bought me—"

Tamura held up a hand, palm outward, and said, "I did not ask for your history. You know who we are, so I am certain you know where you are. You stand on Scorpican soil. Men are not allowed here."

Balicon seemed to find some strength then, some inner steel. He raised his chin again. "I now know my true identity. I am the son of a Scorpican. I come to present myself as a warrior."

Tamura gazed at him. Perhaps what he said was true. It didn't matter either way. Khara would have rebuffed him gently: given him an audience, a kind word, a basket of the small green apples that grew so well in Scorpica, before sending him back through the Bastion's gates to wherever else he belonged in the world. Tamura had no intention of clinging to the old, hollow ceremony.

She looked away from him toward the warriors who were drawing curiously close, forming a loose circle around the action. For a year she had felt uncertain, overmatched. But doubt fell away as she stood facing the intruder. This was a challenge she could meet, no confusion, no ambiguity. A kind of relief flooded her. She knew exactly what to do: give this man what he deserved.

"Perhaps you have heard," she said, "that we are kind to men who come to make a claim on us."

"I make no claim," he said.

"Then what do you want?"

"To be recognized as a warrior. To fight by your side."

"That is indeed a claim," she said. "A brazen one."

"Who would not want to fight alongside you?" he asked, his voice thick with passion, with admiration. "All the queendoms know yours are the strongest warriors, the best warriors. Had I not been told

I had the honor of Scorpican lineage, I still would have known it. I have always longed to fight. All my life I have felt the angry blood of a warrior in my veins."

"There you are wrong," she said. "The strength of a warrior has nothing to do with anger. If you fight because you are angry, you are no better than a pup. So why do you want to fight?"

"I believe it is my calling."

"Fight me, then," she said.

A glint of alarm showed in his eyes for the first time. His nervous gaze darted from Tamura's face to those of other nearby warriors, but he found no reassurance there. "That is not why I came."

"We heard it plain. Did we not, warriors? You are called to fight."

"To fight," he said unsteadily, "in your army. Not to fight against you. I would not win."

"True," she said. "But that is the choice you have made."

"Choice?" he asked, trying to back away now, but held tight by the women on either side. She could see him trying harder and harder. The warriors who held him had to grip tighter to keep him in place, but he was in no danger of breaking free. Wanting to fight was not the same as being trained for it. He might have natural strength, but it had not been nurtured, tested, grown for his whole life the way his captors' had.

"You chose to come here. One does not trip and fall through the gates of the Bastion into Scorpica by accident."

"But other men have come," he blurted. "I've heard of them. Men who wanted the same thing that I want. They have presented themselves as the sons of Scorpicae and asked to fight alongside their kinswomen."

"*Kinswomen,*" sneered Tamura, and the warriors around her laughed. "We have no relationship to you. Our names should not even lie upon your tongue."

"I know my father was a man, but so was yours! You all had fathers! All of you!"

"Warriors have no fathers," she said. Energy sang in her blood; this felt right in a way nothing had felt right to her for an age. "How could you prove who fathered you? Did you fall out between a man's thighs instead of a woman's? Was the precious seed that grew you watered with *woman's* rain?"

The other women laughed at that. Tamura nodded to them, enjoying their appreciation, but did not soften her jibes with a smile.

"Are you such an extraordinary animal?" she continued. "Such a prize?"

"No . . . ," he said, still squirming and still held on both sides with grips as tight as iron. His attempts to escape were getting wilder now, but to no avail. She could see he was already tiring.

"Then who knows who your father is, and who cares who your mother was? You are not of us."

"I'm sorry," he said at last, his eyes downcast, his arms going limp in the grip of the warriors. "I see now I should not have come."

She let the delicious silence lay there a long time, until the warriors around the circle began glancing nervously at her and each other. She kept her eyes fixed on the intruder and nowhere else. She ran the tip of her tongue along the inside of her upper lip.

Then she said, "But you did."

"I will go back where I came from," he said, his voice growing ragged as he understood what she was saying. "I won't bother you again."

She strode up to him, stopping along the way to pick up a shield from the armorer, the usual wooden circle with an iron boss in the center to protect the grip. The armorer's assistant, Marbera, backed away almost as if she were afraid, but the armorer, Golhabi, met Tamura's eyes with a grim smile, placing the shield firmly in her queen's waiting hands.

The man was taller than her by far, but her gaze overmatched his even as she tilted her head back to look up. Her gaze was packed with fury, his with fear.

"You wanted to fight," she said, casting the shield into the dirt. It landed at his feet. "So you will fight."

She drew her sword then and nodded to the women on both sides to release him. They dropped his arms so suddenly he caved in on himself for a moment before he recovered. He was on his feet, but unsteady. He now had the eyes of a trapped animal.

He tried to back away but found the warriors arrayed behind him did not move as he approached. He feinted to the left, then the right. The ring of warriors was closed tight around him. The center of the circle was open, but the walls of the circle did not move. He had no means of escape.

"I refuse!" he shouted, turning outward toward the circle, then back to face Tamura. "I know you will beat me. I will not draw my sword."

"Then die with your sword undrawn," she said, taking one lackadaisical step, then another, closing the space between them. "That is your choice."

"Wait," he said, and put out both hands.

She slowed to a halt with her head cocked, but her eyes burned as they had before, and the point of her sword remained high. No one in the circle doubted the outcome.

He bent to pick up the shield, wrapping his hand around the grip. She could tell by the way he winced that it was an ill fit, his fingers too wide to fit comfortably inside the boss, his overlarge knuckles grazing the metal as he flexed his fist. "May I not choose another weapon? Another time?"

"No. Those are privileges reserved for warriors."

His voice sounded half-strangled, but she admired that he spoke at all, knowing the fate that now awaited him. "Then I can only fight and die?"

"You wanted to fight," she said. "Draw your sword or don't, but the time is upon you. Now."

He drew his sword then with a quavering hand, but he might as well have left it in the scabbard, for all the good it did him.

Her first blow went straight for the hilt of his sword, and even though he brought the shield across his body in an attempt to block her stroke, she was too fast for him by far.

The blow knocked the sword from his hand as if his fingers were nerveless as the dead's. When he turned to follow the tumbling blade, she reached out with her free hand and ripped the shield from his grip. Unprepared, unbraced, he let it go. The shield and sword spun in opposite directions across the ground, each sliding across the dirt to land at the feet of a different spectator.

Deprived of both sword and shield in well under a minute, he was left undefended. Tamura was already in position for a second stroke, but held back, waiting.

What was there to do? He did not even raise his arms across his body nor clench his open palms into fists. His body seemed to go limp even while standing, and after a long moment, he closed his eyes.

Tamura flung her sword down in disgust. "Not even a fight," she said. "Not by half."

He did not open his eyes and so he did not see her lunge toward him, her hands up, not at first. When her foot hooked behind his knee, his eyes opened in surprise, but by then it was too late; her hands had already closed around his throat and he was falling.

Tamura rode his falling body down, tight against him for the instant it took for his taller form to topple and crash in the dirt. When he landed on his back, her hands were already locked on his throat, thumbs pressing his windpipe closed.

She shifted once to kneel on his upper arms, sitting astride his torso. No matter how hard he kicked and flailed, he could not gain purchase. His face turned an ugly, mottled shade of crimson. Blood flecked his open eyes as he struggled silently, unable to gather even enough breath for a scream.

After a long, ugly minute, his limbs falling still, his body under Tamura's going limp, the man who had been called Balicon lay motionless in the dirt.

Only then did Tamura rise to her feet, reach out for her sword, and drive it in one stroke through his body. It met with no resistance.

"The Scorpion drinks the blood of the defeated," she said. "The fight is done."

Tamura braced her foot against his belly to free her sword and sheathed it without wiping it clean. She would do so later, but she wanted the story to spread. She wanted anyone, warrior or otherwise, who looked upon her to know that the blood staining the sheath of her sword belonged to a man who did not know his place. She had killed barehanded because she could and she wanted to; the blood was for show. But the show would fix this moment in their memory as no words could.

The warriors surrounding her neither cheered nor hissed, only looked and waited. Only the armorer's assistant Marbera stumbled away, hand over her mouth as if retching, and everyone knew she lacked a true warrior's temperament. The rest seemed loath to leave the circle they had closed around the intruder. No warrior would want her light snuffed out so decisively, without dignity, like a rat tossed into a pot half-full of rainwater. His very inability to die like a warrior proved that he'd deserved his fate.

The warriors seemed to wait for her words. What should she say? Blood running hot, impulsive, she simply opened her mouth and gave voice to her thoughts.

"Spread the word when you travel," Tamura said to her warriors. "Any man seeking to join the Scorpicae will meet an end like this one. Does anyone here object?"

There were some murmurs, too low and quiet to be understood. Tamura met the gaze of any warrior who dared look at her, but only one spoke.

"We could have used him," grumbled Larakhi, every woman in the circle knowing exactly what she meant.

Her voice ringing out, Tamura addressed the assembled warriors. "Never use a weakling."

Then she spoke directly to Larakhi, nearing her, her voice rising with every phrase. "In times past, I would have told you, if you want to give birth to a warrior, go find a strong man with strong blood and take him. If the first one refuses you, find another. Or find another even if the first one gives himself to you. Even if they all give themselves. You could journey through the entirety of the Five Queendoms in that fashion, if you liked to. You could have hopped from bed to bed until your *muoni* gave way. Perhaps one day when the Drought ends, you could resume that journey."

Larakhi was quiet then, looking at the ground. Her gaze slid over the body of the bleeding man near her feet, then found a new spot on the ground to stare at, one untouched by blood.

Tamura lifted her hand to cup Larakhi's cheek, a tender gesture. She said, "But we must be wiser now. You understand why."

Larakhi nodded.

She turned to address her subjects, knowing the moment had come. She had never realized this before: they were so very ripe to listen when the stink of blood hung in the air. And she had an idea, her first edict as queen, the first thing she wanted. A future for Scorpica.

"This is what the other queendoms have to offer," she said. "Men and weaklings. So you may be thinking, we are so strong, we have nothing to fear. Is that so?"

No one responded. They seemed not to know what answer she

wanted. She wished they would think for themselves, but if not, she was happy to do the thinking for them.

She pushed on, searching for the right words. "You see the writing on the wall. Our youngest girls are six years old now. For ten years, twenty years, even thirty, they will be able to fight. But after that? If things continue on as they have been, in fifty years, there will be no Scorpica."

"It is so," mumbled Larakhi, braver than most.

"We cannot survive. If we have no young, we have no future."

"It is so," several others now chorused.

Tamura said, "So we must have more young warriors."

"But how?" asked that woman Gretti, grim and assertive. She was one of Khara's loyalists from the old days; Tamura had assumed she would step up to speak the words of Challenge, but she never had. If questions like this were all Gretti had to offer, thought Tamura, she had nothing to fear.

Instead of answering, Tamura let the silence hang in the air, let every warrior ask herself what the answer might be.

Gretti clarified, pressing what she seemed to think was an advantage, "My queen, you may not have heard my question. Do you have a suggestion of how we are going to make more warriors?"

"Well, Gretti, I do not know how to *make* them any way we have not already tried," Tamura said, with a dark chuckle.

Gretti looked down, color rising to her cheeks, as a few warriors burst forth with derisive laughs.

Tamura held out her hands to dampen the mirth, though not quickly. Then she said, "Luckily, that is not our only option. What we cannot make, we will take."

Were their slack-jawed stares born of incomprehension or fear? She hoped it was fear. Fear, she could work with.

"The other nations have girls, after all," she said, forging on. "Like us, they birth no new ones, but they have girls of seven and eight, girls of nine and ten, young enough to learn, old enough to train. There is already a supply of what we need, only in other queendoms. We will simply take some of theirs and make them our own."

"Steal them?" asked the stout, tenacious warrior they called Bohara. She was still one of Tamura's favorites, an ox of a woman, loyal and fearless. But since they had returned from the Fingernail, she'd developed a fondness for a kind of fermented millet drink called hammerwine. It weakened her. "In raids, you mean?"

"Steal them if we like. March into their villages and demand them at sword point if we like." Tamura was gathering strength and energy from the waiting faces in the crowd. "The other queendoms are weak. The very warriors who defend their territory are Scorpican-born; we could call them home any minute of any day. So who will stop us?"

Nods around the circle became smiles; those who understood approved. There were those whose faces were impassive or confused, perhaps uncertain, but none of them spoke out.

Only Gretti plainly resisted, her heart-shaped face tight with concern, her hand resting on the hilt of her sword. "Demanding girls at sword point? We would be inviting war."

"And who fears war?" Tamura looked out, imperious. "We are warriors, born to fight. Your previous queen may not have been prepared, but I am."

She heard the words almost as if someone else was saying them. Was she really ready to lead her people into war? They were outnumbered by far, for one thing, and the opposing blades would be borne by Scorpican hands, for another. War was out of the question. She'd let herself go too far, drunk on spilled blood and righteousness. What else could she offer them? She was not sure she had her mother's gift for strategy, but she did the best she could.

Tamura held out her hands, palms forward, toward the waiting warriors as she tried a more temperate approach. "But war is not yet required, not for this purpose. I ask no warrior to compromise her principles. You may decide to take only girls who come willingly. You might choose to pay a family to take a girl. You may decide to take only motherless girls, girls who are unwanted, girls who are unloved. What type of girl and how you get her? That is between you and the Scorpion. But bring girls to join us. To build our nation's future. And you will be rewarded."

The queen scanned the group to see the effects of her words. Bohara's features were set in a fierce, appreciative glare. A grudging agreement, somewhat short of approval, dawned on Gretti's face. Then Tamura saw two warriors near the edge of the crowd, Khitane and Pura, exchange a look with each other. They'd recently been sent home from an assignment in Sestia for taking bribes to look the other way when sheep thieves cut fences; she knew exactly what they were thinking. *Redemption.*

"Here is the cold truth: we cannot go forward exactly as we have been," said Tamura. "Every day we grow closer to a world where Scorpica no longer exists. I will do everything in my power as queen, every day I draw breath, to fight off that world."

"It's never been done," said another warrior, but Tamura noted that this time it was not Gretti, who seemed to have no more objections. This pleased her.

"True, yes, we have always relied on warriors born here, but are we not the greatest nation?" she asked them, the answer obvious to all. "Can we not inspire young women to become warriors, wherever they were born? In this way, we will last. We will live."

Gretti said, "But if the Drought does not end for fifty years, Queen, that is not true. We will not live."

Grumbling and curses rumbled around the circle, sending a thrilling jolt through Tamura. If her warriors would shout someone else down for disagreement, that showed her strength. But she could show it even better by listening, she realized.

"She is right! No, no, let her speak, she is right." She enjoyed the look of shock on Gretti's face. "If the Drought of Girls lasts forever, nothing we do will save us."

"I'm sorry it's so," said Gretti, and she did look genuinely sorry.

"But who knows what the future holds?" Tamura's question was no question. It was a rallying cry. She put all her fire, all her love of Scorpica into her words. "The Drought could end tomorrow! Will it last a year? Five years? Ten? We will only know the day it ends: the day we hear a freshly born warrior howl her greeting to the world. In the meantime, we must do everything we can. For each other. For ourselves. For our nation. For Scorpica."

"For Scorpica!" echoed Larakhi in her deepest, loudest voice. She seemed to unlock something in the crowd that had been pent up, contained, just waiting to flow out like a river.

Cheers started, quietly at first, then rippling like a strong wind across a field of wheat.

"Scorpica!" they shouted, rattling their spears and swords and bows.

Tamura surveyed the warriors around her, their eager faces, their fierce enthusiasm. She had not even known she had it in her. She had turned them, focused them, aimed them. Yes. They would rally for the strength of Scorpica. They were behind her.

And if they were behind her, as their rightful queen, she would lead them.

CHAPTER 17

A SLIP

An island off the coast of Scorpica

Sessadon

S essadon was on the back foot from the beginning, which might account for how bad it got, how fast.

Hana had risen that morning in the dark, as she always did, then headed out to check her traps and lay new ones before the nocturnal creatures settled down to their daytime sleep. She herself slept in the cave, not far from the shell of the sorcerer, which was now recognizable as a body. Plump where it had once been parched, muscled where it had been skeletal, hale where it had been nearly wasted away, the body was almost ready to move. It only lacked the one thing no number of boars or snakes or birds could provide. The All-Mother's creatures varied and so did their life force. There was one more type of life the sorcerer's body required.

A light rain fell as Hana worked her way down to the shore to check the netted traps she'd arrayed in the shallows. These often brought in rock crabs, their flesh sweet and delicate, well worth the labor of cracking their tough, mottled shells. But today, even before she could see if the traps were full or empty, she noticed something out of place. A dull spot on the shining waves. She drew closer and closer until she could identify it.

The round, low shape was a deserted *kupha*, an exact replica of her own craft, beached in the shallows.

Her own *kupha* was hidden away in a cave near the water, anchored securely with a hemp rope. Whose was this? What did it mean? She crept forward, her feet making no sound on the wet sand, which felt as familiar as her own skin. The beach was deserted, but where the sand began to dry, the faint imprint of sandaled feet remained, leading toward a narrow path that disappeared into the tree line.

Hana crept forward, following the path, her senses on alert. Only yards into the wooded area she saw the stranger's form come into view.

Next to the largest tree nearest the path, sheltering under its branches, a woman hunched over a wet knapsack, muttering under her breath. Hana's heart leapt to see a sister warrior. The woman's body was unusually small and slender, not as muscular as most warriors, but the make of her leathers was unmistakable. *Another warrior, after so long! Did fate bring her here? Did she search me out?*

The woman had not seen her yet. Hana's lips began to form a greeting as she moved forward, moved closer.

But in the same moment, Sessadon became aware of the intruder. She snapped to attention, hearing what Hana thought, seeing what Hana did.

Sessadon did not want what Hana wanted.

She wanted the warrior dead.

And so even while Hana extended a friendly hand toward the slender, small warrior, a smile on her face, Sessadon dove into her head to wrench her in the other direction. *Reach for your weapon,* she commanded.

Hana fell still, her arm paused in midair, a look of confusion on her face.

The other woman stood from her crouch, unfolding slowly. When she spoke, her voice trembled. "Hana?"

Hana's hand was on the hilt of her sword, but there was something so familiar about the other woman, the curve of her ear, she . . .

Hana. Your weapon, Sessadon insisted. *Draw it.*

"Hana," the other woman breathed, almost laughing, her eyes bright, delighted. "I found you! I've searched so many islands, and I hoped, but . . . I can't believe it! I have so much to tell you, and it's *you*, and—Hana?"

Inside her mind, Hana was pushing back against Sessadon's command. *No. I couldn't, I can't. She is . . .*

"It's me, Marbera," the other warrior said, her smile less certain, fading. "Don't you know me?"

Hana's mind flooded with memories. Her lips next to the curve of Marbera's delicate ear, whispering, teasing, pledging. Stolen moments in the armorer's hut one long, fierce winter, wrapped around each other flesh to flesh, musk and salt drowning out the scent of worn leather and cold iron. Memories set aside, faded, but never, ever gone. Indelible.

Sessadon pushed harder. *Draw your sword. Now. Do it.*

The sword slid from its sheath and Marbera's lovely eyes went wide.

In the long moment when Hana and Sessadon warred inside Hana's racing mind, a moment so silent the loudest sound was the patter of the morning rain, Marbera made a decision.

She dropped her pack and ran for the woods, hard.

After her, screamed Sessadon to Hana, all gentleness gone. *Now. Go.*

Sessadon forced Hana to give chase after the other warrior, to pursue her through the scrub. Marbera was not as strong nor as lithe as Hana, but she ran like lightning.

It took all the magical energy Sessadon had to focus Hana and push her forward against her will, which was why her concentration in holding the other spell, the grand one, slipped. The web of light on the ceiling of the cave rippled and tore. A few of the bright-lit stars—two in the base of the Cauldron, one from the shoulder of the Dreamer—winked out.

No time for the spell, no time for anything else at all. If the new warrior got away, she would ruin everything. Sessadon needed that life force, and it might be years before another warrior stumbled onto the island. And if this one escaped to tell the tale, the next faces Sessadon saw would be a party sent to kill her. She might be able to fight them all off, but she might not. One could not take such a chance when victory was so near. Sessadon had felt a surge of power from her all-magic descendant, a bright, fierce flash, and she knew the girl was as strong as she'd hoped. Things were falling into place now.

If this intruder didn't ruin it all.

Marbera fled, unsteady, into forest she didn't know. The green leaves were slippery with water, and the scent of wet moss crushed underfoot rose up around the warriors as they ran. They seemed to run forever. The gentle, steady morning rain grew more intense. The fleeing warrior knew her only hope was to loop back to the beach, but she was not sure she could find her way back in the right direction, especially half-blind in the rain.

She almost made it.

Marbera broke free of the tree line and under the open sky, which was pouring down rain now, and as Hana broke out after her, neither had any shelter from the pounding droplets. Their hair was soaked, their leathers, their legs. It was hard even to see in the downpour. They both knew they were on the desolate beach, but it was hard to tell where the sea started, and both were knee-deep into the seawater before they even knew it, wet sand sucking at their feet.

And then finally, at the last moment, as Marbera reached for her *kupha* foundering in the shallows, Hana caught her.

Sessadon knew how to fight, but it had been so long, hundreds of years, and Hana was a born fighter, but she resisted Sessadon's control for the first time, her hands twitching and jerking as they were forced into shapes against her will, and she wailed inside her mind, *Why? Why?*

Sessadon wasted no time in explaining but only told her, *Fight. Hard. Knock her feet out from under so she cannot stand. Throttle her. Hold her head under the salt water. Hold it. Hold it.*

The other warrior fought valiantly. She bucked out of Hana's grasp once, twice, three times. Desperate for air, she thrust her head up out of the water so hard the top of her head drove into Hana's chin and knocked her back. Although Hana's grip did not loosen, for a moment the other woman was above her. Looking down on her. In a desperate flail Marbera slapped her open palm atop Hana's head to shove her, in her turn, under the water, until Hana sputtered and screamed and swallowed a choking gulp of salt water that burned her throat and her lungs.

Could Marbera, small but desperate, actually win the fight? Sessadon realized perhaps she should have tried to control the new arrival instead, but now it was too late to refocus. She couldn't risk losing control of them both. She simply had to force Hana to follow through until the bitter end.

Get up! Fight. Breathe.

Hana got her feet under her and thrust her whole body upward, hard, churning the water as she rose. In the moment she seized the upper hand, she made the best use of it that she and her master could, twisting the other hunter's wrists until she cried out in pain. The cry was the beginning of the end of the fight. Marbera's head went under the water with her mouth wide open.

Drive her down. Hold her under.

The smaller woman's body bucked and twisted, as it had before but so different, rising against Hana's firm hands. Tears ran down Hana's face, salt running into salt, washed by rainwater into seawater. The hunter's body convulsed like a snake suffering a scorpion's venom, a lethal, deadly strike.

Hold. Hold.

Knuckles white, throat thick with anguish, Hana held Marbera down even after she stopped writhing, even after the last bubble broke the surface, even after it was clear that she would not rise again.

Once the intruder was senseless, Sessadon forced Hana to drag the unconscious body back to the cave, which she did, sobbing all the way. The rain slackened and then stopped. Now that things were quieter, the sorcerer finished patching up the spell hastily, then focused on Hana as she drew nearer and nearer with her unspeakably heavy burden. Sessadon had asked too much of her pet, she knew. And yet, and yet. She could not truly be sorry. This was the only possible outcome. There was no other choice.

She snapped her fingers and sucked the last of the life force from the intruder's body, feeling the energy rush into her like a powerful tide. Then Marbera lay fully dead, her breath gone and heart still, the lifeless body limp on the stones like a discarded poppet.

Hana began to scream.

Not just any scream, but the worst Sessadon had ever heard. Unearthly, in its way. This scream was a piercing, shrill wail of anguish, a spreading ocean of terror, seemingly without end. Inside the young woman's mind there was nothing left but the scream. Sessadon recognized the mistake now that it was too late to rectify it. In struggling to hold the spell and force Hana to act against her own wishes, to do something she never would have done, she had pushed her pet too far too fast. So far that now, she saw, there was no coming back.

The hunter's brain was melting now, changing color, red blood swirling into grayish liquid, puddling with something clear; Sessadon could see it all. It looked exactly like that young servant's ruined brain had so long ago, the first time Sessadon had stripped a mind, before she knew or understood the limits of her power. The brain was a muddled pink mash and still there came the scream.

The sorcerer herself felt her own mind threatened by the power of that scream, so high, so savage.

Sessadon pushed her way into the hunter's mind to silence the scream and everything there went dark at once, all the flickering light, the last swirl of color, all the memories, all the words, all the life.

She'd been in the young woman's head since the day Hana arrived on the island, her constant companion, and now it was over. What had she done? Brought one of her worst fears roaring back to life: she was alone again, all alone. Panic rose in her throat. She fought it. There would be time for that, time to mourn, time to regret. But there was no going back; Hana's mind was gone. Only her body remained, and it might or might not last. There was nothing she could do for the hunter. But there was one last thing the hunter could do for her.

Hungrily she gulped Hana's life force, drinking it down like water, feeling the surge well up within her. It quenched a thirst she hadn't known she had, filling her with heady power, as if she had breathed in not just air but a whole new world. She gave a kind of thanks to the dead woman, though Hana was beyond hearing it.

She knew from her years in the hunter's thoughts that Scorpicae believed they would move on after death to some sort of hallowed hunting ground. The battlefield beyond, they called it. She hoped, for Hana's sake, that some part of her was awakening in that sacred place even now. What was left behind on this earth was gruesome. The Scorpican's body, such as it was, lay like a discarded husk on the floor of the cave. The sorcerer's drinking of her spirit had dried out what was left, crumpling it inward like the deflated, limp stomach of a dead animal. Not just dead, but depleted.

And Sessadon's body, rebuilt death by death by death with dark, insidious magic, began to move.

She stepped out of the shallow pool in which she had lived for what seemed like an eternity. The feeling of having arms again, legs, a heart, a throat, the shimmering oddness of it would take some time to deal with. It was both powerful and disorienting. She did not know what to do with this body, how awkward it felt, both limiting and limitless. Had she always been able to feel the movements of her heart within in her chest, lurching unevenly like a colt just learning to stand? But she did not need to know everything, not this minute, she told herself. There would be time.

Because look at her now: moving, stretching, carving out her own space in the air as she walked. That was a strange sensation, to feel the air parting around her, over her, while the earth pushed back against her feet. She blinked and breathed and shuddered. She had her own eyes to see and her own legs to stride. She had a body now to match her expansive mind, and along with both of those, she had a plan.

Sessadon was back from the dead.

CHAPTER 18

THE KITCHENS

The All-Mother's Year 509

Daybreak Palace, Arca

Mirriam

Seven years into the Drought of Girls—for that was the milestone everything was measured from now—Rijs died. Mirriam had not killed her senior husband, but neither did his death, sudden as it was, cause her despair. If she did mourn, she was mourning the Rijs she'd married. He'd had sparkling eyes and a quick tongue, an impish smile. That Rijs had been gone long before her husband drew his final breath. In his later years he'd been still beautiful, but not charming, not quick, not warm. Which had happened first? His descent into bitterness, or her neglect? Or had the two fed on each other in an endless, bleak cycle? Perhaps it would have been a mercy to take him away earlier. She could have breathed in his life force, though there wouldn't have been much of it. The younger the person, the stronger the life force. A man of sixty years would have offered up barely a wisp of future promise.

Rijs had grown so bitter, she even wondered if he'd become one of those upstarts who believed that the men of Arca deserved magic as powerful and plentiful as the women's. Other than those few revolutionaries, most believed that men's magic had been taken away in the earliest days of the world, as the stories said. Mirriam was not sure the stories were true, but she also didn't believe it mattered. For whatever reason, Velja had chosen to bless women differently than men. That was the truth of how things were, and even the Drought did not change the truth. Multiplying the number of men did not change the gifts they did or did not have. Things might be different if the Drought lasted twenty years, but as of yet, there was nothing to be done.

A year or so ago, when she'd first wondered if Rijs's bitterness had made him radical, she'd dipped into his mind briefly. The truth was there. While he wished fervently for more powerful magic, daydreaming about what he would do with power over bodies, over fire, over air, he had done absolutely nothing but daydream. His grumbling was just grumbling. But his attitude had pushed the two apart, until at last they'd been so far apart she found herself, now, surprisingly unmoved at his passing.

Above all else, she found the loss of Rijs tiring. Courtiers would now scramble to improve their standing, offering up their brothers and sons as replacement husbands, hoping to create or strengthen an alliance for their matriclans. The mere thought of fending them all off exhausted her. But at least there would be a state funeral. They, and she, would be distracted by the opportunity to put on one's finest robes and jewels and compare oneself favorably to all others in sight. Here was one area where both women and men could shine. Literally, in her case, she smiled to herself.

The floor-length robe she chose was a shimmering black, its folds glowing faintly with a dark gleam, enchanted by some long-dead magician to shine for decades, maybe centuries. Abstract patterns, picked out in silver stitching as delicate as spiderwebs, ringed her cuffs and hem. As she moved they seemed to leave pale, glowing trails in the air.

It was not only her own appearance she controlled. Because she thought it would be fitting, as well as to make the woman feel favored, she asked Dolse to have her husband Ijahn cast a gray pall over the funeral proceedings. When the queen stood next to the palace's enormous hearth, her hair pulled back in a severe plait down her back, the blue glass snake around her long neck shone like a beacon in the dim gray. No one could look away as she spoke the words of homegoing. She spoke clearly, her voice ringing out, the assembled crowd murmuring their responses in a single hushed, reverent voice.

"No matter who we are or what we do," Mirriam finished, "we return at the end to Velja. We return, at the end, to the hearth."

In the desert villages of Arca, before burial, bodies were wrapped in strips of rag, glued and pasted on with clay. Nothing that still had a use could be consigned to the grave. But earlier queens had refused to display rags in Daybreak Palace, even for the holiest of reasons, and the palace had its own traditions. Rijs's body was laid into the hollow before the hearth without cloth or covering. Others moved to begin to close the earth back over the body. The queen stood, motionless and silent, until the work was done.

She remained standing next to the hearth until the very last courtier, the least powerful magician of the least powerful matriclan in her court, departed. She stood there standing a long while after. When Ever reached out for her elbow, the motion startled her; it was him she had been thinking of.

No flirtation, no teasing, no show. She only said what she thought, this time. "I want you with me tonight." It was not yet time for sleeping, but sleep was not what she intended to do.

"Yes," he said, returning her boldness with boldness, nothing coy in his tone. She asked, he answered, and that was all.

She had thought herself hardened against emotion, but now she realized that she did feel, only not in the way she might have expected. The loss of Rijs made her mindful of Ever, almost painfully so. Her young husband would continue to age while she did not. He would wrinkle, slow, swell, and die. Not for many years yet, perhaps, but it would happen. She had never considered changing that.

But now, her mind returned to it over and over. That was why she had asked for him. Her anticipation mounted as they walked down the long halls together, arm in arm. She would enjoy his young body tonight, running her hands and lips and tongue over every inch; perhaps that would give her clarity on whether she should take unprecedented steps to keep his body exactly this way. Doing so would open a door she'd always assumed she would leave closed. Her own body was taut with desire under the floor-length black robe. Soon she'd let that robe slip to the floor in a dark puddle around her feet, her bare skin meeting the cool air, his lips descending to warm the flesh of her neck. She shivered expectantly as they neared their destination, eager to begin.

But barely had he shut the door to her rooms behind them when a knock, not loud but still insistent, interrupted them. She was still dressed and so was he.

She knew the knock. It was Sobek's.

"A moment, my love," she said to Ever, veiled her mind quickly with a protective shield, and went to let the woman in.

Sobek was the human equivalent of a warm woolen blanket, a woman whose every curve and feature seemed carefully selected by a friendly god to put others at ease. She was a handspan short of average, with merry eyes and generous proportions. Her arms looked meant to cradle, not to crush. Not every woman's gift matched her physical form, but Sobek's did: she was a mind magician with a very specific talent. She could only influence one mind at a time, but that mind trusted her utterly. Any person she shone her gift on would follow her commands without question.

Mirriam did not trust Sobek, of course; she trusted no one but Mirrida and Ever. She was careful to shield her mind every single time she interacted with the woman, just in case. If Mirrida happened to be present, Mirriam would ask her to put up the veil—it was her daughter's strongest talent—but she could easily do it herself, if that was where she chose to direct her energy. In any case, the conversation should be quick. Sobek had a very specific set of responsibilities in Daybreak Palace to go along with her very specific gift. That was why, no matter what her knock might interrupt, Mirriam would always let her in.

Sobek said, "Shall I enter, or would you like to speak elsewhere?"

"Enter."

The woman eased into the room, but there was a hitch in her step when she saw Ever. She slowed, stopped. "Queen?" she asked.

Mirriam made a snap decision. "He can stay."

To her credit, Sobek took the shocking turn of events in stride. She pretended Ever was not in the room and spoke to Mirriam as she ordinarily would. "There's a girl who has asked to leave the kitchens."

"How old?" She did not ask which one; that was not important.

"Ten-and-two."

She needed only a moment to consider before making her decision. "Here, then. Midnight."

Sobek hesitated.

Mirriam prodded her. "Yes?"

"Tanaj is her sponsor," said Sobek, in the same buttery tone she always used, the voice that would have convinced Mirriam of anything if she hadn't shielded her mind from the woman's power. Even with the shield, she felt she listened harder to Sobek, paid her more attention. "She knows the girl's six months have passed, so she has also been asking."

"Tanaj can go hang. Greedy *kafal*. This one is mine."

Sobek said, "She has been quite impatient."

"Give her more patience, then," said Mirriam, her voice pointed, commanding. If Sobek told Tanaj to be at peace with the decision, she would be. "I have plans for this one."

Sobek's eyes flicked over to where Ever lounged against the pale cushions, his watching eyes mica-bright with interest. Mirriam wondered perhaps if she should have hidden her plans from the woman. But let her blab; everyone would figure it out anyway, if she went ahead with this. There were no magicians currently in the court with the gift to halt aging, let alone reverse it. It would be abundantly clear that the queen had stopped her husband's aging process the old-fashioned way. The rumors, and the resentment, would be the same.

"Is that all?" Mirriam asked the woman.

"One other thing. A new all-magic girl, we think."

"Where?"

"A small village, called Adaj."

"And where is that?"

"In the north. Small, fairly isolated. The nearest settlement of any consequence is Sjinja."

"And why haven't you sent Seekers already?"

"I did. They have not returned."

"I see," Mirriam mused. "Do we think the girl's a serious threat?"

"Probably not, but I must admit, our information isn't good. There was a burst, and nothing since. She might have learned how to cloak it. She might be dead. No way to tell."

"Except to send better Seekers."

"I thought you might want to try that, yes."

"You're correct. But this time, let me talk to them first," said Mirriam. "Who does Pom pair with now?"

"Alamaj."

"Those two, then. Have them meet me in my audience chamber right away."

"Very good."

"Should I stay here?" asked Ever. She had entirely forgotten he was there, listening. Not that he could or would do anything about the seeking of a new all-magic girl. But the other matter, that, yes, that would be interesting.

"Stay or go, as you choose," she said, lowering her voice to a purr. "As long as you're here at midnight. There'll be a treat."

"I'll wait right here, then," he said, and stretched like a cat.

It was too bad business called her away, but on the other hand, they both had much to look forward to.

The Seekers were waiting for Mirriam in the audience chamber when she arrived. Both women were dressed in dark clothes, clinging except for their capes, with hoods they had thrown back. Pom wore her hair back in a long plait, her small, dark eyes narrowed almost to slits. The taller one, who had to be Alamaj, had an oval face like a cameo and a short sword on her hip.

Lesser Seekers—those who brought back lost objects, missing pets, and the like—might work alone. But Seekers of all-magic girls always worked in pairs, and in fact, only one of the pair was actually a Seeker. It was simply easier to call them Seekers than to call them what they were: one Seeker and one Bringer, one to find the target and the other to retrieve the target once found.

Seeking magic was not all-magic. Any Seeker with enough talent to scan and read minds en masse wouldn't have body magic that could compel an unwilling target into cooperation. A Seeker might be physically strong, but physical strength was not enough when all-magic girls were in the mix. There was no telling what skills such a girl might exhibit. She might be completely untrained and docile, going along just as she was told; it was equally likely that she could crush hearts, snap bones, or steal souls, possibly even without meaning to. It was necessary, in these pursuits, to be prepared.

"I know your skills," Mirriam said to Pom, and the woman inclined her head in a respectful nod. "Yours, Alamaj, are unfamiliar to me."

"Air," said Alamaj in a cool, quiet voice. She seemed unremarkable at first, like most women who chose long-term partnerships with Seekers, both cultivating their ability to blend in. But the longer Mirriam looked at her, the more authority the woman seemed to exude. Something like a stillness in her eyes. "Wind, to be specific."

"And that's enough?"

Pom interjected, "More than. Her skills are excellent."

Mirriam said, "You vouch for her?"

"Absolutely."

"Then the task is yours," she said, and explained the mission.

They both listened somberly, then asked a few follow-up questions, quickly getting what little information Sobek had received. At the end they nodded and waited for her to dismiss them before taking their leave.

"Send word when you have the girl's name," she told them. The more people knew the name, the more minds could be put to use. Pom's scanning range was about a league, and between the girl's name, age, and gifts—untrained all-magic had a way of erupting, no matter what was done to contain it—they were sure to ferret out their target.

Mirriam could not wait to meet her.

✦

Later that night, when Sobek returned to Mirriam's chambers hand in hand with a stranger, Mirriam did not, at first, understand. Sobek with her rounded curves, her open-seeming face, her mouth naturally settling into a smile, yes, she was as she should be. But next to her stood an unusually short woman, her cheeks gaunt and hair brittle, a deep vertical groove of worry worn between her brows. She appeared to be about thirty years of age, perhaps five-and-thirty, worn down by hard living.

It wasn't until the woman spoke that Mirriam understood.

"My dear friend Sobek would like me to pass the evening with you before I return to my village," she said. Her voice was high and thin, like a child's.

Despite her appearance, a child was what she was.

This was the girl of ten-and-two Sobek had promised, mere hours ago, to bring. An all-magic girl who had been deemed unworthy in the trials and sent to serve in the kitchens for six months. Some girls let themselves lose track of time and remained kitchen servants for years; the luckiest, the most obedient, found themselves assigned to more plum roles in Daybreak Palace. Obstinate ones who tracked every moment of their six months and requested release as soon as the term was up, these always turned out to be trouble. When the girl asked to go home, the request did not mean what she thought it meant. She would not see her village again.

And now this, the wearing-down, the difference between her real age and how she appeared. Distasteful as it was, it was obvious to Mirriam what had happened. Sponsors were allowed to tap discreetly into the life force of the all-magic girls they sponsored. That was the point of sponsorship, the advantage the courtiers enjoyed, and a queen's most important tool for keeping them in line. But this sponsor, Tanaj, had gone much too far.

"Come in," she said, barely able to form the words. Not that she really needed to be convincing. Sobek's gift had taken care of that.

The woman—girl, Mirriam reminded herself—took small, patient steps into the room. Mirriam's heart hurt just to look at her.

The sponsor had drawn down so much of her life force that she had literally taken years off the girl's life. Mirriam realized belatedly that Tanaj had been looking particularly well lately, the glow of health in her round cheeks, a firm confidence in her stride. The girl would never get those years back; they belonged to Tanaj now. Though Mirriam might not let her make use of them. But thoughts of punishment could come later. At a minimum, when Tanaj's next turn to sponsor came, she would be passed over. Though of course, Mirriam reminded herself forcefully, if there were no more all-magic girls, there would be no more sponsoring. Which would make her life easier in some ways, harder in others.

That was a problem for another day. She put it out of her mind, thinking instead of the gift she was about to grant Ever, one she'd never before shared with a husband. Had any other queen done so? The histories were silent. Perhaps no man had ever been so lucky. She felt a wicked delight at breaking the unspoken rule. After so long, few new experiences remained to her. She planned to make the most of this one.

"You may leave us," she said to Sobek.

Her courtier first placed her hand on the girl-woman's shoulder, murmuring gently, "You'll be safe in our queen's hands. Do be good for her, won't you?"

"Yes, Sobek, I will," came the response in that reedy, disconcerting voice. The smile on the worn face was just as disconcerting. Somehow both weary and innocent, cheerful and resigned.

Once Sobek was gone, Mirriam reached both hands out for the girl's hands and drew her toward the pale cushion. "Come here and close your eyes," she said.

The girl obeyed, her lashes lowering, her bony hands warm and limp.

They began.

For a talented woman with all-magic, especially one whose enchantments burned bright enough to make her queen, there was nothing particularly striking or complicated about the process of drawing down someone's life force. Mirriam merely had to think it to make it so.

But the novelty of sharing the experience with Ever changed it, this time. In a way she saw it through his eyes. She saw herself from his vantage point—confident, commanding, hungry—as she began to draw the power into her own body. The force spread through her, a heavy warmth, slow and sweet as honey. Then she placed Ever's hand on the shoulder of the aged girl, fitting his cupped palm over skin beginning to grow papery, bone sharp beneath. She met his gaze and his eyes were as hungry as hers. She let her magic flow, shifting it, curving it into something new. And she whispered commands with soft breath right next to his waiting ear, teaching him how to receive the life force, how to absorb it. They continued by turns—some for her, some for him—until she felt the last breath go out of the body, drained of every day of its future, giving up the last of its energy from her earthly form into theirs. The lifeless body slumped, fell.

Mirriam was nearly breathless from excitement when she turned her full attention to Ever, examining him from only a handspan's distance.

The physical differences were subtle, but she saw them clearly. The gleam in his eyes, the sheen to his skin. More than that. Something beyond the physical, almost like a shift in his consciousness, hers, both. A twinning instinct united the two of them in a way she'd never been united with anyone. Their gazes connected and she could not, would not, look away. The corners of his mouth began to turn up, and his smile spread across both their faces at the same moment. They were alive, joyous, together.

His hand that had rested on the aged girl's shoulder now came to Mirriam, brushing her cheek, cupping her chin. She relished the soft pressure of his fingers. As attuned as they were, sharing a kernel of the same spirit, they were not the same person, she recognized. There would be exquisite pleasure in exploring their differences.

"Come," she said, leading him from the outer chamber, and he followed without letting go.

When they stood next to the bed, his hand slid down to follow the curve of her neck. Then he pushed the shimmering black fabric of the rich robe off her shoulder, exposing bare skin there. A few more movements, smooth and languid, and her other shoulder was bare. Her back. Her legs. One hip and then the other, everything between. Before long, all she wore was the snake necklace, its blue glass cool on her flesh. The stories said that if a man without the right to touch the queen reached for her, the snake would bite. But in all her years wearing it, she had never seen the snake do so much as hiss or rattle. It had slithered onto her neck when she became queen and rested against her flesh in silence ever since. Its pearl eyes bore unseeing witness as Ever's fingers continued to explore, gliding across her flesh until she shivered.

One smooth fingertip traced her hipbone, then her belly, then lower still, moving from soft skin into dark curls. His eyes locked with hers again, that lazy, shared smile coming to their lips again as his newly assured touch struck home. When she gasped, he curled his palm and pushed in harder, perfectly attuned to her desire. She collected herself long enough to form words, just a few.

"How do you feel?" she asked him.

He looked drunk, pleased, glowing. "The best in all my life."

"Then let us see how much life is in you," she said, reaching for the knot of his belt with eager, nimble hands.

✦ CHAPTER 19 ✦

THE QUARTZ HEART

On an island off the coast of Scorpica

Sessadon

Even from the isolation of her island, Sessadon could feel the balance of the world warping, tilting, melting. The spell was working even better than she'd hoped. Not only would her all-magic descendant—the girl called Eminel—stand tall in a world where no challengers could arise to her power, but that world itself was softening, becoming ever more ready for Sessadon to claim it, month by month, year by year.

Back when the queendoms were established, the conflict-ridden world of Sessadon's own time had stabilized into a mostly peaceful set of separate nations, each with its own resources and strengths. But now those borders had lost their stability, become porous, unsound. There was hatred bubbling up between the queendoms, resentment and fear, and Sessadon didn't even need to feed it. Some wanted to blame others for the lack of daughters; others were outright stealing daughters that did not belong to them. Blame and fury were swarming. Women of every stripe—boneburners and scholars, farmers and cooks, lawmakers and air magicians—were furthering her cause without even knowing it. She could feel, everywhere, the pulsating, paranoid fear.

It was perfect.

The weaker the five nations were, the easier it would be for her to sweep them away, to take all five in one motion instead of fighting through them one by one. The fewer queens remained to rise against her, the better; there would, in the end, be only one. And she would not rule one of these fabricated queendoms. She would rule the world.

But to do that, she needed to take her power with her everywhere she went, and for that, she would need a new heart.

She would be leaving Scorpica for the first time in five hundred years, ever since those heathen warriors had chased her off a cliff. Perhaps she'd start her rule by murdering their queen. Someone needed to. Live by the sword, die by the sword, wasn't that how the saying went? Whatever weapon those warriors turned against her, she could and would turn back on them.

Again she thought of her sister, so much like her, yet so different. Their talents were almost the same. It was their temperaments that defined them. Almost as if Sessadon had the blood of a warrior and Kruvesis the blood of a diplomat, though neither was true. Their mother and her husband had both been magicians. They would have been Arcans if there had been an Arca when they were born. But there had been a time before Arca, and now, there would be a time after.

One last thing to do to clear the way.

Sessadon had life force in her body now, but she did not have a power source to sustain the spell she had woven. It could be the mightiest spell this world had ever seen, supported by the mightiest sorcerer, and it would be foolish to let it dissipate if there were another option.

But was this step one step too far?

There was a tremor in her, an unaccustomed fear rising, when she remembered she did not know her limits. She must have them; all magicians did, no matter how talented, no matter how long they'd lived. Old stories from hundreds of years before the Great Peace, when women's magic was more widespread and did not rely on sand to power it, were clear about what happened to a woman who aspired to the power of a god. Velja had struck them down time and again: the earth magician she'd buried under a mountain, the water magician she'd drowned in the Salt Maw, the arrogant all-magic girl whose enchantments she'd turned inside out so that when the girl tried to destroy her enemies, she herself was destroyed. Sessadon did not want to be a god. Velja was still her god. She only wanted to be a queen, the queen of everything. And so she soldiered on, ready. If she reached her limit, that was fine. It would be far worse to create a limit for herself that did not truly exist.

Once the power was within her, traveling with her, she would be able to hold this spell and cast countless others, regardless of where she went. There was a risk to it—if the quartz heart were taken from her body, she would die, no lingering half-alive this time—but the risk was worth it. This was the only way for her to reach the goal she'd been working so long to achieve. She had to go forth into the world. Here, alone, she'd go mad.

Sessadon faced the outcropping of quartz that had first drawn her to the island. She lay her palm flat against the cool quartz, savoring its featureless surface. It was a rich, dense glass, transformed from what had once been sand. This rock had done so much for her. It had brought her back to life and given her enough power to change the future of the entire known world, to the edges of every queendom. Now she would ask it to do one more thing.

She opened the front of her tunic, then reconsidered and removed it entirely. Warmth would be the least of her worries once the spells began. Better not to spoil a decent garment with stone dust and blood.

Before she set to her task, she looked up at the gleaming blue ceiling of the cave one last time. She checked every detail of the spell that lay over the five queendoms like a net, ensuring that it was smooth and steady and that it would be able to sustain itself for the time it would take to power herself to travel.

Satisfied, she began.

First, she summoned dividing magic to the fingertips of her right hand. The power poured forth, ever-so-slightly visible, a kind of radiating shimmer against the air. Without hesitation she plunged the hand directly into the wall of quartz, pushing against the slight resistance, as if her fingers pushed not into solid rock but thick, sluggish mud. She curved and twisted her fingers into the precise shape she wanted, settled her grip into the stone, and yanked.

A chunk of quartz the size of her fist came free from the outcropping. She'd expected a ripping sound, something momentous, but it slid free from its thousand-year home with no more than a whisper. The rush of blood in her ears was louder than the gasp of the torn stone.

She then shifted and bent her magic, allowing the dividing spell to subside and lie in wait while she launched into a capturing spell, summoning this one to her empty left hand. Still her every move was silent; still her tremendous power was no more visible than the faint waves of heat rising from sand in the noonday sun.

Sessadon transferred the quartz lump into her left hand, muttered a few more words of enchantment, gripped the quartz tight, and poured everything she had into it. The life force of all those animals, of Hana, of the entirety of the quartz mountain, all of it. She drew more power from the island's living creatures, from the plants and the animals, to take along.

The quartz began to glow. Now was the moment when everything could go wrong. She hurried into the next step of the enchantment, imagining she might outpace the doubts, and did the thing there was no coming back from.

Sessadon steeled herself, drew the magic of pure force into the fingers of her right hand again, and reached that hand through the bone and flesh and muscle of her own chest to grasp her weakly beating heart and rip it free.

This was the hard part now. The body shut down and she could not see, could not hear, could not breathe. She would have been done for if she were not magic, and even the magic would give her only a few precious moments to bridge the gap. With her strength fading—the body beyond weak, all the power in the quartz heart itself—she plunged the quartz heart into the gap where the beating heart had been.

It was cold and hot at once, her flesh all around the heart burning and freezing, the searing, soaring pain, just pain, all pain. She could not catch breath. There was no breath, not anymore. Everything was gone but the pain. And deep within the pain, its burning kernel, the heart. The heart was here.

There. It was done. All she had to do now was survive it.

Her hands flowed, more feebly than she'd hoped, in the motions of a healing spell. A day and a night should suffice. She put herself to sleep so that when she awoke, the healing would be complete. Her chest would be solid again. Her blood would pump through her veins, flow, bring life everywhere into this twice-revived body. Everything would be as it had been, except that she wore a quartz heart in her chest now instead of a flesh one, and then her journey could begin.

Was the night long? Short? She might as well have died and risen again for all she remembered.

When her eyes opened, a weak sunlight showed in the cave's mouth. Night was over, day had come. She lived.

The pain had faded to a dull, aching roar in her chest, radiating little flickers of fire and rot. Had she been human, looking down at it would have made her queasy. Over her breastbone was a raw, ragged wound two fists across, its borders pulped like fresh meat. But it had healed remarkably well, all things considered. Mere hours from now it would not look nearly so dire. She found she was exactly where she'd hoped to be.

She reached up for the spell, its twinkling blue light she had so enjoyed spread against the ceiling, and drew it down to her, lower, smaller, until all its blue light was drawn into the quartz heart and it no longer had a physical presence outside of her own. In this way she could carry it. She was the spell and the spell was her.

The sorcerer rose and stretched, then dressed herself in a tunic and leggings of deerskin Hana had once made. She buckled sandals onto her feet and slung a pack over her shoulder. She left the cave for the last time, not looking back, and walked south with a steady pace. She knew every inch of the island, every rock and tree, because Hana had known it and she had seen with Hana's eyes. Now she saw with her own, but everything was just as familiar. The sun on her face felt just as glorious, for though it was a different face, it was the same sun.

Down along the beach, she found the *kupha* where she knew Hana had left it. The little round craft seemed precarious, and it wasn't entirely clear how to steer. She did not need to be precise, of course, only aiming for the mainland, but she was starting from a place of complete ignorance. This gave her pause for a moment, for what would have been a heartbeat if her heart were still beating. She would shore up the *kupha*'s present form with the right touches of magic, making it sail straight regardless of winds or waves. She would be as safe on the boat as she was on land. Magic was like that, making the impossible possible.

It wouldn't matter, she told herself, that she'd never sailed before. There were a lot of things she had never done before. With a quartz heart in her chest, her energy bursting with stolen life force, and a softening world out there in which to make her indelible mark, now was the time to do them.

✦ CHAPTER 20 ✦

A REQUEST

In Scorpica
Tamura, Azur

Seven years after the last warrior had been born in Scorpica, two years after she'd risen to become queen, Tamura dha Mada looked out over her dozens of daughters and smiled.

Warriors had scattered far and wide in response to her call for the girls of other queendoms, and when they returned—striding or skulking, proud or chagrined—they brought the girls she'd called for. She'd rewarded those warriors, as she'd said she would. The best tents, best weapons, first pick at meals, all went to those who had brought strong, eager girls for training without upsetting the queendoms or families they'd been born into. Competition between warriors was fierce, but she kept it in line.

And she'd made it clear several months back that deaths in the service of kidnapping were not acceptable, after Khitane and Pura left a body behind in the Bastion and a furious envoy appeared to demand redress from Tamura. She pretended complete ignorance and sent the envoy on her way. She upbraided the clumsy pair in private. One last chance, she told them, and not in the stony warrens of the Bastion, not ever again. Every citizen of the Bastion was known, recorded, classified; it was folly to try to spirit one away. She ordered her warriors to narrow their operations to the remaining three queendoms. They should take good care, but there were still plenty of girls, if one knew where to look. No matter how valuable girls were as a group, there were individual girls to be plucked here and there, the neglected, the misfit, the lonely.

Three years before, there had been a chill, a stillness in the tent city that had set all their teeth on edge. But now girls ran and played, cheered each other on, laughed with pleasure at their own skills in the field. There were still no babies, of course, but it seemed to matter less. Tamura still ignored most of the queen's traditional responsibilities, focusing only on what she desired most. Let them think her a brute or a savant, an arrogant butcher or a softhearted, softheaded child. She did not care what anyone else thought. She would serve her daughters and herself.

If someone had asked her whether she was building a family or an army, she would not have known how to answer. The truth was that she craved both.

Dozens of girls had joined the nation of Scorpica. Before long, the camps and training fields swelling with new recruits, they would be hundreds. Only no matter how many girls came, no matter how many tents they filled with their high-pitched voices and ready, growing bodies, the need still burned. *More,* she thought to herself. *Scorpica needs more.*

Tamura's longing for a family was more complex, buried so deep within her she didn't have words for it. The yawning chasm had always been there, a hungry darkness, deep down.

She'd had a mother, yes, but one who rarely concerned herself with Tamura's care. Even when Mada was alive, Tamura had felt alone. Single-minded and ambitious, hungry to rise, Mada had spent years angling her way forward. Everyone respected Mada's quick mind and ready attitude, but they saw through her feigned affections; she lacked both sincerity and the gift of seeming sincere. When the reckoning came at her death, it was easy to see that while she'd had plenty of comrades in arms, she hadn't left behind a single friend.

When Tamura was a mere child, before her mother's death, a warrior on assignment in Paxim took a bandit's arrow through the throat and never returned home. Tamura still remembered the outpouring of affection for the lost warrior's daughter, Nikhit, who had no shortage of families willing to welcome her. How different things had been when her own mother died. Tamura had not gotten over her burning resentment of Nikhit until the two served together in the Fingernail, an assignment the arrogant, ambitious Nikhit had requested. If the young woman had been less brave, less impressive, Tamura might have been tempted to leave her unguarded during a prison riot or let a hunting accident unfold with fatal results. But Nikhit was strong and smart and a good ally. Only the smallest resentment remained.

Because when Mada had died, no one wanted Tamura. No one had rushed forward to claim her, comfort her, offer support. Her mother was a failed Challenger who had not made any arrangements for her daughter if she should fail, and if Tamura's own mother had not valued her, why should any other Scorpicae? Vishala dha Lulit was the one who had told her of her mother's death, not wanting her to hear it from anyone else. But no one else had even tried. Queens of legend who'd defended their titles sometimes took in the daughters their Challenger's death had orphaned, but Khara had a treasured daughter of her own; as far as Tamura knew, she'd never even considered doing that kindness.

And afterward, oh, the uncertainty, the sidelong glares. She'd had to ask to be taken in, no better than a beggar. Household after household had tolerated her in their tents because no one was better at bringing more food to the cook fire, but after a few months, she always found herself shuffled off to another reluctant host. Sometimes she didn't even know she'd been sent away until she returned to a tent and found her pack gone. She'd considered fleeing Scorpica entirely, except that it was the only home she'd ever known. She'd been born a warrior. There was no use pretending she could be anything else.

But she'd made do, muddled along, until her unexpected assignment. At ten-and-four, as she approached the time of womanhood, Vishala dha Lulit took her aside again. It was the first time the queen's councillor had spoken to her since imparting the news of her mother's death. Even though she was not old enough for an assignment, Vishala said, because of her skill and readiness, she was being sent to the Fingernail. In a way, that had been a great day for Tamura. At least she felt she had a purpose.

Even now, with these girls regarding her like flowers facing the sun, she still felt alone. She was a fraud. How could she be a mother to them when she barely had a memory of what it had been like when someone, long ago, was a mother to her?

But this might be the only form of motherhood she would ever taste. Khara dha Ellimi had robbed her of her mother; the Drought of Girls, whatever its cause, had robbed her of any daughters she might have borne. She'd never feel that swell of life between her hips, to free it from her body and hold it, wet and slick, in her arms. All that was gone now.

This, though, she could have. She could help Scorpica live by gathering these girls to her, showing them the way, bringing them up.

If only she could spend all her time with the girls. But other concerns, other worries, intruded.

Her allies were her allies, and she was not worried they would betray her, but over time, their weaknesses were becoming more clear. Bohara, for one, was letting her taste for hammerwine get the better of her. One day she'd been gone from the camp without warning. It had taken hours to find out that the camp's hammerwine stores were depleted, and Bohara had ridden off to replenish them from the network of caves used for storage, fed by cool springs. Tamura worried she would not be reliable the next time she was needed, whenever that might be.

The one they called Ibis, who had been in the Fingernail with Tamura, had fallen in love with a warrior named Ruya, a fragile-looking woman with features as delicate as clary sage blossoms. Ordinarily Tamura would have been thrilled for a friend to find a companion, especially Ibis, who had always seemed to need company in a way Tamura herself did not. But Ruya was known to disapprove of the way Tamura had come to power. *Butcher* was the word Tamura had heard rumored. If Ibis was called upon one day to choose between her queen and her lover, Tamura was not sure which way the wind would blow.

And that Gretti woman seemed shiftier and shiftier. She almost never spoke directly to Tamura, but she always seemed to be nearby, moving on the periphery. Nearly every day there were whispered conversations, sidelong glances, the frequent sight of Gretti's back vanishing through tent flaps, behind trees, through gatherings. She was sick to death of the sight of that woman's back, narrow and taunting.

With all these pressures, Tamura rarely settled into a good night's sleep. No matter where she slept, in a tent or under the stars, she tossed and turned. Dreams reared up in her head like the ponies of Godsbones, wild and fierce, only settling down into a semblance of tolerant obedience as the sun rose.

In the morning, her first thought was always the same: to walk out to the training ground again. To address the girls. To convince them to love her, a feeling she was growing to need more than food, more than air. If she had their love, that would be the sign that the

Scorpion approved of her queenship. If she had their love, she could do anything.

✦

The Arcan girl who came to them without a name, in the seventh year of the Drought, was a girl of no gifts. That was how it happened. In her matriclan, no girl was named until the gift Velja blessed her with became apparent, and her own gift had not yet manifested. No one in their village had the gift of detecting others' gifts, so she'd been biding her time. When the warriors came to her village, time ran out. Bristling with arms and armor, they said that if enough girls were given freely, they would not take any against their will. She was the first ushered forward. The warriors said her life would be better. The nameless girl was not so sure of them, in this and many other ways.

So she began her journey north, out of Arca and into Paxim and beyond. Everything she saw felt new and strange. What disoriented her at first were the buildings. Instead of vanishing down into the earth like she was used to, they shot up into the sky. And the trees. So many trees. Tall, spreading pines. The pale limbs of birch, the broad sweep of cedar. All were a far cry from the stunted, twisted scrub that they called trees back in eastern Arca, nearly on the lip of Godsbones.

Along the way the warriors gathered more girls: five, then ten. She whispered to these other girls and they whispered to her, nights along the roadside in their bedrolls as they made the journey north. They shared their stories, which differed in detail but not in the main. Like the nameless girl, none of the other Arcans had any great gifts, at least none that had yet been discovered. One had been the child of her mother's less favored second husband, and when the mother had dismissed the husband, the girl had gone with him. When the warriors had taken her in the night, she did not know whether he knew what had happened to her, and if so, whether he cared.

All the girls from Paxim were motherless save one. If possible, her tale was even sadder than the rest.

"I was bought, not stolen," she whispered, each word precise in the darkness, almost tangible. "My mother took payment. Some say a daughter is a jewel without price. I say, that depends on the price, doesn't it?"

Those who had names shared them. The Arcan girl kidnapped from her mother's husband was named Tulian; the young Paximite girl with sleepy eyes, Vira. The Paximite girl sold by her mother was named Ysilef, and among them, she was the only one who ever smiled. After learning Ysilef's story, the nameless girl lay her bedroll next to hers every night, bedding down close enough to hear the Paximite girl's slow, measured breathing as she slept. If one could choose her company, the nameless girl thought, she'd choose a girl who could find her smile even in misery.

"I've never heard you say a name," the sleepy-eyed Vira said to the nameless girl one night. "Don't tell me you don't have one."

If she'd had Ysilef's light heart, perhaps she could have mustered a clever reply. No answer came to mind but the stark truth. "I don't."

"That's absurd," Vira said. "Our neighbor's daughter, four years she was then, once found a baby mouse in a sack of flour. She named it Baby Mouse. Did your family care for you less than that child cared for that animal? Should we call you Baby Mouse, if you need a name?"

The nameless girl struggled again for an answer, but it was no use. She was not accustomed to speaking, and words did not come easily. She knew she was being mocked. She could not strike back.

Then, unexpectedly, the warrior who watched them at night had leaned down and clapped a hand on Vira's shoulder. The warrior was so quiet, they often forgot she was there. When she did speak, her voice was like the rumble in the throat of a mountain lion about to pounce.

"This does not matter. Your names are not yours," she said. "When you become warriors, you will have new names."

"Why?" Tulian asked. "Why new names?"

"You will be new people," said the warrior.

"But I like my name," said Vira.

"You need practice seeing things how a warrior sees them," said the warrior, the purr in her throat like a promise. "You will find that what you like is of little consequence."

That silenced them all for a while.

And when they made it far enough north, what the nameless girl saw pushed her to a new depth of wordlessness. She had never set foot beyond the desert, and now she passed wonder after wonder without even a pause to look closely. At some point she could no longer absorb the new. She could only move forward. So she did exactly that.

Their party walked through the Bastion without stopping, hard stone under their feet making their legs ache. They had walked so far already, but the earth of Arca and Paxim had given under their sandals. This vast swath of stone did not, and it seemed to go on forever. They had heard that this was where each queendom sent their brightest to be educated, but here on the surface they saw no classrooms, no children. Only stone, which stretched beneath them and beyond them into its turrets and corners and impenetrable walls. Not a tree to be seen, nor dirt, nor grass. Stone, all stone.

By the time they arrived in Scorpica—recognizable as land again, thickly forested and beautiful—she was not the only girl in the party with wide-open eyes and a stunned look on her sunburnt face. Ysilef held her hand sometimes to help her keep pace with the long-legged warriors, their brisk strides leading ever more quickly to their destination. A few more days' walk and they arrived at the winter camp, smoke from its cook fires wafting in high, tight spirals, signaling some kind of home. But the warriors did not take them to the tents, not right away. First they visited the training field, where the other warriors awaited them. There, even saucy, cynical Vira was dumbstruck.

The girls of Scorpica, no matter their age, were real fighters.

Ysilef and the nameless girl stood side by side, watching a vast field of girls train. There was no way of knowing who'd been born in Scorpica and who'd been brought, as they had been, from other queendoms. Every one was fit and fierce and glowing with health.

A group of girls pulled back their arrow strings in unison. Another group watched their captain for signals and obeyed in silence: fanning out, crouching, leaping up, drawing together in a knot, back-to-back, blades drawn and eyes watchful. There was a rhythm, almost a music, to how the warriors moved. Even the older women who watched, arms folded and heads nodding, were in sync with it. The newly arrived girls watched in awe. For girls who had grown up in fractured households, parched lands, the harmony of the scene was breathtaking.

Ysilef said, under her breath, "What a wonder."

The nameless girl said, "You think we can be wonders too?"

They looked at each other, both knowing what they wanted the answer to be.

So they obeyed every single instruction. When they were told to walk, they walked. When they were told to sit, they sat.

They lay down to sleep among the other girls, rose among the other girls, drew back their bows to fire and then jogged down the field to retrieve their arrows like the other girls. With the other girls they ate coney stew, thick but bland, that they scooped from a bowl with two fingers. Afterward, they licked both bowl and fingers spotlessly clean.

And when, a week after they'd arrived in Scorpica, they were told they were going to meet the queen, they looked to each other with equal delight and fear.

The nameless girl had heard, already, countless stories about the queen. How ruthless she was, how focused. How she had won her position by defeating the previous queen hand to hand. The nameless girl was frankly terrified at the idea of being in the woman's presence, let alone meeting her. What if the queen spoke directly to her? What should the girl say? What if she wanted—demanded—something the girl could not give?

So when she and the other recent arrivals were gathered to sit in a circle on the soft grass, and she looked up to see a woman approaching them, she did not realize who it was at first. This woman looked fearsome, yes, but so did most of the warriors here. She did not look substantially more fearsome than they. She was not a giant, as some had said. There was no sneer on her face, no ornate braids on her head, no ornament of queenship around her neck. She was simply another warrior, lean with muscle and carrying herself proudly, and when she said to the girls, "Welcome," the girl without a name found her lips forming the words "Thank you" without a thought.

She knelt in front of them, offered up a prayer to the Scorpion, and said in a gentle voice, "I am so glad that you are here."

The queen told them some of the same things they had heard from the warriors who'd brought them here. That they had been unfairly rejected by their old countries, but that Scorpica welcomed them and would embrace them. They would do great things together, she said.

She explained their training and how the rhythm of life in Scorpica ebbed and flowed, surged and settled. How they would each practice each weapon before they found what they were best at. The bow? The spear? The staff? How they would learn to forge weapons themselves, to fletch arrows, to flake stone into sharp points. How they would each be required to participate in the hunt when their turn came. She emphasized how much each warrior's very life de-

pended on her fellow warriors, how the bond between them tran-
scended whatever families they'd been born into, that the blood of
true warriors ran in all their veins.

"And once you train, you will learn things you did not even know
were possible," she said, signaling toward a group of women nearby,
one of whom handed her a polished yew-heart bow.

A woman so heavily pox-scarred that her skin looked like the
bark of a tree stepped forward. She was dressed the same as the other
warriors, in leathers, with her hair cropped close. In her hands she
held three apples, round and red. The girls were rapt.

The woman set the first of the three apples on a flat-topped
stump, and barely had she removed her hand when Tamura shot it
almost effortlessly, her arrowhead splitting its crimson skin to reveal
the pale flesh inside. Then the tree woman threw the second apple
into the air, tossing it with a lazy upward arc high above their heads.
Tamura drew back her bow, released an arrow, and shot the apple
from the sky. Small, juicy chunks scattered across the field, and the
air filled with a bright cider smell.

When the tree woman raised the third apple, every girl wondering what she would do with it, the queen's voice rang out again.

"Gretti!" she called. "Assist me, please."

A voice called back from the gathered group of older women. "I
believe Khadriye has it well in hand."

"I must insist," the queen said in a measured tone.

A moment later, a woman with a heart-shaped face came forward.
She had a sun-warmed leanness to her body, the look of a longtime
warrior, though her manner was more tentative than most. The tree
woman handed off the apple to her and disappeared into the crowd.
The woman with the heart-shaped face looked down at the apple,
then to Tamura's expressionless face, then back to the fruit.

"Very well," she said.

She raised the apple and balanced it squarely on her own head, in the center of her close-cropped curls. She faced Tamura. The girls who watched, including the nameless girl, could not see her face.

"Turn," the queen said, her voice hard and sharp as a splinter of bone.

As commanded, the woman called Gretti turned toward the army of girls, her limbs relaxed but her eyes narrowed. Who was she to the queen? There was no anger on her face, no surprise, but a kind of sorrow, the nameless girl thought. She did not want the queen to do this. But for whatever reason, she could not say no.

Even before she had finished turning, the arrow sang through the air.

The nameless girl heard a sharp intake of breath, and she wasn't sure whether it came from Ysilef next to her, from Gretti, or from her own throat.

Then the apple cleaved in two, one white-fleshed half tumbling off each side of Gretti's head, landing in quick succession on the ground, *thump-thump*.

The woman did not smile or react in any way, merely completed her turn until she was facing the queen again. No bow, no grin. Simply facing off, calm and steady.

"See? All it takes," the queen told them coolly, dangling the bow from her fingers, "is training."

The look on Gretti's face had shifted into something else unreadable. "I thank the Scorpion you are so well trained, my queen."

"Come now." The queen's tone was light, almost teasing. "Don't say you doubted me."

"I never doubted you could do what you set out to do," said Gretti, without any of the lightness.

"Your faith inspires me," said the queen.

Gretti raised her hand in a gesture the girls had recently learned, though they had never seen it done so gracefully. The motion of pulling back a bowstring, a fist to the sky. *Good hunting*, the woman said as she left, without words.

Ysilef and the nameless girl barely had time to exchange a look before the queen spoke again, her voice ringing out over the heads of the gathered girls. "The time has come, girls, for your naming."

The nameless girl leaned forward, eager, at the very word.

"Here in Scorpica," the queen intoned, her voice more serious than it had been, "your mother's name is always part of your name. So when you receive your name, you will receive also your mother's name."

"You." She pointed to a girl sitting cross-legged almost at her feet. "What is your mother's name?"

The girl looked up. "She is called Abeya."

"Wrong!" shouted the warrior queen. It was the first time she had raised her voice to them, reminding them that as familiar as she felt, they did not truly know her. The girl, who had a clubfoot and a shaven head just starting to sprout a dark fuzz, looked like she'd been slapped.

The queen repeated her question. "What is your mother's name?"

This time the girl stayed silent. The fear on her face was plain.

"Better," the warrior said. "I like that you know not to make the same mistake twice. That bodes well for you here. So how will you find out your mother's name?"

The girl said, "If it please you, I'd like you to tell me."

"Very good," said the warrior, bending to kneel in front of the girl. The warrior placed her hands on the girl's shoulders and kissed her solemnly, first on the right cheek, then on the left.

Then she said, "My name is Tamura. And I am your mother now."

The fear in the girl's eyes slipped away, replaced with an open welcome that bordered on desire. She nodded solemnly and held herself in readiness for whatever her new mother might require of her. It was a stunning transformation.

Nodding her approval, the Scorpican queen rose to her feet. Then she turned to the next girl in the line, one who had arrived with the nameless girl, the saucy, sharp-tongued Vira. Now she was unusually subdued, patient, her face upturned.

"I am your mother," Tamura said, caressing Vira's cheek and holding her gaze, just for a moment. The girl was rapt.

Then she went on to the next. "And yours. And yours." She walked from row to row until each girl had been visited, placing her hand on each one's head like a blessing. When the girl with no name felt the queen's palm curl over the crown of her head, a warmth spread under her skin, working its way down her throat toward her heart, easing her, soothing her.

"I am proud of my daughters," said the queen, and now there was no harshness in her voice, only warmth, only love. "I can tell that you will be faithful, powerful warriors. I am sorry for what you suffered in the queendoms that mistreated you. I wish in my heart that you did not have to know that pain. But you are here now, and for that, I can never be sorry."

She closed her eyes and opened them again, looking down at the girls, taking them in. "I welcome you. I choose you. And I feel honored beyond belief that you have chosen me."

When the time came to name the new girls, the girl with no name knelt at her new mother's feet. Her eyes felt wet but she did not let tears fall. That would not befit a warrior.

She knelt with no name. She rose as Azur dha Tamura.

They were all Tamura's daughters now.

✦ CHAPTER 21 ✦

THE TAKERS

In the streets of the Bastion

The Shade, Jehenit

The woman in the high-collared cloak knew a warrior when she saw one, even in disguise, and here were two. She knew how warriors held themselves, how they moved through the world. Heads up straight as if drawn on a string. A ready bounce to their knees. Most importantly, blades strapped to their left hips, at the ideal angle for a swift right-handed draw. In this case the blades were broad, flat daggers, mostly concealed by the folds of the women's long, swinging tunics, which were topped off with dark capes, hoods thrown back. The capes looked Arcan, but these were no Arcans. That they were pretending to be made something in her head vibrate like a struck bell.

Many things about the Bastion had not changed, would never change. It had simply always been. There were no stories of its creation, nothing that explained its massive, complex bulk; it was too large to exist and yet here it was. Leagues upon leagues of dark gray stone, forming an impenetrable border between Scorpica and Paxim, running from Godsbones to the shores of the Salt Maw. Outside, there were thick, curving walls, towers, gates, roads, all made of that same stone, the color of thunderclouds but far more solid. Inside, guard rooms and classrooms, nurseries and palace chambers, dormitories and meeting halls, untold levels extending deep down into the earth. There was life within, teeming life, but no green.

It was that teeming life that had changed. As the woman in the high-collared cloak strolled down the stone paths of the Bastion's main market, she could clearly see the difference from a few years before. Fewer tables and stalls, fewer goods, fewer people. The people, too, had changed. She saw men ranging from white-haired to too young to grow whiskers, but the few women doing business in the market were well past their childbearing years. The stranger remarked on this casually, as if she didn't understand why it might be so, to a woman with flashing eyes stooped behind a fruit cart. For the price of a half-dozen figs, she had all her suspicions confirmed.

First the Bastion had hidden away their girls, which was a simple matter, since all their children were already raised in nurseries until the age of eight. But as the Drought of Girls wore on, the woman whispered, the ruling board had brought a large swath of its adult women behind closed doors as well, salting them away like coin. It was not hard to guess why. When the Drought ended, if it ended, those women would bear the next generation, boys and girls alike, to produce all the generations to come.

Which made these warriors disguised as magicians stand out all the more, when she spotted them. They were the wrong age. Where her face was sun-touched, marked with lines of experience and knowledge, theirs were smooth. When they paused at a cart, she paused a few carts away; in quick succession they made their way through vendors of mint and dill, clementines and lemons, grass-green olive oil, never lingering long. They bought nothing. As she watched, they exchanged a quick flurry of words and headed for the main gate, in the direction of Paxim.

So the woman in the high-collared cloak watched them go without turning her head, gently set the undersized apricot she'd been pretending to examine back on the pile, and followed.

She'd come to the Bastion only for the day, drawn by a sentimental flicker she told herself she shouldn't have indulged, and she'd have to leave through the Paxim gate before nightfall anyway. She might as well go where these imposters were going. They set a fast pace but she had no problem keeping up, even with her slight limp. She left nothing behind to follow them. Everything she owned of value, she wore.

As the imposters wound their way through Paxim, every few leagues she reconsidered. Perhaps they were up to nothing in particular. Perhaps when they stopped at a tavern for a meal, or at an inn for the night, she would turn around and let them go on their way unobserved. Only they did not stop, not at a tavern nor an inn nor anywhere, until long after darkness fell.

Hours later, when she saw them at a distance—she gave them distance, so they would not observe her in return—laying their capes down on the ground to sleep, any shred of doubt she'd had that they were Scorpican warriors fell away. They were not among the best of the nation's warriors, she could tell. The best warriors would have made better time across this easy terrain, for one thing, and for another, the best warriors would have known they were being followed.

She herself did not sleep, not wanting to lose them if they woke before her, since she was not sure in which direction they'd go. Paxim was vast. This close to the Bastionite border, the trade routes crisscrossed one another, leading in every direction. She could miss a night of sleep or two; if this impulsive chase went on for longer, she could always turn back. But having come this far, a dark knot of worry thrumming at the base of her skull, she wanted to see it through.

By the next time the noonday sun was high overhead, she'd reached a new, surprising conclusion: they did not seem to have a set destination. At dawn, they'd seemed to be heading straight southwest, almost as if they intended to walk all the way to Sestia. But when they reached a crossroads, they took a sudden turn due south. If they'd intended to go toward Arca, why had they not used the more direct route from the beginning? Now she knew there was no going back, not until she found out their intent.

They napped in the shade when the sun was at its highest. While they rested, she scouted the immediate area and found a small, welcome pond, which yielded up enough cool water and cress to blunt the edges of both her hunger and her thirst. In her travels she had grown as slender as the blades she carried. She was just about to move into a nearby stand of trees to hunt for blackberries when she saw movement. She turned her back on the glade to regain the trail of the suspect warriors. The road here passed through a long stretch of lightly wooded terrain. Among the skinny-trunked trees, it was easier to remain hidden, so she could follow them more closely than she had on the open plain. The road twisted through the trees and she followed each twist, winding now southwest, now southeast, and back again.

That evening just after sunset, the caped warriors suddenly stepped off the road into the brush, and she stepped off to watch them. Had something made them skittish? She looked up ahead and saw it. Yes. The flickering light of a fire came through the trees. Soft and contained; a campfire, no threat, casting only gentle shadows.

They skulked forward. She skulked behind them, staying low, one hand on the hilt of a short sword, preparing. In the near darkness she could tell they were using hunters' signals but not what they were saying. They were drawing ever nearer to the fire. The shadows were resolving themselves into shapes: a wagon, a fire not far away, a few figures, women and men, silhouetted by the low flames. A slight figure, possibly a child, moved from the fireside to the wagon, the wagon trembling slightly as it took on the small burden of her weight.

She could hear the adults' voices now, soft murmurs and banter, people who were not worried. They should be, though. Or perhaps she was mistaken. Perhaps the two disguised warriors were meeting the group in the wagon, some sort of prearranged rendezvous. Perhaps all was as it should be.

She realized with a start she had lost the shape of the warriors. Her night vision had been warped, disrupted by the flames. The warriors had likely drawn up the hoods of their cloaks. Now they were black on black in the night. She looked away from the fire, blinking, hoping to find their outlines again.

Then a shout split the darkness.

"Mama!" a young voice screamed, high and loud, frayed at the edges with a hoarse panic. A girl's voice.

"Eminel!" came an answering scream.

She sprang forward toward movement, she saw it now: the back of the wagon, one dark-cloaked figure springing to the ground, one already there, one with sword drawn and the other with a bundle, a wriggling human bundle the size of a girl no older than ten, over her shoulder. They were sprinting away from the wagon at top speed.

They were, unknowingly, heading straight for her.

She drew one sword and then the other, and she readied herself in the road.

"Stop!" she shouted. Her voice was rusty from disuse, but they heard her. The one in front, the one with the blade, stopped. They had expected resistance from the wagon party but not from this direction, and she could see their eyes, wild, as they struggled to make sense of her. Had they not planned for this possibility? The best warriors would have. But just because every Scorpican woman was a warrior did not mean they were all equally good at it.

Behind the hooded warriors appeared two more women. One was of average size with haunted eyes. The other was a staggeringly tall giant, a silver scar streaking across her remarkable face, a wickedly large broadsword resting comfortably in one outsize hand.

"Give back the girl," said the giant, almost conversationally.

"You heard her," she found herself calling out, and the hooded warriors, trapped, looked back and forth between the two armed women flanking them on the narrow road.

A sound like a sob emerged from the throat of the unarmed woman alongside the giant. "Don't hurt her," she said.

The giant shushed her gently, then said to the warriors, her voice tight, "Give us the girl and you live. Force us to take her from you and you die."

"*Igni morami,*" said the warrior with the girl over her shoulder. *Die in a fire,* an all-purpose insult, and given the circumstances, a foolish one. But she had raised a dagger to the girl's throat. That the girl was not whimpering with fear spoke well of her.

The woman in the high-collared cloak could see the girl better now: among the youngest she'd seen in years, probably around seven years old, clearly valuable. Likely that was the only reason the hooded warrior hadn't cut her throat already. She met the girl's eyes and tried to make her gaze reassuring.

The shapes of three men loomed in the shadows now, behind the small woman and the giant. The giant held up a hand to warn them back. They obeyed, shifting uneasily, watchful.

"As I was saying," the giant said to the trapped warriors, "you have a choice here."

Did they? The woods were too rough to navigate with this many armed enemies so close by. They could yield the girl and run, take their chances. Or the armed woman without the girl could abandon her fellow warrior, or they could—but even as she thought it, they made their choice.

They were running straight at her, the armed one in the lead, having judged her the lesser obstacle, now hoping to clear her from their path and head back toward Scorpica with their prize.

She was ready for them.

As the armed one charged, she used her first short sword to parry away the approaching blade and then raised her second, almost nonchalantly, cutting through the dark hood and the paler neck beneath. The woman's form crumpled and fell to earth. The woman in the high-collared cloak muttered a prayer—quickly—and turned her attention back, as the battle was not yet done.

The other warrior, who held the precious girl, had had to take her knife away from the girl's throat in order to run, and suddenly the girl was flying—no, not flying, being lifted, held in the capable hands of the giant, ripped away from the kidnapper, who now looked like a doll beside her.

"Twins!" shouted the giant.

The thwarted kidnapper now ran flat out on the level road. She was a strong runner, but she did not stand a chance against the two men who now roared out of the darkness, flanking her from either side and running her down like a doomed hare. This one expired with more screaming and howling than her companion had, but the result, in the end, was much the same. Blood, a great deal of it, then silence. The woman in the high-collared cloak wiped her own short swords on the grass and re-sheathed them before turning back to look down the road again.

The giant was laying the girl into the outstretched arms of the other woman, who cried silently, her shoulders caved and trembling, her face pressed against the girl's hair.

Then the giant turned back to the swordswoman, nodding at her sheathed weapons, and said, "Thank you. You have our gratitude."

She did not know how to respond. What was there to say? They had needed her help. A girl had been in trouble. In these times, to do anything besides what she had done would be unthinkable.

"What's your name?" the giant asked.

Again she did not know how to answer. She could not use her true name. Not with Tamura dha Mada ruling as queen of Scorpica. Not when the name Vishala was a key that might unlock Amankha's whereabouts. She cared more about Ama's life than her own, and their futures were still intertwined, even if she had not seen the girl for two years. She remained silent.

"Well, sometimes it's like that. Not to worry," the giant said, sheathing her sword and extending her arm. "I'm Fasiq."

She gripped Fasiq's forearm and allowed hers to be gripped, sealing their connection, and gave a firm, sharp nod.

Fasiq said, "It's awkward not to have anything to call you, though. You came out of nowhere, all silent, like a ghost. Unless you object, we'll just call you the Shade."

It was as good a name as any. "Yes. The Shade," she echoed.

"We're the Rovers. Perhaps you've heard of us?"

The newly christened Shade shook her head, *no*.

Unfazed, the giant continued, "My Rovers can always use someone who's a dab hand with a sword." She tilted her head and grinned. "Even more so when it's two swords, and two dab hands."

Vishala felt suddenly shy, unused to attention, especially the attention of a charismatic woman like this Fasiq. She could do worse, though, and had. Maybe it would be good to have company for a while. To travel with these—what were they, bandits?—and keep an eye on the girl. Train those twins a bit better, polish their sword technique. No one waited for her back in the Bastion. No one waited for her anywhere.

The Shade pulled her high-collared cloak a little higher around her throat. Her voice was hoarse and soft when she spoke, but she eked out two words, as clearly as she could.

In the end, the two words she spoke were the only two needed. She said to the giant, "Why not?"

✦

In the years after the first Sun Rites of the Drought of Girls—a ceremony that apparently had no effect whatsoever on improving the situation—the charmed life of the Rovers had lost a great deal of its charm. Some of the Scorpican patrols in Paxim had become violent, constantly spoiling for a fight. Others were as they'd always been, inclined to look the other way, but it was impossible to know whether any particular patrol was out for blood until it was too late. And there was far more competition for less traffic. While in the old days, a few well-chosen attacks could net them a month of supplies—the Rovers' mere appearance setting the drivers running—carters now armed themselves, ready to defend their cargo. Plucking a trailing wagon off a loosely assembled caravan was a thing of the past. Jehenit knew that more than one driver had died in defense of the goods she or he transported, falling at the bandits' hands. She tried not to think about it, but that was the bargain she had made. Choosing to live with people fierce enough to protect her daughter at all costs, she could not complain about what those costs might be.

Now the Rovers regularly plundered the cities, relying more heavily on what Hermei could steal, rotating partners from the group. Any one of them, when properly instructed, made an excellent distraction. Jehenit enjoyed her turns with the thief. They fell into an easy rhythm, stripping travelers of coins, jewelry, food, weapons, and trinkets, as the spirit moved them. On one hand, she had a twinge of guilt at taking people's valuables, but on the other, if they wanted to keep such things, why didn't they protect them better? And a person could live without a necklace, a seedcake, an extra dagger in their boot. Again it was a question of living with a decision she had long ago made and couldn't imagine having made any other way.

Drawing limits around Eminel's world was another long-ago decision. But the girl, like the world, was changing. She'd begun to resent her mother's limits. The older Eminel got, the more she chafed at being stuck in the wagon every day, all day. The bandits, of course, did their best. Someone needed to stay with the wagon at all times, and by default that person became Eminel's companion for the day. When a twin stayed behind, he'd play games of chance with her, rolling bones or casting lots, wagering twigs or stones that flowed back and forth for hours, first in her pile, then his, then hers. Hermei was the only one of them who could read, so when it was his turn, he took it upon himself to teach the girl her letters. For a long time they had only one book, a simple adventure story about a girl who rode the wind. When Eminel had mastered it, Hermei stole her a new one, a much longer book about the Great Peace and its architects. Even with these entertainments, Eminel wanted more. To roam the cities, to spar with the swordswoman, even just to ride on the driver's seat and whip the oxen. But none of these were possible. Jehenit longed to tell her the truth—this friendly imprisonment was the only real alternative to the fatal dangers of Daybreak Palace—but she did not believe the girl was old enough yet to understand.

As the Drought dragged on, the Rovers' conversations in the evening more and more often turned to how good they used to have it. When it was safe to stop and gather in a circle, the pattern repeated itself as if the God of Fate had drawn the plans Herself. The twins lit the fire, Fasiq brought out a wineskin if there was one, Jehenit and Hermei handed around the bread and cheese, and the memories almost immediately began to pour forth.

They remembered when careless drivers left their stations for a mug of beer or a nip into the woods to void, putting easy pickings at hand. The twins often told the story of the wagon they'd dismantled so effectively that it was down to boards and wheels inside of ten minutes, the spare parts sold off inside of a day to a traveling repairman who asked no questions. The luck they'd once had seemed enchanted, a bounty of goods showing up everywhere they looked, falling into their hands like raindrops. It had never been that good, not exactly, Jehenit reflected to herself; but in this way they could avoid dwelling on how bad things were, or how much worse they were all worried things could get.

The Scorpican patrols were dangerous now, yes. But how much more dangerous would it be if, as was rumored, the Scorpicae would call all their warriors home? Would patrols of newly armed, hastily trained Paximites be any better? They were sure to be made up of at least half men, in this nation careful to carve out rights for men far beyond those in any other queendom. Jehenit had heard enough Arcan men grumble about their lot to fear what would happen when men who'd spent their lives without weapons found a staff in their hands.

They seemed philosophical, all these *what-if* and *when-they* discussions around a nighttime fire. But then two hooded women had arrived out of the night to steal Eminel, and it seemed their turned luck was to turn even worse, to dive to a depth from which it would never rise again.

But instead, the narrow escape had set things back on the right path. The arrival of the Shade seemed to buoy everyone's spirits. The twins loved her company, constantly asking for pointers on their sword technique. When the party could spare the time she trained them, fighting two-on-one in whatever clearing or grove was handy. Jehenit had never relished the sound of fighting—metal clanging on metal, wood thudding against leather or flesh—but she enjoyed watching the three spar. It was like a dance, a constant succession of graceful arcs. And in their hands, the sounds of battle rang out almost like music: swords like bells or gongs, staffs like a vital drumbeat.

Jehenit was nervous around the Shade in the beginning, desperately grateful and overwhelmed by her inability to pay the woman back in any fair measure. Fasiq seemed nervous too, she noted, after her initial burst of eloquence. In many ways the giant was unchanged. She silvered her scar in the mornings without help, she bossed the group ruthlessly, she planned their next move and the move after that with the nonchalance of an experienced general. But this awkwardness, Jehenit had never seen. The giant stumbled over her words in the presence of the Shade, when before she had always seemed effortlessly charming. Jehenit knew this awkwardness had a different root from her own, and she suspected she knew its cause. She remembered all those stories of Fasiq's former companions, lovers who had traveled with the caravan before the giant had sworn off love; perhaps she was ready to swear it back on again.

Jehenit did not know whether the Shade would welcome Fasiq's attentions; her face and body were impossible to read. But if Fasiq declared herself, Jehenit had no doubt the swordswoman would quickly make her own feelings clear. A woman who could handle herself on the road as capably as the Shade could surely handle herself in other ways.

One evening about a month after the Shade had joined them, when the others had gone off to parley with another group of bandits to turn some stolen baubles into food and drink, Jehenit kissed her daughter good night in the wagon and then climbed down to join the Shade.

The swordswoman had arrived without a pack, Jehenit had noticed. The next time they were near a city, she asked Hermei to steal one and simply leave it with the Shade without comment. Now the woman was taking a moment to unpack and repack it with the scant possessions she'd acquired: another cloak, a tunic from one twin and leggings from the other, a rag for polishing her swords, a few other practical items. Jehenit caught sight of a familiar shape in the small pile and smiled.

"I didn't know she'd given this to you," she said, reaching for the knot of wood. Back in Arca, what seemed like a lifetime ago, it had been their household image of Velja. Two years now they'd had no household but the Rovers' wagon. Eminel must have given it to the swordswoman in gratitude. Jehenit's heart swelled. The girl was so young yet, seven years old, but growing and learning. She'd known some gesture of thanks was required and worked out on her own what it should be.

Wordlessly, the Shade reached out to put her hand over Jehenit's and squeeze the other woman's hand tighter around the wooden image. She gently pushed their hands toward Jehenit's belly. It took a minute for Jehenit to understand.

"No, I don't want it back," she said. "You can keep it."

"Who is it?" asked the Shade quietly.

"Someone very important to us," Jehenit said, but worried about saying more. What would happen if the Seekers came for them? It was better for the Shade, like the rest of the party, not to even know they were Arcans. After all, the Shade had hardly opened up about her own past. It was a safe bet she was Scorpican, given her skills. Beyond that, they knew nothing, not even her name.

The Shade made another gesture of giving, but Jehenit opened both their hands and dropped the knot of wood into the swordswoman's waiting palm.

"I won't hear another word of it," she said. "I have so little else to give you. You saved my daughter. Nothing could repay that."

"I did not do it for pay," the Shade said.

"I'm glad you did it, for whatever reason. And I . . . I worry you may need to do it again."

The Shade's eyes met hers. Jehenit looked down, toward the sheathed twin swords that lay in perfectly parallel lines on the ground.

Jehenit said, "I try my best. But I am no fighter. You saw what happened, when those women came for Eminel. If you hadn't been there ... I ..."

She swallowed against a hard lump, the fear and helplessness flooding her all over again. Raising her gaze to the Shade's, she found the woman still regarding her patiently, waiting for her to continue.

"I thank the All-Mother you were there," Jehenit went on, forcing the words out. "So I must ask. If something happens to me, or I'm not able to—for whatever reason—would you please keep my daughter safe?"

The Shade, her face grave, reached out for Jehenit's arm, gripping her at the elbow. Jehenit knew instinctively why. This was a sacred seal.

"Yes. I will protect her," the Shade said, in that hoarse, soft voice, each word precise as an arrow.

Even as her body flooded with relief, Jehenit wondered about that voice, wondered whether she was right to trust the swordswoman. She could never get a clear look at the woman's throat, given the high-collared cloak. Unlike Fasiq, this one didn't seem to flaunt her scars.

✦

One evening two months after she'd become one of the Rovers, a full moon hanging like a polished silver gong in the sky, the Shade joined the group around a fire for the evening meal. They allowed themselves this luxury when neither running from or to an opportunity. Done this way, it occasioned no suspicion if others happened by. Any group of travelers—pilgrims, traders, merchants—would have done the same. They only indulged on low land where they could see a distance in every direction, so if a light approached, Eminel could climb up into the wagon long before she was seen. It was a precaution they never missed taking.

On this night, they passed warm bread and aged cheese around the circle, washing them down with lily wine Hermei had pilfered from a caravan of traveling priests. From time to time they encountered these knots of practicing worshippers of the minor gods, the vast pantheon beyond the three great daughters of the All-Mother. This particular band worshipped Velja's second consort, the one She had made Herself: the God of Dreams. Hermei had drunk a little of the wine two nights before to test it, making sure it was not enchanted with something that would twist the dreams of the drinker. Once his sleep was untroubled, he shared. It was excellent wine too, neither too heavy nor too sweet. The Shade felt herself relax a little, though she remained vigilant despite the warm feeling in her blood, her eyes restlessly scanning the inky black of the horizon. She remained ready, at a moment's notice, to help the girl disappear.

"When we head out tomorrow, we're moving south," said the giant.

"Why?" asked Hermei.

"Because I said so, that's the reason," Fasiq answered, though her eyes flicked over to Eminel, who was chewing thoughtfully on her torn chunk of bread.

"Away from Scorpica is toward Arca," said Hermei, pointing out the obvious. "You think pickings will be much better there?"

"I wasn't asking for opinions," said the giant, her voice firm.

One of the twins interrupted, "No sense even saying them if we know you won't listen to them, is there?"

The other twin added, "Agreed."

"Of course you agree with each other," said Fasiq. "We should have a rule that if one of you talks, the other doesn't need to."

"Silly rule," said one. "Unnecessary."

With a grin, the other added, "I concur."

Fasiq threw up her hands in mock outrage.

The mood was light enough, but the Shade understood the giant's reasoning. She was worried about more warriors, better warriors, coming to steal Eminel. Better warriors might succeed.

As protective as Fasiq was of Eminel, Vish thought, she herself was now even more so. She was sworn to defend the girl, at her mother's request. Of course, every time she looked at Eminel, she thought of Ama. And every time now there was a pang of—what? Regret? Longing, worry, love? The girls were of an age. Ama would be like this now, finding her own way toward womanhood, learning and growing. Would she and Vish even recognize each other if their paths crossed, two long years later? And though she knew there was no sense in it, not truly, Vish worried about the other mother she'd sworn to. Even though she'd never meet Khara again, not in this life. From the battlefield beyond, if Khara knew what had happened, would she take pride in the fate Vish had chosen for her daughter? Or would she be ashamed, thinking her girl abandoned? Vish had thought it was the right choice at the time, surrendering Ama to a new, fresh future that started at the base of the Orphan Tree. Then, it had felt right. Now, she was far less sure.

Fasiq interrupted Vish's dark reflections by handing her the wineskin. Tonight she'd made a game of handing it over differently each time it came around the circle: now with dash and braggadocio, now as tenderly as a cat bearing its kitten, now with the studied formality of an ambassador presenting a diplomatic offering to a queen. Vish took it every time it was offered, and somehow, it felt like Fasiq was offering her more than wine. She didn't think she was imagining it. She admitted to herself, ruefully, that she'd never had much of an imagination.

She'd also never been the type to long for pleasure, had never been driven by stirrings of the body or the heart. But she was awakening now. Perhaps she was opening up to new possibilities because she felt safer than she had in years. She owed all that to the giant. But when Fasiq's hand curled around hers as she took the wineskin, the current of warmth rippling up her arm had nothing to do with gratitude. She drank and passed it on, feeling the giant's eyes on her as she did so. The warmth remained.

When the meal was nibbled down to crumbs and rind, the party began to disperse. Eminel kissed her mother's brow and made her way with slow, drowsy steps toward her sleeping place in the wagon. She was up late, but would nap in the wagon as she hid from daylight. The twins headed for their bedrolls, arranged beneath the wagon tonight in case the threatening clouds came to rain, and Hermei had gone into the nearby woods to void before he did the same.

Jehenit was holding the wineskin, which was not yet drained. She rose and crossed what was left of the circle, skirting the dying fire, and handed the wineskin to Fasiq. When the giant grasped it, her hand dwarfing Jehenit's, Jehenit did not let go.

As the giant looked at her, puzzled, Jehenit leaned forward to her ear, the one on the unscarred side, away from the Shade, and whispered something the Shade could not hear.

Then Jehenit let go of the wineskin and Fasiq held it in both hands, looking up at her, uncertain.

Jehenit nodded. She said good night to the Shade. Then she walked back to the wagon, thirty feet off in the darkness, and climbed inside.

Then it was just the two of them together by the fire's red embers, the dark night vast around them, their shoulders less than a handspan apart.

The giant sat so long without speaking that Vish grew restless. At last she forced herself to speak.

"Will you keep it for yourself this time?" she asked, gesturing at the wineskin. Her voice was still hoarse and hushed, damaged from her sojourn in Godsbones, but it carried.

"No," Fasiq said, but made no movement to hand it to her.

Vish realized the giant had been reaching out to her all night. If she wanted something to happen, it was her turn to reach out.

She raised her hand and placed it over Fasiq's larger one on the wineskin, her thumb brushing the back of the other woman's hand, marking out a pattern, circling and circling.

Fasiq looked down at their hands in silence.

"You are a plain speaker," Vish prodded her. "Or so I have been told."

"I am," the giant said, not looking up. She turned her hand to grasp Vish's, then brought her other hand over both of them. Slowly she began to mimic Vish's motion, moving her thumb in a regular rhythm across the back of the other woman's hand.

Vish said, "So you can say no."

Softly Fasiq said, "I could."

"Will you?"

A smile crept over the giant's uneven mouth, turning up on the unscarred side, as that mouth drew nearer and nearer to Vish's.

"No," she said with a laugh, and then her mouth was on Vish's, soft lips exploring, and there were no more questions, no more words.

And so the makeup of the Rovers shifted, just slightly, to welcome one more. This group of people who had found each other, through the will of the Holy One or Velja or the Bandit God or none of them whatsoever, carried on as if this were simply the natural order of things. As if a family could this easily be made up of an aging thief who had once been a magician, a watchful girl accustomed to hiding away, a pair of oddly merry well-armed twins, a grateful woman with a secret, a giant with a wicked scar and a careful heart, and the swordswoman to whom she gave that heart gladly.

✦ CHAPTER 22 ✦

HAVOC

The All-Mother's Years 509 to 511
All across the Five Queendoms
Sessadon

In the two years she explored the Five Queendoms, Sessadon discovered many things. Some were about the queendoms and their people; some were about herself. The latter, of course, she found most interesting.

She'd intended to test the limits of her power, but in many cases, she found her interest and attention ran out before her power did. She did not linger in the Bastion; people were always asking her where she belonged, what she was trained for, and flicking away their interest took up too much of her time without teaching either of them anything. So she temporarily blinded both the guards and the scribes at the southern gate and made her way into Paxim, where people were much more welcoming of strangers, or if not welcoming, at least comfortably indifferent.

In one of the rural settlements, far enough from the large cities to avoid drawing too much attention, she set herself to the task of emptying each of the six houses with a different type of magic. The first house was simple: with mind magic, she nudged the family gently to seek better fortune elsewhere. For the second house she used body magic, forcing each resident's limbs into motion. This was less successful, as their protests began to draw attention, so then she needed to use additional magic to silence them, and it was much more exhausting. Earth magic shook the foundations of the third house until the residents ran out screaming; air magic whistled a vicious wind through the fourth house, which had a similar effect. When she realized she needed to use water magic for the fifth house, she wished she'd chosen a settlement on the coast, but there was only one resident, and she was able to heat the water in his blood just hot enough to send him running without doing any permanent damage, or at least not much. Fire magic was no challenge at all, but she made herself complete the task she'd set, even though she was almost too bored to bother. She fetched up a spark and dropped it in a jug of cooking oil; the resulting explosion was far bigger than she'd expected, and no one made it out of the house before it burned. So she failed anyway, at least by the strictest interpretation of the challenge she'd set, and left the abandoned settlement in a funk.

She tried, too, getting what she wanted without magic. The quartz heart meant she would never be dependent on sand to fuel her power, and she'd built up enough life force to power most spells even if there were no living creatures nearby, but she wanted to be ready for anything. Perhaps another sorcerer would try to shut down her magic. Or if she wanted to go undetected by sorcerers who could sense the use of enchantments, it would be helpful to have more arrows in her quiver, as it were. Her most successful gambit was to convince worshippers of any particular god that she was that very god in disguise, and that they would be rewarded for their faithfulness if they would only complete a particular task. Sessadon would never understand people who didn't recognize Velja as the truest power;

did they not see how chaotic the world was? But people would believe what they chose to believe.

Nowhere was this truer than Sestia, which she explored with both wonder and bewilderment. Sessadon had never thought much of the worshippers of Sestia in her own day, and now that they had their own nation, she did not find any greater love for them.

But their land, ah! Their land. She had never seen such lush terrain. She understood why people considered themselves content among these vast green fields, these rolling hills dotted with rams and sheep. But the price was steep: when the time for the Sun Rites came every five years, any child of ten-and-four in the nation might be selected by lottery and fetched to the Holy City to have her or his throat slit in front of a thousand avid watchers hungry for blood. It made no sense to her. Either they didn't believe, but overlooked the murder of children for their own comfort, or they truly did believe that this periodic sacrifice allowed them to live in plenty the rest of their lives. They were willing to accept that their god gave freely as long as she occasionally slaked her thirst for blood. Yet Velja, not Sestia, was the god everyone called whimsical. Idiots, she thought. Fools.

She was beginning to form the outline of a plan. Once she found her heir—how marvelous it would be, at last, to have worthy company—she should establish their prominence in a way that no one could mistake. She would erase the distinctions between the queendoms and unite them; the so-called Great Peace was already dissolving year by year. When the time was right, she would be ready. As she formed the plan, she considered whether she had the skills to complete each part of it. She would have to kill someone to test at least one of the skills she'd need, and if someone had to die, that person might as well be a Sestian.

So she gently killed a boneburner and managed his life force so that he appeared alive, inhabiting his routine, living his life for him.

She was delighted to find her skills up to the task. She could not make him speak, but she could move him in any way she chose—bowing, lifting, gesturing—with movements as natural as life. She could even make his hands strike flint for a fire.

Fire was a boneburner's reason for being. Sestians from nearby farms brought their bones to be burned, trading them for the amount of ash they would produce. The ash they took home would be used for fertilizer on the farm, churned into the earth, tucked into vegetable beds, sprinkled along the grapevines' rows. Worshippers of Sestia were obsessed with the circle of life, the way every action fed or starved the world.

But she stayed only until the first farmer appeared, hauling a cart of bones to burn. Her own form waited out of sight in the woods nearby while she hailed the new arrival from inside the body of the boneburner, moving his limbs, looking out through his eyes. Through those eyes she instantly spotted the bones of a woman nonchalantly scattered among those of animals—a household goat, a horse gone lame, chickens slaughtered for meat. She dove into the farmer's mind, ready to rip him apart, but she saw quickly that he wasn't a murderer. His companion had been ill for months. He'd nursed her as she passed to the Underlands. He missed her terribly, and he was eager to complete his task and get home to care for her children. Sessadon discovered to her horror that what she was witnessing was simply how Sestians lived. *We laid her spirit to rest,* thought the man, his mind tinged with sadness but no regret. *Once the ceremony of homegoing is complete, a person's bones are just bones, no more or less sacred to the Holy One than any other creature's.*

Perhaps there was something to this idea of nations after all, thought Sessadon in disgust. If these people could believe something so wrong, so foolish, wasn't it better to separate them? Shouldn't ridiculous ideas be quarantined, confined? But in the next moment she

reconsidered. That was not how to handle dangerous ideas. Dangerous ideas should be ripped up by the roots, their wrongness exposed.
That way they would die out, leaving the right ideas to find purchase
in the bare soil left behind. When she was queen of all, that was how
she would lead.

She knew she should keep up the illusion, go through the motions
of burning the bones and exchanging the ash, but she just couldn't.
So she swung open the door to the narrow temple, recoiling from the
heat of the blazing fire pit, the leaping orange flames rising from a
squared-off bed of black charcoal and white bone ash. Ignoring the
grieving farmer's shouts, she walked the boneburner's lifeless body
up to the edge of the fire and dropped it in. Let him die as he had
lived, she thought, serving his god through fire.

She had no more appetite to stay in Sestia after that, and thought
carefully about her next step. She did not intend to spend time in
Arca; displays of powerful all-magic too close to Daybreak Palace
were bound to draw attention, and while she had no doubt she could
pick off attacking magicians like sparrows on the wing, now was not
the time. Let her young all-magic heir grow stronger, out there in
the world. She would use the time to prepare. To test. To build her
magical arsenal the way she had rebuilt her body back on the quartz
island.

Thinking of the quartz island sent her in search of another like
it, and she found herself in the loveliest place she would visit in the
whole two years. It was a small island off the south coast of Paxim,
not far from Arca. Not quartz like her own island had been, but
scalloped on both the mainland side and the Mockingwater side by
long beaches of white sand, gleaming against the slick silver-blue of
the water. The center of the island, on a high hill, was occupied by
a gorgeous sandstone temple consecrated to the God of Luck. The
temple's curves were like those of Daybreak Palace, all spires and col-

umns, but instead of emerging from a mountainside, it stood tall into the open sky from every angle. Standing on those towering steps, gazing either back toward the mainland or at the infinite waves of the Mockingwater, one felt lucky indeed.

The priest of the God of Luck was a patient person of no gender, openhearted and pious, who answered every one of Sessadon's questions without guile. Yes, pilgrims came constantly to the island. Yes, the priest spoke with every last one of them, no matter what they sought. Yes, the pilgrims came from all over. No, the priest did not hear the voice of the god in their ear; they read his signs in other ways. No, they did not believe that all luck, good or bad, came from the god. Indeed, people made their own luck in many ways. The priest was so honest, so happy to share, that Sessadon did not even dip into their mind once to check the veracity of what they were saying. Some people in the world actually were who they seemed to be; it appeared that this person was. Indeed, just talking to them went a long way toward building Sessadon's faith that most of the people of this world, wherever they lived, were worth ruling.

At the end of their conversation, Sessadon flipped a Paximite coin to see whether this person truly was favored by the God of Luck. If the coin showed the All-Mother, she told herself, she would slay the priest where they stood. If the coin showed the olive branch, she would let them live. She flipped the coin and looked at the priest's smiling face. When she looked down at the coin, it was the All-Mother's face that showed.

Yet she left the Isle of Luck without killing the priest. She did not want to and so she didn't. In that way, she decided, the priest had proved their own belief correct; the priest, not the god, had made their luck.

What good were the gods anyway? She had been afraid, before she left her island, that the gods might punish her if she dared too much, aimed too high. The more she traveled, the more she learned, the less she feared. Perhaps the God of Luck was not the only one she would defy. Even with all her power, not even Sessadon knew what was to come, not with complete certainty. She had years and miles to go before her story was fully written. Not even she knew what its end would be—or if in fact it had an end at all.

✦

Sessadon visited none of the queens or their palaces in her wanderings. She was curious about them, of course, but she did not need to meet them face-to-face in order to hate them. Or even, if she chose, to destroy them. She could have slain any one of them, even all five of them, from where she stood. But if it were done now, each nation would simply find a new ruler and go on functioning. She wanted them at each other's throats before she took charge. The longer the Drought lasted, the more the queendoms grew to resemble a cluster of ripe fruits, sun-warmed and plump, ready to drop off their branch into her waiting hands.

So she dipped and swooped through each queen's mind from far off, familiarizing herself with their movements, their weaknesses, their courts. It took a great deal of focus and power, so she hunkered down in a forested safe haven where she could work and rest undisturbed. It was never a mistake to get to know one's enemies.

The queen of the Bastion, for example, was an overwhelmed functionary who posed no real threat. In two years there would be another queen anyway, another functionary, and Sessadon expected the same from her. No one ever really wanted to be queen of the Bastion; no scholar-queen had ever truly ruled. Consensus ruled, and by definition, that meant not even the queen was in charge. Scholars they might be in the Bastion, the wisest intellects in the known world—just now their teams were working day and night, desperately attempting to find a cause or cure for the Drought—but they made halfhearted, uninspiring monarchs.

The queen of Sestia, the High Xara who also served as the nation's highest priest and spiritual leader, had the most surprising mind of the five. From the outside she seemed calm and able, effortlessly devout. Inside was a different matter. She spent hours every day sequestered in a sacred chamber only she could enter, consumed with wondering why the Holy One was withholding girls, what she must do to appease the god. She even worried that she herself had somehow caused the Drought with her own actions, her own shortcomings. Did the Holy One hate her? Why did She not speak to her, when She had spoken to every High Xara before? What actions could possibly appease the god, win Her love, return the world to balance? To see the inner workings of the woman's twisted self-hatred was unpleasant in the extreme; to put her out of her anxious, fanatical misery would be a kind of mercy when the time came.

The queen of Paxim's mind was more predictable, utterly occupied with her nation's internal politics, jockeying for position with the senators and assemblywomen in Ursu, Paxim's capital. She wanted to craft the impossible: a future for her son, her only remaining child, as a ruling king. In a way, Sessadon wished her well. It took remarkable energy and grit to see things so differently from how the rest of the world saw them. Heliane was truly a visionary. But even if the boy Paulus, nine years old now, did rise to become the first ruling king of Paxim, there was no real future in it for him: Sessadon would merely destroy four queens and a king to get what she wanted instead of destroying five queens. Besides, if it hadn't been for her Drought of Girls, male succession would not even have been whispered of. Should he rise in time for her to destroy him, she'd merely be taking away something that she herself had made it possible to offer. Everything came back to her, to the Drought, if you looked at it in the right light.

The two queens Sessadon found most interesting were also the two most threatening, surely not coincidental. When she dipped into their minds from afar, both were still in the process of moving toward the Sun Rites, the gathering that brought together all five queens once every five years. The warrior queen was moving southwest, the magician queen due west, and both of them would have been horrified to understand that there was any similarity whatsoever between them. Both of them thought themselves unique in all the world.

The Scorpican was finding her footing as queen, gathering her army of daughters around her, but still deeply uncertain, alone. If she were bold enough, this one queen could do more than anyone else, besides Sessadon herself, to disrupt the balance of the world. The temptation to reach out and nudge Queen Tamura's mind toward the outcome the sorcerer wanted burned in her like a coal. It would be so very easy. But it was unnecessary, she told herself. And if the warrior queen made her own decisions, put herself and her warriors in harm's way purely through her own acts, victory over her would be all the sweeter.

Similarly, Sessadon was sorely tempted to sow discord and mistrust in the court of the queen of Arca, given her hatred of the woman who ruled there. But when the sorcerer looked into the halls of Daybreak Palace, she almost laughed to see there was nothing for her to do. The court was already a nest of vipers, seething with venom. When she recognized the plot afoot, Sessadon had an odd pang of sympathy for the queen of Arca, though it quickly dissipated into an eager, wicked anticipation. Mirriam was a piece of work, whimsically brutal, touched in the head from too much power over too much time. When the time came, Sessadon would enjoy killing her. In the meantime, she could savor the knowledge that the second-oldest magician in the world was both too paranoid and too trusting, and this paradox had produced a nasty surprise that had yet to be revealed.

When she dipped into the mind of Queen Mirriam herself, Sessadon realized with a start that the queen had sent Seekers after Sessadon's heir. Scouring the minds of the villagers of Adaj had turned up little, but Mirriam had at least learned the girl's name, Eminel, and her mother's, Jehenit. Beyond that, there wasn't much of a trail. The Seekers had informed Queen Mirriam that they had thoroughly searched Arca and the girl was absolutely nowhere to be found in the queendom. Mirriam informed them, in return, that four more queendoms remained to search.

Should she interrupt the Seekers, even destroy them? thought Sessadon. She could, of course. But no. Even if they found the girl, they would not harm her. They would only harm the people who she was traveling with, and that did not bother Sessadon in the least. And the Seekers had yet to pick up even a trace of the girl's trail. Unless Eminel's gift manifested, or unless she or her mother told the secret, the Seekers might wander another year, or even longer, before they tracked her down.

So much could happen in that time.

In a way, Sessadon was glad she couldn't tell the future. It made life so much more interesting to experience it as it happened.

✦

Two years after she had installed the quartz heart and started her journey to explore the queendoms, Sessadon felt a tug, a stretching deep inside her chest.

The spell was beginning to strain. It wanted out.

If she stored the spell outside her body, as she had during those years in the cave, she could save strength for other tasks. And those tasks would multiply as soon as she decided to move forward.

She no longer needed sleep—one of the many ways in which her body had been improved by the addition of the quartz heart—but she had found in her travels that it was helpful to lie down in the dark sometimes anyway. A period of rest, free from other stimuli or distractions, helped clarify the mind.

It was during one of these periods of rest, lying in the lush grass of Sestia and staring up at the far-off stars, that she made her next important decision.

The time had come to move on.

In these years of wandering, she had learned what the Five Queendoms as they currently stood could teach her: about herself, about what had changed in five centuries, about how to defeat them. She had changed form many times, looking as she needed to look to accomplish what she wanted, but now it was time to settle on a form. It was foolish to use more magic than needed. So she decided on the shape of a woman in the later half of her fourth decade, dark curly hair shot through with salt-white, features just sharp enough to give the impression of intelligence without cruelty. She had never attained this age in her first life. She wondered if her sister had, and realized she did not know how long her sister had lived. It would be an easy thing to find out, and yet, she believed she'd be happier not knowing.

Her heir was nine years of age now, plenty old enough to begin learning anything she might need to know, and a handful of years would be more than enough time to teach her. Eagerly Sessadon imagined how grateful the girl would be to learn from her, how they could explore her abilities together, how Sessadon would answer every one of her questions patiently. Sessadon could almost taste the girl's raw power, even though it had been years since it had been fully unleashed, since that initial burst of blue sparks shattering the very air around her as she arrived in the world. Even the two later bursts, much smaller, hinted at an untapped reservoir below. It was time to harness that power and teach her who she was. It appalled her that even now, the girl did not know.

And so Sessadon reached out into the darkness, searching.

When she found what she was looking for, deep in Paxim, she made one small change. To act was as easy as thought. She reached out across the miles, a finger of magic extending, and extinguished a light.

There, she thought. *Now we'll see.*

✦ CHAPTER 23 ✦

COMFORT

The All-Mother's Year 511
On the roads of Paxim
Vish, Eminel, Hermei

Though Vish bedded down next to Fasiq, watched over her, shared every moment of her life, it was Jehenit who still made Vish's favorite tea every morning. It was a habit of nearly four years now, not easily broken. Both Fasiq and Vish were glad for it. A few more minutes each morning, those precious, drowsy minutes of intimacy, were theirs alone. A cheek pillowed against a shoulder, a nose pressed into the musky, familiar curve of a neck. Whatever else happened in a day, it could, and often did, start with those half-aware moments of shared peace. Nearly every morning, they were both roused from their last moments of sleep by Jehenit's voice calling, *Tea, tea, I have tea*, as sweet and soft as a chime.

But one autumn morning it was Eminel who woke them, instead, with her screaming.

Vish opened her eyes a heartbeat into the scream and sprang up, her hand finding a short sword even as she swam her way out of sleep. Too much daylight, that was the next thing she noticed. Jehenit always took a long succession of drinks from her waterskin just before she lay down for the night so she would be the first to rise in the morning. But the sun had risen, and, Vish realized with dread, it seemed that Jehenit had not.

Eminel's scream tore through the morning calm again, ragged, raw.

Fasiq rose then, her not-yet-silvered scar gleaming the pink of raw meat, her eyes turning quickly toward the awful sound. In half a moment her foot was on the step of the wagon and one large hand parted the curtains. She disappeared inside. Vish followed, sheathing the sword and pulling a dagger from her boot, the better to engage in close quarters, should it be needed.

But as soon as she saw what lay in the wagon, she knew there was no fighting to be done, at least not that kind.

Jehenit lay on her back, seemingly asleep. Eminel curled next to her on her knees, mouth open, still screaming. The sound was deafening in the small space. Fasiq crouched as best she could, though there was not much room left, and reached for Eminel's hand.

At last the screaming changed to words.

"Get away!" shouted Eminel. "I'm going to heal her!"

Vish could see the blue tinge to Jehenit's skin, everywhere exposed: not just her still lips but curled fingers, upturned wrist, bare legs. Vish knew the look of the dead when she saw it. Jehenit was not alive, had not been for hours, not with that cast to her skin. Hope was a fool's gambit now.

"Let me see," Fasiq said, firmly but not loud.

Eminel ignored her, releasing the cold bluish hand she'd been holding, placing her small palm now on the woman's chest, which they all could see failed to rise and fall as a breathing woman's would. Eminel herself gulped for air, swallowed past the knot in her throat, froze in place. She seemed to concentrate, her brows knit.

At least she was not screaming anymore, thought Vish, but her eyes were still wild. This could not end well.

"I can make it better, Mama," the child said, her voice completely changed. It was heartbreaking how clearly she was struggling to keep her voice under control, how she was, intentionally or not, imitating her mother's own calming tones, soothing as an aloe leaf. "Let me try. I have no great talent. Not like you. But I will try. My very best."

Fasiq stole a look at Vish and the swordswoman returned it. What could they do? Vish had long suspected that Jehenit hailed from Arca—she had that quiet hardiness about her, and no skill whatsoever with weapons—but this was the first hint that she'd been a healer. She'd known the woman and the girl had secrets, but she had respected their need to keep them. Now it was too late to ask. The only question was whether the secrets were just as important, or even more so, now that one of the secret-keepers was dead.

"Velja be with me," said the girl, her voice faltering, becoming a harsh rasp in her throat, "Velja be with me, Velja be with me."

But if the God of Chaos heard, She gave no sign. Eminel shrugged off Fasiq's hand on her shoulder, kept chanting, kept pressing one hand, then both, against Jehenit's unmoving chest. All Fasiq and Vish could do was stay with her. Serve some kind of vigil. Be there when she finally looked up, exhausted, recognizing she was powerless to change the unbelievable but undeniable fact in front of them all: Jehenit was dead.

That recognition took a long, long time.

For hours, Vish and Fasiq stayed with the girl and the body. There was no room for the rest of the party to join them in the wagon, but one by one, each took turns peering inside. Vish was closest to the flap and she met their eyes as they appeared, raised a warning finger to her lips. Each of the remaining bandits—Hermei first, then Luben, then Elechus—gazed at her with blank, aching faces. She nodded to show nothing else was needed for now, then waved off whatever they held out to her, knowing neither she nor the giant would be able to eat or drink until the girl had accepted the heartbreaking truth.

The sun was high overhead by the time Eminel fell completely silent, her breath halting and then coming hard. Vish feared that the girl would simply give out under the strain. It was too much for anyone.

Then at long last, Eminel sat back on her heels, letting her hands fall into her lap. She took her gaze from her mother's still, waxen face.

She turned to Fasiq and said, the single word almost a prayer, "Help."

Fasiq put both palms over her chin and cheeks, the unsilvered scar disappearing, and ran them up over her hair. It seemed to Vish that she was struggling to keep her own sadness under control. For the girl's sake, she managed.

"You need to eat. The men will have food for us," said Fasiq gently to Eminel. "Let's go out."

"I can't," Eminel said.

"There will be many things you think you cannot do in these days," Fasiq told her. "We are here to help you do them."

So the girl began to rise, leaning heavily on the giant, who ushered her out as Vish held back the curtain for them.

Once they stepped down, the twins were waiting.

"We are going to the fire," Fasiq said, not because they could not figure that out for themselves, but simply to have something to say.

One of the twins said, "We will stand guard."

"For as long as it takes," said the other. "No one will get past us."

"We swear," said the first. "On our lives."

Eminel did not respond in any way. Perhaps she did not hear them at all.

"Thank you," Fasiq said, ushering the girl forward, away from the wagon where her mother lay.

Once the giant and the child were seated next to the fire, Hermei appeared and approached them with tentative, measured steps. He offered the girl watered wine and her favorite seedcake, which she ate and drank absently, her gaze unfocused.

Vish said nothing, only watched, looking back and forth between the giant's face and the newly orphaned girl's, her gaze finally coming to rest on Fasiq. The giant was being kind now, but she worried and wondered what her lover would do, in the end. In uncertain, increasingly combative times like these, a girl of not yet ten years—one of the youngest in the five queendoms, surely—was far more of a liability than an asset. Keeping her hidden at all times held the bandits back. Would Fasiq banish Eminel, send her away to fend for herself? It was what anyone sensible and merciless would do. Vish knew the former was true but held out hope against the latter.

But when the girl tired as the last of the day slipped away, Fasiq was still there, holding and stroking her hand, speaking softly. She had not taken any kind of break from the girl, not to tend to her own needs or silver her scar or drink even a sip of tea. Though no one had made tea, Vish realized with a start. With Jehenit gone . . . but perhaps it was better not to finish the thought. There were a thousand ways things would be different without Jehenit among them. Very few of them could be solved by sundown.

The giant said, her voice tender and resigned, "Nothing more to be done today, I'm afraid. Tomorrow we will perform your mother's homegoing. Tonight, I will sit up with you, if you wish."

Eminel could only nod.

They stayed there as the sun sank below the horizon, just the two of them, though Vish continued to watch from nearby. Without speaking, the twins settled their bedrolls in guard positions, one in front of the wagon and one behind. When it got late, Vish took up a position under the wagon, finding Hermei had done so as well. The older man's face was as grave as she'd ever seen it.

Next to the dying fire, the giant sat and folded herself into an awkward package next to Eminel, her legs too long even when crossed. Her arms wrapped around the girl and held her close, her palm dwarfing the girl's head. The newly orphaned girl found herself cradled against the enormous bandit's lean, muscular chest. They stayed that way until the fire went out and the stars above gave the only light.

After she could no longer see them, before she lay down to sleep, Vish took a long pull from her waterskin, then a second, then a third.

In the morning she woke early, shivering in the unaccustomed cold without the shelter of her lover's arms. Then she rose, stretched, and relieved the ache of water in her loins. Then, resolutely, without hurry, she set about making Fasiq's strong, bitter tea.

✦

The third night after the morning she'd awoken curled against her mother's cold, dead form, Eminel lay next to the last red embers of the fire and stared up into the starry night sky. She could not sleep in the wagon where she'd discovered her mother's dead body. Not last night, not tonight, maybe not ever again.

She'd been grateful for the giant's company the first night, when she was too stunned to think, but now she wanted to be alone. The bandits, respecting her wishes, kept their distance. There was no hearth under which to bury Jehenit out here, of course, but they'd done their best with Eminel's vague recollections of Arcan burial traditions. On this front Hermei was also unexpectedly helpful; Eminel had not known until now that he, too, had once chosen to leave Arca behind. She wondered what other secrets her mother had not shared with her. She suspected there had been many. Jehenit had anticipated far more years in which to reveal them, waiting for her daughter to grow into readiness, but that was not to be. Her mother was dead, thought Eminel, the pain hitting her afresh. She was not ready, not for this, not for anything yet to come.

There was no sign of what had killed Jehenit. Not a mark on her anywhere. She'd heard the bandits whisper enough to know that they, too, were mystified. There was no sign of trauma or poison. Jehenit had not eaten or drunk anything in the past few days that the others hadn't also consumed. As far as any of them could tell, no beast or plant had done this: there were no scratches or bites, no signs of fangs or stingers, venom or thorns.

When she'd crouched over Jehenit's still, blue body, Eminel had immediately assumed the cause of death. Those whispered conversations between the bandits confirmed that even after reasoning through it, talking about possibilities, guessing and deducing, they'd all reached the same conclusion she had.

It was magic.

She tried to put thoughts of her dead mother out of her head. She stared up, again, at the stars. The Cup hung high above her head. To the left, the Scorpion reared; at the right, the Dreamer slumbered. So far off, so high. She tried to imagine herself traversing the endless miles between, drifting formless in the cool, thin air above. She tried her best to lose herself completely. After a long time, her vision blurring from exhaustion and smearing the stars above her, she closed her eyes.

Even before she settled into the private darkness of sleep, a vision came to her, as bright and searing as daylight, tinged with blue at the edges.

The bandits without her. Happy. Fasiq with her arm around the Shade, the laughing twins rolling bones, Hermei shaking his head in mock disapproval of the game with an indulgent smile on his face.

Without Jehenit, without Eminel, they were lighthearted. *So much less to worry about,* said the giant in the vision, and Eminel knew without a doubt what she meant.

Then they raised their heads to look at her, one after another. Hermei first, wary. One twin, then the other, their eyes full of doubt. The Shade glanced her way only for a moment, then turned aside, as if she didn't want to see what came next. Eminel found herself dreading the giant's gaze. When Fasiq lifted her head, her face was dark with fury, her body already moving toward Eminel, one enormous hand drawing her sword from its sheath with a scraping sound that seemed to echo into forever.

When Eminel's eyes flew open, the dark night still surrounded her. She gasped in the night air. Only the darkness made her doubt what she'd just seen. It couldn't have happened. It hadn't happened, she told herself. Yet it was too real to be a dream.

But for all its impossibility, to Eminel in that moment, the vision made perfect sense. Certainly the bandits would not want her, not anymore. She had only ever been a burden. If she took to the road before they asked, she'd save everyone the trouble.

The positions of Arca's stars were slightly different from Paxim's, she knew, but she no longer remembered what the sky at home had looked like. Could she even count it as home anymore? Could she, should she, return to Arca after all these years? She wasn't sure, but she knew she had to leave. She'd figure out a direction once she'd started.

One of the twins had brought her pack and her mother's pack out of the wagon so Eminel would not need to go inside to retrieve them. Now she satisfied herself that the bandits were asleep—no one moving, no one watching—and emptied both packs so she could rearrange her belongings to take only what she needed. She left her mother's clothes, all far too big for her, except a thick winter cloak.

That would probably drag on the ground when she wore it, but she would need it as the weather changed.

Keeping the rest of her body still as stone, she slipped her fingers under every lining and pocket of her mother's pack, even picking apart stitches that felt out of place, and found a substantial handful of coppers her mother had tucked away. These she took, along with a small dagger and a hammered silver bracelet she could perhaps sell if needed, secured deep in the folds of her own pack. The stone crow one of her mother's husbands had once carved for her, she gripped in her fist. Instead of taking it, she hurled it into the woods as hard as she could. Then she stood, leaving her mother's disassembled pack where it fell, and began to walk away.

She did not bother to hide what she'd done. When the bandits woke, they would know. She would be gone and they would shrug, relieved, and go on their merry way. Her only moment of hesitation was in deciding which direction to go. She picked the road they hadn't come in on and put one foot in front of the other, heading into the darkness, wherever the road might lead.

By the time the sun came up, she was well beyond tired and getting worse. She lay down in the shade to rest, exhausted, but the moment she fell into a shallow sleep, the dream came. This one was much worse than the last and also it was not a dream. She had heard her mother and Fasiq talking, years ago, when they thought she couldn't hear. The words Eminel heard when she closed her eyes were words she'd heard the giant herself speak on a dark, clouded night: *They cheated me out of my fair share of something. I hung one from a tall tree and hung the second from the first.*

Eminel opened her eyes, still exhausted, but the lightning bolt of fear got her immediately to her feet. The bandits might come after her—not to bring her back, but to punish her, prevent her from turning them in. She thought she'd feel better after she left their encampment behind. Instead paranoia dug its hooks deeper. The way Fasiq's eyes had burned in the vision, her expression as she reached for her weapon. Eminel shivered. She didn't need money just now, but the bandits didn't know that, and that was something people did, wasn't it? Scored a bounty for showing authorities where notorious bandits could be found? Of course she would never do such a thing—they'd been her family—but what if they thought she would?

She forced her feet to the road, forced one foot forward and then the other, kept herself moving.

When she saw a stream she left the road and walked through it for a time, remembering that in the story of the girl who rode the wind, a criminal had done the same to throw hunting dogs off his scent. None of the bandits had the nose of a hunting dog, but why take chances? The less predictable her actions, the better. She found a road on the far side of the stream that wended away. She took it.

By midafternoon she could walk no longer, but as if Velja Herself had intervened with the God of Luck on Eminel's behalf, she found a roadside inn with a sign out front that advertised available rooms with both words and images. She took a room, ignored the innkeeper's obvious curiosity, mounted the stairs. In the last moments before exhaustion took her, she bolted the door from the inside with fumbling, numb fingers, and she tumbled into sleep even as her body was still in the process of falling onto the hard, narrow bed.

When she awoke it was dark. Perfect, she thought. She could not have taken dinner in the main room with other guests; she would have been too obvious. Now, with most guests abed, she could sneak down for bread and cheese from the kitchens. If someone was there to insist on payment, she could spare a copper or two. If no one saw her, all the better. She didn't know where her next meal would come from. It would be wise not to pay for this one.

The inn was quiet, but when she slipped into the kitchen, lit only by its banked fire, she realized she was not alone. She approached with caution, but it was too late not to be seen. There near the hearth were a kitchen boy of perhaps ten-and-three, apple-cheeked and quick, and a silent male figure he was already handing cheese to; with a start, Eminel realized the man was all too familiar. Those worn cheeks, those steady eyes. Hermei.

He had already found her, was already waiting for her. She had not been clever at all. Now the only question was, why was he here? To keep her from leaving their group, or to seal her lips forever?

She thought about running. But if she did, wouldn't he just run after her? He was faster, smarter, more devious. His presence here proved it. She might as well sit and eat.

"Room for one more, if you like," said the kitchen boy. "And plenty to go around, for a coin."

"Thank you," Eminel said.

When the boy turned to the table behind him to reach for a loaf of bread, Eminel snuck a look at Hermei, her face a question. His face was entirely without expression. She realized he was going to pretend they didn't know each other. Instead, as he would with any stranger, he used one hand to indicate the seat next to him, which she silently took.

The boy returned. She was self-conscious, not sure what to do, what to say. The dagger was upstairs in her pack. She had not even thought of bringing it with her. A child's mistake, or a fool's.

After Hermei tore a chunk off the cheese, he handed it to Eminel, again without a word. Then, after the kitchen boy handed it to him, he did the same with the bread. Both times Eminel nodded her thanks but did not speak them. She was not sure she trusted herself to talk, not with these thoughts whirling around in her head, her own vulnerability, her fresh grief, her trust for this man that had for years gone all the way deep into her bones. Better to be silent. Better to wait. And to eat, when she had the chance. Now that her body had satisfied its craving for sleep, food was next, and that craving had grown nearly unbearable.

"Should I stoke the fire, sir?" asked the kitchen boy.

"No need for that," Hermei replied, in a voice no louder than needed. "Perhaps a bit of butter, though?"

"Of course."

The boy handed over the butter, again from the nearby table, and the older man dragged his bread through. Eminel could tell Hermei was perturbed only because she'd known him so long. His eyebrows neared each other by only the smallest of motions.

The kitchen boy was standing just next to Hermei's shoulder, smoothing his apron, appearing to be waiting for something. Hermei turned to the boy. "Where do you keep your ale, young man?"

"Out in the springhouse, sir."

"Ah, that sounds lovely. I fear I am parched."

"I'll fetch a mug," he said.

Turning to Eminel, the thief asked, "Two?"

She didn't know what the right answer was, so she guessed. "Thank you, but no."

"A second for me, then, I suppose, boy. I'd be ever so grateful." His voice was nothing but kind to the boy, but Eminel now understood his aim. He was contriving to get her alone.

The thief waited several moments after the kitchen boy had gone. Silence surrounded them, even the fire's crackle subsiding to a hush.

Then Hermei said, "Oh, Eminel," somehow encompassing a boundless ocean of sadness in a few short syllables. Her name had never been said with such regret before.

To defend herself, she said, "I was saving you the trouble."

"You were never trouble. Everyone's sick with worry."

"Are they?" she asked, letting her skepticism show. "Or is this a trick?"

"Why would it be a trick?" he asked.

"I could turn you all in. For a bounty."

He laughed without humor. "That's ridiculous. You would never."

"I know I wouldn't."

"Then let's talk no more about it. A bounty! Honestly. Oh hush, here he comes."

The kitchen boy returned with two mugs, setting them carefully on the nearby table so nothing sloshed, not even a drop.

Hermei produced a few coppers from nowhere and let them fall, one clinking against the next, into the boy's outstretched hand. "For the ale and our meals. Will this do?"

The boy bobbed his head and said, "Very generous, sir, thank you. I'm to tend the other fires now. But I'm not supposed to leave guests alone in the kitchens."

"I promise we won't tell," Hermei said conspiratorially, and something about his smile must have convinced the boy, because he bobbed his head again and was gone.

Now it was just the two of them in the flickering firelight. Eminel ate her bread in silence, forcing herself not to bolt it down. It was dry and crusty, nearly stale, but with the cheese it would do.

At last Hermei said firmly, "Now. You shouldn't have left us."

"I made it this far."

"Who knows how much farther you would make it? I wouldn't want to find out. This world is dangerous."

"Or perhaps I am the danger," said Eminel, and felt the threat of tears prickling behind her eyes.

"Why would you say that?"

"My mother," Eminel said. "Did she ever tell you why we left Arca?"

"No. I didn't want to know."

"It was because of my curse," said the girl.

"Curse?" There was something about his voice, a kind of tender curiosity, that opened the door for Eminel to tell a truth she'd never told before. Her mother never wanted to talk about it, so they never had. And now, they never would.

But she could talk about it with this man. This man from Arca. Maybe he would understand.

"I did something when I was little," she began. "I tried to heal someone, and I did, but I hurt her too. And then I—I went inside her mind."

Something flickered in Hermei's eyes, and not just the firelight's reflection. Shock, it seemed. She had genuinely surprised him.

"And your mother told you this was a curse?"

"Yes. And that I shouldn't ever use it."

"And you haven't. Not in all the time you've been with us."

"No."

"Let me try something," he said, seeming to make a decision. Deliberately he lined up the fingers of one hand over his jawline. "Watch."

She did as he said, leaning in close to observe him in the firelight. He concentrated, making a small gesture with the hand on his jaw, tapping his blunt fingertips lightly in a pattering motion that reminded her of rain. Then he fanned his fingers out suddenly, flexing each as if he hadn't used them in a long time and wanted to see how far they might stretch.

Then she saw it. A subtle ripple moving across his face, his skin. The depths of his brown eyes grew deeper, the wrinkles around them fading, the leathery folds on each side of his mouth smoothing as he smiled. His face was younger, more charming, than it had been just moments ago. Two different instincts pulled her in opposite directions. This man's face looked open, welcoming, willing her to share her secrets; but he looked like a stranger now, not the Hermei she knew, and that made her instantly wary.

He said, "And?"

"How did you *do* that?" she asked in wonder.

As soon as the question was out of her mouth, he dropped his hand, rapping his knuckles once on the wood of the chair next to him. The changes were gone. He looked tired again, ordinary, familiar. She preferred him this way. Less charming, she supposed, but wholly known.

"Seems there must be a magician in this inn," he said. "Probably asleep upstairs. I borrowed a little bit of power from the sand in her *psama*."

"*Psama*?"

A current of sadness swam across his face. "If you have the gift I think you have—not a curse, Eminel, a gift, though a complicated one—there are some things you need to know."

And so Hermei told her of life force and sand, of magic that could change bodies and minds, earth and water, air and fire. Of Daybreak Palace and the trials and dangers, but also potential, that waited there. Of all-magic girls who, once their families released them to the care of the palace, never came back.

Eminel listened carefully. He asked her questions about what she had done, what she might do. She told him everything, about the winged girl and the bruises, Jorja and her betrayal, what Jehenit had said about her curse. He told her that if she could damage bodies and read minds, she was no ordinary magician. If she could do that, she had all-magic, and it was not just bodies and minds she had the power to reach. All the elements were hers as well, though it was impossible to know to what degree. With water, for example, she might have the power to stir the ocean or barely to heat a teacup. He wanted to test her, and the *psama* upstairs meant he could; but at the same time, it was too dangerous to do so. All-magic was very powerful, and she might accidentally do far more than she meant to, given her complete lack of training. Better to leave it alone, for now.

They left together to go back to the bandits. Nothing was decided except that Eminel belonged with them. That was enough, they agreed, for now.

As they left, once Hermei was already out of the room, Eminel thought about what she'd learned, and she could not help but reach back toward the fire. Wasn't fire magic part of all-magic too?

The girl stared into the brilliant, rippling color of the fire and concentrated on it, wondering why fires were orange, and whether they had to be. She held out her hand, forming a V with her thumb and index finger, and watched the fire through the frame her fingers made.

And for the space of one heartbeat, the orange flames in the hearth blazed blue.

Eminel turned away, satisfied, and followed Hermei from the room. She was overwhelmed, reeling, dizzy from what she'd learned. These revelations, following so soon on the heels of Jehenit's death, drove her deeper into herself. She had believed her mother loved her, still believed it, but she no longer understood what kind of love it had been.

In the shadows, unseen, the wide-eyed kitchen boy looked hard at the fire.

Had he really seen what he thought he saw? Had the flames in the hearth completely changed color, just for a moment, when the young girl stretched out her hand?

He had spied on the two of them talking, as he always spied on the guests. There was so much good information to be gleaned from conversations when people thought they were unobserved. *Nothing to be gained from that one, though,* he thought, and went back to work.

When several months later, two women in black cloaks came to the inn, even if he were asked what he knew about all-magic, the kitchen boy would not have bothered to tell them what he had seen. He would not have made the connection between these two somber magicians—one with a delicate oval face and a shorter one with a braid—and the quiet girl who had eaten bread and cheese in the kitchen late one night, sitting next to an undistinguished man whose face he could not remember.

But the Seekers did not have to ask him. They looked inside his mind, and they knew.

PART III

CRISIS

The All-Mother's Year 511
Second Sun Rites of
the Drought of Girls

CHAPTER 24

THE CHERRY GROVE

Midsummer, the All-Mother's Year 511
In the Holy City, Sestia
Azur, Tamura, Gretti

As the entourage of Scorpicae rode into the Holy City, Azur and Ysilef craned their necks to see. Ysilef was more circumspect, attempting to disguise her curiosity, while Azur stared flat out, hungry for the strange sights. They were not alone. All six of the younger warriors stared up wonderingly, stunned by the bright white stone all around them. Blinding white buildings everywhere, stretching toward the sky. There was nothing like any of this in Scorpica. Even those who had been born elsewhere had never been to the Holy City, and they had seen nothing but the plains of Scorpica for more than two years. They had been born again when Tamura took them as her daughters. If they remembered what life had been like outside of the warrior nation, they chose to forget.

There were people in the streets, but the warriors ignored them. Azur, for her part, had eyes only for how the structures soared. She devoured the differences, the similarities: arches and frames, homes and public buildings, shacks and temples. As they approached the city center, the buildings were clustered even more thickly, huddled together like wolves in winter. When she saw the temple-palace, there was no mistaking it. The largest by far, its stunning white lines undeniable and solid, the temple-palace soared four stories into the overcast sky.

Azur jabbed Ysilef in the side with an outstretched finger to get her attention. "If you fell out a window," she said, "you'd be dead as soon as you hit the ground."

"We'll have to stay away from windows," Ysilef said, ever pragmatic. She was the more cheerful of the two, practical where Azur was ambitious, a versatile but workmanlike fighter where Azur was an absolute genius with the bow and only the bow. If Azur did say so herself, and she did. She might be arrogant, but it wasn't bragging, she told herself, if you really were that good.

The older warrior in front of them turned to hush them, hissing under her breath. Azur looked around, but it was Ysilef who caught on first.

"Be dignified," she muttered under her breath. Both girls sat up taller and aimed their ponies' noses straight down the center of the wide, flat road. There was no breeze to stir the dust of the street, and even with the cloud cover, the veiled sun seemed to lick the backs of their bare necks with a sticky, persistent heat.

They rode in silence the rest of the way to the temple-palace, trying to project the most serious, fearsome image possible to match the more senior warriors. In their hammered leathers, shields hanging from loops on their backs and swords bouncing in their sheaths, the elder Scorpicae looked like a small but deadly force. Azur might not be the most deliberate thinker, and also a mere ten-and-three, but even she knew that this was no accident.

When they arrived at the temple-palace and were shown to their quarters, they heard Tamura muttering under her breath to Larakhi.

"Too many buildings, not enough air. If the All-Mother had intended people to live so high, she'd have made the world with more mountains."

"No wonder the God of Plenty took all the girls away," said Larakhi, without bitterness. "When people make the world over like this."

Azur and Ysilef exchanged a look. They'd heard the rumor before that it was the God of Plenty, also known as the Holy One, who'd caused the Drought of Girls. It was one of many rumors. The Drought was a Bastion experiment gone wrong, it was a bet between the God of Luck and his sister the God of Fate, it was the beginning of the end of the world. But no one knew the truth, and it was not Azur and Ysilef's place to have an opinion. To be part of this trip in the company of these senior warriors was a rare gift. And they two were the youngest two. Too young to be councillors or to seek pleasures, they had nothing to add to the journey. For them, it was pure reward. They'd won trials meant for older girls—Azur with the bow, of course, and Ysilef on a lucky day with a longsword—and improbably, gratefully, here they were.

The other four young warriors were at least ten-and-five. These newly minted women whispered to each other on the road about whether or not they would seek pleasures in the Holy City, as so many other warriors had before them. Tamura had given them no instruction one way or the other.

Azur had even heard one of the young warriors ask Nikhit what she thought, and the older warrior snorted, "Please yourselves." Judging from the rounds of whispers that followed, this answer had left the young women more puzzled than ever.

Strong, veteran warriors like Ghosh and Bohara were also here, which made sense, but the oddest addition was Gretti. Not that Gretti wasn't a capable warrior and a valuable councillor—she was—but she had been included in the entourage as bladebearer, a position the adopted warriors had been told was always reserved for a new woman of ten-and-five. As strange as it seemed, they knew better than to ask for explanations. Tamura had made this choice. She was their commander, their mother, their queen. She had a reason, and if she wanted them to know what it was, she would tell them when the time was right.

When at long last, the Scorpicae reached their temporary chambers, the young warriors lay down on the thick beds and laughed at how they sank into the mattresses. Azur stared across the gap toward Ysilef, who giggled as she lost herself in the thick stuffing. As cheerful as Ysilef always was, Azur wasn't sure she'd ever heard her laugh with such abandon.

Everything about this odd land was different. Everything. And, reflected Azur, they were different here. It was exciting and overwhelming and, she had to admit, just a little bit unsettling.

But if their queen wanted them here, they would be here. They were Azur dha Tamura, Ysilef dha Tamura, not just her followers but her daughters. They owed her everything.

✦

As much as she hated and resented this journey to Sestia, Tamura looked forward to the day before the rites for two reasons. One, because it brought her closer to her goal, and two, because she knew she would see trees again at last. This monstrous city made her miss trees.

When the appointed day came, she walked with her guard to the grove where the five queens were to eat fresh cherries together, staining their lips and fingers with the crimson juice. This would affirm they were participating willingly in these rites. She had been briefed on this aspect as well as the others: for example, tradition dictated that the guards accompany the queens as far as the entrance to the grove but no farther, each queen leaving her guards at that entrance while she proceeded alone into the sacred space.

It was a simple matter, then, to modify tradition for her own ends.

Tamura made sure she was the last to arrive to the grove. She looked at the guards milling around near the entrance, four sets of Queensguards for her four fellow queens. All born Scorpicae, every last one. The pull of tradition was so strong. She'd let herself wonder if any queen might be paranoid enough to bring native-born guards, but it was so unthinkable that a Scorpican would not be faithful to her assignment that no one had. Her plan would not violate this sacred trust; she would not strip good soldiers of their honor. These guards would simply wait for their queens where they'd been told to wait, and she would not ask more of them. To a woman, their cloaks were pale and long, their faces wary, their swords sheathed.

Tamura walked into the sacred grove without pausing, two warriors on each side of her matching her stride, making hers the first and only Queensguard to ever enter the grove, swords swinging from their hips.

It was a bold action, provocative and impossible to ignore, which was why she thought it perfect. It might well outrage the other queens enough that they would leave the grove. But if they did, they would be the ones leaving. Not her.

She, and her guards, would stay. Whatever else happened.

And so, under the spreading beech trees, with heaped bowls of bright red cherries gleaming on the long, smooth tables, the dappled sun shone down not just on five queens, but also on the four warriors in full Scorpican battle dress who flanked them.

Tamura was a lamb among wolves here and she had planned accordingly, worried that the other queens would force her to a reckoning. So she would stand among her enemies, yes, but not alone. She could be a lamb among wolves if that was what they wanted. But she would bring bears with her, bears that could eat the wolves in a noisy, wet gulp.

All four queens were on their feet in an instant, and behind her Tamura heard the rattling of armor as other Queensguards rushed toward the entrance to the grove, but the High Xara stepped forward and raised both hands, palms outward, forbidding entrance. At the same moment her voice rang out. "No! No farther! We will have no further sullying of this Grove."

Tamura could hear the guards behind her arguing, clearly incensed, but she did not turn. She kept her face impassive. She ran her fingertips around the rim of the bowl of cherries in front of her but did not yet dip her fingers in.

Despite the obvious fury of their host the High Xara, the first queen to speak directly to Tamura was the last one she expected: the queen of the Bastion. This new one was awkward, her long body and narrow face all angles, her words unembellished. "Queen of Scorpica, my nation seeks answers."

"To what question?" asked Tamura, all innocence.

"Do you deny stealing girls from our nation?"

"None of us have as many girls as we once did. That is not my doing. Talk to this one's god," she said, jerking a thumb toward the High Xara, whose fingers tugged at the golden-dyed lock of hair over her brow.

"Do not," the High Xara said, her voice sharp, "accuse the Holy One of something you know nothing about."

"I am not here to argue," said Tamura, faux-appeasing. "I am simply here to affirm my participation in these rites. As is my duty, I have brought the sacred blade."

"Indeed," said the queen of Paxim, the one word dripping with displeasure. Thick, intricate braids were piled so high on her head that Tamura marveled she could even raise her chin. But there was no mistaking her seriousness as her eyes flicked toward the dagger at Bohara's hip, mere handspans from her own heart. "And several more."

Tamura said, "My warriors are here to guard me. I have reason to believe there are those here who wish me ill."

"Whether or not that is true," the High Xara interrupted, "I must ask your warriors to leave this holy grove. We cannot have the sacred rites disrupted in any way. And you are disrupting them."

"I would never dream of disrupting the Sun Rites," said Tamura. "Again, am I not here with the blade? Just the same as my southern neighbor has brought the book. You are here to perform the sacrifice; the Arcan is here to represent Chaos. Our predecessors performed these sacred duties for centuries. Are we not here to do the same?"

"We all agree on our duties," said the Arcan queen, speaking for the first time, her voice winter-cold. "But some disagree on how they are carried out."

So far, Tamura had been careful not to give anyone her direct attention. But she could not keep her eyes from turning to the Arcan queen. Next to the rest of them, Mirriam looked so young, even with her formidable, aquiline nose, one might be fooled into not taking her seriously. But Arcans had ways of carrying their power with them. How much power did this one, their queen, carry?

As if she knew what Tamura was thinking—and perhaps she did—the Arcan queen said, "Do not test me, warrior."

Tamura didn't care for the magician's scorn. She would not endure it simply to keep the peace, a peace she wasn't sure she wanted.

"Why would I?" she quipped, then rose from her bench in a swift, brusque movement, knocking it over. It fell with a soft thud in the grass. Seamlessly she stepped over it, backward.

Now she stood between Nikhit and Bohara. Nikhit stood, hips and shoulders wide, her mouth tight and straight and unyielding.

The sword on her hip was wide as well, a thick length of iron too heavy for most women to lift, let alone to yield. Nikhit shifted her sword hip forward and lowered her hand to rest lightly on the hilt, her thumb stroking it like the cheek of a lover. On Tamura's other side, Bohara, stout and strong as a boar, stood with her eyes burning fire. She wore a dagger on each hip, but her gaze was the weapon she used in the moment, staring down the four queens she did not serve.

On the other side of the table stood the remaining queens, unarmed and vulnerable. Like Nikhit, Edda and Ghosh kept their hands on their swords; both were small but fast, and if things went awry, only speed would matter. Tamura felt a spiral of dread move downward within her, but the time had passed for second guesses. Her warriors were near and she drank in the scent of them, the honest sweat and the musk of horseflesh, the iron of the blades they wore, the overlapping amber scales of their scorpion armor. They were with her. She had nothing to fear.

"As I said," she continued, her voice utterly calm, "I came to bring only the blade, not trouble. In this time of need, should we not be united?"

"The dead in the Underlands are *united*," the Arcan muttered. "You will not hear me advance unity as our goal."

Tamura heard false bravado in her words. If the magician queen had wanted to destroy her, she could certainly do that, without conversation. Instead the Arcan glared, and raised her fingers to touch the bump of a pendant under her elegant tunic—yes, she must carry her source of magic there—but she did not act.

Was she afraid her magic was not strong enough to kill Tamura and her warriors where they stood, or did she have other reasons for holding back? Ghosh could draw a longsword fast as lightning. No matter how skilled a magician the queen of Arca might be, she'd lack the power to do spells when her head rolled from her shoulders and landed on the bright green grass. The chance was, perhaps, not worth the risk.

Tamura said, "I am sorry your nation is suffering. Mine suffers too. No one's future is safe as long as the Drought of Girls persists. Until it ends, we should value peace above all."

Folding her long arms, the queen of the Bastion said, "Your words are hollow, warrior queen. My nation's questions remain." She turned her back on Tamura and her Queensguard, addressing the other queens. "Do you not see through this woman's platitudes? She is a smooth liar. Speaking with confidence does not mean one speaks the truth."

The warrior Edda shifted closer to the queen of the Bastion, not a broad motion or a noisy one, but enough so that the queen knew exactly how near she stood, metal so close to tender flesh.

Tamura could see the queen of the Bastion thinking over her situation, evaluating it, logically, as scholars did. Her entire nation was a fortress built to withstand an incursion, but its strength was also its weakness. Its impenetrable walls could keep the Scorpicae, or any invaders, out—but such a bulwark would also keep anything they needed from getting in. Its residents could not grow food, mint coin, earn money from educating outsiders when there were no outsiders to educate. If they were well-placed and patient, no enemy needed to slay a single Bastionite in order for every last one to die.

"And who is attempting distraction now?" Tamura responded. "Don't try to make my confidence sound like weakness. I am confident because right is on my side."

"And the girls who have disappeared?" asked the queen of Paxim, but not sharply. She was giving Tamura an opening.

Tamura took it. "The five queendoms have grown so much more dangerous in the past few years. The Drought has made desperate creatures in every queendom. I worry for my girls as you worry for yours."

They might believe her or they might not, and while she was not the best strategist, she knew a key arrow in any politician's quiver: distraction. She needed to give them something—someone—else to focus on.

"But tell us, High Xara." Tamura shifted her gaze to the saffron-robed one, whose body nearly vibrated with tension. "You are the one who speaks to the All-Mother's daughter, the God of Plenty, who withholds the newborn girls from us. What does She say?"

The eyes of the High Xara raked the gathering, going from warrior to warrior, then sizing up her fellow queens. She did not turn to look toward the entrance to the grove. Instead she met Tamura's gaze, steady and true. It seemed she was working hard to define what she read there.

Do not slit your own throat, thought Tamura. *Save that for your sacrifices.*

At last, her face ever so slightly green, the High Xara said, "I am not answerable to you, warrior queen. Only to Her."

But Tamura had succeeded in shifting the group's focus at last. The energy in the grove changed.

Now Tamura picked up a cherry, pressed it between her fingers until the red juice ran, and said, "Yet we all see what She has sent you for the past nine years. You have no more girls than the rest of us. Are you even still Her darling?"

The High Xara recoiled, but she caught and mastered herself quickly. When she spoke, her voice was level. "The Holy One will never desert Sestia. If we have no girls, it is because She has a reason to withhold them."

Tamura felt, and hid, a small thrill of victory. The High Xara had linked the Drought with her god's actions. Long after these rites ended, every queen would carry that link home with her.

The queen of Paxim interrupted, her voice almost friendly. "Let us have done with this conversation. Warrior queen, you say you have come here only to affirm your participation in the rites. State your affirmation and let us be done."

"Done," echoed Tamura, probably too quickly. She cursed herself for rushing instead of letting the silence sit.

The queen held up a hand. "But your actions in this grove have made your fellow queens . . . nervous. So I ask that you swear to do no violence within the city walls during the Sun Rites. While these rites last, your warriors' blades stay in their sheaths. Are we agreed?"

Tamura knew when to take an opportunity. In a way she was almost disappointed there would not be bloodshed; she had come here today fully prepared for it. But there would be other occasions. If no one else would stir to action, the best end in this moment was exactly what the Paximite offered: a truce.

"Thank you for being clear," said Tamura. "If everyone else here will swear, I will swear."

"Let any queen who does not want to be bound by my grip say so," the queen of Paxim said.

No one spoke.

"A deal, then." The queen of Paxim extended her hand, moving with certainty and poise. Was her hand trembling, though, just a bit? The drape of her purple robes parted neatly at the shoulder, falling aside, as she reached out.

She and Tamura grasped arms, locking their grips on the underside of the arm, index fingers on each other's elbows, the most serious binding. Tamura felt the diplomat queen's fingertips against her flesh, tense and pointed. The deal was made.

"And so," intoned the Scorpican queen, "our negotiation complete, I am now ready to affirm that Scorpica participates freely and openly in these rites for the favor of the God of Plenty."

Their faces drawn and angry, the other queens each gave their own affirmation, but none took her eyes from Tamura as she spoke.

Nothing like this had ever happened. Then again, nothing like the Drought of Girls had happened either. They were all striding blind across an unknown field, wary of hills and holes, fearing a fall with every step. They could not know the dangers ahead.

The last to affirm, as was tradition, was the High Xara. Tamura did not sense even a hint of fear in her as their gazes locked. It crossed Tamura's mind that this woman, holy and placid as she seemed, might be the most dangerous of them all. There was nothing more deadly than a true believer.

The High Xara said, in a sober, ringing tone, "The Holy One recognizes your affirmations and welcomes your contributions. You have Her gratitude. Tomorrow, the Sun Rites begin."

Tamura's warriors righted the bench for her and she sat again, cool and steady, scooping a handful of sun-warmed cherries from the bowl. She began to eat them one by one, savoring each burst of sweetness. They really were delicious. After each, she spat the hard pit to the ground.

Their energy seemingly spent, all five queens ate in utter silence. One could almost hear the pits fall.

✦

It was the oddest feeling, thought Gretti, plodding down the long path to the amphitheater behind her queen. She had taken these same steps on this same ground as a girl of ten-and-five, still aching between her legs from her first pleasures, ten long years ago. Ten years had altered her, and not only her. The steps were the same, yes, but she, a transformed woman, took them through a transformed world.

Still, she remembered those Sun Rites in every inch of her flesh. Those pleasures. She and the young man she'd coupled with had both been clumsy and curious, fumbling their way in the darkness, blind with excitement. Of course at the time she had felt so adult, so mature, a grown woman knowing and known. Now she saw how innocent she'd been. Then, she had followed Khara, who had encouraged her, guided her, protected her. Now, she followed Tamura, and everything was different.

This time, Gretti would not indulge in pleasures with a man, not while the Drought of Girls continued. Bearing and bidding goodbye to a son was not one of her regrets—most warriors did both—but she was not eager to repeat the experience. She would not wear her hair long again, watch her body swell for months, surrender to blind, animal pain, just for a fleeting ecstasy that could be achieved in other ways. And she had Scorpica's future to keep in mind. Tamura doubted her love of country, she knew. Which was why she was here, even though she was ten years past bladebearing age and a full member of the council. Tradition dictated that the bladebearer be a young girl without status, but in this, as in many ways, Tamura thumbed her nose at tradition. This was a punishment, not an honor. Tamura wanted to show Gretti that she had no earned place; her place was whatever Tamura said it was, even the place of an inexperienced near child.

Council membership was largely an honorific these days, in any case. Tamura hadn't called the council in several seasons, maybe a whole year. *Next month,* she always said. Or, *Soon. When it's needed.* It had become clear that the only person who decided what was needed was Tamura.

So she trailed her queen, who bore that holy, ancient blade, the only reason the Scorpicae were welcome at this gathering despite the rumors of what they'd done. That blade would open throats to bless the harvest. If they did this, would the harvest be bountiful? More importantly, would girls be born again? Ultimately, thought Gretti, that was the only harvest that mattered.

As she watched the rites, that strange dance of honor and ritual and blood, unfold in a way they never had before, Gretti was moved to do something she'd never done.

She prayed.

She believed in the All-Mother and her daughters in a loose, general sense, but their will had never meant much to her. She never believed they intervened directly in the affairs of women on earth. And even as she prayed now, she did not address her prayer to anyone in particular. Not to the Sestian god who asked for the sacrifice, nor to the God of the Underlands who readied herself to welcome these souls. Not to the God of Chaos who guided the actions of the Arcan queen and her spell-casting countrywomen. Not even—and oh, how Tamura would condemn her if she knew—to the Eternal Scorpion.

She did not address the prayer to any god or hero. She simply sent it up. The words were in her mind and would not be denied. As she stood there watching blood pump from a young woman's throat down onto the golden pool of grain, Gretti's first prayer spilled out, sang out without sound.

Let this be enough, then, she prayed. *Let us have our girls back at last. Let these lives, let this year's sacrifice, be enough.*

✦

If the walk to the amphitheater following Tamura's footsteps instead of Khara's felt oddly dislocating to Gretti, the road back to Scorpica was doubly so. Everything reminded her, insistently, of ten years before. The past felt as close as her own heartbeat.

When they neared the place where the bandits had made their stand, wounding Khara and panicking an untested Gretti, the now-grown bladebearer recognized it instantly. She could practically see the outline of those ragtag assailants, feel her skittish pony twitch under her tense thighs, hear Mada's shrill *kii-yah* as the warriors plunged toward the bandits and Khara and Gretti turned to flee.

She knew the shades of that moment were not real, yet even so, Gretti found she could not remain on that road. The pull of memory, and darker emotions, overwhelmed her. She tapped her heels against the sides of her pony and turned its head north. Puzzled shouts began to sound from behind her. She ignored them. With distance, they grew faint.

She rode on, as close as she could remember to the path she and Khara had taken, the one that unwittingly changed the world. Because of what had happened here, Khara was dead now. Only the bandits died that very day, but Mada's death, then Khara's, had grown from the same day's seeds. Why should she herself have survived? thought Gretti. What was special about her? Nothing. Only Khara's protective instinct had made the difference, and Gretti had done nothing to earn that, before or after. She had not saved Khara or her daughter. She had not Challenged Tamura, Khara's killer, though she had been asked to. She would have had plenty of seconds.

As she swayed with the pony's movements, leaving the column behind, Gretti pictured the face of the man in the hut. Even before Khara's belly had begun to swell, she'd guessed what had passed between the two of them. She could even remember his face, the spidering lines near his eyes. Funny how he was easier to picture than the fumbling boy she herself had coupled with. She remembered the feel of the boy's hands on her, the sound of his panting, eager breath in her ear, but she did not remember his face.

She wondered if the man still lived in the hut. She toyed with the idea of riding all the way there, dismounting in his yard, walking up to his door to inform him of the daughter he surely could not know he'd sired. For just a moment she allowed herself a ridiculous fantasy: Khara had not died, had not been slain by Tamura in the ugliest way possible, that was just a misunderstanding. Instead she had escaped with her daughter, Amankha, and the three of them had been living in harmony in this hut for years, untouched by the world. She pictured herself knocking on the door, a beaming Khara stepping out to welcome her, throwing her arms wide.

"Gretti!" barked a sharp, familiar voice behind her, with none of the warmth of Khara's imagined greeting, which lingered only a fleeting, aching moment in her mind.

The fantasy vanished. Slowly, reluctantly, Gretti turned to face reality in the form of her angry queen, glowering at her from the back of her own pony.

"Come on," said Tamura. "You and I are going on a hunt."

Gretti glanced back toward the column in the distance, uneasy. The other warriors did indeed seem to be pairing off, riding toward their own destinations, some moving toward a stand of nearby trees on foot, others galloping off across the open ground. In deep midsummer no caravan of any size, especially a Scorpican one, would attempt to carry all its own food. Hunting along the way was an absolute necessity. It was the timing that was odd, and the request that they hunt together. And she supposed, as she looked into Tamura's angry face, this wasn't exactly a request.

Had she drawn Tamura's ire with her actions, or had the queen already planned to take her into the woods alone? She supposed it didn't matter. Whatever happened to her, perhaps she deserved it. This was the place she could easily have died ten years ago. It would be a grim sort of justice if she died here now.

They trotted in silence for a good quarter of an hour, leaving the other Scorpicae well behind, until Gretti could no longer hear even the faintest echo of other hoofbeats. They reached the forest at last and Tamura led her in.

Once they were in the shadow of the trees, Gretti could no longer stand the tension. Their ponies balked at the nearness of the trees on the thin, narrow path. Tamura did not even scan the area for quarry. That made sense, realized Gretti, if she herself was the quarry Tamura sought. She drew her pony to a halt. Tamura stopped immediately beside her, uncomfortably close.

"Get down," the queen said.

Was there any point in protesting? They both dismounted. The dappled half shade of the trees all around them cooled the air, and if her blood hadn't been rushing in her ears, Gretti suspected she'd be able to hear songbirds nesting in the low, lovely branches. They were alone. The woods themselves were welcoming, but the presence of the angry queen drained every mote of pleasure from the scene. Tamura's full attention continued to be on Gretti, even as she notched an arrow onto the string of her bow without looking into the nearby trees for movement.

"Why did you bring me here?" Gretti blurted, sick of waiting and worrying, no matter what the consequences of speaking might be. "It wasn't to hunt."

Tamura said, "Wasn't it?"

Gretti shrugged. She was not as nonchalant as she pretended, but she knew Tamura. The queen would respond better to confidence than fear. "Kill me or don't kill me. I suppose that's up to you."

Tamura drew her bow then, the sharp point of her arrow leveled straight into the center of Gretti's chest. The sick satisfaction of being right drained the last reserves of calm from Gretti's body. She watched in rising fear as the string vibrated with tension. All Tamura had to do was let go, and it would all end. This charade, this struggle, this life.

Sighting her down the arrow's length, Tamura said, "Don't tempt me."

Slowly raising her hands in a motion of surrender, Gretti said, "Stay your weapon. You misunderstand."

"Don't talk to me like I'm a child," snapped Tamura. "I am your queen."

"Yes. And I'm trying to keep you that way."

Tamura's brow knitted and the point of her arrow sank just slightly. It was the first moment since she'd drawn the bow that Gretti genuinely hoped she might live.

The bladebearer seized her chance. "I suppose you've seen me talking with others on the council."

"Not just the council."

"Talking with other warriors, then." Gretti felt increasingly foolish with her hands in the air, but matters felt too delicate for her to drop them. She could do nothing right in this situation, but she had to try. Her words were her only weapons. "And you're suspicious of me? Is that right?"

"You've been against me from the start," growled the queen.

Though she wasn't quite wrong, neither did she understand Gretti's position. Her patience strained, Gretti yelled, "Tamura dha Mada, don't be a fool!"

The arrow came back up again, and Gretti sucked in a hopeless breath, sure that it was her last, that the arrow would disappear into her chest at any moment, the sharp stone point burying itself to one side of her breastbone, puncturing softer, vital places within.

But the moment went on for one more breath, then two, and she let herself hope for more.

"The truth is," Gretti said with utmost care, "I am trying to keep you queen. I'm happy to tell you everything. But one thing first."

"Yes?"

"Put down the bow."

At long last Tamura lowered the point of the arrow so it hovered around Gretti's feet.

"Close," said Gretti. She could feel the frayed edge of a hysterical laugh threatening to burst from her throat. If it succeeded, she knew that laugh would be her last. "Now the rest of the way."

"And if I don't?"

"This!" she burst out, then struggled to shift her tone. "This is what you need to change." She paused a moment, let the cool of the shadowed woods wash over her. The past was not here in the glade, she reminded herself. It was the future she needed to think of. If she, or Scorpica, were to have one.

"Don't you tell me what I *need.*"

Gretti said, "I will say what I have to say, and *mokh* the consequences. That is my choice. Now make yours. Put down the bow. Or go ahead and put an arrow through me, and forever wonder what I would have told you, if you'd let me speak."

Tamura glared at her for a long time. There was no sound in the grove now, no birdsong, not even the whispering of the wind through the dappled leaves.

Then the queen swallowed a hard knot, nodded once, and let the arrow fly.

It plunged into the ground between Gretti's feet, right between her sandals, where it vibrated with a *thwang.*

Then the queen said, "Fine. Happy now?"

"Happier, yes," Gretti said, faking calm. She yanked the arrow from the ground, flipped it in a smooth motion, and handed it back to Tamura, fletched end first. As the queen took it, she said easily, "You are correct. My conversations with other warriors are nearly constant. They see me as a representative of the previous regime."

"Which you are."

"In some ways, yes," Gretti said, looking up at the shivering leaves of the canopy overhead to settle herself. "Some warriors—many, to be honest—have tried to convince me that you need to be Challenged."

Tamura said, "And they want you to be my Challenger."

"Exactly."

The queen cocked her head. "What do you say in return?"

Grimly, Gretti said, "I tell them I do not believe any warrior alive could Challenge you and win."

Tamura nodded, her satisfaction plain.

Gretti went on, "I believed in Khara when she was queen, believed with my whole heart. And I still miss her. She and my sister Hana shaped who I am and who I still might become. I think of them both every day."

"Fools love the dead," said Tamura, annoyed. "I vanquished her. The queendom is mine by right. And you still wish she were queen instead of me?"

"That is not what I said," Gretti told her. "And it is not what I mean. The world has changed. Khara is not the queen, and if she were, I'm not sure she could be the queen Scorpica needs to survive this Drought. But I think maybe you can."

Tamura stared at her.

Gretti said, "And I think I can help."

For a long time Tamura was silent. The wind rustled the leaves. At last the queen said in a quiet voice, "Could you not have mentioned this before the Sun Rites?"

"Frankly," said Gretti, with the bitter satisfaction of one who had nothing to lose by telling the absolute truth, "I thought you might get yourself slain by one of the other queens. That would have solved the whole problem."

"Sad for you, then."

Gretti shrugged. "You know it's only because the queen of Paxim can't resist making a deal that you even survived, don't you? You posture too much. That scene in the grove could have ended in a dozen different disasters."

"My warriors respect me for my passion."

"Some do, yes. Others are worried it shows you are too hot-tempered to rule."

"Who thinks that? How many? Are they on the council?"

Gretti shook her head. "You're missing the point. A queen's job is not to root out and punish her enemies. It is to serve so wisely and so well that she has none."

"Like your beloved Khara?"

"Much like her, yes. And yet . . . not like her at all."

"You sound like a riddling Arcan," Tamura said in disgust. She lifted her gaze to look Gretti in the eye. "Be clear. Tell me how you can help me."

"It's the Drought that's changed everything. We need a ruthless queen, a fighter, to lead Scorpica through it. So I will swear not to Challenge you. If you agree, I will advise you, serve loyally on your council, stand beside you, as long as the Drought of Girls continues."

Tamura's face was serious, clearly considering. "And if it lasts until one of us dies?"

"Then my fealty is lifelong," said Gretti grimly. "But I look forward to the day when our agreement is void."

"Likewise," Tamura said.

"Swear on what matters most to you, then," said Gretti. "Swear on your mother's memory."

"If you knew me at all," said Tamura, almost smiling, "you would know the Scorpion comes first."

✦

For nearly six months, the air of Scorpica rang over and over with shouts of welcome. As much as Tamura hated to admit it, Gretti's advice was excellent. When Tamura called the council and presented her new adviser's plan—bring Scorpica's warriors home, but in a carefully planned, deliberate sequence with no public fanfare, so the other queendoms did not see the action as a threat—the council offered no objections.

"We have been cautious," Tamura informed her council. "And we had reason. But there is no longer plenty, and we must choose who gets what we have. It is time for us to close ranks."

Murmurs of approval rippled around the gathering. Tamura met Gretti's eyes. There was no smile on the woman's heart-shaped face, but she gave a short nod of satisfaction. Tamura wondered for the hundredth time whether she could truly trust Gretti. She had sworn to follow her counsel until the Drought of Girls was over, and who knew when that would be? Had she gotten in over her head, bound herself with a promise that could hamstring her just when she needed freedom most? Only time would tell.

But for now, she followed the plan as Gretti had suggested it. The only assigned warriors Tamura did not recall were those guarding the northern border. The Pale might not have been seen in hundreds of years, but just because none came today didn't mean none would come tomorrow. No one was willing to risk that.

So, called home, the warriors came. They returned from all corners of all queendoms, each in their turn. Dirty or clean, angry or relieved, graceful or brutish, they all came.

It was not their intent to start a war, the councillors told each other, but to stay out of any war others might start. Let the other queendoms declare war on one another, if it came to that. But any queendom that chose to fight could sacrifice their own citizenry, not Scorpica's.

It had not been Gretti's idea to call the warriors home, but the details of the plan were hers, including the requirement for every group to report intelligence as it returned. No warrior would be asked to betray the country she'd come to know, only to say what she'd seen and heard. It would be a moment in time, and Tamura and her advisers would know everything there was to know in that moment.

Paxim, reported the women who had been stationed there, was building an army. Notwithstanding their reputation as dealmakers and diplomats, the Paximites were training two forces: one to keep the peace at home, protecting trading posts and highways, and another to defend the homeland against any foreign invaders. Who these foreign invaders might be, relayed the Scorpicae who had lived there, no one said but everyone knew. It was the Arcans that Paxim feared most.

A strong anti-Arcan undercurrent was sweeping the country, from the Senate to the servants' quarters. It did not matter that Arca itself did not have any kind of military force. Its very nature was a threat. Rumors rippled through every part of Paxim, along every trade route, through every outpost and village: gods aside, who could have caused the Drought of Girls but some Arcan? Who else would have such a power? Few really understood that most Arcan gifts were modest, cooperative, meant by Velja—if one believed in Velja—to produce and reinforce community, not to give any woman or group of women power over others. Non-Arcans everywhere, on edge from the Drought, felt threatened by the mere existence of magical powers, never mind whether such powers had ever been or would ever be wielded against them.

As the warriors returned home to stay, the nation of Scorpica was transformed. Hundreds more warriors, edging past a thousand, had come to live where far fewer had lived before. Camps were far larger. More of everything was needed. Scorpica had never before hosted so many warriors at once, and the money from boys had dried up when the boys did, but nonetheless, none wanted. The land was generous, and they were more careful than ever to live lightly upon it. Tamura gave commands, based on guidance from Gretti, that kept their homeland from being overwhelmed. They were never to take more game from the forest than they needed to live. They were to use and reuse the same tents, the same leathers, the same weapons until such goods could not last another moment in service. Not every woman had a sword—they'd left their arms back in the nations that had once armed them—but Gretti's plans called for warrior smiths who would make enough swords for warriors to defend the home-land, and they were already hard at work.

But as Tamura watched the smiths laboring, she saw other pos-sibilities. Perhaps yet more swords would be needed. Armor, too, if it came to that. All this would take time. Preparation. Focus. But if she took Gretti's plans and added to them, could they not achieve more than safety? More than mere defense?

She looked out over the ocean of women and pictured them as a breaking wave on a foreign shore. *What if?* With patience and pas-sion and the blessings of the Scorpion, what if they could turn this Drought of Girls, the worst thing that had ever happened to their nation, into the best?

CHAPTER 25

BLOOD

Approaching Daybreak Palace, Arca
Mirriam

Now that the Sun Rites were over—and what strange, awful rites they'd been, this time—Mirriam simply could not wait to be home in Daybreak Palace. They were quickly out of Sestia, leaving its green, sheep-dotted pastures behind, but the trip across Paxim seemed three times as long as it ever had. Every night, every morning, she pictured herself hastening with quick footsteps over the palace's threshold, disappearing into the doorway, striding down the long halls, to find Ever waiting for her. Sometimes, in her imagination, she came upon him clothed, sometimes not. But in every imagining, he looked up at her and smiled. A warmth spread through her at the smile, its intimacy, its sly invitation. The smile was her world. There her imagination drew a curtain over the possibilities and brought the fantasy to a close. The maddening, tantalizing disobedience of her mind only made her more desperate to move the column more quickly toward home and make her fiction real.

She had been away from him for this long before, of course, five years ago. But five years ago, her return home had been nothing like this. She had moved along at a stately pace, barely even noticing the country roll by from the private luxury of her curtained wagon. If she'd had any eagerness then, it was only concern that Mirrida might lose control of Daybreak Palace in her absence, but this time, she barely gave Mirrida a second thought. All her thoughts were of her young husband. The man he was now was not the man he had been. Ever since she'd let him drink the life force of that girl two years ago, ever since they'd shared her energy, he'd been transformed.

The differences in his body were minor; it was how he used that body that had changed. How he carried himself. Confidence now showed itself in his every movement, not just during pleasures, though that was where his new attitude made quite the difference. She had enjoyed him before, but with the new life force inside him, she enjoyed him enjoying her, a whole new plane of lustful indulgence.

Her magic had never been any good at a distance, a secret she'd managed all these years to keep. She had no spies she could trust as runners to bring her news when she was away. Even as they crossed the border of Paxim into Arca at last, green hills giving way to golden sand, she knew no more of what was happening in Daybreak Palace than any villager in her bolt-hole. She could not bear it.

So she didn't. When night fell, she snuck away from her entourage—fools, not to protect her, even from herself—and entered the city the night before she was due to return.

On the way home, she had been toying with a dangerous magic, sending the spark of her essence outside the confines of her body. No one in the court had such an ability, and all the old legends' mentions of it were warnings: the ways the spark could be lost on the way back to its body were legion. But she was powerful and bored and she toyed with it, this intoxicating power, in case it might ever come in handy.

As she approached the palace from a distance, fairly bursting with eagerness to be back within its walls, she decided that sending her spark was a needless risk. She would go in conventionally but secretly, cloaked in two different, overlapping spells to hide her both from the eyes and the minds of any observers.

And so, unseen, Queen Mirriam of Arca, Well of All-Magic, Master of Sand, and Destroyer, simply walked through the dark doorway of Daybreak Palace the way she had in so many dreams.

There was something both delicious and unsettling about entering her palace this way. She had never come in before unannounced. Before there had always been courtiers waiting, servants with cool cloths in the summer and warm in winter, fanfare and expectation. Her Queensguard had always surrounded her at moments like this. Now they were back at the distant camp with the rest of her entourage, of course—oh, how she would upbraid them for letting her slip away—and she heard the sound of her own footsteps on the sandstone, shuffling and dry. A quick enchantment silenced the steps. Now to decide where to start.

The warm, kind face of Sobek flickered in her mind. Should she visit her first, see if those Seekers had brought back the new all-magic girl at last? No, that could wait. She dreamed so insistently, almost obsessively, of Ever. Let his rooms be her first destination. There would be time for other things later. After they got reacquainted.

She glided through the shadows, unnoticed, back to her own rooms and his. As silent as she was, as she drew near the doorway, the voices were impossible not to notice. She slowed down and hesitated. She would not have mistaken those two voices for any others in the world. Mirrida, her daughter, and Ever, her love.

Arguing. Not violently, not petulantly, but with some fundamental disagreement that radiated off both of them like heat. She paused outside the door. Even with the enchantments she had cast, a shiver of trepidation kept her from entering the room. Mirrida was so good at shields, and if she had shielded her mind—why would she, but what if?—she might see through the spells that kept Mirriam hidden from view. Better not to risk it.

"It's just one more time," Ever was saying, his anger a low smolder. "You did it before with no complaint. Every day, like it was nothing. And now you're pulling the rug out? I need this, Mirrida."

"Watch your tone," she said frostily, and Mirriam had a curious reaction. Part of her was fearful—what in the name of Velja could they be talking about? But that tone of voice, that regal distance, she recognized it. She'd taught her daughter that, without knowing until now that she'd learned. Maybe Mirrida did, somewhere deep down, have it in her to be queen. If she could be convinced to extend her life after all . . . but they were still talking, and she had to pay attention.

"I'm sorry," he said. "Of course. I don't mean to push. But if you don't, everything else will have been for nothing."

"I didn't shield your mind for fun," she said. "Or for you. I did it on principle. Because people have a right to think privately without her inside their heads."

"Which is still the case." His voice was smoother now, more ingratiating. He was just around the corner, Mirriam realized, so close. If she passed through the doorway, she could touch him in three strides. But her desire to touch him had gone cold like a coal doused in water. Now she was hungry not for him, but for facts, for knowledge.

"But where does it end, Ever? Once she's back, do I have to shield you from her every single day, until . . . when? Until one of you dies, or I do?"

Now she knew what they fought about, at least partly, and it was a stunning realization. Her daughter had been helping her husband hide his thoughts from her. For what purpose she didn't know, but she didn't need to. She had been betrayed. That was all that mattered. She almost strode into the room then, but Ever was still talking. She listened.

"No," he said. "Don't worry about that. It's almost over."

"What does that mean?"

"I'll only ask you once more, I swear. Shield me tomorrow."

Mirrida, her voice thick with suspicion, said, "What happens after tomorrow?"

"Nothing you need worry about."

"Tell me," Mirrida said. "I want to know."

It was time. Shedding her enchantments like a robe before the bath, Mirriam crossed through the doorway and entered the room.

They stood facing each other near the couch upon which Ever had so often reclined, her husband and her daughter, anger crackling in the air between them. The confidence of Ever's stolen life force still radiated from him like a glow, but there was something distorted about it now, something disturbing. Confidence had grown into entitlement, assurance into arrogance. She had not seen it clearly before she left, or perhaps it had grown, but there was no mistaking it now. Ever had come to think the world of himself, and it had led somewhere ugly.

"Shield me," he said to Mirrida, not a shout but a quiet, urgent command, as if keeping his voice low meant the crime was not a grave one, as if volume were the thing that would undo them.

But Mirrida had seen her mother, and her face crumpled. For a moment, her mother saw her as she'd been at five years old, the day Mirriam found her in the kitchens attempting to scale the shelves to reach for a forbidden sweet. But then she was an adult again, one who'd done wrong. Regret and resentment played across her face, then intense guilt, followed by the simmering of an anger she herself probably didn't fully understand.

"It's too late," Mirrida said sadly.

Starting at the unexpected sight of his wife and queen, Ever lifted his hand as if to slap her face. But it hung in the air, fingers spread, before he dropped it again. Then he edged one foot toward the doorway.

With a flick of her wrist, Mirriam slammed the door to the outside without touching it.

To Ever's credit, he seemed to recognize the futility of escape quickly. His handsome face went blank. He did not even scowl, only stood, and avoided meeting the queen's eyes.

Mirriam said to her daughter, "So he told you he wanted privacy in his thoughts. That was the only reason he gave when he asked you to shield him?"

"Yes."

"And you believed him?"

Mirrida faced her with more resolve than she'd seen in a long time, again with the regal air that impressed Mirriam even as it irritated her. "He's not the only one who asked. Many of the courtiers would rather not have you in their minds all the time. It's an invasion, Mother, a violation."

"It is my right as queen."

"There we disagree," Mirrida said.

Mirriam said, "But returning to this . . . issue. You have asked a question he refuses to answer. Do you want me to tell you what's in his mind? I don't think you'll like it."

"Pay her no attention," Ever said to Mirrida, a gleam of desperation entering his gaze, his facade of disinterest slipping. "She'll lie."

"Why would I lie?" Mirriam said. "I do many things. I hurt people. I kill them, if I have to. I do not pretend to be other than what I am. Mirrida, you are my daughter. You rarely like me and I doubt you love me, but I think you know you can trust me to be honest."

Mirrida's mouth was a tight, flat line. "Yes."

"Ever," said Mirriam, not gently, "why did you really ask Mirrida to shield you?"

Don't think it don't think it don't think it. He was trying his best to conceal his thoughts from her, but she dove into his mind with ease, curled imaginary fingers into its depths to scoop out the truth. What she found was shocking and ugly. But she had to face it, and so did the two other people in this room. She withdrew from his mind—it was a relief, to be out of it—and spoke the truth aloud.

"They would have killed me first," the queen said to her daughter in a tense, steady voice. "And you second."

"What?" asked Mirrida, clearly shocked.

Mirriam opened her mouth to tell her the rest—*you were next in line*—but something pressed against her back and she'd begun to fall . . . what was happening?

Pain ripped through her before she even realized that Ever had moved, that he had a dagger in his hand, that his hand was still wrapped around the hilt but the blade was nowhere to be seen because he'd sunk it into her body just below the shoulder and it burned oh Velja how it burned. She thought she had wrung the whole truth from his mind, but he had managed to hide this one part from her. It seemed now a very important part.

He managed to pull the dagger from her back as she fell. Now she was on the floor, him kneeling beside her. Faintly she could hear Mirrida screaming. The dagger came down again, this time in the soft flesh of her belly. Then up it flashed, rising and hovering in his white-knuckled hand, aimed for one more plunge toward her heart.

Her last chance to act. She took it.

Magic poured forth from her, seizing the blade, turning it in his hand. She was weak but she could manage, just barely, to draw power from elsewhere, using Ever's own life force to fuel the spell she needed to kill him.

When he lost control of the dagger, Ever cried out in rage, too late.

The blade leapt free and speared the hollow of his throat, a place she had pressed kiss after kiss into, a place she had loved, but now the place she buried his own blade to silence him forever.

Blood streamed down from the hole, running over his chest, soaking his tunic, as he fell. Then Ever's body slumped on the floor beside her own, that running blood oozing into the pattern of the colorful, elegant carpet, staining it deeper than any dye.

"Mother," Mirrida was saying urgently, her face close by now, though her voice sounded far off. "Mother."

Mirriam reached her hand up toward her daughter and splayed her fingers across the younger woman's neck. She was all instinct now, her reason fading.

A last thought: Could she?

She curled her fingers inward, gathered all her force. One chance. Her only way to live. She had to try.

✦

The servant who found the bodies raised the alarm.

Mirriam and Ever lay entwined in death, utterly still. On the richest carpet in Queen Mirriam's chamber, soaked and wrecked by blood, their bodies were draped over each other. What had happened seemed obvious, though not why. The violence had been swift and fatal. Ever's open eyes stared up at the ceiling, the hilt of the dagger protruding from the hollow of his throat like some odd, outsize ornament, a pendant without its chain. The queen's mouth hung open as if in shock. With her skin drained of color she looked like a god's statue, an image one might find on a temple altar, though what god was a matter of some dispute. To some, she looked like Rapture, to others, Fear.

The queen's long, cool neck, they noted with surprise, was bare.

No one alive had ever seen her without the snake necklace. The servant who discovered the bodies worried that he would be accused of stealing it, though only a fool would steal the most famous jewelry in the queendom, and an item of powerful, unknown magic to boot.

But it was found quickly, and in the most sensible place. The servants who woke Mirrida from her slumber to give her the news of her mother's murder saw it first. As the queen's daughter opened her eyes drowsily, her sleep-shift falling away from her shoulders and her dark hair tumbled in a cloud, a blue, glassy gleam could be seen around her neck. The snake necklace had found its new home.

The new queen dressed with quick but clumsy movements, as if her limbs would not quite obey her commands. This, the servants attributed to her fresh grief. She had gone to bed yesterday the queen's daughter and awoken today the queen. How disorienting it must be, how jarring. By afternoon she had determined a course of action and issued commands. Whatever her personal grief, the affairs of the court must come first. Actions had to be taken.

Servants gathered the courtiers in the queen's audience chamber, and they stood shifting, whispering, unsettled. Their gazes slid around the room, hovered and sought, looking for anyone who might know what any of this meant. They could not remain above the fray as they usually did; even the most jaded lost their breezy composure in the face of so much uncertainty, especially as their wait wore on.

What happened? they asked each other, over and over. The most intelligent ones, those who had been at the court the longest, asked the more unsettling question, *And what now?*

Then the new queen entered, flanked by the stone-faced Queensguard, and her footsteps were attended by whispers and gasps.

"Quiet," she said, and they obeyed.

The glistening glass snake around her neck was echoed in the glistening tears on her face, but her voice was firm and steady.

"I am sorry to deliver bad news," began the new queen. "I will not dress it up with pretty words. It saddens me to report that my mother and her husband are dead."

The courtiers stifled their gasps but their eyes went wide, searching each other's faces, then hers, for reassurance. They found none.

She went on. "Last night she slipped away from her Queens-guard—these women are not at fault, do not blame them—and arrived unexpectedly, which appears to have led to a confrontation. My understanding is that she found out Ever was a traitor."

This time any attempts to stifle gasps were unsuccessful.

As the new queen continued to speak, even through the haze of their own panic, courtiers began to notice that she was surprisingly controlled and poised, considering her newness to the role. She'd been tentative before, but no longer. Perhaps she would make a better queen than her mother, they thought now, the cloud beginning to lift.

"My mother's husband, Velja rest his blighted soul, was part of a ring of men who were planning to grab power from the rightful queen. Our Seekers are investigating. Offenders will be dealt with swiftly. We must cleanse our court of this rot."

The optimism of moments before quickly vanished. The powerful women of the key matriclans of the court looked around at each other, panic and doubt plain on their faces. They hoped their husbands wouldn't be implicated, but could they swear to their innocence? Did they know for sure their own mates—Duveen, Ijahn, Malloi—had not been desperate for power, hoping, plotting against their queen, their system of law, the women themselves?

As if by agreement, women began to step away from their husbands and toward each other, joining hands. Fingers stretched out for fingers, grasped, squeezed. Heads turned. Gazes met and slipped away. The shape of the crowd moved like an animal, reconstituting itself, nudging the men of the court forward whether or not they wanted to go. But it was not only the men who would be questioned. All minds would be opened in the search, all secrets revealed.

Among the movements were the swift, decisive steps of the palace guards, who moved in two solid wedges to block the exits of the audience chamber. They took up positions with their shields and swords and remained still, watching, until the proceedings were complete.

Once the guards were in place, the queen indicated the royal scribe, a mere girl named Beyda, who would record the names of the guilty and the innocent as they were determined. The girl did not look like she would relish the work.

It was a brutal afternoon in Daybreak Palace. Even those whose names were recorded in the list of innocents by the scribe did not leave completely unscathed. What they had seen would stay with them for years. While the Scorpica-born security forces were generally called into service on the rare occasions Arca needed executioners, today would be different. In this case, the queen insisted she would deliver the death blow herself. All the courtiers knew Mirrida had all-magic, but she had been hesitant about showing its extent. Now that she was queen, it seemed, things would be different.

"Because of your plot, betrayers, my mother is no longer here to punish your wrongdoing," the queen called out. "So it falls to me to avenge her."

When the first of the guilty was led forward to face the queen, she looked down at him, her expression thick with sorrow. She raised one hand, palm outward. The sentence was pronounced.

Then a barely visible ripple of force came through the air from the queen's flat palm, rocked the conspirator back, and burned off his head.

His shoulders gave one last shuddering twitch, a smoking hole between them, and then the body crumpled to the ground. The searing was so thorough that what was left of him did not bleed.

As they slumped to the tiles, the headless bodies of each of the guilty were left, not moved. They accumulated, heaped on each other, sprawled where they fell. When the final name on the list of guilty was called—the only woman discovered to be part of the plot, Tanaj of the Sukru matriclan—it was hard to find a place to put her feet. When her headless body fell, it made no noise, landing on the heap of bodies without touching the painted tile.

When the grim work was done, the queen gestured for the guards to move aside from the exits, and the doors were opened for all remaining to leave. Even then, weighed down by what they'd witnessed, they dragged their feet. It took a long time for the room to empty.

And when she settled down that night to sleep in her daughter's chamber, alive in her daughter's body, Mirriam breathed a heady mix of satisfaction, sorrow, anger, and gratification, but most of all, relief.

She had done the magic she intended to do.

It had been a frantic, mad attempt fueled by desperation, but it had succeeded, and now everything was different. Sending her spark out of her body was dangerous magic because the spark might not find its way back. Sending it out of her body into another body with no intention of retrieving it had turned out to be, if not easy, at least possible. The hard part had been finding the spark of her daughter in the body and pushing it out, placing it in the dying body as blood flowed out of it, making the trade complete. She knew it worked. She saw her daughter looking back at her out of what had been her own eyes moments before, the dying face contorted with surprise and helplessness, before the light went out.

Now Mirriam looked out from new eyes upon a new world. She would miss her daughter and her husband. They had been the only people she trusted, and she would not recover from how much they'd hurt her, how they'd violated that trust.

But at least their deaths had not been for naught. She had wiped the slate clean, settled her debts, carved out the rot from inside the walls of Daybreak Palace. It had been the only satisfying answer. It took a while for her to get used to being called by her daughter's name, but she did. That was what one learned, Mirri mused, being alive more than a century. One could get used to anything.

✦ CHAPTER 26 ✦

THE FESTIVAL

The All-Mother's Year 512

The city of Hayk, Paxim

Vish

The first day in years that Vishala dha Lulit truly relaxed—truly felt herself free from any trace of the care and worry that had weighed so heavily on her shoulders since she'd fled Scorpica five long years earlier—was the day the world came apart under her feet once more.

She had never been to the city of Hayk, never even heard of it, not in all her wanderings. She was given to understand that on any other day of the year, it looked like any other city. Buildings and alleys, yards and animals, markets and ditches, wagons and crowds. It was only once a year in late springtime, for the Festival of Dolomi, that it transformed.

The village square was a sea of faces, none of which could fully be seen: all were obscured by masks, giving the entire scene an otherworldly, dreamlike feel. The array was dizzying. Feathered eye masks and glistening gilt half masks, masks that made their wearers look like mountain lions or rams. Tragic, comic, elegant, grotesque.

Vish was stunned by wonderment as she looked out on this crowd, so alien but so warm, all these strangers together for the single purpose of celebrating the festival of the Bandit God. Rumors of tension between the queendoms grew worse every year—students had been called home from the Bastion, Scorpican warriors withdrawn from their assignments—but such matters seemed far off on a day like today. Even the newly trained Paximite enforcers she spotted at the edge of the crowd, keeping an eye on the revelers, seemed amiable.

All around her, her family of Rovers hid in plain sight among the law-abiding people of Hayk. In the masked crowd they did not stand out; no one knew, or even wondered, who they were or why they were here.

The twins dressed differently to de-emphasize their sameness, a trick they often took to in cities to make them less memorable. Elechus's crimson mask was elegant and eye-catching, a face-covering *bauta* covered with red rose petals so fresh their heady scent still lingered; Luben wore a sort of hood low over his eyes, which made it hard for him to see others but even harder for them to get a good look at him.

Vish's own mask was the beaked half-mask shape known as a *pantalo*, heavily feathered in black and tan, giving her the look of a patient hawk. She wore it with a shapeless robe the color of autumn ryegrass. More than once she felt Fasiq's fingers graze tenderly down her back, the closeness of the crowd an excuse to touch where everyone and no one could see them.

Because in this crowd, for once, Fasiq did not stand out. Her brilliant disguise made her look like a woman sitting upon a man's shoulders. The costume hid both her scar and her size, rendering her unrecognizable, with the added bonus of making people smile. Even Eminel laughed when she saw it, though she had smiled rarely and laughed less in the six months since her mother's death. Vish herself had grown more serious alongside her, thinking of Ama every time she looked at Eminel, wondering if Ama too seemed to carry a weight in her chest that drew her down, every moment, every step. Vish realized she might never know, which was itself a sadness.

Poor, motherless Eminel. She had been so quiet these past months, Vish suspected Fasiq had steered them to the festival solely to cheer up the girl. At least for now, it seemed to be working. The girl was in love with the ornate mask Fasiq had given her, a gilt affair of swirling, fragile scrollwork, almost certainly too valuable an item to wear in this crowd. Everywhere Eminel went, Hermei was only steps away, wearing a plain black domino. Practically invisible, he was well positioned to protect both mask and girl.

All the Rovers kept Eminel well in sight, though the immediate danger seemed slim. In this past year, approaching ten years of age, she'd shot up and filled out, losing some of the childlike softness in her limbs and cheeks. With the mask on, no one could tell how young she was; she was among the shorter figures in the crowd but blended in with them well enough. Perhaps, thought Vish, they could all relax a little. It would do them good.

Relax they did. When the players set to their instruments and the music rang through the village square, Luben beckoned to Eminel and swept the girl up in a Paximite reel. Elechus gallantly extended his hand to Vish, and after a nod and a sly smile exchanged with the disguised Fasiq, she let him sweep her into the dance as well. He was a surprisingly competent partner, with an innate sense of musicality she would not have suspected. If her old leg injury hampered her attempts at grace, he overlooked any awkwardness with good cheer.

On a whim, she said, "Tell me your story."

With characteristic coyness, Elechus answered, "Story? Once upon a time, a boy was born, and then another boy right after."

"I know how twins work," she said with a laugh. They pivoted in time with the music, the heady scent of roses following everywhere they went. "But where were you born?"

"You should not ask a question you are not willing to answer."

"Yet I just did," she said.

From this close, even with his face mostly covered, she could easily read the expression in his eyes, and she saw him choose not to spoil the lighthearted mood. "We were raised, but not born, here in Paxim. Our parents bought us from the warriors."

A man over her left shoulder spun close, then away again, shadows and light crossing one another. She shifted and settled back into the rhythm. "When did they tell you?"

"We were ten," he said with a wry smile. "We should have known sooner. We fought constantly; more than once they poured water on us like we were dogs tangling in the street. Perhaps we banged our heads a few too many times doing so. You may have noticed, we aren't the sharpest arrows in the quiver."

"You're smart enough," she said.

His steps were as quick as ever, but his eyes looked away. "We get by. Hard not to feel slow sometimes when you've got deuced clever thieves and giants ordering you about."

She felt he'd honored her with a confidence. As they wove in and out of the crowd, among the dancing couples, she searched for the right response. "We each have our strengths."

"Yes," he laughed, relaxing again. "We appreciate the lessons, you know. You make us better."

"Credit yourselves, not me. You've worked hard."

The song ended, the crowd applauding, and rowdy dancers began calling out to the musicians for their favorites.

Suddenly parched, Vish said, "I'll get us something to drink."

Elechus nodded, turning to scan the crowd for his twin and Eminel as she went.

She headed for the side of the square where wine barrels were stacked high, a wall of them so solid it echoed the Bastion. The crowd there was thick and boisterous. As she neared, a man in a *bauta* mask the color of spring leaves was pouring from a barrel on a tap-stand, aiming its contents into sloshing cups, cupped hands, and in one case, directly into a reveler's mouth.

That barrel ran dry, to the loud displeasure of the drinkers. The man in the green *bauta* gestured at a nearby helper, thick-armed and fox-masked, to trade the empty barrel for a full one. They rolled one forward that had already been pulled down from the impressive wall. Meanwhile, the man swept up his spike and mallet and shouted good-naturedly for some elbow room. Vish hung back. No need to be crushed by her fellow revelers, who jostled impatiently as the fox-masked figure levered the full barrel into place.

Then, faint among the smells of wine and sweat and roses in sunlight, Vish thought she caught the scent of burning.

She scanned the crowd, all her senses on high alert now, but saw nothing. Where were the Rovers? The twins she spotted first, chatting amiably with strangers. She caught the top half of Fasiq's costume far off, high above the other heads and shoulders, painted smile bobbing. The others were too short to make out in the mass of revelers, which had grown thick. Should she search for them, or for the source of the burning smell? She could still detect it, no stronger but no weaker, maddeningly faint.

Out of the corner of her eye she caught a swinging motion as the man in the leaf-green mask moved to hammer his spike into the new barrel, and as he struck it, it burst into flame.

A licking tongue of fire erupted all around the man, clearly not planned; the green mask was gone, the man had fallen, the fire was spreading. Stacked barrels fell and rolled, a few breaking open to spill wine harmlessly onto the ground, but at least half a dozen exploded, as the tapped one had, into fountains and rivers of fire.

People who had been dancing, laughing, drinking only a minute before were running now, panicked, fire climbing their robes as they searched for a safe direction to flee and guessed wrong.

Then, something stranger: a wind swept down, unnatural, spreading the flame. Vish gasped at its force but could not figure out its source or direction.

Smoke roiled the world, the blue sky gray. Nothing felt real. Not with masked figures running hard, toward or away from the danger, no one knowing which was which. Some people reached up to rip off their masks. These seemed the most unreal of all, the bare faces. Like wild creatures with even wilder creatures underneath.

Eminel? Where was Eminel? That was all that mattered. Fasiq could take care of herself, and she had been nowhere near the flame. The girl was another matter.

Vish caught the wink of light on gold and pushed in that direction as hard as she could.

Yes. It was Eminel's mask. She struggled toward it, shoving aside anyone in her way. The girl was too small in the vast crowd, shoulders of dozens jostling her, threatening to crush her from every direction.

Wind swept down and raised a cloud of dust all around her, swirling with the smoke, burning her eyes. No natural wind had ever moved like this. It was too precise, too punishing. Was an air magician working with whoever had booby-trapped the barrels, or was it a coincidence? She wasn't sure it mattered, at least not right now. Right now, they needed to run.

Wind swept toward her from the other direction—the direction of the girl—and parted the crowd between.

"Help!" cried Eminel, her voice shrieking above both the human din and the unnatural wind.

Vish rushed into the gap as fast as her imperfect legs would carry her. She grabbed the girl's hand. Then they ran as if Death itself were on their heels. Perhaps He was.

✦

Leaving the square behind, Vish fled the pandemonium, heading for the safest, quietest place she could find. Around the corner, away from the square, down a narrow alleyway thronged with noise and confusion. Running until the crowd thinned out, until they'd gotten far enough away that people stood talking without desperation, without terror.

There. She saw it. A temple to the Bandit God.

She recognized the shape and type of the temple right away; they'd been to dozens of them, all across Paxim, because of the giant. Fasiq worshipped the Bandit God, the god of thieves, with more dedication and devotion than the Xaras in Sestia worshipped the God of Plenty. She made offerings wherever they went, giving away a percentage of their take so large it made the other bandits grumble. No one was grumbling now. In the current situation, to the Shade, this haven felt like a literal godsend.

Temples on the road were generally unguarded, but in cities it could go either way. A thick-handled pike lay in the dirt against the side of the building, hard to spot among all the frippery and glitter, as if a guard had dropped the weapon and run in haste either toward or away from the pandemonium.

She ducked through the low doorway and headed for the door in the floor she knew was behind the altar. Knowledge was power. She whispered to Eminel, *Quiet now*, and the girl made a soft noise of assent.

The door to the hiding place behind the altar was already open. Vish did not care why.

She tucked the girl into the groove, whispering to her the impor-tance of staying quiet, and closed the door over her. There were slats enough in the door to let the girl breathe. There always were, in a Bandit God's hiding place.

That done, she went outside to stand guard at the door of the temple, trying to ignore the insistent pain flaring up in her old leg wound. Pain was temporary. She could have jammed herself into that small space with Eminel, hid them both, but her conscience wouldn't let her. If she were slain in this madness—which she doubted would happen, but just in case—the girl would be safe, and that was the only important thing. She had promised Jehenit. The death of the person who charged her did not remove the charge.

She should not look like a reveler, she realized as she took up her position outside. She removed her mask. Her robe had no pockets large enough to keep it, so she tossed the beaked, feathered *pantalo* through the doorway into the temple's darkened interior. If anyone asked her who she was and why she was there, she would have to lie. Subterfuge was not her strength. She had been so honest in the life she'd lived before. She was always having to learn new skills in this one.

Hefting the heavy pike, she let out a long, bracing breath. She always felt better with a weapon. This was a good one, too, its sharp iron head bound securely to the thick oaken staff. It was hers now, and it completed the illusion. She was pretending to guard this place. This would make the pretense real.

And just in time, as a tall woman in a dark cloak strode down the alleyway directly toward the temple, her brows drawn down in concentration, so focused on the temple itself that she did not seem to notice Vish standing guard.

Only when the long shaft of the pike lowered to block the door-way in front of her did the cloaked woman have no choice but to stop.

Had she kept walking, the pike would have folded her in half along the ribs.

Vish said, "No, ma'am. There's nothing in there to see."

"Isn't there?" The woman cocked her head, her concentration now on Vish. Her oval face was classically lovely, but everything about her was somehow dulled. Her eyes did not sparkle and her black hair did not shine. Her dark cloak draped loosely over her indistinct form. In a way, everything about her was so calculated to blend in that it made her stand out. In a mild voice, as undistinguished as her appearance, she said, "I simply want to make a sacrifice to the god."

Vish did not drop her guard, nor her weapon. "In the midst of all this?"

"Is there a better time to pray than in disaster?"

"Surely some other god would be better able to help you than the god of thieves."

Her voice still remarkably free of any affect, the dulled woman said, "I have stolen and regretted it. Now I want to make my atonement."

"Again—how could this be the best time?"

"Now is when I am here. This day, this hour. And what business is it of yours?"

"I am the guard here," lied Vish.

The woman laid two fingers on the shaft of the pike and pushed down gently until its point touched the dirt, then said, "So let me see what it is you are guarding."

Vish calculated. If the woman was this insistent, there would be a reckoning, and better that it should not happen in the street where anyone could see. She let the woman shoulder past her into the temple. A moment later, she followed.

As the two of them entered the temple's confines, she breathed a sigh of relief. The girl was invisible, still tucked away in the hole beneath the floor. How many treasures had it hidden over the years? Many, she guessed, but none quite so valuable.

In the half dark of the temple, it was hard to see exactly what the woman was doing, but the way she moved only made Vish more wary. Most of the tall figure's steps were like a dancer's, graceful and smooth, but every once in a while there was an occasional, sudden hesitation, then a turn. Almost as if she moved in thrall to something invisible, a guiding influence that told her where to go.

The woman approached the altar. She stood in front of it with a curious expression, cocking her head again. She was only steps from finding Eminel. Vish could wait no longer.

Abandoning her pretense, Vish said, "I will make this as painless as I can."

Without turning, the cloaked woman said, "Oh, there will be pain."

A mighty wind rose up inside the temple, lifting Vish into the air and slamming her against a highly decorated wall. A shower of pottery shards fell like rain behind her body and she plunged down with them, thudding on the ground.

Wind whipped around the inside of the temple, buffeting the decorations, shaking them loose. The magician advanced, pressing her enemy toward the far corner of the room, the wind she created shoving her and holding her against the wall. Vish could feel countless sharp edges pressing into her back. If she moved, or if the magician moved her, they would cut.

The woman's oval face was curious now, watching her struggle. But the wind she had raised had loosened so many of the small decorations that it was hard to see—ribbons and beads and coppers flying through the air—and the very confines of the temple that had made it easy for the wind magician to buffet her opponent now turned against her. Vish moved her arm and curled her fingers against the wall, scraping whatever she could find there—glass beads, it felt like?—and tossed the handful of tiny, hard shapes straight at the Arcan's face.

For a moment, when it counted, she was stronger than the wind.

The Arcan raised a hand to clear the spray from her eyes, wincing as the scatter of beads struck. In the moment when she was distracted, the warrior pushed off from the wall with her feet, pushed hard, flew. She launched herself and her weapon straight at the distracted Arcan. Her aim had to be true. There would be no second chance.

The pike pushed the woman backward several feet and knocked her to the ground, sliding in through her belly with no resistance. Vish felt the iron tip thud against the dirt floor, stop hard, leaving her arm trembling. She did not let go.

The wind rose, swirled even harder, slammed every surface, but Vish was crouched low over the fallen woman with the pike in her stomach, and she would not be moved.

The woman's eyes went wide. Her hands gripped the thick shaft of the weapon that had entered her in the soft place under her ribs. To her credit, she did not try to move it.

Vish said, "You don't think I recognize a Seeker when I see one?"

The Seeker shifted her gaze upward from the weapon to the woman who wielded it and said, nearly spitting the words, "As I recognize a killer and a thief."

"I am no thief," Vish answered her with mild indignation.

"We all. Steal something."

"You've stolen trouble, it seems," Vish said wryly.

"I came where I. Was sent."

The Seeker's words became more labored as her body went into shock. Judging by her pallor, Vish expected she had few, or maybe no, words left to say. The wind was subsiding now as the woman's energy drained. It faded to a breeze, a murmur, and disturbed nothing more.

The air stilled. Vish could not see the door from this side of the altar, but it seemed the girl was being smart, staying hidden. Good. Once this intruder was dealt with, they would move together to a new place of safety.

Still keeping one hand on the shaft of the pike, Vish bent over and pulled on the black leather cord around the Seeker's neck, then drew out the small glass vial of sand at the end of it, wrapping her hand around its double-teardrop shape. She knew what it was and she knew what it did. She also knew the *psama* would do her no good; she had not been born with the magic to use it. But she could at least take it away from the Seeker so *she* could not use it. That was important.

She turned her attention back to the Seeker. "Well, I'm sorry you haven't found what you're looking for."

The woman just glared. Her eyes rolled back, then toward Vish again, fighting to hold her gaze.

When she looked away, in the dark of the temple, Vish was starting to see things. Shadows that seemed to move even though her logical mind insisted they hadn't. Shapes that slunk around the borders of the room. Perhaps it was an aftereffect from everything flying through the air, from breathing the awful dust from the earlier chaos followed by scattered debris stripped from the temple's walls. It was a good reminder not to linger.

She turned back to the Seeker, whose face had gone waxen. "When you die, the Eternal Scorpion will drink your blood, and it will strengthen her. I know that doesn't mean much to you, but it does to me. You have my thanks."

The Seeker did not meet her eyes this time, her attention fixed on the weapon. The wound bled little, plugged up by the thick handle of the pike, but blood was now leaking from the corner of the magician's mouth. She mustered the strength to speak again, for what seemed like it might be the last time. "You know. So much. Scorpican. I am surprised. There is one thing. You seem not. To know."

"Oh?"

"We work. In pairs," said the woman, and gave a bloody, ugly laugh.

Knowledge dawned on Vish and it was a miserable, wretched dawn. She should have known. She should have remembered. She'd been distracted by the wind, the fight. She should have kept her eye on the door in the floor. Even still crouched here over the dying Arcan, even before she rose to force herself to look at the other side of the altar, she knew what she would find there. She knew the door would be open. She knew the hiding place would be empty. Eminel, her charge, would be gone.

And she was.

Jehenit had given her a sacred charge and she had not kept her end of the bargain. She had let the girl be stolen away. Once, her best friend in the world had given her a similar charge to protect her daughter, Amankha, and she was no longer sure whether she'd done right by her. This time there was no question. She had failed.

And what about Fasiq? There, yes, a question. Did Fasiq love her enough to forgive such an error? It was too awful to contemplate. She forced herself to contemplate it. If their positions had been reversed, she was not sure her heart was strong enough to forgive. The giant had not been born a warrior, but she had a warrior's heart: fierce and loyal, hard as iron when needed, burning day-bright like a firebrand until it burned itself out. The giant would understand what it meant that she had failed, how terrible that was, how final.

She let herself hope for a moment. Perhaps if she went back to Fasiq and threw herself on her lover's mercy, begged her for absolution, perhaps Fasiq would grant it. She never doubted the giant loved her. She knew her to the core. She had basked in her scarred lover's tender, unguarded gaze, treasured her secrets, savored the other woman's cries of passion as she yielded herself up helplessly to pleasure, to slick fingers, a nimble tongue. Slack in each other's arms afterward, spent and sleepy, they traded whispered endearments, lips against ears, breath warm on skin. There was so much between them. But Vish knew she could not accept Fasiq's love after this failure, no matter how desperately she wanted to. She could not accept forgiveness when she could not forgive herself.

The realization was a physical pain in her chest, a sharp ache, like a muscle stretched too far, too fast: the most loving thing she could do for Fasiq now was not to put her to the test.

It was Fasiq who had named her the Shade. She would be the Shade no longer. She would have to let go of the woman who loved her, of the Rovers who had become like a family to her, of the name they had known her by. Let go of all of it. Go far from them, far from here.

She heard her own voice, hoarse and failing, and the words sounded hollow, but she had to say them. One last thing to do before she'd leave.

"The Scorpion drinks the blood of the defeated," said Vishala dha Lulit, standing over the Seeker's limp body. "The fight is done."

She yanked out the pike.

CHAPTER 27

RESCUED

Leaving Paxim for Arca
Eminel

In the mad, fast moment, Eminel mistook her abductor for a friend. As she'd hunched in the space behind the Bandit God's altar, the terrifying wind whistling above her, violence crashing and thudding all around, the door in the floor opened. A woman's hand appeared. The woman extending the hand wore the Shade's feathered mask. Eminel never would have followed her otherwise. In the thick fog of the unknown, she'd thought she was reaching out for safety.

Then, as they fled the scene of the disaster, Eminel had staggered behind the mask-wearing woman at a brisk pace, following blindly. It had not seemed so odd that the Shade said nothing; the Shade often went entire days without speaking. That was one of the reasons she and Fasiq were so well suited. The loquacious giant talked enough for both of them.

By the time she realized the woman who was leading her by the hand into the growing darkness wasn't the Shade at all, wasn't taking her back to safety to meet the twins and the rest of their companions, it was too late. There was no way to know how far they'd gone or where they were going.

At the first moment they faced each other, on the outskirts of Hayk, the woman wordlessly knotted a rope tight around Eminel's wrists. There was no emotion on the face of her captor, even as she pulled her bonds so tight it hurt. When the stranger drew out a long stretch of the rope between the two of them, then tugged hard to show the girl how she would lead her forward like a pack animal, despair hit Eminel in a wave. She struggled to keep from drowning. She had never let her emotions run away with her, Eminel reminded herself, and she would not start now. She had still not cried over losing Jehenit, though she believed it had been half a year since her death. The passage of time was hard to track with any certainty. And now this. A kind of numbness reached through her, tingling into her extremities. She told herself what she always told herself in these moments: *simply accept, do not try to understand.*

It almost felt, somehow, like she deserved it. She'd been running and hiding for years now, dodging a fate she did not in the least understand. It was all her fault. Her mother had died from mysterious, untraceable magic; that was likely her fault as well. Now to be taken from the only family she knew, dragged across the open road to an unknown destination, that seemed of a piece with everything that had happened so far.

As the sun set and the wrecked festival town disappeared behind them, she'd opened her mouth to protest a dozen times, but never made a sound. Any question, any complaint, died on her lips before she made it. What could she say? *Return me to my family?* They weren't really her family, as much as they'd felt like one; they had no blood relationship to her or the dead mother who'd foisted her on them. *Where are you taking me?* If the woman had wanted her to know, she would have said so already. In all her ten years, Eminel had been watchful, thoughtful, always sure to consider before she acted.

She would be no different today, just because everything she'd known in the world was lost to her. Again.

"You're good and quiet," the woman said, stopping in the shade of a tree near a river to fill her waterskin. Her dark braid swung as she moved. She removed the robe she'd worn over her tunic and leggings, folded it into her pack, shrugged back into the pack's straps, all with effortless grace. "I'll give you that."

Eminel stared at her blankly. If only she had real power, now would be the time to unleash its force. Her mother had said, *You must do all that you can not to use it.* Her mother had called it *your curse.* But Hermei had told her it could be something completely different, something almost beyond imagining. In one sense, the message was the same—she was not to even try using it—but there was something potent, almost intoxicating, about the idea that she might be secretly powerful enough to fear.

And her abductor, she finally realized in this moment, was a magician. As the woman threw back her head to drink, Eminel could see the *psama* swinging in the deep V of her tunic. The hourglass of sand dangled from a black leather thong, glimmered as it caught the dying rays of the day's sun. Whoever this woman was, she had powers of some kind. So what did she want with Eminel? Did she know what Eminel's power really was? Would she tell her if she asked?

"Velja's teeth, stop gawking," the magician said, annoyance finally creasing her unnaturally steady brow.

Eminel forced herself to look away, but found she could not keep her eyes from returning to the stranger, who let out an exasperated sigh.

"Fine. Stare. But stay quiet," said the magician, starting again, tugging on Eminel's rope so the girl was forced to stumble after her. "I have to deliver you. I don't have to deliver you with a tongue in your head. See how much good your power will do you that way."

My power? thought Eminel. *My curse, you mean.*

"Whatever you call it," said the woman.

Stunned, Eminel couldn't contain her reaction, even though it was a silent one. *You can hear my thoughts?*

"What kind of Seeker would I be if I couldn't?"

I didn't know you were a Seeker.

As pleasantly calm as her face was, the Seeker's voice was the opposite: thick with emotion, angry, snide. "What you don't know, little girl, could fill a thousand of the Bastion's books."

I know you must not be able to speak into my mind.

"What makes you say that?"

You wouldn't bother speaking out loud if you could.

"*Igni morami,*" spat the Seeker. "Just because a woman can do something with magic doesn't mean she won't do it without. You think everyone goes around just spending their magic freely, slinging it around like a knapsack? For what? For *fun*?"

Eminel was suitably chastened. *I see.*

"Well, I suppose then we're getting somewhere."

So where are you taking me?

"Daybreak Palace," said the Seeker.

Eminel planted her feet so hard that the rope grew taut between them, stopping the Seeker short. She lowered her brow, turned back to Eminel, and gave the rope a sharp, low jerk that yanked the girl clear off her feet, burning her wrists as she fell.

"Don't try that again, please," the Seeker said. It was the first time she had said *please* in Eminel's hearing. The word sounded bitter, almost nasty, on her lips.

Face in the dirt, Eminel thought all the words her mother had ever warned her not to say, all the creative epithets she'd heard from Fasiq's crooked, colorful lips. *Pust. Cock-for-brains. Fig-face. Kafal. Knob-nose.*

"Call me whatever you like," the Seeker told her, her voice verging again on a snarl, "but do it walking."

And so Eminel set one foot in front of the other, following along as she had done before, biting back her questions. She knew more now, but knowledge had not improved her situation. Perhaps she would have been better off, she told herself grimly, not knowing.

✦

It had been years since Eminel had seen Arca, but when she did, she recognized it in an instant.

Where they crossed, the border was not marked in any clear way; the road was more or less the same on both sides. They walked a bumpy road in the scrub, the sun shining above them, both on the Paxim side of the invisible border and the Arcan side.

But when they crossed over, two things happened.

Eminel heard the Seeker let out a sigh, almost imperceptible. And she herself felt something click into place.

It was nearly impossible to describe, this feeling. Maybe it was less of a click. More of a surge. A shimmer. Was this her curse returning as she entered her homeland? Was this what her mother had whisked her away from, all those years before? Well, she couldn't run now, not tethered to this stone-faced Seeker, whose name she still did not know.

As they journeyed deeper into Arca, the sparse vegetation became even more rare, the scrub dotting the landscape less and less often. The road under Eminel's feet became visibly sandy. When she first realized it was shifting sand she felt under her feet, another feeling overwhelmed her, a knot from the past coming loose. She nearly cried.

What came next was an overwhelming fear. The shock of it coursed through her veins, so harsh and cold it made her want to cry out. Then she realized with a start what was so strange about the fear.

It wasn't hers.

The fear radiated from the Seeker. Along with it were words. The woman's own private thoughts, in words Eminel could hear as clearly as any spoken, the same way the Seeker must have heard Eminel's thoughts before. Never meant to be out in the open at all, and yet, here they were.

Velja preserve me, the Seeker thought, her fear pulsing in her throat. *This girl's all-magic. It's—so strong. Too strong. If she had any idea, she'd choke me with that rope in a heartbeat. Better stay out of her mind. Safer that way.*

Eminel plodded along behind the Seeker, afraid to breathe wrong, afraid to move wrong, afraid to give anything away. Blessedly, the Seeker simply continued to walk forward. Both of them walked as if they were calm and steady. Ironic that Eminel wasn't sure which of them was the more terrified.

The queen didn't warn me, the Seeker thought. *I wonder if she even knows.*

Fear rippled between them, magnifying, skipping and swooping, until Eminel thought she would faint from it. *Did my mother know how strong my all-magic is? Is that why we were hiding all those years? Why didn't she tell me?*

Eminel couldn't possibly act on the Seeker's fears; she was too busy with her own swirling thoughts, struggling to make sense of any of this. Whatever her powers, whatever her mother's reasons for hiding them from her, Eminel couldn't let the Seeker drag her to Daybreak Palace. No one returned from there. Everyone knew it. Was that why Jehenit had hidden her true nature from her? Had she feared losing Eminel to Daybreak Palace so much that she would rather keep her daughter leashed and ignorant than take the chance?

Even so, thought Eminel, competing ideas fighting toward the forefront of her reeling, dizzied mind: the future her mother feared was not the only future that might be. She'd thought herself an incompetent healer, a drain on her mother's goodwill, a disappointment. But what was she really? A girl doomed to stumble and fall under the burden of a power she didn't understand, or a girl blessed with magic so rare and wild, so immense, it might carry her all the way to the throne?

The strength of an all-magic girl's gifts wrote her fate, and Eminel knew the extremes, thanks to Hermei's explanations that night at the inn. At worst she might die a gruesome, quick death in the trials, crushed or ripped open or burned alive by her own enchantments. But on the other end of the scale, oh, what might await. She might rise to rule the entire nation. As a practical matter, thought Eminel, she was one of the youngest Arcans left. No one knew when girls might be born again. If the queen needed a successor, and she would eventually, wouldn't it be wise to find the youngest one possible? And why shouldn't that be Eminel?

The farther they walked into Arca, the more her confidence grew. The Seeker eventually stopped panicking, her thoughts dropping from a shout to a whisper and then fading out completely. But those early, overheard thoughts had already told Eminel everything she needed to know: the Seeker would be helpless against the all-magic that Eminel had, if only Eminel could figure out how to use it.

Unfortunately, she had no idea.

The landscape grew more barren, sandier, as they walked on. There was no more green to see. Eminel's mouth was dry and even her skin felt different in the harsh light of the unforgiving, untempered sun. She had been too long in Paxim. Arca felt otherworldly to her now, when it had once been home.

She thought she might try to act when they settled down for the night, when the Seeker would be most vulnerable. But it was only late afternoon, the sun still fully present in the sky, when she heard the Seeker's breath catch. She focused all her attention on the back of the Seeker's skull and was shocked to realize that she could make herself hear the woman's thoughts by choice.

Finally, the woman thought. *An hour or so to the palace. We'll be able to see it over this next hill. Then I'll hand off this tinder, get my reward, and be shut of her for eternity. Velja be praised.*

Hearing this, Eminel's fear reached a fever pitch, spreading to every corner of her being in an instant.

Everyone she'd loved, every home she'd known, was gone. It was barely possible that riches untold awaited her at Daybreak Palace; it was like a joke to hope. Far more likely those sandstone spires meant her death. She'd lost so much. She was about to lose everything she had left. She was sick of being powerless, tossed around, a burden.

Her sadness and anger burst forth, impossible to contain.

Blue light rippled out from her like cloth, sheets of it, yards of it, spilling out in every direction, and it raced across the landscape, burning.

The Seeker went up in orange flame, so quickly the scream died on her lips even as she drew breath to fuel it. Her form simply erupted in fire and consumed itself, leaving only ash, which the swirling air quickly scattered.

As soon as the rope dropped away, singed into nothingness, Eminel turned and fled back toward Paxim. She did not understand who had killed the Seeker or why, but there was no point in hanging around so that same unknown force could slay her in turn. She did not see the figure in the shadows nearby, watching with hungry eyes and a delighted smile. She had no way of knowing she herself was capable of such destruction. That she had, in fact, wreaked it all with her own, now unfettered, all-magic power.

What Eminel left behind, she never knew or saw; she was gone before it cooled. The next day, and all the days after, others would see it, but they would not understand. They did not know why the marks started where they did, in a valley of no particular import, and wiped away the sand that had been there for a league in every direction.

Eminel ran away from what she'd done, not even knowing she'd done it, leaving a lake of glass—gleaming, flawless—in her wake.

✦ CHAPTER 28 ✦

TRAINING

Near the Arcan border with Paxim
Sessadon, Eminel

Hair in wet tangles like seaweed. Slow pulse, faint breath. No sign of her potential on the outside, but within, a thrumming in her blood, all-magic swirling in her veins, lying in wait to howl, to thunder, to roar.

In a way, thought Sessadon, looking at Eminel was like looking at a memory of herself. Her form limp and settled in sleep, the girl looked like Sessadon herself must have looked when she washed up on the shore of the quartz island, hundreds of years before.

After she slew the Seeker, Eminel had simply run, blind with desperate uncertainty, taking wrong turn after wrong turn until she stumbled onto the shore of the Mockingwater and there was nowhere else to run. Much farther into the water and she would have drowned herself, a ridiculous end for an all-magic girl with the world in the palm of her hand. Had she planned to put out her own light? Had she feared the fire so much she thought only to extinguish it, even though it had not touched her? But she had dropped onto the flat, wet sand at the edge of the water just as the tide went out. She was safe from the lapping tongue of the Mockingwater, though help-less in her unconsciousness if any other dangers came.

As Eminel slept, exhausted, the sorcerer could truly take a good, long look at the girl she had waited so long to meet. In a sense, every-thing she'd done since awaking on that lonely island was all for her, all because of her. Eminel would grow mighty like an oak from an acorn, and now, here was that acorn of a girl. The family resemblance was there, carried through generations upon generations. Sessadon thought she recognized her sister's proud, straight nose, their moth-er's blunt-tipped fingers. The large, watchful eyes, she did not know where those came from. Some other branch of the family tree. Her body looked strong enough: good thick legs, broad shoulders. This was the girl she had waited for. Now she was finally here.

When Eminel's eyes opened, she looked around in alarm, but she did not scream or run. She took her time examining the stranger who knelt in the wet sand beside her. Sessadon had done nothing to her mind, not since she'd planted one precise, powerful vision in the girl's head shortly after her mother's death to encourage her to leave those bandits behind. Since then, she'd refrained from guiding the girl's course. She wanted to try letting Eminel make her own decisions. It would be better for both of them.

"Who are you?" Eminel asked, with more calm than Sessadon would have expected. "A Seeker?"

"No. No, not at all. A friend."

"I don't—have friends," the girl said haltingly, and though Ses-sadon was not inside her mind, it was obvious how she wanted to complete that sentence. *Anymore.*

"Are you all right? Hurt anywhere? Do you remember how you came here?"

"There was—I saw—" She searched for the words. "Someone set the world on fire. It might—it might have been me."

"It might have been," Sessadon confirmed, speaking quietly so as not to scare the girl. Eminel's energy was like a colt's: skittish, fragile. But the sorcerer could feel Eminel's simmering potential warm on her face like sunshine. It was hard not to tell the girl everything; they had to make the right beginning.

Eminel's eyes narrowed. "How do you know?"

"I can tell you have all-magic." Sessadon put her hand gently on the girl's.

Eminel pulled her hand away. "How?"

"Because I have it too."

"Wait. Who are you?" asked Eminel. She sat straight up now, alert and aware, the haze of her unconsciousness shed like a blanket.

Sessadon felt for the line between truth and lie, walked it carefully. Truth, here. "My name is Sessadon."

"Like the sister of the first queen of Arca."

Sessadon felt a pang. "Yes, like that."

"And do you know my name?"

"Yes. You're Eminel."

The girl stood upright, fully herself, and brushed roughly at the wet sand clinging to her garments. Sessadon could even feel a tingle in the air as her energies shifted. Consciously or unconsciously, she was gathering her power. She might try to cast an enchantment. Disaster could result.

"It's not an accident that I found you," Sessadon said, letting the truth land hard to prove her sincerity. She stayed on her knees in the sand as the girl stood, sending the message with her body that she held back sending with her mind: *I am no threat.* "I want to help you. Keep you safe."

Eminel stared down, her face clouded. "And why would you do that? For a girl you don't even know?"

"We are of the same line, you and I."

Now the girl's eyes were wide. The force that had been simmering up subsided. "My mother never . . . She said there was no one left."

"Your mother tried so hard to keep you safe." Sessadon kept her voice low and urgent, looking up at the girl earnestly. "But you're in more danger than ever now. What will happen if the queen finds you? She could name you the next queen, or she could slay you where you stand."

"Do you know about the Seekers? Can you keep Seekers from finding me?"

"I can." Sessadon nodded. She thought about standing, but stayed on her knees, keeping the girl above her. "But the queen will stop at nothing. She's terrified of how powerful you might become. Your— your poor mother. May she rest in Velja's arms."

Eminel's eyes were locked on Sessadon's upturned face, her mouth open in shock and horror. The sorcerer felt again for the line between truth and lie, settled on the side that would close the deal. The right words spoken in this moment would forge a bond as strong as any enchantment.

"It was the queen," Sessadon said. "The queen killed her."

Now the girl fell to her knees, back in the sand next to the sorcerer. Sessadon resisted the urge to reach out. Instead, she watched carefully, gave the girl time and space to feel. Who she was in this moment could show who she would become.

There. Even as the girl's eyes spilled over with tears, Sessadon saw how they narrowed, how her gaze sharpened to grim iron. For all her softness, there was something hard at the girl's core. And that was very good. For both of them.

Eminel wiped the tears from her eyes with two quick, forceful motions, much like she had brushed the sand from her clothes. All business. "You said I could be powerful?"

"No one knows yet what you can do. But if you train—yes. Very powerful."

The girl held Sessadon's gaze, and the sorcerer felt the tremble of magic in her intensity. It was time for the crux of it. The final argument, the moment that would tell whether words would be enough.

"You can defeat her," she told Eminel. "Someday. You can be strong enough."

"Me? *I* could defeat the queen?" Her body shifted, facing Sessadon, almost knees to knees.

"And the nation of Arca will thank you. She's hurt so many innocents."

Eminel made to stand, but Sessadon caught her by the hand. The girl paused, let herself be kept on her knees.

"But Eminel, you're not ready yet." She put regret in her voice, as if she were sorry to break the bad news. "It will take time. Maybe years."

Eminel nodded soberly.

Not daunted. Good. It was time to make her offer. "I can teach you. I can show you, help you tame your power, master it. And when you're ready—"

"That monster. She'll be sorry," said Eminel, eyes gleaming.

Sessadon replied, "She won't even have the chance to be sorry. She'll be dead."

The girl's gaze was solemn, but the sorcerer caught a twitch at the corner of her mouth. Just a hint, a beginning, of a smile.

That was it, then. She had her heir.

Sessadon's long journey alone had ended; it was time for their journey together to begin.

✦

The Isle of Luck was just as beautiful as Sessadon remembered it, a sparkling gem just off Paxim's quiet southern coast, its gorgeous sandstone temple stark against the blue, blue sky. But she did not see the priest she had spared several years before. This worried her. She had not planned to kill anyone to take possession of the temple, at least not where the girl could see. Eminel changed everything.

Sessadon was so used to being alone, simply doing what needed to be done. Now she needed to think of how her actions would look to her innocent, untutored heir, who had so much to learn. This was a welcome complexity, at least. The sorcerer would only grow stronger from this kind of challenge. If she had wanted only vengeance, all this would have been settled long ago. Eminel made it so much more. She had no regrets.

As they mounted the steps, a young man in an undyed, rough-spun calf-length robe came out to meet them. His features were pleasant enough, but unfamiliar; Sessadon did not recognize him. His attire was that of a servant, not a priest, and she had paid little attention to the temple servants' faces on her previous visit.

"Who are you?" Sessadon asked rudely. "Where is the priest?"

"I regret to inform you, faithful ones," said the young man, hands clasped. "Our priest is ill just now. We have attempted to spread the word; if you've come for a blessing, I am sorry you've come all this way. You could come back another day, perhaps. You are welcome to pray, of course, and leave an offering for the god."

"Ill?" asked Sessadon. "In what way?"

"Ill," he repeated, his pleasant face a mask.

"Take me to the priest, please," said Sessadon.

"I don't think I can do that."

Magic it would have to be then, but subtle magic should be enough. "I'm sure you can," Sessadon nudged. She felt a hitch in her chest, almost like the quartz heart was beating. "We're old friends, the priest and I."

The young man's tension eased. "Yes, of course. You're right. They'll be glad to see you."

Sessadon could feel Eminel's eyes on her. Had she sensed the magic? There would be time, later, to explain. First things first.

Sunlight did not reach the room where the priest lay, deep in the temple's inner warrens, and the lamp near their head provided scant light. Sessadon drew closer to get a better look, motioning for Eminel to stay back.

At first, the priest did not look like they were dying—their skin was golden and dewy, their color all tawny health—which made Sessadon skeptical. She looked back at the young man, prepared to enter his mind. He might be lying, not knowing who she was. It would be simple to find out the truth.

But then the priest took a breath inward, and the awful sound, somehow both a hiss and a rattle, told the tale.

Sessadon went to their side and knelt. "Honored one. I am so sorry to hear you are unwell."

The priest looked at her, their eyes deep and still. They did not respond—but of course, forcing enough breath through their throat to make words must be impossible.

Sessadon turned to the young man. "How long have they been like this?"

"Weeks," he said.

"Did they eat something, drink something, that made them like this?" asked Eminel.

"Not that we know of," he said sadly.

"What have you done to heal them?"

"We have prayed."

Eminel walked forward, put her hand on Sessadon's shoulder. "Can I help heal them? Can you teach me how? I couldn't when I was young, but—maybe now—I'd like to try."

Sessadon stopped her. She was surprised by the girl's forwardness, and it pleased her, but now was not the time. "Not yet."

"But they need—"

"Let me."

As Sessadon spoke the words, the priest's hand rose—not quickly, but it rose—until their fingertips brushed Sessadon's wrist. The sorcerer looked down in surprise. The priest's cool fingertips spider-walked to the palm of the sorcerer's hand, lay curled on the heel for a moment, and then, with little force but clear intent, pushed her away.

She let her mind slip inside the mind of the priest, as gently as she could, a feather landing softly in the curve of a nest.

No, thought the priest. *My god has willed it.*

No one else heard. Eminel was saying to the young man, "You said weeks? How many?"

"Since the harvest," said the young man.

Sessadon said to him, "You may leave us."

"You presume," he said in confusion, his smooth young face clouding. "It is you who should leave."

Her voice changing, Sessadon said, "Oh, but we are trustworthy. Aren't we, Eminel?"

"Oh yes," the girl said. Her voice did not carry the magic that Sessadon's did. She did not know how to put it there, not yet. But Sessadon was pleased that the girl instinctively followed her lead. Spoken agreement magnified the effect of the persuasion enchantment. It was one of the countless little nuances the sorcerer looked forward to teaching her heir.

"Why don't you show Eminel where we'll be sleeping?" Sessadon suggested to the young man, the force of enchantment behind her words now close to irresistible. "We'll be staying for a while."

His face untroubled now, the young man bowed at the waist. When he raised his head again, he gestured with an arm for Eminel to proceed him, and the two walked off.

Alone with the ill priest at last, Sessadon crouched next to their unmoving form. Words seemed unnecessary, since the priest could not speak. It would be unkind to make them try. Conversation in the comfort of their own mind could be, would be, easier.

Is there much pain? Sessadon asked.

Much.

Would you like me to take it away?

No. I told you. Their thoughts were firm, even as another of those awful, labored breaths rasped out of their barely open mouth. *The god has willed it.*

The god would not want you to suffer.

How are any of us to know what He wants? The priest's thoughts had a chiding tone, their lips the shade of a smile. *We only read the signs.*

This is how I read the signs, Honored One. It was Sessadon's turn to be firm. *You have been ill and will not recover. Now my charge and I are here. We will take over for you. We will welcome the pilgrims and interpret the signs. I will take good care of your temple, I swear to you.*

You will? And then, *Yes. You will.*

And so, Honored One, Sessadon told them, offering a push of magic so gentle it felt loving, almost intimate, *now you may go.*

On a last rattling breath turning into a soft moan, a sigh, an absence, they went.

✦

It was hard to believe, thought Eminel, but with the benefit of hindsight, she was glad she'd been stolen from the Rovers.

She had been so foolish to risk their lives. How could she never have thought about the danger she put them in? Hiding and dodging would not have kept them safe forever. The queen would have sent more Seekers, perhaps even come herself. Sessadon told Eminel she would one day be capable of fighting the queen—imagine that!—but not yet. She could not have borne those deaths on her conscience. The merry twins, the quiet swordswoman, the kind thief, the spirited giant. Without her, they could go back to their marauding lives, happier, safer. Did she have Velja to thank for this? She hadn't worshipped Velja a single day since she and her mother had left Arca; Jehenit insisted she not do so in Paxim, not wanting to give their origins away. And certainly she'd seen no sign of the god's favor when magic had murdered Jehenit. Perhaps, if Eminel was finally starting to come into her own, there was no one but Sessadon to thank.

She did not know much of the sorcerer's history, not yet, but she knew she'd been alone. The sorcerer had told her the bare bones of the tale. Like Eminel, she'd once been kidnapped, taken away from all she held dear, and like Eminel, she had fled her captors. That was how she'd ended up on the road. Instead of risking life and limb to find her way back to a home where no family waited for her—again, their stories were so similar—she had continued to wander, until her all-magic made her aware of Eminel. And then finding her last remaining relative had become the only thing left that mattered.

Now they had landed on the Isle of Luck, and it seemed like the God of Luck Himself approved of their presence. Here on the isle they had everything they needed, starting with privacy to hide from prying eyes. The more isolated a place, Sessadon told her, the easier it was to ward. And they were going to be throwing off a great deal of magical power as they tested and learned what Eminel was capable of. Pilgrims would bring sacrifices of animals and fruits, bread and prayers, Sessadon told her, which would bring them two more things they needed: food for their own needs and life force to feed the experiments with Eminel's magic. The handful of temple servants, like the young man who had greeted them, could help with any other needs.

It seemed like the perfect arrangement.

Was it too perfect?

Eminel quashed the niggling snake of worry in her mind. Sessadon was a relative, she'd said so, that was why she wanted to help. They were of the same matriclan: a line that was not just healers, as her mother had claimed, but women of all-magic as well. That power that her mother had hidden from her was the very power that, properly nurtured, could take down a queen who did not deserve to rule. It was time to stop hiding from her destiny. It was time to build and grow and learn, and eventually, attack. If Sessadon meant Eminel harm, she could have been rid of her a thousand times by now. Or not gone looking for her in the first place.

But now they were here together, and Sessadon had promised to start training her as soon as she was comfortable. A week after she'd fled the Seeker, they were ready to begin.

They walked downhill from the temple, facing out toward the Mockingwater. The day was lovely, sunny but not hot, with a gentle breeze off the open sea. Once they left the sandstone steps behind, small trails branched into the green of the grass and woods, forking and forking again like lightning. Unsure of their destination, Eminel simply followed.

Sessadon looked out over the possibilities, seemed to consider, and turned the two of them toward the woods. Once inside the shade of the trees, the sorcerer led Eminel to a nearby grove of birches, their pale trunks bending inward, forming a kind of shelter. "Perfect," she pronounced. "A place like this will help us concentrate."

"But is there sand here? Enough?"

"Smart girl. The beach down there will suffice. My power can draw on it without trouble from here."

"But we don't know if mine can," Eminel said.

"Well," said Sessadon, a comforting smile spreading across her angular face, "let's find out."

The sorcerer seated herself on the ground, folding her legs, and motioned for Eminel to do the same. They faced each other, and Sessadon reached out her hands for Eminel's, grasping them lightly, letting their entwined hands sink gently to the ground. The earth was cool here where the sunlight did not reach, and Eminel could feel its coolness under her hands along with the other woman's warmth. She was aware of everything, feeling everything. Finally she would learn about her all-magic. Finally she could start becoming who she was meant to be.

"Let's begin with something simple. Sing."

"Sing what?"

"Anything. Whatever comes first to mind," said Sessadon.

Eminel closed her eyes and opened her mouth, singing the lullaby she remembered her mother and her mother's husbands singing when she was very small, just two verses, which she'd heard over and over and over again:

> *When an Arcan calls on all her magic*
> *Nothing stands in the way of the true.*
> *When a lake of glass swallows the desert*
> *Then my girl, you will know I love you.*
> *When an Arcan calls on all her magic*
> *And the answer's a thousand leagues deep*
> *When a girl helps a girl helps a girl*
> *Peace be upon the land, and sleep.*

She'd lost herself in the memory, but as she sang the last word, she became aware that the sorcerer had dropped her hands.

Eminel opened her eyes and saw that other woman's eyes were wide. She had never seen her look this way—startled, almost frightened? Could it be?

Sessadon said in a hesitant voice, "That is . . . powerful magic you sing."

"It's just a lullaby."

"It was never a lullaby," she said, with force. She considered and spoke again, a bit more gently. "Not when I was a child, anyway. When I was a child, people died for that rhyme."

"What?"

"Not that exact rhyme, but parts of it. It has changed. I suppose that over the years it has been taught and learned a thousand times, and each time, it was corrupted. But those words—Eminel, you should not sing that anymore."

"I won't, if it's dangerous," Eminel said.

"Danger is a matter of perspective."

Eminel admitted, "I don't understand."

"And you don't need to. Not now." Falsely cheerful now, abrupt, Sessadon said, "But I was going to teach you something! Sing a harmless scrap of song, that's what we need. Sing 'My Mother Was a Stone.'"

"I don't know that one," said Eminel, a shadow of worry crossing her brow.

"Here, I'll teach it to you." Sessadon sang in a thin but passable soprano:

My mother was a stone
My father was a tree
I am a rushing river
Come drown yourself in me.

This song seemed far darker to Eminel than the lullaby she had chosen, but Sessadon's smile remained broad, and the melody was certainly simple to learn. Sessadon reached out for her hands again, gripping them lightly, and had her sing the words over and over.

"The song is not really important," said Sessadon, speaking low and clear, just loud enough to be heard between Eminel's sung words. "It is to occupy your mind so you can free yourself from interfering thoughts. All-magic demands a lot of you. I won't lie, Eminel; all-magic is by no means a pure gift. It is a challenge. I will help you through it, but it is still very dangerous, to you and others, so you must follow my instructions carefully. All right?"

Eminel nodded without ceasing her song. *"Come drown yourself in me. My mother was a stone . . ."*

Sessadon pressed on Eminel's hands in a way Eminel could not quite define, not a pinch or squeeze, somehow a pressing all over, even though no one's hands could fully envelop another person's hands so evenly. The pressing was on her knuckles and the backs and the palms of her hands all at the same time, on her fingertips and inside her nails—inside? How?

"Don't stop singing," warned Sessadon.

"My father was a tree, I am a rushing river, Come drown yourself . . ."

The pressing feeling spread from her hands up her arms, racing, covering her like moss or oil or water, right up over her face, the pressure, everywhere, into her eyes and nose and mouth, and she worried she wouldn't be able to breathe—

"Sing," Sessadon said hoarsely.

"My mother was a stone . . ."

And then, for the first time, Eminel could *feel* her power.

It was intoxicating.

The pressure turned both inward and outward, suffusing her, embracing everything around her, soaring in every direction at once. Everything was the clearest, most beautiful blue, and she was everywhere and everything lived in her, breathed, pulsed, joined, and everything was blue light.

She cried to feel its warmth and she cried when it left her, all that blue fading into black, then white, then a mottled pattern of greens and browns around her. She found herself back in her body, her mere body, her hands slipped free from Sessadon's and lying on the cool, dry ground. She was no longer singing. She heard no sound at all.

Her young face shining with tears, Eminel looked at Sessadon, unable to put any of what she'd just felt into words. The well of power, the connection with everything everywhere, the way the light expanded her very being. It was too much. And yet, in some way, it was not yet enough.

"You have more potential than I'd even dreamed of," Sessadon said. "You are remarkable."

At the sorcerer's words, Eminel felt something in her chest she'd never felt before: pride. Swelling, expanding. The knowledge of all this *possibility* inside her spread like unchecked fire across a parched grass field.

Sessadon said, "You felt it, didn't you? Your potential."

And Eminel put her hands back into Sessadon's, wet eyes glittering bright, and said, "Show me more."

CHAPTER 29

A MISSION

The All-Mother's Year 514
The north of Paxim
Azur, Tamura

Watching the tip of her arrow disappear into her first enemy's throat, Azur dha Tamura finally knew what she was born for. She'd felt a rush of satisfaction on the hunt, ending the lives of creatures, but this was far better, an intoxication that suffused her from the tips of her fingers to her very core. She was instantly addicted to the feeling of dealing death, snuffing out a life equal to her own. Again she gave thanks to the Scorpion for bringing her to her sister warriors, freeing her from those nameless, shapeless years in Arca. The idea that she could have lived her whole life without feeling this way was blasphemy.

The night before, their journey over on the *kuphai* had been terrifying, sailing through the dark on the bobbing crafts. The empty raft they pulled behind them rode high in the water, constantly bumping and nudging their own *kuphai*, and Azur was convinced she would slide off into the water and sink to the bottom before she even had a chance to scream. But Ysilef, riding next to her, saw her fear. She launched into a long, rambling, filthy joke about a Sestian boneburner, an Arcan fire magician, and a Paximite senator. By the time they beached on the silent shore of Paxim, Azur was chuckling, and when Ysilef repeated under her breath, "Forgive me, Senator, that's no bone," she had to stifle a true laugh.

They had trained so long for their first mission, and Azur was ready. This was a fitting way to wet her first arrows with human blood. The returned Scorpicae had brought much intelligence from their time in other queendoms, and Queen Tamura had sifted through it to make a plan. This was not an act of war, she impressed upon them. This was merely a test. Take the weapons by any means necessary, then go. One discreet mission, sharp and brief, like the sting of a scorpion's tail.

Not far from the northern shore of Paxim, a returned warrior had told them, there was a huge cache of weapons that had been collected at the nearby trading post, called Centralia, over the years. A local merchant, rightly or no, had never trusted the Scorpican enforcers. He'd been stockpiling weapons that came through the post, keeping them in a shed on his own property, a good distance from the post. Everyone in the area knew about it, but no one beyond, and the cache was not heavily guarded, said the returned warrior. The merchant and a nearby farmer had argued in public many times about the hoarded weapons; if the weapons were stolen and the merchant slain, suspicion would fall heavily on the farmer's head. The only people on the property were the merchant, his wife, and five or six sons, most of whom were too young to know how to fight. Paximite women were apparently less able to refrain from pleasures with men than the Scorpicae, or perhaps they didn't understand the results thereof; even with fewer births overall, Paxim was still crawling with young sons.

Bohara was their captain for the mission, commanding a group of only five, with Azur and Ysilef the youngest among them. A few more

warriors might have been useful, if only to carry the looted weap-
onry, but Bohara liked the number five for good luck, and Tamura
had approved the choice. Three swordswomen would attack directly,
Bohara in the lead, and two archers would rain down arrows from a
nearby perch. For the situation the returned warrior had described,
that would be plenty.

And had that been the true situation, it would have been.

At first, everything unfolded according to plan. The element of
surprise was on their side. In the light of early morning, they found
the men of the family loading barrels onto a cart, carefree and singing. Bohara led the charge, her sword taking a full-grown man—the
merchant, Azur supposed—through the belly before he could even
raise his own weapon. The three younger swordswomen came behind her, locating and eliminating targets in a flurry of tight, focused
action. That was when Azur's first arrow found one young man's
throat and he fell dead, the hot feeling pulsing through her, and she
notched another arrow quickly, ready to repeat that joy.

But as she squinted down the next arrow she saw there were far
more men than there were supposed to be. Not just young sons, either, but men full-grown, streaming from a nearby building. They'd
taken it for just another storage building, and it clearly once had
been, but was it being used as some sort of bunkhouse? She had no
mind for strategy, just a blind guess. Had the merchant been training
other men with the weapons he'd stockpiled, now that the Scorpican
guards were gone?

She fired another arrow, missed this time in her panic, gave a
shout and drew another, squinted down the shaft again.

Swords clashed, metal on metal ringing so loud it hurt her ears,
even from this distance.

She let fly, hooted in satisfaction when her arrow took another
man in the stomach, and she let her bow dangle for a moment while

she watched his death throes. He twisted and fell, thrashing in the dirt. He took longer than the first to die and fought death harder, yanking out the arrow and cramming his clenched fist against the wound, as if his bare knuckles could keep the blood inside. When at last he lay still and she looked up, the battle had raged on without her, and she realized her mistake.

She saw Ysilef, shield fallen to the ground, facing off against an opponent. Her face was grim, determined. The opponent raised his sword, taunting, dancing. Azur's blood pounded, a rushing sound in her ears, the world swirling around her dizzied head. The fighters were too closely packed and her bow was useless now. She raised it anyway, notching an arrow on the string out of habit, but she was too late.

Ysilef didn't see the man behind her until he struck. The second man had no sword, only a dagger, but he sank the small blade deep into the meat of Ysilef's thigh. Then he leapt back, almost as if surprised at his success, stunned by the blood. As she turned in shock at the pain, that was when the opponent in front of her raised his sword and ran her through. Her mouth opened, her scream silent. By instinct, or that was what it looked like to Azur, Ysilef wrapped her hands around the sword. Then there was blood on her hands and in her mouth and on her thigh and she toppled sideways, suddenly clumsy, falling.

Azur was running, she was flying, abandoning her post. Arrows whistled past her ears—the other archer must be trying to cover her—but she could see nothing but those men standing over Ysilef. Were they laughing with satisfaction? Actually *laughing*? She ran harder, faster, bile in her throat. The roaring in her ears grew loud enough to drown out the whole world.

But by the time she got there, it was all over. She blinked as the scene stilled, came into focus. The man who had stabbed Ysilef's thigh with the dagger now wore that same dagger buried in his own gut, and the Scorpican archer who'd remained at her post had taken out the swordsman. Bohara and the other swordswomen had dispatched the rest of the men and cleared the house, sure there were no other fighters hiding. They drove their swords through the sightless fallen to make sure they would not rise, offering them up with the sacred words. *The fight is done, the fight is done, the fight is done.*

"Bad information. We were in the dark," spat Bohara. "Blind and dumb as a forest of cocks."

Azur roared her anger as she drew the dagger from the man's gut and stabbed him it with over and over. His wet blood sprayed in her face, streaking where the tears rolled down. Again and again she stabbed, frenzied with rage, until she felt fingers digging into her shoulders. A voice was shouting behind her. The hands wrenched her away from the dead man, hard, letting her fall in the dirt. When she blinked, she saw Bohara squatting next to her, her expression disapproving.

"Come away," Bohara shouted in Azur's face, snapping her out of her trance. "Do you hear me? Come away. It is done. Be a warrior. Say the words."

She had to. She couldn't. She had to.

"The Scorpion drinks the blood of the defeated," sobbed Azur, jabbing once more, then pulling back her bloody hands, leaving the dagger behind.

Bohara grabbed the back of Azur's neck and pulled her up to a standing position.

"All of it," she ordered.

Azur forced out the last four words. "The fight is . . . done."

Then Bohara told them what to do. Hide the bodies in a shed, get the weapons, go. Disappear. Azur moved as if someone else's mind controlled her. In a way, it did. She simply moved when and how her captain told her to move. Bohara ordered her to retrieve the dagger from the man's body where she'd left it; she did. Some moments she was conscious, but there were moments of blackness, too, even as she swayed on her feet, somehow upright.

They took Ysilef's body with them—the other swordswomen lifted her, Azur was not allowed—so no one could prove Scorpicae had been here. As they crossed back to Scorpica, their raft piled high with plunder, Bohara herself weighted the body with stones and pushed it off a *kupha*. Azur was still crying, on the edge of mania. Her dead friend's body sank exactly as she'd imagined her own body sinking on the crossing over. That felt like years ago now. It had not even been a day.

Once they were safe in Scorpica, their *kuphai* carefully beached along with the raft of weapons they'd plundered, Bohara pointed inland and ordered them to set up camp. "We'll stay overnight," she said. "Hunt a bit, take our time, rest up. Gather our energy for the trip back."

Instead of following her fellow warriors toward safe camping ground, Azur turned her back and stared at the water. She did not go inland. She could not even watch the other warriors set up camp, eat cold meats, congratulate each other on a battle well fought. She could not pretend the world still made sense with Ysilef gone. Instead she sat down on the sand and remained on the beach for hours, staring back toward Paxim, the salt sting in her nostrils smelling like iron and blood.

Over time, the sky dimmed; the waves on the beach crept closer as the tide rose. Time did nothing to cool the mania still bubbling up inside her, her furious blood still demanding that she *do something*. She did not know how to handle it, how to tamp it down. She only knew how to fight and there was nothing to fight now, no one to stab or slash. Only her pain. She wanted to put a dagger under her ribs and lean into it until darkness, then death, blotted out the world's light. It was only then that she realized Bohara had not left her a dagger. Or any other weapon. Her bow was gone, her quiver empty. Her commander had not said a word when she stayed behind on the beach, but apparently before that, she'd taken away anything Azur could use to hurt herself or anyone else.

When the sun began to sink over the Salt Maw and her entire body was still aflame, Azur decided it was time. Her body kept demanding action. She could think of no other action to take without a weapon at hand. So first she stood on the beach and walked to where the sand changed color under her feet. The pain in her chest was still there. So she took a few more steps until the water covered her ankles, her feet. Still pain. She tried going up to her knees next, the water warm as blood, then her waist, but because it kept hurting, she kept going.

She was up to her shoulders when she felt a strong, familiar hand grab her by the scruff of the neck and float her protesting body, kicking wildly, back to the shallows.

Bohara flung her down on the sand, panting slightly, and said, "You are too good a warrior for us to lose. You stay in this world."

Azur raised one shoulder enough to shrug, difficult to do when lying half-drowned at her captain's feet.

Bohara grabbed a wineskin, half-full and still plump, from a flat rock where she'd clearly left it before chasing Azur into the surf. Even from where she lay, now that the salt water had drained from her nose, Azur could smell the heavy bite of hammerwine on her captain's breath.

After a long drink from the wineskin, Bohara tried again. "There are things you can do."

"Yes," said Azur. "I was trying."

"Not that. To live in the world after loss."

"Don't tell me to forget her. She was my friend."

"And you are angry," said Bohara, clenching a fist to echo her words. "Turn your anger into action."

"What action?"

"When we return to Tamura, tell her about Ysilef. Tell her of your loss, of your sorrow. Tell her she never should have sent untested warriors, precious girls, on a mission like that. And see what she says."

"She is our queen," said Azur, "and my mother. I would never show disrespect."

"Accountability is respect. She needs to answer for her actions," Bohara said, her voice forceful. "No one is immune to that, not even a queen."

Azur ran her hand over her wet hair and stared out at the water. Every time she rested her mind, even for a moment, she saw that man with the dagger standing behind Ysilef, ready to strike. She saw her friend's silent scream.

"For tonight," said Bohara more gently, "do not think of it."

"Easy to say."

"There are ways. For example, this one," Bohara said, dangling the hammerwine down toward the younger woman. "Want some?"

"I don't like the taste."

"Who drinks it for the taste?" Bohara said, clearly not expecting an answer, tilting back her head to gulp another mouthful.

When Bohara offered her the drink again, Azur finally righted herself, sitting with her legs outstretched, feet pointed toward the water, so she could take it with both hands. She raised the wineskin to her lips and swallowed. Then she handed it back, shaking her head.

"No good?"

"No good."

"Still thinking of what you shouldn't?"

"Yes," Azur said, the pain inside her welling, and it shamed her. She had thought herself a warrior. She had been born in the wrong queendom, but fate had brought her to the right one and she had found her joy, her purpose, with bow in hand. She was dishonoring Scorpica with this weakness. And all she wanted to do at this moment was fill her tunic with stones and run back into the water, all the way in this time. To join her friend in death, leaving behind a world that did not seem to want her.

"There is only one other thing that works as well to free the mind from worry," said Bohara, setting down the wineskin as she crouched next to Azur on the sand.

From her belt she drew a carven form, something like a small club. It was as long as an index finger but much thicker around, with a loop on one end large enough to hook a finger through. It was made of some kind of bone or horn, probably horn, ringed with thick ridges all the way from the loop to the far, rounded end.

"Oh," Azur said, pointing at it, clinging to the chance for distraction. "I always did wonder what that was. What kind of weapon."

"It is . . . not a weapon."

"What is it?"

Something crept into Bohara's grin that Azur didn't recognize. "It is an instrument of pleasure. A little something I picked up in Sestia at the rites one year. Made of ram's horn, specially polished and shaped for the purpose. Not god-approved, of course, but very good for what the god likes them to do down there."

"Down there?"

Bohara barked a laugh. "I meant Sestia, but yes, also . . . down there."

She reached out with the length of horn and touched it to Azur's knee. Playfully, at first. Then the air seemed to still around them. She touched the horn to her knee again, this time toward the inside, and dragged its tip gently against the bare skin in slow, small circles.

"Part your knees," said Bohara, almost conversationally.

Azur did, shifting to put one hand on the sand behind her, bearing part of her weight. She felt very far away as she watched the length of horn wandering upward with a soft, steady pressure, tracing circles up the inside of her thigh until it disappeared under the soft leather of her half-skirt.

"I will give you pleasure if you wish it," Bohara said. "I will show you a way to forget."

Azur felt the horn reach the place where her legs met and nudge at her opening, still circling, triggering a soft gush of wetness there.

Bohara asked quietly, "Do you wish it?"

Azur nodded, once, twice.

"Lie back."

She lowered herself onto the sand, arms at her sides, knees parted, face upturned toward the sky. Eyes closed, she heard Bohara move closer. After a moment Azur felt a second hand slide under her skirt. This one moved in lines, not circles, fingertips gliding over tender, soft skin until the pad of Bohara's thumb, softer and more nimble than the horn, reached the join. When it landed, pressed, teased the swollen nub there, a heavy, lush warmth took hold of Azur.

All at once the pattern of the stroking changed, thumb and horn moving together in rhythmic sympathy, and the sensation made her gasp out loud. As her mouth fell open, the back of her head pressed harder into the sand. Without meaning to, she tilted her hips back, turned her whole body upward, hungry for more.

As she stroked, Bohara said quietly, "Just this once, you understand. The one who holds my heart is on assignment at the Scorpion's Pass. I wait for her. Whatever we do here, we form no further attachments."

Even as Azur's body yielded up to the more experienced woman's touch, inside she gave a grim laugh. How foolish Bohara was to think Azur would form an attachment to her just because of pleasures. Azur's attachment to Ysilef was the strongest one she would ever feel, just as strong in death, even though they had never laid hands on each other in this way. Pleasure had nothing to do with attachment. She could touch herself like this whenever she wanted, though it had never been even close to this good, this powerful, only a sort of mechanical release. Ecstasy, this type of ecstasy, seemed to have little connection with true joy.

She had taken joy in Ysilef's friendship and in the satisfaction of battle. The first was forever lost to her. She was not sure whether she would regain the second. There was such luxurious relief in letting the warmth take her. Letting herself stop wondering, stop caring, just for now. She spread her palms against the sand, sank her fingers into it, thrust her hips high again for more of what she wanted.

Bohara worked the length of horn expertly, sliding its ridges in and out, her thumb rubbing the throbbing spot above in close, tight circles. Tension gathered in Azur's body, hard and hot. The world around her disappeared—the salt air, the smell of leather and musk, the lingering iron stink of the battle, even the other woman seemed to be at a great distance, irrelevant. She was alone with pleasure.

Everything shrank to that small, hard knot, and then as it drew too tight to bear, that last light in the world exploded.

Azur lost herself in the release, stunned by its power, which held her suspended in a world outside the world for she did not know how long. She might or might not have made sounds. The horn pressed deep into her and she bucked hard, her hips riding out the pulsing sensation until it subsided, fading away, and of its own accord her lower body slowed and stilled.

"There," Bohara said. "Was I right?"

Azur could not find the words, but she nodded, her short, wet hair rubbing against the sand.

Bohara laughed, turned away, and in the same motion, swept up the skin of hammerwine.

"The world is a big place," Bohara said. "Don't think you've seen it all just yet, youngling."

A moment later she was already gone, walking away from Azur's limp form toward the warriors' camp in the distance. Azur heard her laugh again as she went, chuckling to herself, as if she'd heard a joke worth savoring.

Azur lay still, spent, considering. Distance had crept in between her and the events of the day. Tomorrow would be soon enough to think of them. She was drowsy now, maybe a little bit from the hammerwine, but mostly, she assumed, from the pleasure. She let herself linger in its warm shadow, thinking only of that sensation, that lifting out of herself. A moment that this world had let her have, even though she'd felt outside the world. She was already hungry to find a way to feel that again. It was the only thing that felt as good as killing felt, and it blunted the edges of everything.

The feeling did not last, but for the moment, it was enough.

✦

Azur should have felt triumph as they brought the cache of weapons back into Scorpica. Instead she felt hollow inside. The gap left by Ysilef was a dark, unfathomable cavern. Yet no one else seemed to be thinking of their loss, only their victory. Bohara and the others swaggered into the camp, proud of their success, accepting praise and wonder as their just due.

"Behold!" shouted one, and the others echoed her, *behold, behold, behold.*

Warriors cheered them, hailed them, welcomed them back. The weapons were spread out on a length of spare tent cloth so Golhabi the armorer could look over them, lifting blades to inspect them for nicks, rubbing her thumbs over hilts and handles. Warriors of all ages gathered to murmur approvingly.

Azur alone stood grimly aside. There was only one weapon that mattered to her, and only one warrior with whom she would discuss it. More than a warrior, much more, of course, but a warrior the same as the rest of them, deep down.

It took an hour or so for the queen to appear. When she did, she raised her arms in triumph, hailing the returned warriors from the mission, and clapped Bohara on the shoulder.

"Well done! I see the fruits of your mission and I am pleased. May I speak with the warriors who brought this blessing to pass?" she asked, and Bohara urged the four of them forward.

The queen's brow knit instantly at seeing the four. Azur saw recognition dawn on her face: a captain and four warriors, one fewer than those who had left. Now was the time to strike. Bohara, counseling her again on the return trip, had urged her to act quickly.

If she cannot make a good answer, her captain had said, *it will look bad for her. And if she lets her anger show, if she blames you, or hurts you, well. You may then take any action you are moved to. Even if you want to Challenge her. You would be within your rights as a warrior.*

Azur stepped out of line, rushed forward, and stood in front of Tamura, her dead friend's sheathed sword gripped in her fists.

"We did not all return," she addressed the queen, her voice sharp and strident. "There were not enough of us. You sent us—we five, plus our captain—we were not enough."

Dozens of warriors had gathered to look over the cache of weapons, and at the sound of Azur's angry, accusing voice, every single one fell silent.

"She was my *friend*," Azur said, though she knew that made no difference. A warrior was a warrior. But the loss ripped through her, and she needed to do something to let it out. Speaking the truth, that was something she could do. "And she's *dead* now. If you had—if you had—"

Azur did not know what she expected to see in Tamura's eyes at the accusation. Bohara had made it sound easy. The young woman's anger had carried her this far. Now the pain of her loss was dwarfing the anger, weakening her. The sword was heavy in her hands, and she did not know what to do with it.

Tamura met her gaze. There Azur saw deep sadness. No anger, even with the daughter she'd done so much for challenging her so openly, not even a trace.

"Is this her weapon?" the queen asked. Her eyes were wet, Azur saw now. Warriors should not cry, they had all been told so, and yet, at the mere mention of this one lost warrior, their queen was moved to tears.

"Yes."

Tamura put out her hands, and Azur laid the sheathed sword across them.

Still and sorrowful, the queen looked down at the sword. "Speak the name of my fallen daughter." Then she added, "Please."

Azur could barely choke out her response. She was holding her own tears back as best she could, afraid that if she let them free she would descend back into the darkness that had gripped her on that shore after the crossing. But her queen, her mother, had asked her to speak. She would speak. "Ysilef."

"Ysilef dha Tamura," the queen said. "My first fallen daughter, may she never be forgotten. She died a hero?"

"She did."

"And her body?"

"At the bottom of the Salt Maw."

Tamura's face twisted with grief and pain, but she steadied herself. "Thank you for bringing her weapon home. Her loss must be marked."

Turning to the assembled warriors, Tamura called out, "We will honor her sacrifice. Join me in honoring our fallen sister, daughter, friend. Ysilef dha Tamura, may you brandish a sword more beautiful than this one on the battlefield beyond."

Her hands gripping the sword so tightly her knuckles turned pale, Tamura sank to her knees. She laid the sword on the ground and her forehead on the sword.

Azur fell to her knees beside her, pressing her forehead to the ground. She felt the queen's hand reach out for hers and hold it as they lay there, bent to the earth, together. All around them, warriors joined in mourning: falling to their knees, heads pressed to the earth, silent in memory of their slain sister.

From the back of the crowd, Gretti watched the warriors fall like downed trees. One after another after another, they went to their knees, then placed their foreheads on the ground to mimic their queen. Yet the last warrior to fall was not the one Gretti would have expected.

Bohara, of all of them, went to her knees reluctantly. There was something on her face besides sadness. It was a stray moment, but it was enough to worry Gretti. She knew all the possibilities of history were written and rewritten in stray moments: who caught them, who ignored them, who missed them because they saw only what they wanted to see.

Once, she had failed a queen whose Challenge she had not been smart enough to outflank when she saw it coming. She would not make that mistake again.

✦

Deep in the woods nearest the summer camp, the day after the mission to Paxim brought back an impressive cache of weapons, Tamura drew back her bow and let fly. Her arrow took the coney through the right side of the neck and emerged from the left. The animal only stopped running three steps after it was already dead: tripping, tumbling, then falling still.

Standing beside her queen in the forest's cool shadow, Gretti had been waiting for her moment to speak. A moment when Tamura was no longer armed seemed like the right time.

"Listen to me," she said. "You have to do something about Bohara."

"'Do something'?" Tamura said, trotting over to pick up the fallen coney. She removed the arrow with a practiced hand and slung the carcass into the waiting hammock where she was collecting the game she brought in. A half-dozen pairs of long, limp ears now dangled earthward. "You'll need to be more specific."

"She wants to Challenge you."

"She's said so?"

"No. But she had a hand in what that girl did yesterday, I can tell."

"The girl saw her friend die," said Tamura matter-of-factly. "We trained her, but you know the difference between training and a real fight. Of course she's distraught. I'm her mother and she brought her grief to me, as she should have."

"It's more than that." Gretti shook her head in frustration. "You think a warrior that young, one of your own daughters, would have confronted you if someone didn't put her up to it? Those words weren't hers. Bohara was her captain mere days ago. Think it through."

"Don't be ridiculous. Bohara would never betray me. We were in the Fingernail together. And have you forgotten, she stood as my second?"

"You went to the Fingernail together almost ten years ago."

"Nine, and we served there two years, so it's only been seven since. You think women forget their loyalties in seven years? Tell me, how many years has it been since you served Khara? I bet you could tell me to the day."

"Those same seven years," Gretti said, her gaze fire, "since you killed her."

Tamura saw her misstep but did not let the regret show on her face. She kept her face impassive, her voice sharp. "And you would rather be advising her, yes, yes. Don't you think I know that? My point is that—"

"I know your point," Gretti said, her voice simmering with real anger, perhaps the most Tamura had ever heard from her. "And here's mine. You know I'd rather sail the Salt Maw on a rusty shield than be queen. But Bohara, she's different. I think she may have plans for you, plans you won't like."

"You're so sure?"

"No. I'm not sure. I'm saying, pay attention. Watch her. Make your own decision. Come back to me and tell me she's still with you, and we'll never have this conversation again."

Watching Bohara the next few days, Tamura had to admit she had changed. She'd always taken an active hand in the training of the girls, but now, she seemed to be rallying them for her own sake, not the queen's. When Tamura joked, Bohara laughed, but as soon as she thought the queen had turned away, her face settled back into a thoughtful look, one without amusement. When she did not know she was being observed, she swept her gaze over the camp in a way that made Tamura nervous—what was she looking for? Keeping track of? Each of these things might be nothing, Tamura thought. But taken together, they were cause for worry. Better to act before they turned into something else entirely.

Three days later, in the quiet safety of her own tent, Tamura said to Gretti, "All right. I think Bohara is planning something. What do you think we should do with her? Kill her?"

Her adviser reacted without shock, but there was another unpleasant emotion on her face, somewhere between disappointment and disgust. "Not wise. She is, after all, one of your most trusted captains."

"You're the one who told me she was plotting to take over!"

"I said she might be. And it sounds like you agree."

"I don't disagree," Tamura said irritably. "What would you have me do?"

"Assign her to the Scorpion's Pass."

In a way, Scorpica only existed because of the Scorpion's Pass. Scorpica had been created in the Great Peace to reward the world's best warriors with their own nation, with excellent hunting and open land to roam. In return, these warriors would live astride the place from which, according to the stories, the only attack on the queendoms had ever come. The high mountains in the country's far northeast formed a natural wall between the Five Queendoms and anything that might lie beyond. The only way through the wall was one narrow mountain pass. They'd named it for the Eternal Scorpion.

All these centuries later, guarding the pass was a two-year assignment like any other for a Scorpican warrior, except that the assignment was technically within the borders of the nation instead of outside them. Warriors assigned to the pass hunted, dallied, trained, gamed. But because the Pale had not been spotted in centuries, the one thing they never did was fight. To hear the returned warriors tell it, they spent the majority of their time gambling on dice made from knucklebones, trading the same few possessions back and forth among each other almost ceaselessly.

"Up there?" Tamura's voice was heavy with doubt. "She's one of our best warriors. Nothing ever happens at the pass, and Scorpion willing, nothing ever will. It's an obvious punishment."

"No, because the woman she loves serves there. Her name is Sefikha. Renew Sefikha's assignment, send Bohara to join her, and announce that it's a reward for a job well done."

"She'll see through it."

"Everyone will. But it's plausible enough, and they'll let it go. Everyone saves face."

Grudgingly, Tamura nodded. She reached out to grip Gretti's arm, but the smaller woman hesitated before returning the gesture, and her grip was loose, tentative.

"Oh, look at you," sneered Tamura, angry at the slight. She hated to be reminded that Gretti merely tolerated her. That in this woman's eyes, she would never measure up to Khara, her mother's murderer. "So hungry for the Drought to end so you can finally be rid of me."

"Of course I want it to end. If it doesn't, we're all doomed," said Gretti.

"I know that," Tamura snapped. "Speaking of things we want to end, I think we're done with this conversation." She pointed toward the tent flap, and with a careless shrug, Gretti went.

But that night, Tamura could not stop thinking about what Gretti had said. Not about Bohara and the pass, but the Drought itself, and what its end would mean for them all.

Of course she wanted the Drought to end. She had to believe it would. One day she would see young warriors' faces again, she told herself. She would sing the warrior's lullaby. She would put bows and spears and swords in the hands of young girls just learning for the first time what it meant to be a warrior, to take part in this proud and powerful tradition. Scorpica's best days could not be behind. They must be ahead. Whenever she flagged, whenever she thought she couldn't bear the strain any longer, she looked forward to that day after the Drought ended, the first day a new warrior's cry was heard.

But if that day didn't come right away, not until after she'd made some strides into the other queendoms, gathered more wealth and glory for her sister and daughter warriors—would that be so bad?

Their military strength was their greatest asset. If they used that strength to strike fear in the hearts of the other queendoms, they could extort other assets they needed—coin, goods, food, even more warriors—while heading off the threat of future violence. A few strikes, while potential enemies were still weak. A few decisive victories. That could be all it took. They just needed the backbone to see it through.

Scorpion willing, she told herself, *we'll have girls again. But . . . not just yet.*

✦ CHAPTER 30 ✦

THE ISLE OF LUCK

The All-Mother's Year 516

Paxim

Vish, Eminel

Of all five queendoms, Paxim was the easiest by far to get lost in, thought Vish. She'd been visiting the Bastion when she spotted and followed the disguised warriors who attacked Eminel—a decision that had changed the course of her life—but she'd never intended to stay. Vish, so clearly a warrior, stood out in the Bastion like a goat among coneys. Paxim had given her what she'd needed. In the years when she'd traveled with the bandits, hiding young Eminel from danger, anonymity had been her salvation. But now that she was actively looking for someone, those same vast miles had turned against her. Perhaps it served her right. This was her penance, her quest. She'd find Eminel or die trying.

After a year of fruitless searching, she'd come within a hairbreadth of giving up. In the moment Eminel was stolen, she'd impulsively decided that she would not go back to the Rovers. That choice had become permanent. Though her resolve had long since faded, there was no finding the nomadic, opportunistic Rovers, who could be literally anywhere. Even if a miracle led their paths to cross, she told herself, she would not be welcomed back. Fasiq would never forgive her this second insult, this desertion, on top of her failure to keep Eminel safe. She would never relax into the shelter of Fasiq's warm, muscular arms again. So she threw her whole self into the search for Eminel, far and wide, high and low, in the trading posts and towns, hoping against hope to find her.

Indeed, her task was so hopeless that she found herself growing superstitious, and possibly worse, religious. She had always laughed at Fasiq—ah, that pang, just thinking of the giant's tender, sleepy eyes when they awoke next to each other in the blush of dawn—when the giant had insisted on stopping at every temple of the Bandit God. But now Vish found herself seeking out temples of the God of Luck, bending at the altar with an offering, at every single opportunity across the miles.

Each temple had its own rules, but in many, one coin meant one question. Flip a coin, south or north? Flip a coin, stay or go? Flip a coin, left or right? And the oracle would give her some kind of answer, or tell her to read the coin herself, or purr that the results were unclear and more coin was needed. It gave a rhythm to Vish's days and nights, something to interrupt the otherwise interminable journey that, unless she found the girl, would have no earthly end.

She came close to giving up again when she'd heard a crier calling for recruits for the Paximite army. This, of course, she would excel at. She could fight, train others to fight, work out her frustration and aggression by wielding her long-dormant short swords.

She'd made it as far as a training field, watching the soldiers spar, and saw a glimpse of an ugly future. Hundreds of Paximite men were training hungrily, whipping swords and spears through the air with the eager shouts of gleeful boys. Undisciplined, unfettered, thirsty for blood. When a captain waved her away dismissively, saying, *You look like a Scorpican, and we've had enough of those*, she felt not insult but relief. If the foul day came when Paxim and Scorpican swords would clash, she could not see herself on either side. She would not fight in an army led by Tamura and she could not fight against women Khara had once ruled. It was as simple as that.

And so she left the training field, went back to her foolhardy search. She crossed the border into Arca on a whim, witnessing a glass lake that the locals told her was a promise from Velja to destroy those who had taken advantage of the Drought of Girls to improve their own lot. What she saw was only the obvious: a lake of glass, born of heated sand, the aftermath of burning. There was no way to tell its cause. Perhaps that was why people needed stories.

Heading north again, she heard tell of an Isle of Luck, dominated by a large temple to the God of Luck, and two wise oracles who called it home. *Why not give it a try?* thought Vish. Perhaps all her sacrifices at all those temples along the way would pay off. If not, well, the island sounded lovely. And perhaps these oracles would prove better than the rest at answering her questions. *Is she south or north? Near or far? Living or dead?*

She'd been thinking her questions were about Eminel. But couldn't they just as easily be about Ama?

How many girls would she swear to protect and then lose to fate? Perhaps there was a god who had it in for her after all. Luck, or Chaos, or someone. Perhaps her good fortune in having such a solid friend in Khara, such a unique love in Fasiq, meant she was now doomed to bad fortune to balance the cosmic scales.

She'd walk up the steps to that temple and ask.

Near or far? Here or there? Doomed or destined? She wasn't sure she'd like the answers, but then again, she wasn't even sure she had the right questions.

✦

Soon to be ten-and-four, Eminel now stood as tall as Sessadon and was nearly indistinguishable from her relative at a distance except for the peppering of white scattered in Sessadon's black hair. Indeed, the pilgrims did not seem to be able to tell them apart, not that they needed to. In many ways, now, they were the same.

Sessadon had been a patient and persistent teacher, helping Eminel gain mastery first over the applications of all-magic she had already instinctively tried, like listening to thoughts, manipulating fire, and healing small injuries. Word of her success as a healer had spread, and though the God of Luck was not traditionally known for healing, more and more injured and suffering pilgrims began to appear. This was a boon, because the more pilgrims came, the more gifts and sacrifices they brought, making things easier for Sessadon and Eminel. Now the sorcerers wasted no time growing or hunting food. They simply ate what was given and went back to work, tending to pilgrims or practicing magic, usually both.

When crowds gathered, Sessadon used them as an opportunity to demonstrate mind magic, and Eminel went slack-jawed at how easily her teacher seemed to be able to make dozens of people do her will. The touch had to be gentle, Sessadon explained, and groups of people were much harder than individuals. Eminel herself was allowed to practice on only one pilgrim at a time, nudging them to do things they might already want to do, like fall to the ground weeping, stand all night on the sandstone as penitence, give gold to the God of Luck. It was starting to feel repetitive, as a matter of fact, but Sessadon was an exacting taskmaster. Until she could do mind magic perfectly, the sorcerer said, any attempt would be a risk. Hearing people's thoughts, which she'd once done by instinct as a child, was a far cry from taking action. Though she did not elaborate, Sessadon told her in firm, brisk tones that she would not want to see what happened when mind magic went wrong.

And as she practiced, Eminel's attempts were far from perfect. One day, with Sessadon watching, Eminel attempted to nudge the mind of a thirsty penitent to drink from the shallow pool. But when the penitent moved at the last minute, Eminel had to shift her nudge unexpectedly, overcompensating and sending the penitent's head underwater with a sudden thrust. The girl scowled and pouted, turning her discontent inward. Only when Sessadon snapped her fingers in front of Eminel's face to remind her to release the spell did she do so; only then did the penitent come up, desperate and gasping for air.

After a long moment, the penitent's gasps audible even from a distance, Sessadon spoke calmly, clearly. "Do you understand your error?"

"Of course," Eminel said crossly. In the moment, she was only annoyed with the sorcerer for interrupting her; it did not occur to her to regret that she could have killed an innocent with her mistake.

Sessadon went on, "And do you think the queen of Arca will stand still for you while you nudge her?"

"Of course not."

"Then do it again," Sessadon said, and they went back to practice without delay.

The next penitent who mounted the steps was a tall woman in a high-collared cloak, slender and taut. She walked like a warrior.

When she threw back her hood, Eminel recognized her face, and it took everything she had not to cry out.

It was the Shade.

Emotions bloomed in Eminel's mind, sending her reeling. What to do? When Eminel had first explained the Rovers, Sessadon had condemned them without hesitation for failing to save her from the Seeker. If she found out that this was one of those friends—the very one who had let her slip, in fact—would she hurt her? She could not let that happen. Seeing the Shade's face again, that intelligent, wary face, she was almost overcome. No harm could be allowed to come to this woman. It would not be fair. She had done the best she could.

"Kneel, penitent," Eminel said aloud.

The Shade knelt, her face down, and Eminel seized the moment. Did she have the skills for this magic? Only one way to be sure.

I know you, she said into the woman's mind. *And you know me. But we must not show it.*

The Shade's mind was aswirl, suspicious. *How could I know you, priest?*

I am not a priest. I am . . . Eminel. She added, almost unable to keep her body under the white robe still while she did so, *I am safe.*

The Shade's head stayed down, but her hand began to move toward the hilt of one of her swords.

Stop! thought Eminel.

The hand froze, then withdrew. The line between speaking into someone's mind and pushing that mind into action was a thin one, and she was far from expert. Had she accidentally pushed the Shade? What happened if she pushed too hard? A new wave of panic roiled through her.

Sessadon put her hand on Eminel's shoulder and spoke aloud. They stayed out of each other's minds by agreement; Sessadon called it a gesture of trust. To her it must have looked like Eminel was frozen with uncertainty. The sorcerer's voice was guileless, tender. At least it sounded that way to Eminel as she asked, her words low, "Do you need assistance?"

Eminel patted Sessadon's hand and shook her head. Seemingly unbothered, the sorcerer withdrew one step to watch, her priest's robes swirling around her ankles as she moved and stopped again.

With Sessadon's eyes on her, the Shade kneeling at her feet, Eminel struggled to make even the smallest movement. Any action, any word, could be wrong. She was torn between the girl she had once been and the one she'd become, the all-magic girl, brimming with power.

She remembered the Seeker who had told her that even people with great magic didn't use it when they didn't have to. She reminded herself of the task. She was supposed to be guiding a penitent into action. Whatever she did, it should look like that.

"The day is warm," she said to the kneeling woman. "Will you not drink from the pool?"

She narrowed the spell to make it harder to detect and easier to manage. Just enough to hear the Shade's thoughts, not enough to make her voice heard. *I can't believe you're here*, thought the Shade. *You've grown so much, I wouldn't have known you, but it's you, it's really you. I'm so sorry.*

The Shade raised her gaze to Eminel's, and even if she hadn't been able to hear the anguish in the Shade's thoughts, Eminel would have seen it in her eyes.

"Wait," said Sessadon.

Eminel turned. Had the look given the Shade away? Was that all it took, with a sorcerer this powerful?

"I apologize," the sorcerer said smoothly to the Shade. "This girl is still learning. Girl, what is the first question we ask of all pilgrims who come to seek the god's help?"

There was no way around it. Eminel forced herself to speak and to do it quickly, as she would if the Shade were a stranger, just another pilgrim.

"Welcome, penitent," she said. "What boon do you seek from the God of Luck?"

The Shade's eyes looked back and forth between Sessadon and Eminel. She no longer looked anguished, only mildly confused. She had to be calculating exactly how much to say and who to say it to. Eminel hoped desperately the Shade would keep her expression steady, no matter what.

"I am searching," she said. *For you, Eminel. I have never stopped searching.*

"Pilgrims often are," Sessadon said, her tone indulgent. "What do you search for?"

"A girl," the Shade said, "who needs my help."

Something twisted inside Eminel, her heart squeezing, her throat drawn tight. Did Sessadon think it odd that the penitent looked at Eminel when she said the word *girl*? What could she do to make this all seem normal?

"You are a warrior," she said aloud. This was something any oracle would guess from the Shade's clothing; it would not surprise Sessadon to hear. "And a hero."

The Shade inclined her head in a kind of bow, accepting what the girl was saying, as a humble penitent receiving the word of the god would do.

"But you are misguided," Eminel went on.

Eminel saw the Shade catch herself then, smothering the surprise Eminel's words triggered in her. She kept her head down and her eyes on the sandstone steps. *Good,* thought Eminel. *Good.*

"You must abandon this mission," Eminel said, matching the ringing tones Sessadon liked to use when playing priest. "Turn back."

"But, honored Oracle," said the Shade, still looking down, pretending humility, "how can you be so sure? I am equally certain my mission is noble and right. Without me, the person I seek will be in grave danger."

Eminel knew she was the person the Shade meant. She wasn't in danger; she was coming into her own, taking possession of power she'd never dreamed possible. In her tones of false prophecy she said, "The girl you have been seeking does not need you. There is another who needs you more."

"Another?"

Eminel let herself ease just a hairbreadth further into the Shade's thoughts, gently, easily. Two regrets leapt out. She brushed away the face of Fasiq, which struck at her own heart like a viper, and focused on the murmuring, unfamiliar warrior smiling down at a sleeping young girl. There.

"One you swore to, many years ago. That is the mission to which you must return." She raised a hand and pointed to what she hoped was north. She didn't know exactly what the Shade regretted and it didn't matter. The warrior would be safer anywhere but here.

"How shall I—"

"The God has spoken," Eminel said over the Shade's head, over the heads of the crowd beyond.

And she turned her back on the Shade, on the crowd, on the steps, on all of it. She faced Sessadon but did not meet her gaze, and instead of walking to meet her mentor, she passed her and kept going.

Eminel did not stop until she reached the altar of the God of Luck. She drew a coin from the bowl on the altar and flipped it into the air, catching it easily in one palm, consulted it.

What should she do next? Pretend the God of Luck was giving her some other sort of instruction?

Then Sessadon walked up next to her, their backs to the penitents, their shoulders nearly touching.

She met Sessadon's eyes. Did she know, after all? Who the Shade was? What Eminel had done?

"You'll do better with the next," Sessadon said in a quiet voice only Eminel could hear. "You needn't spend so much time on each one. Take a moment's rest and prepare."

Eminel nodded. Sessadon took the coin from her and tossed it down the stairs. After it bounced twice, she heard the Shade catch the coin out of the air, its metallic *thunk* muffled by her quick fingers.

Sessadon intoned, "Go forth, penitent."

Without a word, the Shade was gone. The entire encounter had lasted mere minutes.

Eminel felt hollowed out. She could not let it show. Instead she breathed in, breathed out, and came down the stairs again to where she had stood before, ready to greet the next pilgrim.

He mounted the steps toward her, a stout man with a friendly face, leaning heavily on a staff as he came. She readied herself to nudge his mind, to practice the skill she had not yet mastered. And she should not linger in doing so, she thought, remembering Sessadon's reprimand.

She would not let herself think about the Shade, who she was, what it meant that Eminel had sent her away. About the life they'd both had with the Rovers. That might weaken her resolve.

She had time and focus enough for only one thing: building her strength to defeat the queen of Arca. The goal she had been working toward since the moment Sessadon told her it was possible. The goal she would not rest until she achieved.

"Welcome, penitent," she said to the man with the staff, her tone serious but warm. "What boon do you seek from the God of Luck?"

Beside her, she could see Sessadon's nod of approval.

✦

When springtime came to the Isle of Luck for the fourth time since she and her heir had claimed the island, Sessadon told herself it was finally time.

Eminel had been an excellent pupil, everything Sessadon could have hoped for, learning a great deal in their time together so far. She'd gone from an untutored girl who always hung back as if afraid to take up space to a confident, curious sorcerer. No one could ask for a pupil hungrier to learn. When Sessadon showed her a simple enchantment, like moving a pebble inch by inch across the sand, she could mimic it straightaway. More complex, risky magic, like breathing underwater, came with more practice, but it still came. And her magic was strong, so strong. She could boil a pond, call a storm, grow a tree, all by drawing whatever life force she needed with no apparent effort and no visible ill effects.

There were flaws, of course, and missteps. The storm did not go where Eminel wanted it to go, and once she started the pond boiling, she could not stop it. These glitches did not worry Sessadon, not in the long run. The longer Eminel lived, the more she would learn. She was a mere ten-and-four now. How powerful would she be five years, ten years, fifty years on?

All the more reason to force the confrontation with her nemesis now, while Sessadon could best control the outcome. Sessadon would bring Eminel face-to-face with the queen of Arca as promised, but she did not intend for the girl to best the queen. She expected her to try and fail. If Eminel truly understood how powerful she could become, feared Sessadon, the girl might strike out on her own. That was the one thing Sessadon feared she would not survive, being abandoned again. The best way to keep Eminel close would be to show the girl her own weakness in a way she would not soon forget.

It was time to meet the queen of Arca in the flesh. Despite more than a hundred years on the earth, Sessadon knew, she was still as vibrant as ever, thanks to the life force she'd drawn from so many all-magic girls. And now, with the third Sun Rites of the Drought only months away, she was on the move.

When Sessadon had checked in to see what had happened with Mirriam, her confused daughter, and her faithless husband, she was shocked to see how it had all turned out. She'd known the queen was somewhat mad, but she would never have guessed her so ruthless, to kill her own daughter and steal her earthly form. She was both disgusted and reluctantly impressed. She had already been excited to kill Mirri, or whatever one had to call her now that she walked the earth in a different body. This was just one more thrill. And once Sessadon had all that stolen life force for herself, who knew what limits there would be? None at all, she mused. None at all.

Even outside of Arca, Mirri sent up a signal easy to detect at any distance, a resonance of peripheral magic that buzzed and hummed. She must have a *psama* enchanted to hold a remarkable amount of sand, powering her magic as she traveled. Well, Sessadon might not have a *psama*, but she had much, much more.

All it would take was a journey. She and the girl would attend the Sun Rites, taking their positions when the time came. Standing beside those who needed to fall in order for Sessadon's line, Eminel's line, to rise. Then those who should fall, would fall. It all unfolded in front of Sessadon like a flat green plain to walk across, bright future shining on the horizon.

✦ CHAPTER 31 ✦

BAIT

In Paxim, traveling to Sestia
Sessadon, Mirri, Eminel

On the open plains of Paxim, the familiar stars at unfamiliar angles above her in the night sky, the queen of Arca desperately missed her Queensguard. Not just because she had loved to look at them, which she had—gazing upon their lovely Scorpican faces was like staring into the sun—but because their solid presence was reassuring on nights like this, thick with unexplained noises in the darkness. This was the first time she'd had to make do without a Queensguard on the road to Sestia, and she did not care for it.

Sarkh and the others were two years gone now, but the wound still felt fresh. The Scorpicae had been honest, steady, reliable in all the ways one expected and needed warriors to be. Arcans could not be trusted, no matter who they were. Her return from the last Sun Rites had certainly driven that point home. She'd heard that other queens had assembled Queensguards of their own citizens once the Scorpicae had called their warriors home, but as she trusted no one in the entirety of Arca, no guard would keep her safer than she could keep herself.

Of course, everyone believed this was her first time attending the Sun Rites; it was Mirrida the daughter, not Mirriam the mother, who they saw as their queen. So she sat through the interminable descriptions, warnings, briefings, and let her mind wander. Without a Queensguard, especially when relations between queendoms grew more tense by the day, they warned her the road had grown dangerous. Of course the most common dangers were not dangerous to her.

By custom she slept alone in a small tent as she traveled, the other tents of her entourage arranged in a ring around hers. She pretended to be the daughter adopting her mother's custom—she had done this in many areas—and the repetition soothed her. All was in order. The higher the courtiers ranked, the nearer their tents lay to the queen's, with servants, drivers, and pilgrims each arrayed in place.

In the innermost ring, mere handspans from her own tent, slept the last two all-magic girls of high birth who remained in the nation. She had refused to take another husband to replace the faithless Ever, and there were no more all-magic candidates to sponsor, so these young women were important to keeping the court matriclans in balance. She had publicly praised both Archis and Elif, honored them, let everyone think they were contenders for the queenship. Everyone believed these were the youngest remaining all-magic girls in Arca, one ten-and-eight years of age, one ten-and-seven.

Mirri, of course, knew there was a younger all-magic girl out there somewhere. This still bothered her a great deal. It had been years now since Pom and Alamaj had vanished, and the next Seeker and Bringer she'd sent reported all leads had gone cold. But the girl had to be somewhere, didn't she? Unless she was dead, but what could kill an all-magic girl whose power was strong enough to keep her hidden? Perhaps the queen needed yet another pair of Seekers, a better pair. The girl would slip up at some point, show her hand. It was simply not possible to hide forever.

If Mirri grew sick of ruling—could it ever be so?—Archis or Elif were her only options. She herself had been a niece of an earlier queen, a sister's daughter, and while blood helped in these situations, only talent truly mattered. She'd watched these girls their whole lives, since they were born into some of the finest matriclans at court. They'd been casting spells before they could walk. Once they'd spoken their first real words—not just *mama* and *milk* but *light* and *breath*—they began undergoing trials shortly thereafter.

Archis was the older of the two, with a white streak in her hair and a wicked scar on her arm. She'd earned the scar in a customary all-magic trial: at eight years of age, she'd been locked in an enclosed space with a tiger, a ram, and a bear. She'd emerged victorious, but only by a narrow margin, and her healing powers were barely enough to bring her back in the aftermath. She was a brash young woman now, confident, unpredictable. Some felt that the white streak in her hair was a mark from Velja that she was a worthy magician; the queen, who'd been there at her trial, believed it marked a spot where the bear's claw had sunk into her skull.

Elif, on the other hand, was dour and focused. Her talents were strong—in the same trial, she'd simply floated upward while both the tiger and bear attacked the ram, then used mind magic to turn the predators against each other—but she used her magic sparingly, as if it might run out. When she did use enchantments, she was slow and deliberate in her casting, almost too much of a perfectionist. Deep down, the queen now known as Mirri was not sure the girl had it in her to rule the queendom. If one was going to brandish her power over an entire nation of magical, powerful women, one should at least be willing to have a little fun.

By keeping both girls close, she aligned the factions that supported them, keeping everything in balance. The matriclans of Jale, Kutsi, and Binaj supported Archis; Merve, Sabit, and Volkan preferred Elif. One of the all-magic girls could, of course, bow out to allow the other to ascend, but how many generations had it been since a possible queen had graciously allowed another possible queen to rise uncontested? Ten, twenty? As a matter of course, all-magic and selflessness did not seem to be born into the same set of girls.

Was the other all-magic girl, the one called Eminel, selfish like the rest? What was she like? Mirri burned to know. It would change everything if she found that girl. Perhaps she'd been dragging her feet on finding new Seekers because she harbored a fantasy of finding Eminel, full to bursting with all-magic, herself. That would mean Velja truly smiled on the queen, approved of everything she'd done so far, if She brought the girl to Mirri's feet. Oh, the fun Mirri would have then.

Eyes open in the dark, thinking of girls and stars and stretching magic until it snapped, Mirri thought she heard a noise. A thud, was it? Perhaps she was imagining things. She had heard voices more and more lately, near her ear, clear as a copper gong. Perhaps it was her age, or something about the way her spark had transferred into her daughter's body, something off-kilter in this new host. She had searched for a magical cause but failed to identify one. Sometimes the voices were low and rumbling, sometimes high and shrill, generally quiet and unclear. She could rarely make out a word. Sometimes she heard *Now* or *Yes*. Once there was a *Me*. The voice had said it over and over: *me, me, me, me.*

Tonight she could not make out what the voice was saying. It was a harsh, raspy whisper. Was it even a voice, she wondered, or the wind?

There it was again, some kind of noise. Not a voice this time. The sound of something heavy falling against the ground, halfway between a thud and a slump. Not wood, not metal, nothing so harsh as that. Softer, she thought, but still solid. More like bone and flesh.

Whatever it was, it did not scare her. She was the oldest and most powerful magician on earth. What could she have to fear?

The queen of Arca rose to her feet. She bent to exit through the tent flap, lowering her head as she held the heavy cloth aside. Then she went out curiously to meet whatever was waiting for her in the darkness.

The rings of tents lay still and dark, and as she walked, the silence was thick around her. But beyond the tents she spied a glowing blue light. A torch of some kind? No. The light was too cool and steady. Automatically her hand flew up to touch the glass snake around her neck. It did not generate light, only reflected it, but it was the exact same shade of blue. Curious.

She wove between the tents, moving outward through the darkness. Was the light growing, or was she nearing its source? It loomed larger, brighter. How silent the tent camp was, how still. There was only her and the light. It was meant for her, it had to be. She stepped between the last two tents in the outer ring, into the clearing beyond. Nothing between her and the light now. Then, against the blue light, someone appeared in silhouette.

A girl.

Broad-shouldered but not large. Solid. In outline Mirri could not tell the girl's age or her expression, could not make out her features, but she could feel her power. And in that moment, with a rush of awe, she knew.

Eminel, she whispered under her breath, and quickened her step until she was almost running.

✦

At last, at long last, the queen of Arca was coming toward her. Eminel told herself she was ready. She had to be. If she wasn't ready, she was dead.

"Go ahead," Sessadon whispered from her position twenty yards away.

The queen's expression was all eagerness, and she was closing the space between them with striking speed. It was only when she drew near enough to read the look on the girl's face and see the patterns in which she moved her hands that she slowed, her expression growing dark and grim.

The moment had come to strike.

Hands dancing, Eminel gathered a storm the way Sessadon had taught her: drawing water into the air, swirling the air in currents, forcing the cool and warm air to clash in the right area to bring the moisture tumbling down. The sky shimmered with its potential. The air above them felt warm and heavy, ready to explode with rain, the torrent only heartbeats away. Then the lightning began to strike, one, two, three forks of brilliant white light jabbing down silent and sudden, and it was glorious. It was the largest storm Eminel had ever drawn, and she'd never drawn one so quickly. Staring up at what she'd made, a perfect object of intense danger, she saw exactly what she'd wanted for so long.

Until Mirrida extended both hands, slapped her palms together with mighty force, and dispersed the storm, almost instantly, into nothingness.

Eminel panicked.

"Help!" she yelled to Sessadon, and the older woman was somehow already there, stepping in front of her smoothly, eagerly, as if flinging wide a gate she'd been longing to open.

She gestured at Eminel to step back and the girl did, haltingly, unready for how this was unfolding so differently from what she'd expected. Was she really so weak? All that work, to fail in moments? She took another step back, stumbled, almost fell, but regained her footing, hot blood rushing to her cheeks.

Stay back! And be sure to stay out of her mind, Sessadon warned Eminel as she moved closer to the queen of Arca. *She's stronger than we thought.*

"But," murmured Eminel, too shaken to use her magic, falling back on clumsy words instead, her tongue thick and sluggish in her mouth, "I want to watch her suffer."

I know, and you will, said Sessadon. *But from afar. Shield yourself. I will show you everything.*

Resolved, Eminel did as she was told and retreated. Then she flicked her fingers once and drew a shield around herself, a simple spell Sessadon had drilled into her until it came as naturally as breathing, even as tears began to course down her flaming cheeks.

"I don't know who you are and I don't care," the queen said to Sessadon. "But if I have to kill you to get to her, rest assured, I will. Step aside and you will go unharmed."

Instead of responding to the queen's parley, Sessadon turned her head and spoke over her shoulder to Eminel, her voice loud and clear. "The first thing I will do is break her wrists."

The sorcerer's hands thrust out ahead of her, twisted the air, and even from her distance Eminel heard the sickening crack of bone.

The queen bellowed with pain as if her throat itself were afire.

Then she raised her hands, which dangled at ugly angles. With a second, tighter bellow, she snapped them back into place.

"Old woman," she said. "If you think I cannot take a little pain, you have no idea who I really am."

"It is she," the sorcerer announced aloud to Eminel, "who has no idea who *I* really am."

Another wave of magic rippled through the air, this one visible, between the sorcerer and the queen.

Eminel braced herself, but the queen did not seem to. She seemed mildly amused, even, as if wondering idly what was to come.

"I will set her aflame," said Sessadon, her voice matter-of-fact, but this time loud enough for only Eminel to hear.

The queen did indeed go up in flames. This time there was not even a bellow before the fire faded to an unnatural greenish glow, the queen's smooth skin still visible through its miasma. After another blink it was as if the fire had never been.

Sessadon smiled, and Eminel knew: the real death blow was coming. She had to be there. She would.

With only a tiny flick of her finger, invisible, Eminel dropped her shield and leapt into the queen's mind. This was the moment Eminel had wanted for so long and she would not miss it, even after Sessadon's warning, no matter how great the risk.

This, Eminel hissed to the queen with wicked delight. *This is what happens. You have earned this fate. This is for killing Jehenit of Adaj.*

And she heard the queen's answer clear as day: *Your mother? I didn't even know she was dead.*

Time stretched out for Eminel, expanded, collapsed. She could think of nothing but the pure surprise of the queen's thoughts. Sincere. Shocked.

Her own mind went blank, her body still.

Each breath went on forever.

Then Sessadon said quietly, "Now she will melt from the inside out."

It was as if a burning coal had lodged itself just under the queen's ribs, but it wasn't a coal, and it didn't only burn where it touched. It burned everywhere.

"Her body will not burn," Sessadon added dispassionately. "But her mind believes in the fire."

Eminel felt it as the queen felt it, as her thoughts erupted into pure pain, pure horror, and there were no more words and no more thoughts and only moments later, no more queen.

✦

Eminel bowed her head as Sessadon lowered the delicate *psama* over it, the thin black leather thong around her neck, the bright glass of the pendant falling squarely between the twin curves of her small breasts.

"There," said Sessadon. "It looks well on you."

Eminel lifted the *psama* between finger and thumb. The glass pendant was no bigger than the first joint of her smallest finger. Like all *psama*s, it was shaped like the symbol of infinite chaos, two teardrops attached at their narrowest points. But this was an extraordinarily small *psama*, fine and dainty, meant to disappear. Eminel could not even see the sand inside, but she knew it was there. "I've never worn one."

"As it should be," Sessadon responded. "This one was meant for you."

There was a small smear of something dark on the glass, Eminel saw now. Blood, it looked like, dried brown and crusted. But she had watched the queen of Arca die, both from the outside and inside her enemy's mind, and the woman had not bled, not one drop. This blood must have been someone else's, from some time before.

Sessadon herself had no *psama*, Eminel had not failed to notice. The sorcerer didn't need to draw power from sand. Eminel knew now, though she was not supposed to know, that was because Sessadon had a heart made of quartz in her chest. The power it yielded up to Sessadon would never run out, never fade. She no more needed a *psama* than the Bastion needed a bucket of gravel.

The sorcerer's graceful hands reached toward Eminel, and now it took all her self-control, every last spark that did not fuel her magic, not to flinch. With one hand the sorcerer lifted the *psama*. The other pulled the fabric at the front of Eminel's tunic away from her neck, less than a handspan. Smoothly the sorcerer dropped the glass pendant to lay inside the fabric instead of atop it.

"Let's keep this hidden," she said. "For now."

Eminel replied, her tone as level as she could make it, "Everyone will see soon enough."

"When the time is right, yes," the sorcerer agreed. "Everyone will see."

They were alone, or almost so. The elegant carriage in which they rode rumbled forward on its tall, slim wheels. The gossamer-thin curtains at the windows swayed, settled, swayed. The queen of Arca's traveling carriage was utterly luxurious, lush with ornate details. Its benches were deeply cushioned. One could stare at the intricately painted designs on the ceiling for hours and constantly discover something new. An enchanted pitcher of clear, clean water on the side table never ran dry; a bowl of perfectly ripened fruit sat next to it, its pears the greenest Eminel had ever seen, its apples a shining crimson without blemish. Whether the fruit was magically produced or natural, Eminel did not know, but when Sessadon selected a pear and sank her teeth into it, the scent of its yielding flesh perfumed the very air.

Eminel, however, had no appetite. Perhaps she would have relished the carriage's comforts more had they not been sharing its confines with the dead queen of Arca, whose body Sessadon had animated to walk from tent to carriage when the caravan decamped and had not bothered with since. Slumped on the opposite seat, looking as fresh as life with the blue glass snake of royalty still in place around her pulseless neck, the queen made for an unsettling companion.

The revelations of the queen's last moments weighed heavily on Eminel. And the information she'd extracted from Sessadon's mind afterward left her reeling. As soon as she'd realized that the queen hadn't killed Jehenit, Eminel knew there was only one reason that

Sessadon would have told that lie. She could no longer hold to their agreement. She slipped into her mentor's mind like a thief, plucking out the truth.

Sessadon wasn't named for the ancient, exiled sorcerer; she *was* that sorcerer, risen and power-mad, and she was a danger to every last woman on earth. Without remorse, she'd slain anyone who stood in her way. Eminel had seen their deaths when she looked into the sorcerer's mind. The empty, hollow skin of that poor hunter, the one whose brain had gone liquid inside her skull, still flashed behind her eyes.

What to do with this awful knowledge now that she had it, that would be the true challenge.

How did one defeat the world's most powerful sorcerer? It seemed foolhardy to think she could trick a trickster. But with Eminel's fledgling all-magic matched against Sessadon's centuries of all-magic in a fair fight, the girl would be wiped from the earth. So trickery it would have to be. Could one play on Sessadon's confidence, her arrogance, as she had just done to the queen of Arca, who now sat lifeless a few handspans away, proving how well the stratagem worked?

These thoughts ricocheted around the inside of Eminel's skull, but she took steps to make sure Sessadon could not hear them. The younger woman shielded her thoughts from the sorcerer, then shielded the fact that there was a shield. She built a steady undercurrent of harmless thoughts to loop and scurry through her head in a layer outside the layer where her true thoughts swam.

Sessadon had not taught her a spell for that, but she saw how it could be done: once she'd dipped into Sessadon's head, the spells the woman knew made sense to her, and she copied their structure more or less instinctively. The skittering layer of harmless thoughts—*the day is long; the sun is high; travel is better with a good companion; I wonder when we will arrive at last*—were the thoughts that, if the sorcerer violated their agreement, as Eminel had, she would see.

When the caravan stopped for a rest and a light knock sounded on the outer door, Eminel tensed.

"Enter," commanded the queen's voice, though Eminel was looking directly at the dead queen and she knew she was not the one who had spoken.

The woman who stepped up into the carriage had a sharp white streak that stood out against the rest of her ink-black hair. At first Eminel thought she was middle-aged, but when she looked at her face more closely, she saw the new arrival was only a few years older than she.

"Queen, good companions," the young woman greeted them with graceful nods. "We're to stop for just an hour or so, to rest the oxen. Given the heat of the day."

Eminel was both surprised and not surprised that the visitor showed no alarm. Of course Sessadon had a spell in place to protect them. They were not rendered invisible, merely unremarkable, giving the impression that they belonged.

"Thank you, Archis," came the queen's voice, and again, only Eminel seemed to notice that her lips did not move.

"Would you care to stretch your legs? Any of you?" Archis extended the question.

"We'll just rest here, thank you," Sessadon told her, this time speaking as herself. After a pause, she echoed Archis's earlier words. "Given the heat of the day."

Archis said, "I'll just tidy a bit, begging your pardon, my queen."

Her hands moved in short bursts, independently of one another, the left making a graceful loop as she plucked the air repeatedly with the finger and thumb of her right. Cushions were plumped, the discreet waste chamber emptied, curtains straightened. The direction of her motions changed and her brow creased in concentration; a small handful of plump figs, streaked pale green, joined the apples and pears already in the bowl.

The queen's body gave a solemn, approving nod. Then her hand flicked out in a clear dismissal.

Archis bobbed her head, first to the queen, then to the other two, and backed gracefully out of the lush carriage, closing the door behind her.

"Show-off," said Sessadon after she was gone. "Wasting all-magic on feces and figs. More insulting than impressive, honestly."

The stranger's arrival had increased Eminel's tension, but her departure brought no relief. Sessadon only looked bored, pouring herself a cup of water from the enchanted pitcher, rubbing at a spot of something on the side of the cup with the pad of her thumb.

"Don't worry," said Sessadon to Eminel. "We'll be there soon."

"Soon," Eminel echoed.

"Why don't you lie down? It may be easier to fall asleep now, while we're still. Go on." Her voice was tender, gentle.

Obediently Eminel moved toward the far wall of the carriage and rested her head on an enormous plush cushion. She knew there was no chance whatsoever she would sleep. But with her eyes closed, it was far easier to pretend everything was all right.

As far as Eminel could tell, her shields were keeping her safe, but she had no way of knowing for sure. If her magic wasn't up to the task of keeping the sorcerer from enchanting her mind, Eminel realized, she would not have thoughts of doubt or confusion. She would simply think whatever Sessadon wanted her to think. And if that happened, far worse, she would do whatever Sessadon wanted her to do.

She did not know the limits of Sessadon's magic, and that terrified her. But she found some measure of comfort in the corollary: neither did Sessadon know the limits of Eminel's.

Now Eminel was a double agent in her own life, pushing her imperfect magic to what she suspected were its very limits. She needed to find the first possible opportunity to stop the sorcerer, to kill her if necessary—and it would almost certainly be necessary—without giving any hint that she did not agree with her mentor's intentions.

It was a balancing act on a dagger's edge, drawing on emotional and magical reserves she'd never suspected she'd need. Even yesterday she would not have known she could recline, smiling, on a luxuriously padded bench inside an elegant carriage with the corpse of a queen and the woman who had made the queen a corpse. Yesterday she could not have pictured it. Today it was simply what she had to do. So she did.

And there was no telling, after a day like this, what tomorrow might bring.

At the Sun Rites, she knew, there would be a reckoning.

PART IV

CLASH

The All-Mother's Year 516
Third Sun Rites of the Drought of Girls

CHAPTER 32

RITES

Midsummer, the All-Mother's Year 516
In the Holy City, Sestia

One hundred times in the first five hundred years of the Five Queendoms, the Sun Rites brought together the world to celebrate and confirm the queendoms' future. Each time, the queen of Paxim negotiated and secured promises of attendance. Each time, the queen of the Bastion brought the precious Book of Worlds to record the ceremony. The Arcan queen came as the messenger of Chaos. The queen of Scorpica delivered the holy blade. The queen of Sestia, the High Xara, performed the sacrifice. So it went for five centuries, the cycle steadily repeating, predictable, plain.

The hundred and first time, when the Drought was still in its early days, the queens and their people came reluctantly, their gazes laden with doubt. The hundred and second time, the warrior queen brought her guards into the sacred grove the day before the rites, and only the quick thinking of the queen of Paxim kept tensions from bubbling over.

As the hundred and third Sun Rites approached, therefore, every delegation had given serious thought to how best to prepare for violence. Every queen worried that such preparations would become a self-fulfilling prophecy; every queen prepared anyway. As it happened, these rites would become known as the Rites of the Bloody-Handed, but not for any reason that any of the five queens could foresee. And none of the preparations of any entourage would have prevented the kind of blood that would be spilled once these unholy rites got underway.

This time, when the queens gathered to eat cherries in the sacred grove, the High Xara had posted guards at the grove's entrance, ensuring that no Queensguard would enter. She herself had chosen not to have a Queensguard, and the Arcan queen had made the same choice; but the Paximite Queensguard, the Scorpican Queensguard, and the Bastionite Queensguard all complied with their host's demands. All three groups milled about on the grass, pretending nonchalance, and shot each other furtive looks without ever removing their hands from the hilts of their swords.

Once inside the grove, tension was thick in the air. The queens did not speak to or even look at each other. They ate in silence, departed in haste. In this way the peace was kept and the ritual was satisfied, strictly speaking.

The fear and dread that accompanied these rites, long before their damage was known, manifested differently among representatives of the queendoms. The Sestians tended to spend more time in prayer, sending up plea after plea to the Holy One that She would find the next day's sacrifice sufficient and girls could finally be born again. The Scorpicae kept to themselves more than usual, with only three of the delegation sneaking away to pursue pleasures, when years before everyone but the queen had done so. Still, not all Scorpicae were of the same mind. The warrior of ten-and-eight named Azur undertook her pleasures with such vigor and enthusiasm that at least a dozen young men and several young women would later claim to have bedded her in the Holy City, and remarkably few were mistaken.

Two of the youngest girls left in the Five Queendoms, born the very last day before the Drought—the fourth day of the fourth month—were present in the city of Sestia for the third Sun Rites of the Drought of Girls. They were ten-and-four years old, on the cusp of womanhood. Soon there would be no girls left in the Five Queendoms. They would all, even the youngest, be women.

One of the two, Eminel, rode into the city in the lushly appointed wagon of the queen of Arca, eyeing the dead queen's body and the sorcerer who controlled it, dreading the moment of reckoning she alone knew would come.

The other, Olivi, had been brought to the city to die. Selected by the lottery that all Sestians of ten-and-four were subject to, she was bound to the bone bed with cords, her neck fitted into the notch that would funnel her spilled blood onto the grain to bless the next year's harvest and honor the Holy One.

When the Sun Rites went wrong, it was Olivi who first understood.

After the dances, once she was firmly bound to the bone bed, the sacrifice saw the High Xara approaching. As regal a priest as any Sestian would expect, her profile was noble, her air commanding. She wore the finest of her saffron robes, light as a whisper, weighed down only by ornate embroidery, a repeating pattern of ram's horns circling her neck, wrists, hem.

The High Xara Concordia crossed the platform and leaned over the boy first, testing and retesting his bonds. She stroked each loop of the rope with an almost sensuous care. Olivi looked away. What could possibly be going through this woman's mind? She was looking down at both of them, the girl and the boy, with something that looked like fondness, like care. How could it seem like she loved them? In mere minutes she would kill them with her own two hands. She could love them and kill them both, it seemed.

She was absolutely going to die, Olivi realized. There was no going back now. No loose knots, no last-minute pardon from the god. While she was tied here she would be stabbed, killed, bled. Her flowing blood would be mixed with next year's seed corn, left in the open air to dry. All during the long winter, that blood would lie in readiness, like the seeds it coated, full of invisible possibilities. In the spring when the corn was planted and watered, encouraged by hours and days of sun, then she would at last reach her potential.

Her bones would be burned and sprinkled on the land as well, to feed the growing plants when they arose. Months after she died, after her shade had slipped away through the gate to the Underlands, once she was only blood and bones without spirit, that was her future. Her mother would not save her; no one would. Here now, with the sun readying itself to rise and the chorus of a thousand spectators breathing in the dark beyond, she felt what was waited for. The land was hungry for her to die.

"Come," called the High Xara softly, not to her. "Test the bonds. Bear witness."

These new figures—queens, Olivi realized—hovered over her. A gray-haired woman in regal purple, an iron-eyed warrior in leathers, a scribe in her scholar's robe, a hooded woman in a dark, shapeless garment. The only thing they had in common was their air of absolute command.

Hands lay on her each in turn. A gentle stroke in some cases, a fierce tug in others. The hooded one, hands inflexible and somehow waxy, seemed to only drag the backs of her fingernails across Olivi's bonds. Whether this was typical the girl did not know, but wondering was a necessary distraction from the humming, haunting fear that filled her. In the open space beyond distraction lay only the final certainty of death.

"You are satisfied?" said the High Xara, louder now.

"We are," came several voices, none distinct.

There must have been some signal given. A horn blared out again, commanding attention, ringing pure and strong through the morning's clear, cool predawn air.

"Queen of Paxim, diplomat and dealmaker," the High Xara said.

"Yes."

"Have you brought forth all the queens from across the known world to play their roles today?"

The woman's voice sounded proud, determined. "I have."

After a pause, the priest called, "Queen of the Bastion, the scribe of our holy rite."

"Yes." A younger voice, very close by.

"Stand you ready to record what we do here today?"

"I do."

"Queen of Scorpica, battle-driven and strong."

"Yes." This one unmistakably fierce, with a note of challenge she'd heard in none of the others, as if the woman's very voice were hammered from iron.

The High Xara asked her, "Will you bring forth the blade sacred to the Holy One for the sanctified task before us today?"

"I will."

Olivi let her eyes open again, not that she could force herself to keep them closed, and she saw the thick iron blade, more brutish than she'd expected. Its handle was of clean, pale bone, so close she could smell it. It smelled like death.

"Queen of Arca," called the High Xara in a formal, proclaiming tone, "I call upon you to speak with the lips of Chaos."

This time, nothing happened.

The pause lengthened and stretched, opening up under the just-lightening sky, seeming to go on forever. The other queens had responded to the priest's call with immediate, utter confidence. The first, the second, the third, they had all stepped up, delivered their responses, as soon as the High Xara had spoken.

This time there was no motion, no action, nothing at all. The only answer was silence.

And then even Olivi—as frightened as she was, as innocent, as mystified—could tell that something was going horribly wrong.

✦ CHAPTER 33 ✦

THE SORCERER SPEAKS

Sessadon

No words came from the mouth of the queen of Arca.

Behind her, another hooded figure moved, stepping up to stand next to the silent queen. As she lowered her hood, the crowd could see that this one had dark, suspicious eyes and dark hair shot through with white coiling curls. Her expression was unreadable, but whatever it was, it was unkind.

The High Xara said, too quietly for the crowd to hear, "What is this?" She spoke not to the woman who had lowered her hood, but to the queen of Arca, who still said nothing.

"Don't bother with her," said the woman with the lowered hood. She lifted a finger, looped it through the air in a careless, almost lazy way, and the queen of Arca fell.

Murmurs rippled across the dais as she collapsed to the ground like a poppet. As she slumped and came to rest, the hood fell back from her face, and the murmurs turned to gasps.

The queen was not just dead, but drained. Flesh barely clung to her bones. Her eyes had gone dry and white. What was left of her hair, thin as grass, fell off in clumps inside her hood and down

400 ◆ G. R. MACALLISTER

around her shoulders. A blue necklace in the form of a snake had hung around her neck, but it dropped away when the body fell. There was not enough neck left to hang on to.

Just off the dais, in the area reserved for the Arcan delegation, a young woman with a white streak in her hair screamed.

The unhooded woman made another motion and the head of the woman with the white streak rocked back as if she had been slapped. She fell to the ground with a cry.

"One warning," murmured the unhooded woman. "There won't be a second."

Eyes wide and terrified, the young woman looked up, her eyes roaming from face to face. The outline of a hand, red and raw, blossomed on her cheek.

"Now," said the unhooded woman. Her hands wove a pattern in the air, ornate and somehow beautiful, until the crowd listened to her, rapt.

◆

Her mind magic was working perfectly, even in a crowd this large, thought Sessadon, gratified. She'd felt a tickle of uncertainty at undertaking a mind spell this far-reaching, and success was intoxicating. She had softened the thousand minds in front of her just a little, making them more receptive, so she could be sure her words landed on fertile ground. They were not hypnotized or controlled. That was not her aim. They were simply opened. Her actual words would have to do the rest. This was the final challenge she had set for herself before she took power.

"Listen well," she began. "Your lives depend on it."

She soaked in their shock and terror. The quartz heart in her chest fairly sang with the energy they yielded up to her, unaware of the offering. Like sheep, they were. Very well. She could work with sheep.

"My name is Sessadon," she said. She heard the gasp from the young woman she had slapped, the one called Archis. It pleased her to know her name was known. Her sister had not wiped her from the earth entirely, and now, it was her star that was ascendant. Sessadon's pleasure was great enough that she chose not to kill Archis yet, though of course no potential rival to Eminel could be allowed to live. There would be time later for that. She was not without mercy, Sessadon thought.

She looked down toward Eminel in the front row of the spectators and met her gaze. The girl was steady, so steady. She did not look afraid. Her eyes shone, bright and ready, prepared for anything that might come. There was so much to love about her. Years or decades or centuries from now, after she tired of ruling, Sessadon would make her queen of this whole world.

Looking out over her new subjects arrayed in lines throughout the amphitheater, raising her hands high, Sessadon proclaimed, "I am not the queen of Arca. But I am your queen. I was born—long before the Five Queendoms, I was born—to reign over you all."

Then, too close to Eminel, she felt the energy of a different Arcan begin to shimmer and swell. Elif, the serious-faced one, slowly drew her hands apart and back together, graceful, menacing. This could not be tolerated. Without moving the bulk of her body, Sessadon raised a single finger and snuffed out the woman's magic, and with it, her life. Another body tumbling to the ground with a thud, another surge of fear from the crowd. She did not even turn to watch the death she caused, and she knew this scared them as much as anything she did or said. Death was nothing to her. It was everything to them. The gap between the two was a black expanse of terror. She would use that.

"Your magic cannot compete with mine. If you doubt my power, I ask you, why have no girls been born to you in a generation?"

Whispers sang and zoomed and swarmed all around the amphitheater. The crowd's fear rose now like wind in a wheat field. She fed on the feeling, as intoxicating as any wine, any powder. If she'd had a flesh heart in her chest instead of a quartz one, it would have swelled with pride.

"You thought it was some faceless being. Some god," she shouted over their heads, anger filling her at the mere thought, a snarl on her face. "It was me. It was only, always, me."

She paused to make sure they had all heard. They had. She continued.

"I am more powerful than this Sestia some of you worship. More than the Scorpion you warriors praise. I am more powerful than life or war or death itself. Watch."

She wrenched the sacred blade in the hand of the High Xara. Stunningly, the woman did not let go. There was something in Sessadon that admired that. And something equally as strong that made her want to kill the priest for her disobedience.

But she did not really care whether this idiot priest released her grip; all she needed was the knife, and if it had a person attached, so be it. She flicked her fingers and made the knife go where she wanted it to. The priest stumbled behind. Sessadon held the knife and the priest for a moment between the two sacrifices, swaying them back and forth, and then made her decision.

When the knife buried itself up to the hilt in the young man's chest, the priest fell to her knees with a rough, low cry.

"Whatever god you worship is nothing next to me," called Sessadon, her voice proud, commanding. "I can cancel out the gifts of the God of Plenty. I can create Chaos to rival anything Velja has and ever will bring forth. I can deal death and send anyone I wish to join Eresh in the Underlands as easily as I can think it. Who will be next? One of your queens? They are liars, your queens, and hypocrites. I know all their secrets. Shall I tell you about their licentious behavior, their forbidden desires? How they have murdered their way into rule? Their trickery and deception? Or should I do you a favor, citizens of every one of these foolishly constructed queendoms, and kill them all?"

Sounds echoed all around, noises of shock and surprise, some let loose, some held in. Sessadon could hear every last one, her mind-magic so attuned to the crowd she could sense them all simultaneously. The spectators, the queens, the girl bound to the other bone bed, a girl Eminel's age. This last girl cried out with her soul but made almost no outward noise at all, her gasp stifled. The girl's eyes were wild.

She had them now. Or, she realized, most of them. There was a jarring wave of something resistant behind her, someone avoiding her thrall, pushing back. She turned.

"Please," said the queen of Paxim, her thick gray-and-black tresses flowing down her back like a length of cloth, her papery skin flushed with what Sessadon could plainly see was terror. She was afraid but she was fighting it, just as she was fighting Sessadon's control.

"Please what?" *Patience, patience, let the crowd see this unfold,* she told herself. *It's part of the game.*

"Please, let's stop for a moment. Consider what you're doing, consider what you want."

"Oh, I know what I want," said Sessadon, suppressing the urge to grin. She could easily have spoken directly into the woman's mind, but she was reveling in the theater of it, in showing the spectators how overmatched this one was—how all of them were.

"Power," said the queen of Paxim. "I feel that from you. You are an enormously powerful woman and you want more power."

What a simpleton, she thought. "Indeed."

"We can discuss this."

"Can we? Can we discuss your surrender?"

The queen blinked then. Her terror rose again, cresting like a wave, and Sessadon savored every trembling, helpless drop.

"That is not what I mean," the woman went on, pushing forward heedlessly. "I can do better. Let me explain."

Sessadon had to credit Heliane's willingness to persevere, even as it bordered on foolishness. Highborn women like her were incapable of telling the difference between being stupid and being brave.

The queen put her hands out, palms up. "I mean to say, I understand what you're asking for, what you want. Perhaps there is a better way to get it."

Sessadon said, "Yes, I think there is a better way."

The diplomat had a pacifying, pandering smile on her face. The smile began to fade as she rose up into the air. By the time she was ten feet up, only the ghost of the smile remained. By fifteen feet her mouth was a hard line. By twenty, it gaped open, a silent O that could have meant any one of a dozen different emotions, but by this point, it was getting hard to make out her expression from the ground. Her hair flowed around her in a grayish cloud, which, to amuse herself, Sessadon turned snow-white. To her credit, the queen did not cry out anything foolish like *Let me down*, though Sessadon, tiring of this game, did just that.

When the sorcerer loosened her magical grip, from twenty-five feet high, the queen of Paxim plummeted out of the sky like a rotted tree branch. The sound she made when she hit the dais was surprisingly muffled. Sessadon would have expected more. The queen's expression could be seen again, now that she was down on the ground with the rest of them. Her brown eyes were glazed, glassy. Whether she still viewed the world through them, it was not yet possible to tell.

Some kind of Paximite attendant rushed forward, falling to her knees to reach out her hands toward the face of the fallen queen. From this position, she twisted toward Sessadon with hatred, her glare burning.

Such disrespect. Sessadon flicked a finger. The glare remained even as a bright line of blood appeared at one side of the attendant's throat and then zinged across to the other. The line cut fast and straight and deep. Some of the blood that cascaded from the wound fell onto the newly white hair of the fallen queen, staining its pristine whiteness with splashes of crimson, standing out like berries in snow.

The attendant's last breath escaped her so quickly that when she fell to the ground lifeless, her eyes still stared with the same intensity. Only gradually did the stillness of death fog them over. The cut across her throat opened like a second mouth below the real one, gaping, red.

"There," Sessadon said. "Better."

More panic, more screaming, and Sessadon fed off the chaos like a starving mouse dropped into a sack of cornmeal. There was so much and she wanted it all, even though it threatened to choke her. So wonderful. So delicious. And she'd been waiting so, so long.

She turned back to address the crowd, watching them gape and tremble, sending a gentle, warm wave of magic into their minds to ensure that even in their panic, they were able to listen.

"The Arcans will understand that I come from the original line of queens," she explained, her tone patient, instructive. "I have chosen another to rule after me who also comes from this line. But we will not just be queens of Arca. The time of Arca is over. You have heard of the time before the five queendoms, but you do not truly understand. I understand because I was there. And I will bring back those golden days, uniting all our strengths into one again. No more warriors against magicians against scribes. All together. All powerful. Every last one of you can be part of this dream. Your allegiance is all I require."

Some at the back of the amphitheater were running. She had let a few out initially to spread the word throughout the city and beyond, but now she had a different message to send.

"Let me make your choices clear," she called out toward the top of the stands.

She reached up her hands and slammed the doors to the outside, sending waves of slashing blue energy across the archways, cutting down the people streaming for the exits. She could not quite see their figures clearly, but she could smell the blood and hear the screams, and she knew she was communicating precisely what she intended.

"Every citizen of every queendom may choose."

She pulled energy from everyone around, weakening them without hurting them, gathering her magic, which roiled and spun with the life force of thousands. She had felt merciful before. Now the time had passed for mercy.

And so she put the choice in front of them. The simplest choice, bold and straightforward, the choice that each of them would need to make. And if they refused to choose, well, that was a choice too.

"Choose your death," she called out, "or follow me!"

CHAPTER 34

THE ONLY WAY

Eminel

I was born—long before the Five Queendoms, I was born—to reign over you all, said Sessadon to the captive crowd, and Eminel knew it was time to take action, even if she died trying.

So much death, fear, destruction. It sickened her that she'd let it happen. She'd been reeling since she saw the truth inside the mind of the queen of Arca, since the entirety of Sessadon's plan had been revealed. She should have stopped this before it began, if she'd only known how.

Instead she'd focused on her own safety, trailing Sessadon across the land and into the Holy City, letting the sorcerer believe she was a willing, even eager, follower—all the while building shields upon shields in her mind. Eminel had been terrified of what would happen if she let those shields down, even for a moment, to focus her magic on an attack. Even the smallest gap in a turtle's shell was wide enough to slip a knife's blade in, then twist. Once Sessadon realized Eminel's loyalties had changed—that she'd woken up to reality—the young woman would turn from heir to target.

Eminel was still terrified, but now she didn't care what happened to her. There was no way around it: too many had died. So many more would die if she didn't act. *So let me die,* she thought. Let the sorcerer rip her in two like a scrap of worn-out nettlecloth. As long as it gave someone else the chance to finish the job.

What spell could she summon? Time was short but the possibilities nearly limitless. She wore the *psama* of the former queen of Arca under her tunic. Its sand would power any magic she could dream of doing. The life force of a thousand people pulsed and swirled around her. Now she needed only one thing, one that might well be impossible: a spell to best a master.

She remembered, in a flash, herself as a five-year-old; what had happened when she had tried to heal the little girl with the broken wings. There was something so sad, so troubled about the girl, Eminel hadn't been able to stop herself from reaching out. But she'd done it all wrong. She'd hurt the girl while trying to heal her, stolen the breath from a grown man while trying to make it right. She could have killed that man so easily, and if Jehenit hadn't stopped her, she would have. After that, there had been so many years of thinking she wasn't good enough, so many years of failing.

And now she understood why she'd failed. She was never meant to be a healer. Her destiny lay elsewhere. But where? Was it her destiny to follow this power-mad sorcerer, this ageless woman who tossed human lives aside like weeds in a garden? She couldn't, not now that she knew the truth. Was she meant to kill Sessadon, then? Was that what this power had been born in her to do?

That felt right, Eminel decided. That was her fate. Stop this destruction, stop the sorcerer's reign of terror before it truly started. She might not beat Sessadon, but she was the only one with a chance. She could not waste one more moment wondering.

As Sessadon raged and shouted, Eminel laid her fingertips atop her *psama* and began with a quick modification to her shielding. Before, she had planted the notion in Sessadon's mind that Eminel was steadfast, worthy, trusted. Now she made a slight twist: the sorcerer would not think of Eminel at all, not while Sessadon was busy rampaging through the amphitheater, making her mad desires clear to the people of the Five Queendoms. The girl might as well be invisible, with all the power of the unseen.

If the spell held.

Absent now from her mentor's mind, Eminel thought of the ways she'd seen the woman deal death. Gently, with the priest of the God of Luck, a death she'd witnessed in the sorcerer's memories. Violently, like when she'd set the mind of the queen of Arca on fire, murder Eminel had seen unfold before her very eyes. Life could be plucked out, torn out, snuffed out, drained. There were so many ways. She was not at all sure what she'd be capable of. Perhaps, knowing her own nature, the best way was the gentle way.

Eminel brought her hands together in front of her, drawing on the memory of Sessadon with the priest to mirror the brief incantation, then extended her right palm to face the sorcerer and sent a focused, seeking wave that would snuff out whatever life it found.

She felt it land where she aimed it, right on Sessadon's chest, and silently mouthed the unlocking words.

Now you may go.

She held her breath, watching the sorcerer's face for the impact, two beats, three, five, and still . . . nothing.

The spell had no visible effect. Sessadon's eyes still glittered with want and fury as she turned on the queen of Paxim, who seemed to be trying to reason with her. There would be no reasoning with the sorcerer, of course, and Eminel felt her heart squeeze at the realization that her failure almost certainly meant one more death, one she should have prevented. At least she'd tried.

She let out her held breath, her disappointment flooding out along with it, and readied herself to try again.

Perhaps her magic didn't work at a distance, like the queen of Arca's. She had to get closer, she decided.

But the moment she tried, she saw this was futile too. Behind her was a crush of humanity where she wouldn't even attempt to venture, but in front of her was something nearly as impenetrable; a chain of Queensguards who had locked arms to separate those on the dais from the rest of the amphitheater. Did they think they were protecting their countrywomen from the sorcerer? Was the sorcerer herself using them to keep others from getting closer? It didn't matter, in any case. Eminel tentatively reached out to nudge their minds and found no purchase. Either there was a strong spell protecting them or her own magic was too weak to make a difference. She was panicking now, her grip on the calm she so badly needed slipping away, and she knew she was no good to anyone in this state, but the panic around her infected her like a venom. She was not good enough. She was too young. Too inexperienced. She might be the only magician trained and motivated enough to fight the sorcerer, but even she was not strong enough to fight and win.

As she watched, the sorcerer lifted the queen of Paxim high, high, high in the air and then dropped her like a stone.

Without conscious thought, Eminel's hands shot out as if she were standing close enough to catch the falling queen, and though she was a dozen yards away, she *felt* the queen landing on her arms, even as the woman's actual body fell unimpeded onto the platform. Alive. Eminel could feel that too. The impact hadn't killed the queen of Paxim, though it should have, because Eminel's instinctual magic had cushioned her fall.

When she tried to use magic, she couldn't. When she didn't try, she succeeded. She'd been training for years and she was still incompetent; what if the only way she could reliably do magic was under the direction of a murderer and madwoman? Had her certainty about her own fate, only minutes ago, been completely wrong after all?

With a feeling of furious helplessness that reminded her of her mother's death, of the Seeker stealing her away, of those last moments in the mind of the dying queen of Arca when she discovered Sessadon's worst lie, Eminel thought, *I'll choke her to death with my own two hands.*

But she could never reach the dais. Even if she could grab hold of the minds in her way, which seemed beyond her, the enchantment she was using to keep Sessadon from thinking of her couldn't possibly hold if they were staring each other in the face. Even as she struggled to think of another option, she watched Sessadon slash the throat of the queen of Paxim's attendant—another senseless death, another failure—splashing red blood onto white hair.

Yet she had managed to save one life, Eminel reminded herself, and used that thought to force away the panic. However inadvertently, she had, in that moment, succeeded. She was not completely without magic. She had to calm herself down, choose one action she could handle. There had to be a way.

Could she touch one mind? If she chose wisely, chose perfectly, could one be enough?

She closed her eyes, shutting out the chaos around her, and forced herself to think deliberately, slowly. Surely she could touch one mind. For years on the Isle of Luck she'd done it, practicing with the penitents. It was possible to make a person do almost anything, but it was easiest to nudge them to do something they might have done anyway. To flow with their nature instead of against it. To ask of a woman no more, or at least not much more, than she would ask of herself.

The right mind, the right nudge. If she could make those two good choices, she could succeed. She had to.

She opened her eyes and looked up at the dais.

The wild-eyed sorcerer. The skeletal waste of the queen of Arca. The dead attendant. The barely breathing queen of Paxim. The dead sacrifice, the boy, and the live one, the girl. The High Xara, hunched between the two of them, muttering under her breath the same words over and over, clearly some kind of prayer.

Behind the sorcerer were two figures. One, the queen of the Bastion, crouched in obvious fear. The other stood as tall and still as a statue.

Tamura, queen of Scorpica.

Yes.

Eminel thought of a prayer she'd heard her mother utter. Not a long prayer, nothing complicated, but what she'd said when she laid her hands upon a patient to heal them. Jehenit had always said it aloud, so Eminel said it aloud. Funny how she had never thought of this, how it hadn't occurred to her, when she was learning Sessadon's magic, following the ways of the sorcerer. But she was not Sessadon's creature now. If this worked, if she lived, she would be her own.

Eminel summoned all her magic, drew it into a knot of potential in her core, ready to act.

"Velja, be with me," she prayed.

Then she reached out to touch the mind of the warrior queen, careful not to push too hard—she knew the dangers—but just to plant a seed, to nudge, to encourage what was already there. She saw the warrior's eyes lock on Sessadon. She saw her turn her body, as tense and coiled as a lion's, ready to spring.

Now she needed to distract Sessadon. Would it take her own death to do it? The sorcerer must not perceive Tamura as a threat or she would have killed her already, but once the warrior queen began to move forward, her intent would be clear. Eminel couldn't risk it. She swallowed hard and readied herself.

An immense power came into her, through her, unexpected.

It wasn't Sessadon's; she knew the feeling of Sessadon's power, which prickled somehow, like the bristles of a boar. This power was smooth and fluid, laden with steady heat, like dark polished ebon wood left in the sun. This was something else entirely.

She had only the length of a heartbeat to make the decision. But it seemed right—necessary, somehow—to let the power in.

And it seemed right, in that moment, to speak—to say three words that would capture Sessadon's attention until the reckoning was complete.

She spoke with the voice then, or the voice spoke with her, the power flowing, burning, shining.

Three words.

I. See. You.

And Eminel understood that the *I* was not her. Who it was, she did not know. What mattered was that the sorcerer raised her head and met Eminel's gaze.

If Eminel had looked down in all the madness, she would have seen a blue glass snake slithering toward her. She would have felt it traveling by magic to coil up her leg, between skin and robe, until it emerged from the neckline to form a loose, comfortable coil around her young throat. She would have seen it settle itself into place, pearl eyes catching the light with a gleam. But she did not look, did not move, did not notice anything that was not the gaze of the sorcerer. In that moment there was nothing in the world but the two of them, and the message, deceptively simple, that resonated inside and between their minds.

I. See. You.

The die was cast. The enchantment hammered home.

CHAPTER 35

THE BAREHANDED

Tamura

Mere steps from Tamura, the back of the unholy, unnatural sorcerer loomed. She had watched in horror with the rest as Sessadon made a spectacle of the lifeless body of the queen of Arca, forced the High Xara's hand, and then, horror of horrors, lifted the queen of Paxim into the sky overhead and flung her down like a petulant child would fling a rag doll. That queen might or might not be dead; her attendant certainly was. Tamura had had no particular love for Paxim's queen, but to see her body flopped around like a poppet's roiled Tamura's blood.

She kept her own body stock-still like a downwind doe's. Catching the sorcerer's attention would almost certainly be fatal, and she had no wish to die today. Yet her inner fury rose and rose with every moment. This would-be usurper had spoiled the most sacred ceremonies of their world. The sorcerer claimed she would be queen of them all, and she showed no respect for the true queens of these lands, women who had toiled, ruled, led for years. Yet the artless hordes in the amphitheater could only watch like sheep. She was a powerful magician—was she controlling their minds? Was it possible? All too possible, Tamura told herself. Somehow her own mind was unencumbered, but she was tucked away on the dais behind the interloper. There had been three of them on this high step before the queen of Paxim had stepped down to confront the madwoman, who had flung her to the hard earth. Only Tamura and the queen of the Bastion stood higher, a step higher than this Sessadon who now commanded the crowd, and she seemed to take no notice of them. Her attention was on the dais and beyond.

This ancient sorcerer was poised to take all of their queendoms from them, to rule them all with a cruel, bloody fist, even Tamura's beloved warriors. It could not stand.

And worst, she—this woman only steps away—claimed to be the one responsible for the Drought of Girls. She had stolen so much from Scorpica, thought Tamura, all those warriors they would have raised in the long stretch of years since she'd become queen. Dozens, hundreds, of young, fierce women who were now never to be. Her spell had held Scorpica hostage all these years; next, she claimed all the years to come. The woman was too powerful for even the strongest magicians to fight her. What could anyone else do against the sorcerer? What hope was there?

The answer sprang into Tamura's head like a flint-struck spark, almost as if someone else had planted it.

Mokh this, she was Tamura the Barehanded. She knew what to do.

Before she could think on it a moment longer, afraid she'd give herself away, she leapt.

Landing behind the sorcerer, without even stopping to make sure her landing was sound, she grabbed.

Sessadon's neck was slender in her hands.

A voice—it was a woman's voice, but somehow deep and high at the same time, booming, full of both fierce threat and profound sadness—said three words.

I. See. You.

Tamura understood that wherever the voice came from, whoever it was, it did not speak to her. The sorcerer snapped to attention, her entire body instantly yearning toward the voice, which seemed to come from the front row of the crowd. From a girl there, a smooth-browed girl? Though Tamura's hands were around the sorcerer's neck, the warmth of her skin pulsing, the sorcerer did not turn to her. Every element of her being was focused on the voice.

It was a gift. Tamura did not need to understand it to receive it gratefully and put it to use.

Sliding one palm under the woman's chin and running the other over the back of her hair, she put all her weight and all her force into twisting the two hands in opposite directions.

A sudden fire seemed to roar in her own head, a blast of light, an awful howl, but the sorcerer was too late. Tamura's hands were already in motion, already twisting.

The sorcerer's neck, bless the Scorpion, was already broken.

Even as the body sagged, Tamura did not let go. The head dangled limply from the neck, no longer straight and defiant, no longer even connected. Like a broken doll she dangled, the line of her body long and bending.

Tamura had never snapped a standing woman's neck before, but she had broken the necks of countless animals on the hunt, and she had seen a woman die this way during a failed escape back at the Fingernail. Human and animal alike died when their spines no longer ran straight. Breath was gone, thought was gone, and with them, instantly, life.

Except in this case, the dead woman turned her head on her snapped neck and stared straight into Tamura's eyes.

The warrior queen was so shocked she dropped the body, a gasp fighting free of her throat before she could think to muffle it.

The body she'd thought was dead opened its mouth as if to mirror hers. No sound followed in that first moment, thank the Scorpion. Tamura thought that if the body actually spoke, she might run. Her heart had never fluttered in her chest this way, like a trapped bird, wild for release.

Then in her head she heard a calming voice speak, not the same as the voice that had said *I see you*, but infused with some of the same qualities, dark and steady.

Put your hands on her shoulders, said the voice, and Tamura obeyed.

As soon as she did, she realized that the body's head dangled brokenly and although its eyes and mouth were open, it had little strength; she was easily able to pin it in place. She saw the body try to lift its hands, and even without instruction she knew what to do. She raised her own hands from one shoulder at a time and tucked the body's flapping hands under her calves, kneeling astride the body to keep it down until she could think clearly about what to do. The legs kicked, but weakly. Magic kept the sorcerer alive, or something like it, but the disconnect between the mind and the body slowed her into something ineffectual, at least for the moment. How long would the moment last?

That was when Tamura saw the light gleaming in the woman's chest. It was a blue light, throbbing, under the skin. Unnatural. Pulsing.

Once you remove the light, the voice said, not a command, just a statement, *it will be done.*

Tamura looked up and around, searching, and saw that smooth-browed girl again, the only still person in a sea of chaos, her gaze steady. She must be the source of the voice, but who was she? The answer was important but not urgently so. Tamura weighed the desires of the unknown girl against the mad statements of the sorcerer who now lay pinned beneath her. The choice was easy.

Ready to cut out the light, Tamura reached to her belt for her dagger, but it was not there. Of course. She'd surrendered her weapons, as was the custom. She had just taken a life—most of a life—on the grounds of the sacred amphitheater, on the holiest of sites on the holiest of days. The God of Plenty, if She existed, could strike her dead for what she'd already done. She might as well see it to the bitter end.

The one weapon here was sunk to the hilt in the body of the young man who lay sacrificed. Stretching out her arm the few handspans needed to reach it, struggling to keep the wriggling, mostly dead sorcerer immobile beneath her, the warrior queen of Scorpica grabbed once more.

The sorcerer's body bucked free for a moment as Tamura leaned too far, and cursing, she threw herself back onto the weakened woman and pinned her hands before making another attempt at the knife. She could not put one hand against the dead boy's body to brace it, but she could reach the knife if she twisted herself just past the point of pain, and she was more than willing to do so.

Tamura whispered something soft, prayer or apology or both, and used her free hand to yank out the bone-handled blade, its shining iron gleaming red with fresh blood.

Then in the same breath she turned and sank the blade into the chest of the sorcerer whose neck she had just broken. She dug toward the source of the light.

A little more, now, encouraged the voice, sounding younger and brighter, pleased. *Almost there. Almost over.*

Someone was screaming. Many someones. One was close by, and she glanced up. The girl sacrifice bucked and twisted against her restraints. The warrior queen did not honor the God of Plenty. That didn't mean she would untie a girl who had been earmarked for the god's use. Leave it to the priest as to whether the girl's life was to be spared. Tamura had her own mission to complete.

Focused, Tamura went back to her work. She cut where the glow was, deep and swift, and peeled back the flesh. With the surrounding skin gone, the glow was even brighter. Blood pumped around and over the glow but she did not let its slickness stop her from her intent. She slid her fingers in on either side of the gleam and freed—what was it?—a chunk of quartz the size of a heart from the dead woman's chest.

As Tamura lifted the quartz, it glowed blue, but after three pulses, four, five, the glow ebbed away. Her hands had looked black in the light. Once the light was gone, their true color showed. Bloodred.

The quartz in Tamura's hands went cold. The world around her leapt back into focus.

She looked up and two thousand eyes were upon her.

Mouths moved, arms waved, but she could hear nothing. Were they cheering her or shouting for her blood? Either way she would not stay for it. The sacred blade was slick in her bloody hands and she dropped it carelessly to the earth.

Heedless, driven, she leapt down from the dais and sprinted across the floor of the amphitheater. No one stopped her. Some looked but did not move. Some did not even look. She took the stairs at a run and flung open the doors to the outside, running like a fleet fox. She only paused to retrieve her weapons from the now-unguarded place she'd left them. Buckling them on felt exactly right.

Now she knew what else needed doing.

The world had just opened up like a flower, and she would not waste a minute explaining herself, defending her decision. No one else could have done what she'd done, and she felt no shame. She did what had to be done to save the Five Queendoms.

Now she would do what needed to be done to save Scorpica.

Gifts upon gifts. She would not turn away from them. She would not shame the unknown giver.

She was up the stairs, out the doors, into the streets of the Holy City, not stopping.

Behind her, in her wake: pandemonium.

CHAPTER 36

FREE

Three months later

In Scorpica

Gretti, Tamura, Azur

The birthing warrior Lamidha labored in the open air, the autumn morning cool around her, though she was beyond feeling it two minutes out of every three. Every time she cried out, her voice rippled and thinned into the middle distance, fading away, swallowed by the horizon. Occasionally she rose to walk but never made it far. She sank again to her knees, bracing her palms against the dirt, and before long, another howl went up, another sound for the vast sky to swallow.

All around her, hundreds of eyes followed every movement. The midwife kept the throng of warriors back, but there were so many, their breathing was an audible, almost tangible thing. Gretti clenched her hands so tightly her short nails left deep pink half-moons against her palms. She did not look at the warriors to the left and right of her. She knew who was there and who was not. Hardly anyone could stay away.

Labor had started near sunrise. It was early afternoon, the sun's thin rays fighting the clustering clouds overhead, when Gretti felt a strong hand grip her shoulder. She turned.

Sarkh looked back at her with piercing, direct eyes. "She wants you."

Gretti gestured toward Lamidha, whose cries were growing fainter now, hoarse with exhaustion, though the midwife said nothing to suggest the child was near coming. "She should be here."

"I didn't ask for your thoughts. I came to tell you, she wants you. Don't make me say it a third time."

What point was there in resisting? She went.

The air in Tamura's tent felt stale at first, but Gretti quickly realized the scent was simply one she was not used to: the smell of paper, in quantity. Maps drawn on thin sheets of pounded reeds were spread all over the tent. They lined the walls, the cot, the trunks, every surface. One was even tacked to the center pole that held the roof aloft.

"Gretti," Tamura said, gesturing at that map, the most prominent, "I need your thoughts on this approach."

The older woman came to stand by her queen, but she did not even glance at where Tamura's finger pointed. "There's no need for an approach," she said. "We could have a new warrior in mere minutes."

"And if we don't?"

Gretti answered, "I'd like to hope."

"We'd all *like* to," Tamura said. "But I am queen. I am responsible. And you promised to help until the Drought ends. The Drought has not ended."

"Scorpion willing," said Gretti, "it ends today."

Tamura clenched a fist. Gretti had the uneasy feeling that this might be the time she'd been dreading for years now, the moment when Tamura finally tired of jockeying with her and simply put that fist through Gretti's face. It would have been a relief, in a way.

But Tamura relaxed her fingers, with what looked like considerable effort, and said, "The Scorpion may have other plans."

Gretti thought about making her arguments, but she'd made them before. The sorcerer was dead, and with her gone, it was only a matter of time until the Drought ended—everyone knew it. She'd even come upon Lamidha painting a circle on her belly with a bloodied fingertip, the old practice for encouraging the child inside to emerge a girl. Gretti hadn't seen anyone bother with that in a decade. Of course, it was much more likely that a mother from another queendom would bear a girl first; Gretti expected any day for a messenger to bring that news. They all expected it, she could feel. Every day the sun rose in hope, but hours later, it set on disappointed silence.

But perhaps, perhaps today would be different. If no hope remained, she thought, all those warriors would have gone about their business hunting and training, tending fires and sharpening swords, making their preparations for war. Lamidha was the first of the Scorpicae to give birth since what had become known as the Rites of the Bloody-Handed. She'd confessed to having a lover in the Bastion, a scholar who'd pleasured her time and again in some secret meeting place tucked away in a corner of the fortress, cold stone against his back or hers. If it weren't for the death of the sorcerer, Tamura likely would have punished her. Instead she ignored the woman, never once remarking on her swelling belly or uncut hair. Gretti knew most warriors prayed for this baby to be the first girl born in Scorpica in nearly fifteen years. She could usher in a new generation.

She could free Gretti from her promise.

What would Gretti do then? Not Challenge Tamura, no—she still couldn't win—but she fantasized about her other options. She could simply walk away. As much as she loved Scorpica, she could disappear into the vastness of Paxim, throw herself on the mercy of the Bastionites, even reinvent herself as a Sestian farmer. To be unknown would be freedom. Or she could steal a *kupha* and hide, a hermit until the end of her days, in the western islands where her sister Hana had once disappeared. She even thought about hiking to the Scorpion's Pass and walking through it, ignoring the warning shouts of the northernmost warriors, becoming the first to discover what was on the other side. She dreamed of that sometimes, though she always woke up thwarted: either her own countrywomen shot her in the back, or the dream simply ended, as if even in imagination, the other side of the pass had to remain a mystery.

But so far, the Drought still reigned. While it did, Gretti was honor-bound to look at Tamura's maps, give her opinion of war preparations, counsel her wisely on how to defeat their enemies. She did so reluctantly, but she did it. Tamura wanted to attack while the other countries were still weak. A girl at the edge of womanhood had been named queen of Arca, but she was completely untrained, without a single ally in the palace, or so the rumors went. Tamura's spies had told her that the queen of Paxim had survived her terrifying fall from the sky, but her health was fragile in the wake of the resulting injuries. If Arca and Paxim were weak, Scorpica had a chance against one or the other, but not both. If war was necessary, Gretti had to agree, now was a good time for it, before the other queendoms rebuilt their strength. But it would have to be executed with smart, bold action. Gretti did not want the Scorpican forces to fight, but if they had to, she needed to make sure they'd win.

After another hour, with a quick flash of sunlight through the tent's front flap, Sarkh entered.

Tamura turned to look at her, slowly. Gretti saw the queen trying to hide her excitement and nervousness, but acting was not one of her greatest strengths. Her eyes were bright and her voice quavered ever so slightly as she said, "And?"

"A boy," said Sarkh without preamble. "I am sorry."

"Take him to the Orphan Tree," said Tamura, her voice steady as iron now, already turning back to her maps.

Sarkh nodded and left.

Impulsively, as the tent flap began to fall closed behind her, Gretti turned and caught it. Without a word to the queen, she ducked through the gap and left Tamura's tent.

She fully expected the queen to shout after her, but there was only silence. And why should Tamura bother to shout anyway? thought Gretti. The queen knew Gretti would return. Tamura knew that, bound by her promise, Gretti would support her, would make these plans for war the strongest they could be. Leaving her tent provided only a temporary respite. In leaving, Gretti was not trying to escape her fate. She knew there was no escape.

She simply wanted to cry in peace.

✦

Six months later, as spring arrived, thousands of Scorpican feet marched, relentless, across the red soil of Godsbones.

These women did not march in files and lines, but in swarms and clusters, like the animals who watched them pass. Some of the groups marched in silence; others chattered and whispered among themselves. More than one warrior tapped another on the shoulder and pointed to a far-off shape in the rocks or a disappearing tail or wing, murmuring nervously.

Not all of them believed the tales word for word, but they'd all grown up hearing about the hazards of Godsbones. Now that their feet were coated in its red dust, it was easy to imagine the stories unfolding all around them. The arch of red stone over there, couldn't it be the outermost gate to the Underlands? Didn't that dry, jagged riverbed look like the path Eresh's second consort Dreams had once walked, searching for wanderers, reaching out with long fingers to draw them to his emaciated, welcoming chest?

For their part, the creatures of Godsbones observed them from afar. A vulture might soar over the heads of a knot of warriors and then alight in a nearby scrub tree to cluck and call at their retreating backs. A nest of shrews, disrupted by a sandaled foot, rioted and swarmed across the red clay, scattering as dozens, hundreds, of other feet came down the same path, hard, steady, plentiful. But it was not the possibility of vultures or shrews that worried certain Scorpicae.

The heroic Scorpion had earned her immortality with five crushing, near-fatal Labors, and one of them had involved defeating the five impossible creatures of Godsbones. To the more suggestible warriors setting foot in Godsbones for the first time, any creature in the distance might be one of the five. The venomed fox. The two-headed bull. The flesh-eating hawk. The enormous, horned white wolf. And the fifth creature, an invisible asp, they would never see before it was too late. Older Scorpicae teased younger ones, pretending to spot the fabled white wolf's horns, mimicking its far-off howls.

The real hazards were silent, watching from farther away. Resenting the disruption, their ire beginning to simmer. They would do nothing for now. But the day would come when their limit was reached. When it did, the hard-packed soil of Godsbones would run with a different shade of red.

For now, thousands of Scorpicae marched down much of the length of Godsbones, the sun glinting off their armor. Even those who said nothing did not move in silence. Their swords and spears clinked and thudded, auguring the noises they would make once the battle joined.

The native-born Scorpicae, and their mothers before them, had trained for this literally their entire lives. Generations of dedication, of focus, underpinned their strength. They marched determined to put that training and that strength to use, whether or not they survived the exercise.

Among them walked women and girls born outside Scorpica:

whoever they had been before, they were Scorpicae now. Once they took the field, they would be indistinguishable from their fellow warriors, and if they died on the tip of a sword or spear, they expected the same just reward: an eternal, blissful afterlife in the battlefield beyond.

In general, there was no telling a former Arcan or a former Paximite apart from the warriors born Scorpican; that was the point of making them all warriors. But Tamura made one exception as she mustered the army, sniffing out young women born in Arca. These she included in the caravan, every last one, instead of leaving them to guard the homeland, skirmish in the north of Paxim, or hone their gambling skills on watch at the Scorpion's Pass. Once they neared Arcan sand, perhaps they had powers that would manifest, lending further strength to the Scorpican army.

And so the young warrior known as Azur dha Tamura rode with the army despite her heavy belly, as round and tight as an apple writ large. Eight years before, she'd come to Scorpica with no name, undersized and nearly silent, but as Azur dha Tamura, she'd blossomed: demonstrating a born archer's skill with the bow, drawing first blood in the early northern missions, even standing toe to toe with her own queen to argue passionately for recognition of a warrior sister's sacrifice. She'd earned the right to attend the Sun Rites with Tamura's delegation twice now, pursuing pleasures by her own choice while there once she'd entered womanhood. If she bore a girl—and there were those who still prayed and hoped, passionately, that she might—it would be a Scorpican girl.

Tamura treated Azur much like she'd treated the last pregnant Scorpican warrior, pretending to take no notice of her condition, but of course she was keenly aware. All day long as they marched and every night as she lay down to sleep, her thoughts turned to when Azur might give birth and what would happen when she did.

Regardless, Tamura reminded herself, there was no planning one way or the other. War was an absolute necessity until the moment the Drought was over. And if anyone was ready to deal death with a steady hand, it was Tamura. She had slain both a queen and a centuries-old sorcerer, one with nothing more than a shield and the other with her bare hands. She reminded herself of this fact in the rare moments when her resolve began to flag. She would need all her anger, her spirit, her pride to carry out this war and win it.

Gretti no longer failed to hide her reluctance whenever they talked strategy, but the council was more enthusiastic, approving Tamura's plan for war with no objections. Several advisers told Tamura they would agree to anything she proposed, given her heroism at the Sun Rites. Her hands had killed the sorcerer who would have taken over the world; hers was the glory, hers was the right.

And now was the time.

Troops were dispatched to skirmish at the northern coast of Paxim, taking to their *kuphai* under cover of darkness, but they were a mere distraction. Paxim, with its trained forces, was too strong to invade outright.

But Arca was a plum ripe to be picked, despite its risks. In a way, it was the most dangerous country to invade, given its untold magical capabilities. Based on the intelligence assigned warriors brought back, thousands of women in Arca had no magic more fearsome than the ability to make pumpkins grow faster, or the power to strike a flame with one's fingertip instead of a flint. It was the remaining thousands who concerned Tamura. Body magicians or mind magicians, air or water, earth or fire: any magic could be a deadly magic in talented hands. Water could be fatal if it was enough water. Earth could be fatal if it were enough earth. Magical gifts that seemed innocuous in isolation could be combined with other gifts to form deadly weapons, sturdy defenses, a fatal surprise.

Yet the time would never be better than now. The new Arcan

queen, Eminel, young and unready, had not yet established herself as a force to be reckoned with. Tamura could not help but feel good about Scorpica's chances to prevail.

And though Paxim was too strong to invade, it was too weak to intervene in this war, at least for now. Their queen still lay abed, healing ever so slowly, or at least that was the word the spies carried. There were rumors that Queen Heliane had actually died and the court was just hiding it, though to be fair, Tamura had started those rumors herself. Internal squabbles would keep their Senate and Assembly distracted, too disarrayed to effectively argue against a war. They would not be able to organize the other queendoms to put Scorpica at a disadvantage.

Every door was wide open. It would be foolish, Tamura told herself, not to walk through.

She still had a shiver of indecision every once in a while at leaving those warriors to guard the Scorpion's Pass. Were they wasted? Would it be better to have them here, approaching Arca? Those same old tales of the Pale attacks in the past had been told a thousand times—the group of three strangers who approached together, the Pale scout whose horned helm had not protected him from the Scorpican sharpshooter's deadly arrow—but they'd never been seen by anyone alive. Tamura couldn't help but wonder if the Pale were just a story, an invention to keep the earliest Scorpicae in line. But if she made the wrong bet and some outside force took advantage of the unguarded pass to spread like wildfire through the queendoms, she would be the queen who let it happen. Then songs would be sung about her, but not any song she would want to hear. There were ways she would not want her name to live on.

The goal of their march was easy to choose; choosing their path was more complicated. News of an army passing through the gates of the Bastion would move as fast as the fastest runner, to every capital, every corner. Tamura did not relish the idea of tramping the long miles through Godsbones, nor did her warriors, but it was the only way to keep their forces secret for any length of time. No one could report to their enemies if they were not seen. It only made sense to go where vultures and shrews were the only living creatures that could observe them. She didn't believe the stories, and didn't believe they were being observed by any other eyes. No one had ever seen the entrance to the Underlands in Godsbones; probably it was not there at all. If there even were Underlands. When it came right down to it, Tamura believed in nothing but the Scorpion, her sister warriors, and her own two hands.

At long last they came to the range of hills that marked the border between Arca and Godsbones, hanging back at the base of the rocky, half-forested red hills where the land began to slope downward. Here they would have their final rest before pushing over the border. As they had along the way, they bedded down in the open without tents, ate their provisions cold, and slept in tight, neat lines under blankets in order to keep and share the warmth they made.

One more night they would rest, to be ready when the next day dawned.

✦

During the day Azur walked with the others. To ride would have shown weakness, and she refused to appear weak among her sister warriors. But at night, when fewer eyes were open to see, while other warriors lay their bedrolls on unyielding ground, the drivers of the supply wagons let her nestle among the sacks of grain. Other allowances, each small, had been made. Several goats trotted alongside the supply wagons in case the new mother's milk did not come in. Once the child was born, if he was not a warrior, the goats would not be long for this world. Games-loving warriors had even laid bets on whether the child would be a boy, and if so, exactly how many hours the goats could expect to live before they were killed and eaten. The most popular bet was five hours, but only because five was a lucky number.

Because Azur slept alone among the grain sacks, when an abrupt wave of pain woke her, she awoke alone. Her first thought was of Ysilef, dead almost three years now but still missed every day. *If only Ysilef were with me. If only she were here to hold my hand.*

But the pain was here and her friend was not. Ysilef was a distant shade and the pain was all too present, too real, inside Azur's body, wringing her out.

When she thought back, she realized there had been other pangs late in the last day, shimmering and not infrequent, which she had ignored. Ignoring was what one did with pain on the march. After walking the red earth of Godsbones for weeks now, everything in Azur's body hurt, brow to belly to heels, and she had not made any distinction between discomforts. But this new pain, ah. This pain would no longer be ignored.

The next one went through her like a blade. She did her best not to scream, but the wringing, the wrenching, they were more than she'd ever expected, more than she'd ever known. Was this how it should be, or was something terribly wrong? No one had prepared her. Again she wished Ysilef were here. Perhaps Azur should have wished for the mother who bore her, but she no longer remembered that woman, only that she'd allowed her to be handed over to strangers. It was only good luck that those strangers were worthy. Warriors were her family, her friends, her everything. And now, as her child was born, they would be her witnesses.

As long as she could, Azur held in her cries. When she howled loud enough for someone to understand the urgency, some warrior— she would never know who—raised the alarm and carried her to their sister warriors. Dozens surrounded her, supporting her when she needed to walk, shouting encouragement when she flagged. She let herself scream then, because she knew they wanted to hear. And when she called out, it was Tamura—her mother, commander, and queen—who she called for.

Azur dha Tamura labored through the dark of the night, the rosy light of dawn, the bright sun of day. The hours stretched, coiled, thinned, collapsed. At last the pain crested, different somehow, and the ache centered down into a heavy pressure between her spread legs.

"Push," called her sister warriors as one, their chanting low and urgent. "Push. Push."

That was all she knew to do and all she did. The rest of the world was gone. There was only the pain and the pressure, that giant squeezing fist, the exhausting feeling that she had not a single breath left in her, except that when she tried hard enough, she did.

Then the pressure eased and she felt a wet, slick weight move against her thighs, and without even pushing, the rest of the body eased out, and the baby was born.

Azur cradled the child and gasped, falling into laughter, what felt like a great burden rising from her shoulders even as the child's weight rested wetly on her chest. It took her some time to open her eyes. She had labored so long. It was over, but it was hard to believe it was over; she needed time, just these few moments, a break between the old life and the new.

She rested there in the break, adrift in a long stretch of chosen darkness.

It was not until the child's mewling cry reached her, a high, thin sound, that Azur was able to gather her last reserves of will and open her eyes to look her child in the face.

When she did, somehow, after it all, she found the strength to smile.

Her child was a warrior.

The next face Azur saw belonged to the queen, who crouched down next to the two of them, her gaze locked on the baby. "Welcome," said Tamura to the newborn girl, her voice hoarse and reverent.

The crowd of warriors encircling the new mother were silent, awed. They had all hoped for this outcome but had not been sure of it. They were stunned to see their hopes made flesh—a living body so vulnerable and small, but still flesh, still here, still true.

"You may not know the lullaby we sing," Tamura said, this time to Azur. "For so long we lacked a newborn warrior to sing it to. If you will allow me, I will sing it to your daughter."

Azur, holding back tears, inclined her head.

Her eyes riveted to the girl's tiny, scrunched face, Tamura sang:

When the warrior has brought in the victory
Climbed the road home so rocky and steep
Lain herself down surrounded by sisters
Peace be upon the land, and sleep.
When the Scorpion calls us to battle
Wipe the sleep from your slumbering eyes
When a girl helps a girl helps a girl
Strength be in your arm, and rise.

Tamura raised two fingers to her lips, kissed them, then laid them gently on the baby's forehead.

She looked up at the gathered crowd. She caught sight of Gretti, rapture on the other woman's face, tears shining on her cheeks. She knew what was in Gretti's mind as surely as if she were an Arcan Seeker, thoughts as clear as spoken words. Gretti was grateful, thrilled, relieved. The Drought was over and she was free now, released from her promise, and she believed that this war, which she'd supported only reluctantly, was no longer needed. To Gretti, in that moment, everything had changed.

But to Tamura, though this change opened up new possibilities, it did not erase the old ones. Yesterday war had been a certainty; she could not let go of it in an instant, no matter what miracle that instant had brought. She felt the iron sting of blood in her nostrils, saw its red stain on the earth. Blood had always been her portent. This was like the moment when she killed Khara, took on her queenship. The moment she'd slain that man, the one who'd claimed Scorpican heritage, before sending off her warriors to bring her daughters. The moment she'd broken the neck of that sorcerer, carved out her quartz heart, saved the world. When she spoke with the scent of blood in the air, her warriors would listen. It did not escape her notice that childbirth, like battle, soaked the earth in blood.

So Tamura dha Mada, queen of Scorpica, decided.

Rising to her feet, opening her arms, Tamura turned to the gathered warriors, all rapt and ready. They looked at her with anticipation, eager for her to tell them what to do next. Wherever she led, they would follow.

"This is our sign, warriors!" Tamura shouted to the crowd, her words ringing across the red, inhospitable rocks. Her shouts were proud, ferocious. "We are blessed and we will not fail! We are ready! We dedicate our fight to the Scorpion!"

Her warriors shouted in reply, their voices a clap of thunder. "To the Scorpion!"

Gretti's expression shifted from expectation to blunt horror, and to keep from seeing it change further, Tamura turned her back. If Gretti said anything, she was too far off to hear. Any words softer than a shout were lost, drowned, in the chants of eager warriors.

"To your companies!" she called, and the warriors began to rearrange themselves, searching out their captains, settling like with like:

riders together, archers together, those too precious to risk, like Azur and her new, still-nameless warrior, staying behind in safety.

Once her warriors were all arrayed, their queen looked back at them. She surveyed the forces she had brought together—created, in so many ways—and then turned to look out over the land they were about to invade. From here, there would be no going back. She should have felt more fear at that, she told herself, but instead she was blissfully eager, all heat and impatience.

Waves of battle-ready women at her back, Tamura looked toward the horizon where the golden sand of Arca waited. She drew her sword in a smooth motion, raised it high over her head, the sun's light glinting off the blade.

And she roared to her waiting warriors, "In the name of the Scorpion, let war begin!"

✦ END OF BOOK ONE ✦

ACKNOWLEDGMENTS

So many people contribute in so many ways to making my books what they are; I'm always afraid of leaving someone out. And I probably have. But as with writing the book itself, while writing acknowledgments feels impossible when you're in the middle of it, it's equally impossible to imagine not even trying.

Many, many thanks to the dream team responsible for launching Scorpica into the world: Holly Root of Root Literary and Joe Monti and Madison Penico of Saga Press. Can't wait to do this again (and again, and again) as we introduce readers everywhere to the Five Queendoms. I'm also deeply grateful to Elisabeth Weed and Hallie Schaeffer of The Book Group for providing early editorial feedback, Kat Howard, Shelley Nolden, and Tracey Kelley for reading versions of the manuscript along the way, Alyssa Moore and Kate Quinn for sharing their enthusiastic support exactly when I needed it, intern extraordinaire Maddie Aitken for researching both this world and ours, Melissa Marr for generously sharing her swordfighting expertise, Heather Baror for taking the Queendoms international, and my husband, Jonathan, for hours upon hours of collaborative world-building.

I'd also like to thank the extended team at S&S, including Jennifer Bergstrom, Jennifer Long, Jamie Putorti, Caroline Pallotta, Allison Green, Iris Chen, production wizards Kaitlyn Snowden and Sarah

Wright, and subsidiary rights wranglers Paul O'Halloran and Cordia Leung. Art directors Lisa Litwack and John Vairo and cover artist Victo Ngai are responsible for making the book so beautiful. Eagle-eyed copyeditor Valerie Shea saved me from myself in more ways than I can count (and would no doubt catch any errors in said count if I did attempt it).

And thanks to the booksellers, librarians, readers, fellow authors, and other booklovers who've supported my previous work so enthusiastically. The best part of this whole writing thing is sharing it. I hope you love this complicated, fantastical matriarchal world. I made it for you.